Marie Romero Cash

THE MARIACHI MURDER

"*The Mariachi Murder*, Marie Romero Cash's new mystery, offers readers the pleasures we have come to expect from her Jemimah Hodge series: a vivid physical and cultural landscape populated with true-to-life characters in a fast-paced story. Set in New Mexico, in and around Santa Fe, the familiar—Cash's family has lived here for generations—meets the mysterious when a mariachi musician turns up dead in the high desert. Forensic psychologist Jemimah Hodge and her sheriff's detective *amor* Rick Romero need to solve a murder, and that requires their ability to sort through the Hispanic, Anglo, and Pueblo eccentricities of New Mexico. All the details—from the deceased macho mariachi in silver-tipped cowboy boots to the gaudy sunset horizons of the Southwest to the sometimes uneasy relations within or between cultures—are absolutely dead-on. Marie Romero Cash knows her material intimately and crafts an entertaining ride through the mystery of death and life in a fascinating world. Don't miss it!"
—Michael Pettit, winner of the New Mexico Book Award for *Riding for the Brand*

"Marie Romero Cash has created a set of well-drawn characters for her Jemimah Hodge mystery series in this, her fourth installment. Her descriptions of the breathtaking scenery, familiar to all New Mexicans, paint vivid pictures for her readers to enjoy. I, for one, am anxious to try one of the several restaurants she uses to nourish her characters while they struggle to solve the murder of a popular mariachi from Santa Fe. Heart-stopping action threads its way through the story right up to the minute they catch their killer, just in time to save the next victim."
—Patricia Smith Wood, author of *The Easter Egg Murder* and *Murder on Sagebrush Lane*

"Full disclosure—I'm a junkie when it comes to stories set in New Mexico. Give me a book by Rudolfo Anaya, Anne Hillerman, Michael McGarrity, Patricia Wood Smith.... Add to that list Marie Romero Cash. Her two key characters, Santa Fe County Sheriff's Detective Rick Romero and his girlfriend, Dr. Jemimah Hodge, are protagonists I would love to have created. Marie's series, which just gets better with each book, captures the food, the landscape and—particularly in this latest episode—the music of the land of enchantment. I'm already looking forward to the next one."
—Mike Orenduff, Author of the Pot Thief series.

TREASURE AMONG THE SHADOWS

"A fictional take on the controversial, real-life hunt for a treasure buried by Forrest Fenn that has attracted the attention of treasure seekers worldwide as well as the FBI. The author knows Fenn in real life; in the book he is renamed Tim McCabe and has strong ties to law enforcement, specifically Santa Fe County Sheriff's Deputy Rick Romero, a straight-arrow local boy who is dating his esteemed colleague, forensic psychologist Jemimah Hodge.... Joining this crew as McCabe's foil—and then the story's next murder victim—is Gilda Humphreys, the frumpy, tyrannical state archaeologist who's been leading a double life as a sex kitten. She's fixated on the treasures to be found on McCabe's ranch—property he bought from a pueblo and to which he insists the state has no claim. When real treasure is indeed found, the fun begins."
—*Pasatiempo*, the New Mexican's Weekly Magazine of Arts, Entertainment & Culture

"The essence of northern New Mexico permeates the pages of this nonstop murder mystery.... Marie Romero Cash paints new shades into the rich New Mexico canvas."
—Robert J. Ray, author of the Matt Murdock Murder Mysteries

"A relaxed, interesting and light summer read that any detective lover will enjoy."
—Fenny, Hopscotching Blog

"The book brings the area of Taos and New Mexico to life! You will find yourself wanting to go back and read the previous two books. You'll love the team of Jemimah and Rick."
—Bless Their Hearts Mom Blog

"Jemimah Hodge has guts, heart and a brilliant sense of direction when she's on the trail of something buried. Cash delivers a thrilling ride from start to finish. Riveting."
—Chris Rogers, author, the Dixie Flannigan series

"Jemimah is an interesting character with an unusual background, having run from a polygamous cult as a teenager.... The Southwest locale is as important to the story as the characters themselves. This series should be enjoyed by fans of Tony Hillerman."
—The Self-Taught Cook Blog

"Jemimah Hodge and Sheriff Rick Romero are a great team. The two of them remind me a lot of 'McCloud' from the old TV show.... a wonderful thriller."
—Vic's Media Room

DEADLY DECEPTION

"A superb investigative thriller.... Readers will appreciate this entertaining whodunit"
—Harriet Klausner

SHADOWS AMONG THE RUINS

"*Shadows among the Ruins* is a fast-paced and old-school fun mystery read, highly recommended."
—Midwest Book Review

"This 'who-done-it' has cops, a surprise ending, great dialog, and stunning vistas. This is the kind of book to dive into in front of a fire or to take on a plane and tune everything out."
—*Tradición Revista Magazine*

"Cash is an author who knows Santa Fe inside and out, from its Canyon Road art dealers selling million-dollar paintings to its drug-dealing bar scene and hard-working cops. She's not afraid to pile up the dead bodies and sling the slang around."
—Wolf Schneider, Reviewer for *New Mexico Magazine* and former Editor-in-Chief of the *Santa Fean*

"Marie Romero Cash writes about Santa Fe with a local's razor-sharp insights, and peoples her exciting mystery with a gallery of colorful, authentic New Mexico characters. The plot moves with the speed and force of a Southwestern thunderstorm."
—Kirk Ellis, Co-Executive Producer/Screenwriter, HBO's *John Adams*

"A gifted writer has entered the ranks of the best of Southwest Mystery Writers. From the first chapters I found myself caught up in the action, stifling a catch in my throat, actually hyperventilating. This book has the kick of a high-powered rifle."
—Tal Streeter, sculptor and author

"*Shadows among the Ruins* is a great read whose real characters and honest dialog capture the intrigue of New Mexico. Throw in a great plot with a surprise ending, and mystery lovers will be clamoring for the sequel. Marie Romero Cash has taken the gift for prose she demonstrated in Lowrider Blues and applied it to the mystery genre with spectacular results."
—J. Michael Orenduff, Author, The Pot Thief Murder Mystery Series

"*Shadows among the Ruins* will compel some Southwestern mystery writers take another look at their own work. Marie Cash made me sit up and take notice. Her come-along plot made me miss dinner, but it was worth it. Now, after I get something to eat, I'm going to read it again. You have to like this book."
—Forrest Fenn, Santa Fe resident and owner of San Lazaro Pueblo, the setting for *Shadows*. He has written eight books on history, art, and archaeology.

The Mariachi Murder

The Mariachi Murder

A Jemimah Hodge Mystery

MARIE ROMERO CASH

CAMEL PRESS

Seattle, WA

Camel Press
PO Box 70515
Seattle, WA 98127

For more information go to: www.camelpress.com
marieromerocash.camelpress.com

Cover design by Sabrina Sun

The Mariachi Murder
Copyright © 2016 by Marie Romero Cash

ISBN: 978-1-60381-300-6 (Trade Paper)
ISBN: 978-1-60381-299-3 (eBook)

Library of Congress Control Number: 2015948380

Printed in the United States of America

For the City of Santa Fe, my hometown and inspiration for my art and my writing. And for my children, like Sun Mountain across the way, always there, looking over my shoulder, cheering me on.

Also by the author:

Shadows among the Ruins

Deadly Deception

Treasure among the Shadows

Chapter One

———◆———

IT WAS FIVE thirty on a cool September day in Santa Fe. The last of the seasonal wildflowers undulated through the landscape in waves of color.

The annual Santa Fe Fiesta was in full swing on the downtown Plaza, and vendors worked throughout the day to set up food booths beneath the shade of the massive elm trees. The smell of green chiles roasting on makeshift grills was propelled through the air by a gentle breeze. Hundreds of burger bun bags sat in stacks behind the booths, alongside cases of ketchup, mustard, and pickles. The hirelings hurriedly sliced away at succulent white onions, which filled their eyes with tears as they chopped. It would be dark in a few hours and the crowds would soon be closing in for the first sales of the weekend.

Santa Fe County Sheriff's Detective Rick Romero left the Cerrillos substation and turned down Highway 14 in the direction of Santa Fe. He had just picked up his girlfriend, Dr. Jemimah Hodge, at her ranchette at the base of the Ortiz Mountains a few miles north of Madrid. They were headed to Fort Marcy, a historic site about a mile north of Santa Fe Plaza.

The annual burning of Zozobra was scheduled to commence at sundown, a fitting time for thirty thousand residents and tourists to gather and witness his demise. Zozobra, aka Old Man Gloom, was a fifty-some foot giant marionette constructed by Fiesta volunteers from sticks, glue, chicken wire, and cloth. Its body was crammed full with over a ton of shredded paper, much of which consisted of old police reports, home mortgages, bills, Dear John letters, divorce decrees, and a multitude of other gloomy subjects. Onlookers gathered for the opportunity to send their own troubles up in smoke by writing them on slips of paper and offering them up to the soon-to-be-ashes effigy.

This would be the second year the couple attended the event. Detective Romero parked his vehicle in front of the Burrito Company on Washington Avenue in a space he scored when a delivery truck moved forward. As they began their walk, they soon merged with a large, exuberant crowd moving steadily toward the bright pink Masonic Temple building up ahead, where the road would narrow and lead them to Fort Marcy Park. It was a steep climb for many, but City officials had decided some years earlier that allowing traffic within three miles of Fort Marcy could be dangerous. It had therefore become a foot-traffic-only event, much to the chagrin of out-of-shape residents who struggled to make the climb.

Romero spread a blanket out on a grassy clump where the slope provided a good view. Jemimah sat cross-legged, wrapping part of the blanket around her.

She shivered. "Should have brought that sweater, but didn't think it was going to be this cool," she said.

He reached into the backpack and pulled out a windbreaker. "This should help," he said, and wrapped it around her shoulders.

Jemimah leaned against him and smiled. "You must have been a Boy Scout ... always prepared," she said.

He chuckled. "Nah, I've just frozen my butt off more times

than I can remember pursuing investigations after sundown."

They snuggled closer as the celebration commenced, watching for more than an hour as fire dancers with flaming torches pranced around the massive figure, working their way toward lighting the bonfires strategically placed at its base. At first the crowd was subdued. Then, one by one, each of the dancers hurled a torch, igniting the fires and causing Zozobra to awkwardly flail its elongated puppet arms and groan loudly in dismay. Onlookers began a thunderous chant and cheered in tandem, *Burn him! Burn him! Burn him!* A roar went up as a fireworks display spewed into the sky from the burning figure. As the giant gloom-monger burned down into cinders, the crowd began to dissipate. The satisfied onlookers gathered their belongings and made their way toward the exit.

As they strolled toward the center of town, the couple walked past the Palace of the Governors and the kiosks in the park, where artists would hawk their wares first thing in the morning. Romero squeezed Jemimah's hand. "Hungry?"

She grinned. "Kind of. What do you have in mind? I'm pretty much up for anything as long as it has green chile on it, in it or over it."

He motioned toward the hotel whose shadow loomed over the next block. "The bar at the La Fonda has a fiesta buffet until midnight. I imagine there's an abundance of smother-ready chile," he said.

Jemimah rubbed her stomach. "Sounds yummy to me."

Five minutes later they stopped at their vehicle and deposited the blanket and backpack in the trunk. "We can eat, have a few drinks, and enjoy the music," Romero said, directing her across the cobblestone street toward the entrance of the hotel.

She took his hand as they walked into the lobby. Music blared through the speakers around the hotel.

"The place is really jumping," Jemimah said. "Either everyone from Zozobra followed us in or we followed them."

Romero laughed. "Looks that way, doesn't it?"

They strolled past the La Plazuela Restaurant south of the entrance. Jemimah gazed at the hundreds of painted windowpanes surrounding the enclosure, their colorful scenes depicting birds, animals, and flowers. The lounge next door was an open concept design, bordered only by a small half-wall that also served as a *banco* for extra seating. From floor to ceiling, the walls were covered with *azulehos*—hand-painted Mexican tiles. He guided her to the center of the lounge where he spotted the last remaining table. "Looks like we lucked out," he said. "This one's vacant."

He pulled out a chair for Jemimah and edged the other closer to her and the table. He reached over and stroked her hair, and their eyes met. Neither wanted the evening to end.

The mariachi band returned from their break and stepped up on the stage. Excited chatter filled the room. The crowd's energy seemed to spur the musicians on.

Romero cupped his ear over hers. "I love this music," he said.

She nodded. "Me, too."

He grabbed her hand. "Come on, let's dance."

She laughed. "Hey, I can do a Texas two-step. I'm not sure I can keep up with a mariachi polka."

He skillfully spun her around the dance floor.

"Not much difference between country and Tex-Mex," he said.

The audience applauded, and as the music came to a halt, they were both out of breath. His hand grasping her elbow, he guided her back to the table. The cocktail waitress brought their drinks and pointed them to the buffet, where they could partake of an abundance of Mexican food when they were ready.

Jemimah took a sip of her drink. "Mmm. They do make a great margarita."

"Yeah, great girlie drinks," Romero teased and took a swallow of his beer.

Onlookers clapped, trumpets blared, and guitars twanged. A

roar went up from the audience as a lone mariachi took center stage and belted out a popular Mexican song. The stage itself was small, one third the size of the dance floor. Because the lounge opened into the lobby, hotel guests stood in the hallway, swaying to the music.

Jemimah was fascinated by the crowd's reaction, particularly the women. She turned to Romero. "Who is this guy? He seems to be really popular."

Romero leaned toward her. "His name is Eduardo Sanchez. A couple of us guys on the force went to high school with him."

They walked over to the buffet and filled their plates with steaming-hot Mexican food.

At ten o'clock, the band took a break. Sanchez walked over to greet Romero.

"Hey, Buddy, long time no see. Still fighting crime and keeping the city's neighborhoods safe?"

Romero stood, shook his hand, and introduced Jemimah. For the next five minutes Sanchez focused his attention on her. Romero merely smiled. When the entertainer returned to his equipment, she leaned over toward Romero and said, "He does think he's something special, doesn't he?"

"Yes," Romero said, "he's quite a ladies' man and famous in his own mind. Always been that way, ever since I can remember." He winked at her. "Looks like he's a little smitten with you."

She grinned and fluffed her hair. "Oh, yes. I do seem to have that effect on men."

Romero pulled her up from her seat, put his arm around her shoulder, and gave it a squeeze. "Yeah, I'll vouch for that." He pointed toward the exit. "Let's get out of here. I need to experience that effect you have on men."

"My place or yours?"

"My brother's still camping out at my place, so let's do yours, sweetie," he said, planting a kiss on her lips.

Following their passionate lovemaking, the couple settled into each other's arms, where sleep came easily.

Chapter Two

———◆———

Guadalajara, Jalisco, Mexico
A month later, November 1
Official Dia de los Muertos

DEEPLY ENGROSSED IN her work since early morning, Carmen de la Torre sat at the Singer sewing machine in the converted bedroom of her residence on La Paz Street. Every available inch of space in the room was stacked with reams of material for jackets and trousers. A professional seamstress for more than twenty years, she'd learned the craft by watching her mother toil fifteen hours a day on outfits for the *Americanos ricos*. The income she generated was less than a thousand pesos per month, but Carmen's mother kept the pantry stocked from the fruits of her labors.

Decades later, it was Carmen who had become famous, if indeed one could become famous as a seamstress. Nonetheless, she was sought out by mariachi bands throughout Mexico, the southwestern United States, and California. Carmen was the Mexican version of Ann Taylor.

In anticipation of the upcoming Day of the Dead celebration,

Carmen's ten-year-old daughter, Dulce, sat pensively at the shrine in the adjoining room. She had followed her mother's instructions to the letter and lit every candle on the shrine. A sweet-smelling cloud of copal incense hung in the air. Dozens of decorated sugar skulls and crepe-paper flowers in boxes waited to be placed on the altar. Dulce's task was to remove the cellophane wrapping and wait for further instructions from her mother.

Carmen took a minute to check on Dulce. "*Mi hija*, be careful not to burn yourself, and make sure you put the matches where your brother can't reach them."

"*Sí, Mama*, I already lit all the candles. I'm just waiting for you to hurry up so we can get dressed for the procession," Dulce said, her voice impatient.

Carmen stroked her daughter's head. "Ah, *mi querida*, I'm afraid I might have to ask Tia Loyda to take you. I'll catch up with you two when I'm done here. I'm expecting a man from Nuevo Mexico to stop by for his outfit. He's in a big hurry and wants to wear it for a concert next weekend." She was excited that her handiwork would be seen by everyone attending the concert.

Dulce stomped her feet in mock indignation. "*Aieee*, we never get anywhere on time."

"I'm sorry, Dulce. There's nothing I can do about it. So run over to Tia Loyda's and see if they've left yet."

Before her mother could formulate another sentence, Dulce turned and rushed out the door. It was no coincidence her name meant *the sweets of the sweet*. She knew her Auntie Loyda, who had no children of her own, would lavish her with every available sweet confection.

Carmen had worked feverishly for the past three days adding the final touches to the *charro* suit ordered by Eduardo Sanchez, a mariachi musician from Santa Fe. All that remained was to sew on sterling silver *botonaduras*. Sanchez was one of the few mariachis willing to pay extra for button adornments specially designed by a *platero* in the village.

Carmen and Sanchez had met in the spring of the previous year when he placed an order for a suit and asked her to recommend a *zapatero* to fashion a pair of boots to match the new outfit.

He was tall and handsome, and his deep hazel eyes sparkled with mischief. She assumed he was a good musician, as he had a booming melodious voice. When he showed her some photos of his group, she wondered if he was married, but didn't want to appear forward. Carmen didn't know then how her life would change because of her association with this attractive musician.

Chapter Three

———◆———

CARLOS ROMERO HAD been living in the spare bedroom of his brother Rick's house. The detective took Carlos in following his release from prison the previous year after he completed an eighteen-month sentence for possession of marijuana. Although he denied the bulk of the charges, Carlos was certain someone had set him up for the collar to get back at his brother. No matter. It was about time he moved into his own place. Rick seemed to be ragging on him more than usual about picking up after himself. Carlos had signed a lease on a condo on the east side of the city and was almost finished moving. He knew his brother would be happy about that.

It was late Friday afternoon when he stepped out of the shower and toweled himself off. At five feet eleven, he wasn't quite a mirror image of his brother. His eyes were a deeper green, and his straight hair was a darker shade of brownish black. Of the two siblings, he fit more in the category of eye candy than Rick, who was considered handsome in a rugged kind of way. He moved closer to the mirror, leaned forward and plucked a lone gray hair from his head. "Too young for that," he said out loud, turning his head in all directions to make sure there weren't any others. His cellphone vibrated on the dresser. It was Rick.

"Hey, Brother. Long time no hear," he said.

"I've been busy, Carlos, and you're never up by the time I leave and always gone by the time I get home," Romero said. "I was thinking you might want to catch something to eat, maybe have a few beers?"

"Ah, sorry. My immediate plan is to head to Albuquerque and check out the club action. Heard they opened a new place down on Central Avenue. You want to come along?"

"Not hardly. I gave up the party scene a long time ago. A bit too wild for my liking," Romero said.

"I knew that, Rick. Just wanted to see if you'd bite," he said. "Never know what sweet little dish is going to be ready to pull my heart strings."

"Seems to me it's about time you settle down and stick to one woman instead of playing the field," Romero said.

"Yeah, sure, Rick. Like you have, Mister Afraid of Commitment."

"Hey, I am in a committed relationship, Carlos," he said.

"Yeah, me too. Committed to sampling all the delicacies out there. Besides, that last involvement I had left a sour taste in my mouth. She couldn't pull herself away from constant gaming and texting on her iPhone long enough to focus on our relationship." Carlos didn't see the need to convince his brother of the fun he had nightclubbing. Albuquerque was the nearest place a guy could party that offered variety. The city was almost ten times the size of Santa Fe. Rows of busy nightclubs lined Central Avenue—the historic Route 66, which wound its way through the center of town. More importantly, it was a mere sixty minutes from his front door.

"Okay, Carlos. So take it easy."

Putting down the phone, Carlos walked into the bedroom and smiled at himself in the full-length mirror on the closet door. He reached for his keys and headed out the door.

Traffic was heavy for the weekend, and by the time he reached the off-ramp on Interstate 25 to the Central Avenue exit, he found that the Albuquerque Police Department had already barricaded off an eight-block section of the popular downtown area. Officers on horseback patrolled the streets with eyes peeled for any sign of a disturbance. Dubbed the Party Patrol, the task force was designed to keep revelers from raising too much hell on city streets. With a criminal record under his belt, Carlos was ever careful to keep his hot temper under wraps, particularly around saddle-bound law enforcement. His personal goal for the evening wasn't so much to raise hell as it was to just get laid.

He rolled into the municipal parking lot, paid the ten dollar fee, alarmed his car, and walked down Central Avenue. The area buzzed with activity. The Friday night art walk was in full swing, with galleries featuring live bands filled to capacity. At the end of a two-block walk, he found himself in front of Sprig, a trendy club smack dab in the middle of downtown. The line at the door stretched for half a block. A pair of hefty bouncers ushered patrons in one at a time, while deftly weeding out any shabbily dressed undesirables. Carlos noticed that most of those allowed in line were dressed to impress. He was surrounded by a gaggle of expensively attired twenty-somethings—shapely, well-tanned women in short cocktail skirts and Aldo heels. Their male counterparts were dressed in Ed Hardy or Affliction shirts, clean shaven with spiked hair and bulging biceps. Although he was dressed in an expensive white Canali shirt, Diesel jeans, and black Chuck Taylors, Carlos felt a little out of place. At least he was smooth-shaven like the rest of the guys in line and his clothes didn't come from a cheap outlet store.

It took a while to reach the front of the line, where the no-personality bouncer droned his admonitions to the crowd. "Hey, stay in line. Get forward or get out." The intimidating six-foot, two-hundred pounder seemed to be caught up in his own fantasy of being some celebrity's bodyguard, not a ten-dollar-an-hour flunky for a seedy nightclub.

"Let me see your ID, boss," he said to Carlos.

A surprised Carlos complied. "So how's it going tonight? Looks like the place is rockin'," he said.

Foregoing the courtesy of a response, the bouncer handed back his ID, stamped the top of his hand with a blue star, and motioned him forward. As Carlos entered the club, a comely barely eighteen girl smiled broadly at him.

"Coat check?" she said, her heavy lashes fluttering.

Carlos returned the smile and winked. "No, but thank you."

The club looked bigger from the outside. A spiky haired tattooed DJ dressed in black entertained from an enclosure halfway between the floor and the fifteen-foot ceiling. A pair of go-go boxes occupied the space on either side as visually privileged female dancers performed a provocative bump and grind in time with the music. The scantiness of their outfits didn't escape Carlos.

If he thought the clubs in Santa Fe were noisy, they were quiet compared to the thunderous din in this place. Winding his way to the bar, he waited fifteen minutes to order a drink and another ten for the bartender to hand it to him. The DJ was spinning his own version of a convoluted mix of a popular song with no apparent rhythm—an obnoxious baseline with a robotic voice in the background that could easily drive a person nuts if they were stone cold sober, which at that point, Carlos was. Between the flashing strobe lights and the fog machine, and for all the hype surrounding this place, Carlos had expected an ultra-clone of a Las Vegas night club. He figured he'd better lower his expectations. *I'd probably be better off if I'd caught the red-eye to Las Vegas and partied at TAO. A lot better class of people than these wannabes.*

And then the most beautiful creature he'd ever seen almost knocked him over on her way to the bathroom.

She looked like she belonged in a centerfold. Her shapely

legs, small waist, and ample bosom were capable of stopping traffic on any main street in America. Thunderstruck, Carlos watched her comely hips sway as she made her way back. She winked as she passed his table. Carlos stood, almost blocking her path. Lush lashes bordered her deep green eyes as she looked up at him.

"Excuse me, miss. I hope you don't think I'm being too forward, but can I buy you a drink?" he said.

She tossed her blond hair back and laughed. "Sure, if you'll introduce yourself properly. I do love a gentleman."

Carlos bowed from the waist. "My name is Carlos, and I'm from Santa Fe."

"So am I," she said. "Just came out here to take a break from the dull nightlife." She stuck out her hand. "Annae … Rivers."

He pulled a chair out for her to sit. "See, we already have something in common," Carlos said. "I don't think I could take another night talking to myself. I'm sure you've never had that problem, though."

"Just the opposite. Sometimes I just want to sit and enjoy the music. You wouldn't believe how many times I can get hit on during the night."

Carlos smiled and leaned toward her. "Yes, I would. I'm sure you hear this a lot, but you're quite beautiful."

Over two rounds of drinks, Carlos would learn that in recent months Annae had settled into a new apartment in Santa Fe and taken a job as hostess for a downtown gallery. When the bartender yelled "last call," the couple looked up in surprise.

"My God, we've been talking for two hours," she said.

"Yes, and apparently it's time to call it a night. Would you care to have breakfast?" he said. "I'm staying the night at the Hilton."

"Let me check. I came here with a friend, but last time I saw her, she had her eyes on one of the DJs. Do you mind waiting a few minutes?"

"Not at all," Carlos said. "Take your time." As he waited, he found himself caught up in the fantasy of love at first sight. There was no doubt in his mind that this was "the one."

Chapter Four

———◆———

THE TINY VILLAGE of Cerrillos lies eighteen miles south of Santa Fe, New Mexico, halfway up Highway 14, a narrow winding road dubbed The Turquoise Trail because the area was originally an ancient source of blue-green turquoise. The town itself hasn't changed much over the years. Most of the dwellings are surrounded by acreage, so neighbors aren't usually within an arm's length of each other as they are in the city. The residents are mostly long-time Spanish-speaking individuals along with a few *gringo* throwbacks to the hippie era. It is an old town, with historic hotel and opera house buildings, curio stores and an age-old Catholic church, all lined up along the dusty dirt road that serves as its main street. The sound of horses, goats and chickens can usually be heard in the background.

Overlooking the town, the Ortiz Mountain Range juts from the earth, its translucent triangular peaks reaching upward like jagged edges of broken glass. The scorching sun hides under gray-scaled clouds gathered together in a futile attempt to wash away the sins of the day with a sudden downpour. A light breeze gently scatters the clouds to the four directions.

Eight miles south, up the highway from Cerrillos, is the Mine Shaft Tavern, a popular bar situated on a half-acre plot on the outskirts of Madrid. For over half a century it has provided liquor and entertainment for a broad cross-section of residents, passersby and tourists alike. The town is like a born-again Christian, ready to embrace everyone with a pulse. From a derelict state in the 1970s, it emerged as a mecca for present-day glassblowers, weavers, and a bevy of arts and crafters. Colorful shop façades lined the lazy highway that ran through the center of town. Road signs varied from *slow down or die* to *caution: fat dog crossing*, each equally ignored by drivers who resented the slowed-down posted speed.

Along a country road several miles northeast of Madrid, Simon Garcia walked along the border of the Crawford and Butler ranches. Since sunup that Tuesday morning, he had meandered along miles of fence line searching for a break where cattle had been skipping off to greener pastures. After trudging around for an inordinate distance, he spotted a section of open fence up ahead. As he approached, he saw several downed posts, the barbed wire fencing between them having been cut.

Garcia, the foreman of the Butler Ranch, surveyed the damage a few minutes longer. He kicked at the dirt, generating a small puff of dust. *Son of a bitch. Who the hell's been out here? Old man Butler's going to be pissed about this. It's going to cost him a bundle to fix this mess, and I'll probably be the one busting my ass to get it done.*

In order to mark the location of the break when he brought the repair material in, he tied a couple of blue plastic streamers to the barbed wire fence. He turned to hike back to his vehicle, which was parked about a mile away near the Galisteo River.

As he hiked, he thought about the weekend and Cinco de Mayo. It wasn't often that May 5th fell on a Friday, which meant that he and his friends could really tie one on and celebrate in style. He smiled at the thought and made a mental note to call his girlfriend when he finished here.

Garcia forgot all about his plans for the weekend when he spotted something shiny a few yards away.

Hell, might as well take my sweet time getting back to the ranch. I can squeeze out another hour wandering around here. Don't get paid enough to hurry. Garcia's hobby was collecting Indian artifacts. He'd spent most of last summer at nearby San Lazaro Pueblo, excavating with the University archaeological team on the Indian ruins.

He approached the gleaming object at the edge of a patch of spiny cholla cactus. Leaning forward for closer inspection, he yelped as the needles reached out and poked his hand. He pulled back in pain, then rifled through his backpack for a pair of leather gloves. He reached down and grasped the egg-sized triangular piece of metal but it appeared to be deeply embedded in the dirt. Undaunted, Garcia kicked at the sides a few times but failed to dislodge it. It might just be deeper than he thought. Excited, he recalled that some years before at the Tesuque Flea Market, a collector had bought a pair of silver stirrups from a picker that turned out to be worth twenty-five grand.

He looked around for a sharp rock or stick, anything he could dig with and found a metal lid and a flat rock. Garcia sniggered as he knelt on the rocky ground and proceeded to scrape around the edges, careful not to scratch or damage his treasure in any way. "All right, sucker," he muttered. "You're mine now."

He was a patient man. He knocked away a few branches of cactus with his pocket knife and used the flat rock in an attempt to unearth the piece. A half hour and several handfuls of soil later, he placed both hands on the object and gave it a hard pull. He hoped it was a silver relic, a thought which flew out of his mind as quickly as it blinked in.

"Jesus Christ," Garcia yelled. He jerked so violently that the movement propelled him back a few feet, landing him on his rear end. A loud, guttural sound emanated from deep within his being. When the dust settled and he stopped trembling, he stared down at the human leg jutting from the ground, the sterling silver wingtip on the cowboy boot glinting in the sun.

Chapter Five

———•———

THAT TUESDAY AFTERNOON Detective Rick Romero was traveling in heavy five o'clock traffic between Interstate 25 and Highway 14 on a winding washboard dirt road a few miles southwest of Cerrillos near the Town of Waldo. He glanced over at Devil's Throne, a dark looming group of obsidian mountains, where the previous year Jemimah Hodge had escaped a hired killer. A shudder ran through him as he gripped the wheel with both hands and checked the rearview mirror for traffic. He was driving the silver and black county sheriff's cruiser, and the condition of the road caused it to fishtail repeatedly. He was en route to the substation after a long day in Albuquerque and was looking forward to dropping off his gear and heading home for a cold beer, a green chile and sausage pizza, and a wide berth in front of his television. The NCAA Mountain West Championships in Reno, Nevada, were scheduled to begin and the seventh seeded UNM Lobos were slated to go up against heavily favored San Diego State. An avid baseball fan, he wasn't going to miss this game. He had a hundred bucks riding on his UNM alma mater.

Just on the outskirts of Cerrillos, he groaned as the cell phone shrieked its incoming call ring. It was a few minutes after five. His office was officially closed. He debated about answering. Probably another domestic altercation, shoplifter- or alcohol-related auto collision. He thought for a moment about letting it go to message. Dispatch could forward it on to Detectives Chacon or Martinez.

Oh hell, he muttered before answering, "Romero."

***

JUST AN HOUR before at four o'clock, Tim McCabe was parked on the side of the gravel road leading to Kennedy Hill, rearranging files that had slid off the passenger seat onto the floor. He was on his way to serve a handful of warrants, and like his fellow deputies, he wasn't too happy about going up that remote mountain for any reason. You never knew what to expect from the crazies who resided there.

Kennedy Hill was a small burg in the knolls southeast of Cerrillos, just this side of the county line, nestled between the Ortiz Mountains and Galisteo Creek. One road in, one road out, and sparsely populated. Residing in trailer homes, largely without indoor facilities, they were mostly pot cultivators and drug dealers who preferred to live in secluded areas of Santa Fe County not easily accessible to the general public. Trespassers generally found themselves face to face with a double-barreled shotgun wielded by a not too friendly septuagenarian whose tanned and wrinkled skin bore the ravages of rough country living.

That particular area, like much of the acreage off northern New Mexico's beaten path, had originally been U.S. Forest Service or privately owned land. The town was established by a land grant in the 1860s that allowed qualifying individuals 160 acres for farming. Unfortunately, gold panning in the Cerrillos hills had been potentially more enticing and lucrative, and after a few years, pretty much all the homesteads in and around Kennedy Hill had been abandoned. Then, in the mid-sixties, small-time entrepreneurs decided the town was the perfect place to cultivate marijuana crops. Approaching vehicles could be spotted from any vantage point on the hill.

Tim McCabe was a lanky cowpuncher with silver specked hair and piercing blue eyes … and a former Idaho lawman. He and his wife Laura had retired to Santa Fe over a decade before. They met when he traveled to Ruidoso to assist her father in developing security for the horse-racing industry. Some months later, he sold the ranch in Idaho, cashed in all his investments, and moved to Ruidoso to marry the woman of his dreams. After Laura's parents were killed in an automobile accident, he retired from law enforcement and they moved to a home on the east side of Santa Fe. For the past two years McCabe had been on the payroll of the Santa Fe County Sheriff's Office as a part-time special deputy, much to his wife's dismay. She would have preferred he devote his time to running the Canyon Road ethnographic gallery they sold last year.

It had been a long day and so far he hadn't been able to corner even one person to serve a warrant on. The steep hills and rutted roads were slow going, and his stomach was growling. He figured it was time to head back to the San Marcos Café for a late lunch. McCabe took in a deep breath and fanned himself with his cowboy hat, mulling over the idea of calling it a day and serving the papers another time. *Oh, what the heck. I'm already out this far, might as well just do it and get it over with.*

The sun was blazing hot, unusual for so early in the springtime. Global warming, he presumed. The cloud cover had drifted south, dashing any hope of a sudden storm to cool things off. McCabe was particularly fond of this part of the county, just a couple of miles from the property he'd purchased a few years ago, which consisted primarily of the remnants of an ancient Indian ruin, San Lazaro Pueblo. More recently, he and Laura had bought the adjoining ranch, upgraded it and made it their part-time residence.

He was about to pull onto the main road when off in the distance he observed a red Jeep coming at him like a bat out of hell, a cloud of dust blowing in its wake. McCabe blocked the road with his Hummer and whirred a few blasts of the siren. The Jeep slammed to a stop. He walked toward the vehicle as the driver rolled down the window and made with a get-out-of-the-way motion with his arms.

McCabe responded with a hold-your-horses gesture of his own. "Whoa there, fellow. Where're you headed in such a danged hurry? At that speed and on this road, you could easily flip your vehicle."

"Going into Madrid to call the cops. Would you mind moving your car, sir?" Garcia said.

"I am a cop," said McCabe, flashing his badge. "Now what's your hurry?"

"Left my cellphone at work. I, ah…" Garcia babbled.

"Slow down a minute there, son. Let me have your driver's license." The man complied. "You need a drink of water? You look pretty shook up, Mr. Garcia … Simon," he added, glancing at the driver's license.

"No, I just need to get into town."

"What are you doing out here? This is private property. You see those signs there?" McCabe pointed in the direction of the fence.

"I work for the Butler Ranch in Galisteo. I was out looking for a break in the fence line."

McCabe introduced himself. "Are those your cattle that have been determined to gobble up all the grass on the Crawford Ranch? Which I happen to own, by the way."

"Yes, yeah, I g-guess," the man stammered. "But listen, I need to get the hell into town." Garcia's fists were clenched around the steering wheel.

McCabe reached through the driver's side window and placed his hand on Garcia's shoulder. "Hey, take it easy, there. Relax. Tell me what's got you all spooked."

Even after McCabe's attempt at small-talking him down, Garcia still appeared shaken. Dribbles of sweat trickled down his forehead. "Like I said, I was out looking for a break in the fence, and when I found it, I started to head back. Then I saw this shiny thing in the ground and decided to dig it up."

"What was it, a relic of some sort?" said McCabe, himself familiar with the thrill of finding an old piece of Indian something or other.

"No, no. It was a boot tip. But I didn't know that until I started digging around it. There was a guy attached to it."

McCabe was incredulous. "You mean a human leg?" he said.

"Yeah, yeah. I think there's a whole body. A dead guy. Someone must have buried him out there. Oh, Jesus. I don't even want to think about it." Garcia wrung his hands, gripping the steering wheel even tighter. "I think I'm going to throw up."

McCabe pulled open the Jeep door. "Here, let me help you."

Garcia plunked himself down on the running board.

McCabe handed him a bottle of water. "Have a few slow sips of water. Maybe take a few deep breaths. I'm going to call this in to the sheriff's office, and when they get here, you can show us exactly where this body is."

Chapter Six

———◆———

Rɪᴄᴋ Rᴏᴍᴇʀᴏ ʜᴀᴅ been a SFCSO deputy for over fifteen years, having come up through the ranks to Detective Lieutenant. He was well aware that every time he answered the phone, he increased the chances of his day going all to hell. This was no different. Tim McCabe was on the other end of the line.

"What is it, Tim? I'm on my way home after a damned long day in Albuquerque. Can't you handle this?"

" 'Fraid not, Rick. We have a ten-fifty-four out here in the boonies off Highway 14. Need you to get out here, pronto," McCabe said. "Fellow might have found a body on the ranch that adjoins mine on the southeast side."

Romero grunted. "All right. Give me your twenty and I'll be there as fast as I can. I'm just pulling into Cerrillos."

McCabe was on the phone for another couple of minutes. "I'll flag you down when I see you. Can't miss us. Red Jeep parked next to my Hummer."

Romero dialed Jemimah's number. She answered on the first ring. Her voice had a musical lilt to it. He would have preferred to have a nice conversation with her but it wasn't the time. Their romantic relationship had to take a back burner to their duties as county employees. He explained McCabe's call. "I'll be by your place in about ten minutes. No use taking two vehicles."

Jemimah hung up the phone, slipped into her boots, and grabbed a light jacket. She hurried over to the corral, where her horse Mandy neighed a greeting. She stroked the Appaloosa's neck and made sure the water trough and feed sack were both full. She was grateful that the teenager from the adjoining ranch came by a few times a week to take care of chores she had little time for. She regretted neglecting the horse, the dog, and the resident cat, Gato. Hopefully life would slow down soon and give her a chance to ride the range.

Romero tapped his horn just as she reached the end of the gravel driveway. Putting the vehicle in park and sliding out of the driver's seat, he gave her a quick embrace and opened the passenger door. She looked at him as she buckled her seatbelt.

"What's going on, Rick? I thought you'd be home by now."

"You and me both," he said. "Unfortunately McCabe called me about a possible homicide out near Galisteo."

"Sorry to hear that. Any more info?" she said.

"Nope. We'll know more when we get there." He blasted the siren to alert a slow-moving trail of vehicles.

Jemimah moistened her lips. "Hope it's a false alarm. The county's already caught up to last year's homicide count."

Romero nodded. "I gathered that from the sheriff's newsletter."

They drove in silence until Romero spotted McCabe's vehicle. McCabe greeted them both—a handshake for Romero and a hug for Jemimah.

McCabe gave them a quick recap of the events of the last hour. "This guy's going to show us where he thinks there's a body."

He directed Garcia to the Hummer and pulled open the back passenger door. "Come on, Mr. Garcia. Climb in there.

Lean back and try to relax. I'll bring you back to your vehicle when we're done. I'm thinking you're still a little too shook up to drive."

"Yeah, thanks. I am," said Garcia, his knees wobbling visibly as he stood up and walked toward McCabe's Humvee. McCabe slid into the driver's seat, spun the vehicle around, and headed across the property. Romero and Jemimah followed suit.

They were noticeably jittery as they traveled along the fence line. Garcia gestured to McCabe. "There, over there. You see the break in the fence where I tied those blue ribbons? Right across from that. Next to that clump of cactuses."

McCabe slowed to a stop, and parking about fifty yards from where Garcia indicated, he stuck his arm out the window and pointed Romero toward the empty space next to them. The four exited the vehicles. Romero walked up to Garcia and introduced himself and Jemimah.

"Mr. Garcia, would you mind showing us where you think this body is located?" Romero said. "Let me remind you that if this is indeed a crime scene, you need to be careful where you step."

As he walked around the area, Romero zeroed in on the scene. To his trained eye, it appeared that the body hadn't been there too long, since the coyotes hadn't yet dug it up. He motioned to McCabe. "He's right. There's a foot attached to this boot," he said. "Probably a whole body."

McCabe nodded. "Looks that way."

Romero noticed Garcia was still shaking. "Mr. Garcia, you can go back and sit in the Hummer. We shouldn't be too long here. And then, if you don't mind, you can answer a few questions."

Garcia jumped at the chance. He had seen enough. As if nauseated, he leaned his head back on the headrest and closed his eyes.

Detective Romero returned to his own vehicle and radioed the location into headquarters. He pulled a clipboard and pen from the glove box and called Jemimah over. Then he poked his head into the window of McCabe's vehicle.

"Mr. Garcia, we're going to be here a while longer. As soon as the medical examiner and the crime scene techs get here, I'll let you be on your way. While we're waiting, Dr. Hodge here will take your statement. It'll save some time and get you back on the road sooner."

Jemimah sat in the seat next to Garcia. She small-talked him for a while, hoping he would calm down enough to give a coherent narrative of how he had discovered the body. His hands shook as he related what had happened after he arrived in the area to check for the broken fences. Jemimah noticed the man's shirt was drenched in sweat and his face was ashen. *Not a very tough cowboy*, she thought.

At half past six, Romero turned his attention to the billowing dust trail of the medical examiner's van winding its way toward them. McCabe motioned for them to park; otherwise it appeared as though the driver would have driven to within inches of the scene. He watched as Chief Medical Examiner Harry Donlon stepped ceremoniously out of the van. He hadn't changed much—a large man with a modified Beatles haircut infused with salt and pepper fringing an acne-scarred face. Known for his reprehensible bedside manner, He had been the chief medical examiner for more years than Romero had been in law enforcement. He thrust his hand out to greet Donlon.

"Mr. Donlon?" Romero said. "I was expecting the second-in-command. I was under the impression you never left your office after lunch."

Donlon snorted and brushed past him, ignoring the outstretched hand. "For your information, I was just about to sit down to dinner." He thumped his bag on the ground and looked down at the crime scene, his long-suffering assistant standing by. "Hey, you. Get your ass in gear, boy. We don't have all afternoon. Once it starts getting dark, you'll have to pull out the floodlights."

"Yes, sir," the young man responded. Romero rolled his eyes at McCabe.

The techs gloved up and deposited their equipment along the fence line. The ME instructed them to carefully dig a trench around the dead man to expose the body. The corpse had been buried in a shallow grave no deeper than two feet. The techs followed the ME's instructions, dusting the body off with whisk brooms as they revealed more and more of it. In a few days the harsh spring winds would have all but blown the top layer away, exposing the body to the elements.

When the techs had finished unearthing the body, Donlon scowled. "Anything of interest strewn around here?"

"Didn't find anything," Romero said.

Donlon gazed up at him. "So everyone's been stomping around here scattering evidence?"

Romero could feel the heat rising to his face. "I'm saying we checked the area to see if anything was lying around. Of course we knew better than to dig him up before you got here."

The ME grumbled, "All right, all right. Just asking. Don't get your *huevos* in an uproar." He gave the body a cursory exam, turning him to the side.

"Couple of gunshot wounds. Poor guy probably never had a chance. No question it's a homicide. Skull seems to be fractured, more than likely by a high-velocity bullet." He conducted a few tests on the body and looked over at the techs. "Bag him. Not much we can do out here." Donlon snapped his satchel shut, stood up, and started to walk back to the van. Jemimah stopped him mid-step.

"Excuse me, Dr. Donlon."

"Yes, what is it? I'm done here," he huffed.

"Could you take a look at the fellow who found the body? He's having a pretty hard time calming down," she said.

Donlon held back a scowl. "Oh, all right. Where is he?"

Jemimah led him to the Hummer. Donlon grunted a greeting, pulled out his stethoscope, and pressed the end against Garcia's chest. He raised his hand and lifted an eyelid with his thumb and shone a small flashlight on each eye, directing Garcia to look straight ahead. Donlon turned to Jemimah.

"I would venture a guess that he's in shock. Heart rate's not too high, though. Should be all right. Nothing to worry about." He shifted his gaze to Garcia. "Mr. Garcia, get yourself home and fix yourself a nice stiff drink. Get some sleep. You'll be fine in a couple of hours." With that, he turned and headed for his van, gripping the black leather case in one hand.

Romero and McCabe watched as the techs placed the partially decomposed body on the plastic sheet and slid it into a blue Ziploc body bag. Post-mortem lividity had long set in. The tech pressed the seal together and scribbled something on the tag with a purple Sharpie. They lifted the body onto the gurney and wheeled it across the terrain to a waiting ambulance. Donlon had already driven off into the sunset, radio blaring some she-done-me-wrong country song.

Chapter Seven

———◆———

Though hampered by his nervousness, Jemimah had completed her interview of the witness. By seven thirty she was certain Garcia had calmed down enough to be able to drive home. She escorted him back to his Jeep.

She poked her head into the passenger side as he started up the engine and buckled his seatbelt. "Are you sure you're going to be all right, Mr. Garcia? I'd be glad to drop you off somewhere."

Garcia smiled weakly. "I'll be all right. Thanks. I'm going straight home to try to forget all this," he said.

Romero looked up as Jemimah joined him and McCabe while they secured the area.

"Anything of interest?" Romero asked.

"Nothing other than the guy was out here minding his own business hoping to peel off a few more hours before he returned to his job. Shock of his life. I imagine it's going to take him a while to get over it."

McCabe wiped his forehead. "Yeah, looking at bodies is second nature with law enforcement, but even after all these years, it doesn't get any easier."

Jemimah stood for a moment and looked around the entire scene. She viewed the indentation in the ground left by the victim. Dried blood mingled with the desert sand, leaving no question where the body had been. "I wonder why the killer would pick this particular spot to bury the victim, next to a fence line bordering two ranches each with a bit of acreage."

"It's off the beaten path, but hardly one that seems too isolated," McCabe replied. "From the tire tracks and scattered beer cans in the nearby field, I get the impression it's probably a popular make-out spot. Most of those cans have bullet holes through them, so a lot of random target practice must take place out here too."

Romero scratched his head. "Whoever did this had to know that the body would be discovered at some point, don't you think?"

McCabe nodded. "Darn right. My ranch hand checks the fence lines every couple of weeks, and I'm sure the adjoining rancher does the same. On the other hand, if the killers weren't familiar with this part of the county, they might have just dumped the body and figured it would never be discovered."

"Sure would hate to be the one to notify the family. Good thing that's not part of Donlon's job description," said Romero.

"Poor bastard. From the looks of it, he probably never had a chance, you think?" said McCabe.

"Looks that way," said Romero. "Off the cuff, it appears this wasn't about money, but more personal. A coward shoots a victim without warning. Revenge? Getting even? Time will tell, if we're lucky."

"Gonna have to figure out what he was doing out here on the Butler ranch. I heard the old guy doesn't cotton to trespassers on his land, especially dead ones," said McCabe. "Looks like whoever did this had plenty of time to dig a hole and bury him, being careful to leave that cactus on top."

Romero nodded. "Yeah, some warped sense of humor. You know this Butler guy, the ranch owner? Any chance he might be involved?"

"Doubt it," McCabe said. "He's got to be in his eighties. Ranch hands do all the work. He spends most his days at the town hall in Galisteo, sending out literature on fracking and other environmental issues."

A brisk May wind was revving up, and it was starting to get dark. Jemimah zipped up her windbreaker, adjusting the collar around her neck. "We'll still have to talk to him. See if he knows anything."

"You know, Jemimah, this section of the ranch is some distance from Butler's main house. Even though there's a bunch of No Trespassing signs posted, these remote areas get a bit of random traffic. They're not as isolated as one might think. Someone's always driving around here shooting rabbits or using the signs for target practice."

She leaned against the fender of Romero's vehicle. "You think maybe this could have happened in broad daylight? Hard to bury someone right out in the open without worrying about being seen."

He scanned the area as he replied, "Either that or they used their headlights to light up the place. But don't dismiss the daylight theory. These ranches cover a hell of a lot of acreage. It's impossible for the property owner to patrol all of it. If it hadn't been for the break in the fence and a couple of head of cattle wandering off, that fellow who found the body wouldn't have had a need to be here."

"You're probably right. I hadn't thought of that," Jemimah said.

McCabe pointed toward the site. "I took a look at the break in the fence. It was an old cut. Probably a couple of poachers who bagged a deer last winter and couldn't figure how to get it out other than to cut the fence."

Jemimah pulled on the handle of the cruiser and smiled at McCabe. "Helps to know these things."

"Yep," McCabe said. "Took the cows about a month to wander in this direction, but if they hadn't, we wouldn't be having this conversation."

Romero climbed in the driver's side and looked over at Jemimah, who was fastening her seatbelt. "Well, I guess we're done here. I'll drop you off on my way home. It's been a damned long day."

She leaned her head back. "Yes, it has. Do you want to come by the house? I can throw something together for dinner."

He shook his head. "I'll take a rain check. I'm so tired I probably wouldn't be very good company."

She nodded. "Yeah, I know what you mean. All I want to do is wash all this dust off, feed my animals, and call it a night." He gave her a quick kiss on the lips and rested his hand on her cheek.

The couple had been dating for almost a year. Jemimah, a forensic psychologist for the county, had been with the Santa Fe County Sheriff's Office for three years. She worked directly under Sheriff Medrano, as did Romero. They were thrown together on a regular basis for most homicide cases, as it was her job to formulate a profile for any suspects. She wondered what surprises this new case would bring.

Romero started up the engine and maneuvered onto the main road. He glanced at his watch and wondered if he could make it home in time to catch the last quarter of the baseball game. There would be time enough to ponder about the investigation in the morning.

Chapter Eight

———◆———

IT WAS THE day after the body had been discovered. In almost every murder case in the county, Detective Artie Chacon served as lead detective and reported first to Sheriff Medrano and then to Romero, who trusted him to wrap everything up and tie it with a yellow ribbon. He was a seasoned detective and chief of the county forensic unit, and like many of his co-workers, a Santa Fe native. In previous months, Chacon had proven his worth by solving a number of high-profile cases. Unlike Romero, he was dark-skinned. He was shorter in stature than Romero, who stood a little over five-ten, with coal-black hair pulled back into a neat ponytail. He'd recently shaved off his handlebar moustache after years of constant ribbing from his peers that he resembled an old-time movie villain. That morning he had been assigned to return to the scene of the crime.

He parked his vehicle near where the body had been discovered and scoured the perimeter beyond the crime scene for anything the techs might have missed. This was one of the many times it annoyed him to adhere to the SFCSO dress code. It was a pain in the ass to climb over or crawl under a barbed-wire fence wearing dress pants and a white shirt. After roaming around the perimeter for more than half an hour, he dusted himself off and walked the hundred yards or so to his cruiser. Whatever clues the harsh overnight winds hadn't scattered, the accompanying torrential rain managed to obliterate. The yellow tape secured around the juniper bushes and fence seemed out of place in the wide open desert. *Nothing more to accomplish here. Might as well go see what the boss has cooking.* He hoisted himself up into his vehicle.

Back on Highway 14, within ten minutes he was a few blocks from the satellite office in Cerrillos. He smiled as he observed how the panhandlers scattered in front of the general store as he drove by. He parked his truck in front of the substation, making sure he locked the doors. It would be an embarrassment if his weapon or even his vehicle disappeared from in front of the sheriff's office. He walked up the gravel driveway and through the glass door.

The front office was empty. He walked toward the back. Romero was in his office. "In here, Artie. Come on back," he hollered.

Chacon stuck his head in the door, turning his head to each side in an exaggerated motion. "I'm surprised our Doctor Hodge isn't here playing Nancy Grace, that television reporter who likes to get herself involved in every case that comes down the pike. And where's that pretty secretary of yours?"

Romero's eyebrows furrowed. "Clarissa is out picking up office supplies. And what's up with these comments about Dr. Hodge, Artie? I thought you liked her."

Chacon pulled out a chair, sat, and put his palms up. "Don't get me wrong, boss. I admire the heck out of her. She's a very intelligent lady."

"But?" Romero said.

Chacon fidgeted in his seat. "Well, it seems like she's always poking around, asking questions," he said. "Like she's more detective than whatever her job description says she is."

Romero cocked his head. "For instance?"

"For instance, why was she one of the first ones on the crime scene?"

"Dr. Hodge's job description encompasses a number of things, Detective, which include conducting interviews of potential suspects and then using those interviews to develop criminal profiles. These have been proven to be very effective in solving crimes. Viewing the victim's body helps her craft these profiles so that they are even more useful to us. Being on the scene can be more enlightening than viewing photographs of the body. We both know it takes the trained eye of a good detective to pick up on the clues left at a crime scene. But a forensic psychologist can pick up on the subtleties about both the victim and the criminal. In case none of you have noticed, her work has been instrumental in helping the Department solve a couple of high profile cases."

Chacon got the impression he might have hit a nerve with his boss. He waved his hand. "I don't mean anything by it. Just having a rough day, I guess."

Romero was aware how some of his detectives perceived Jemimah's efforts regarding their caseload. Even more so once they became a couple. He leaned back in his chair. "Look, Artie. I'm fully aware your crew has done some solid work in solving a bunch of these high priority cases."

Chacon nodded. "Thank you, boss. We appreciate that."

"I have a great deal of respect for all of you," Romero continued. "I know damned well how difficult it is to come up the ranks, particularly in a county where politics rule. That damned board of supervisors is populated by a group of self-serving politicians who are of the opinion that Sheriff Medrano already has too much power, so hiring additional deputies or promoting those already employed is out of the question. The muckety-mucks from the county cite the recession, the necessity to cut down on unnecessary expenses, and anything else they think bolsters their position."

Chacon flinched. "Yeah, don't get me started on that subject. Fewer deputies and higher salaries for the commissioners. Santa Fe politics at its best. And yet they continue to wonder why cases take such a long time to solve. No manpower. No progress."

"My point exactly. That's why we need all the help we can get. That said, Artie, I would appreciate it if you guys would give Dr. Hodge some slack. She's just doing her job, and she exhibits a lot more enthusiasm than most people."

Chacon shifted in his chair. Romero changed the subject. "I see you've been rolling around in the dirt again, *hombre*?"

The detective looked down at his dusty boots. "Yeah, I have. So answer me this: how come the employees at the main office get to wear jeans and t-shirts and we have to dress up like altar boys?"

"Sheriff Medrano likes his deputies to appear professional, even though some of them can't pull it off," Romero said in his best faux-authoritative voice. "Besides, have you seen the price they're charging for Levis these days?"

The detective grunted as he bent down and pulled a file from his briefcase. "I guess, but it pisses me off that every time we have an investigation going out in the boonies, my dry cleaning bill goes up," he said. "Anyway, no use beating a dead horse." He handed the file to Romero. "Here's the info you requested, boss. I went out to the site and didn't find anything more than what the techs gathered, which was pretty much nothing. The boonies don't hold onto stuff like something that happens indoors. The landscape can change from night to morning with a rainstorm or strong wind."

Romero reached for the sheaf of papers and scanned down the pages. He browsed through the photographs, and although the body appeared to be partially decomposed, the tall male corpse was still fully clothed. The ravages of decomposition, along with the blood and mud caked over his head and neck, made him unrecognizable.

"Ranch hand was out there checking for stray cattle on the property," Romero explained for the record, since he wasn't sure how much Chacon had been told already. "Located the broken fence, hung around a while hunting for pottery chards and discovered the guy's boot protruding from the earth. Ended up being human remains."

Chacon leaned over and glanced at the photographs. "Any sign of foul play?"

"Being covered with dirt and a couple of bullet holes in your body, that's foul enough," Romero said flatly.

Chacon smiled. "You know what I mean."

"Yeah, just couldn't resist," said Romero. "According to the ME's report here, they found the guy's wallet in his back pocket." He read down the list. "Driver's license was intact, along with a small wad of bills and loose change. It's pretty obvious robbery wasn't the motive. Not really a lot to go on."

Romero pulled a couple of photos from the pile.

Chacon pointed to one. "Mariachi, don't you think? Even covered with dirt, looks like this guy was a musician."

"What's his ID say?" Romero asked. "Anyone of importance?"

Chacon picked up the driver's license. "Eduardo Sanchez, age forty, address indicates those pricey condos out there by the National Cemetery. Gotta have a few bucks to live anywhere around there."

Romero scooted his chair back. "You're kidding me. *Eduardo Sanchez*? Let me see that license." He paused to examine it. "I'll be damned. I went to school with this guy. So did Detective Martinez. Dr. Hodge and I saw him perform last year during Fiesta weekend at the La Fonda Lounge. Sheriff Medrano probably knows both him and his family. Damn! We were right there looking at the body. I would have never guessed."

"I gathered as much," Chacon said. "I spoke to Medrano earlier. He was going to make sure the family was notified before they heard it on the five o'clock news."

"I suppose we'd better shift things into high gear before the media starts to make mincemeat out of the sheriff. Damned reporters have the public believing it only takes ten minutes to solve a crime."

"The preliminary coroner's report indicated Sanchez was shot twice," Chacon said. "One bullet entered through the side of his head and the other lodged in the spine. Looks like someone caught this guy off guard. Nothing to indicate it was self-defense, as he didn't seem to be armed himself. A couple of shell casings were recovered near the site, but it's hard to say if they're from our perp's weapon. Have to wait for the lab's results. Lot of target practice goes on in that area, mostly beer cans and no trespassing signs."

Romero grimaced. "Yeah. We considered the victim could have been murdered somewhere else and the body buried out there, but that didn't make sense. To top it off, we've had wind and rain and everything else lately to mess up the site, including the guy who discovered the body traipsing around there for a good hour before he found the break in the fence. I'll bet you a burrito there's going to be very little in the way of usable evidence."

Chacon shrugged. "We'll just have to see what happens when we start turning over a few rocks."

"This would be a good case for one of those rookie detectives to cut their teeth on," Romero said. "How about Gary Granito? He's due for a change right about now."

Chacon groaned. "Christ, boss. I'd rather take Clarissa. Granito is such a pussy. I gotta babysit him on every move he makes."

Romero waved him off. "Deal with it, *Artie*. He's got to start honing his skills as a detective. What the hell good is working toward a promotion if a guy has to spend all his time doing menial tasks? And check in with Dr. Hodge every so often. Keep her in the loop. Sometimes it takes a village to solve a case."

Chacon smirked. "Maybe we could have Dr. Hodge babysit him."

Ignoring Chacon's crack, Romero scribbled on the yellow pad in front of him. "I'll have Clarissa get you two hooked up. By the way, Sheriff Medrano's called a meeting for noon today. I'll see you there."

Chapter Nine

———◆———

I T WAS THE second day of the investigation, which had gotten off to a slow start as detectives waited for the ME to perform the autopsy. So far, it hadn't been scheduled. Around noon that day Romero and his detectives entered the squad room at the county sheriff's main compound on Highway 14, across from the old state penitentiary. The building housed not only the sheriff's offices but also the county jail, recently reclassified as the Adult Detention Center. A wide variety of criminals could be found there on any given day: rapists, wife beaters, thieves, and perverts. In time, any one of them would be transferred across the street to the state prison. The jail had a slanted green roof above a long line of rectangular windows. Sheriff Medrano's office overlooked the fenced yard where inmates were allowed two hours a day to have a smoke, exercise, or mingle with fellow prisoners to catch up on the latest gossip.

The three men sauntered single file into the squad room. Romero was first, with Martinez close behind. Chacon, lugging more poundage, squeezed across the narrow row between the chairs. The room reeked of stale cigarette smoke and scorched coffee. Sheriff Bobby Medrano was in the middle of briefing his deputies on the status of recent crimes in the county. He looked up as the three took their seats.

"Glad you all could grace us with your presence," he bellowed. "When I say ten o'clock, I don't mean ten-oh-five."

Romero scanned the room, looking to see who was in attendance. "Sorry, boss. Had to wade through a State Police blockade. Guess they haven't met their monthly quota of speeding tickets."

On the podium Medrano adjusted the microphone, which emitted a loud screech. "We're discussing the Sanchez case here. Someone can bring you up to speed." He motioned for the detectives to sit. "Soon as the autopsy is scheduled and we receive final word from the coroner, we need to get the task force moving. Doesn't look as though there's a chance the weapon was discarded somewhere near the scene. Maybe someone who's been a guest in our facilities slipped up and left us a nice chubby fingerprint. That probably sits high on the list in the Fat Chance Department."

The detectives never looked forward to these weekly meetings with Medrano. Romero could see the veins in the sheriff's forehead pulsating. Nobody was smiling as he continued, "The whole damned department is up to their asses in unsolved cases. The media's having a field day. Channel Thirteen's watchdog mentioned us on the news again last night. *Just WHAT is it Sheriff Medrano's deputies do all day?*" he said in a mocking voice.

"And then, dear deputies, there was a clear shot of Rodriguez, Wilson, DeLeon and oh yeah, Martinez, all sitting at the Dunkin' Donuts counter stuffing their faces. And don't try to deny it, the cameras don't lie." Medrano's voice was just shy of a holler.

"Hey, it was sheer coincidence that we all landed there at the same time," Martinez said, finishing the last bite of a cheese pastry from the box on the table. "Most of the time we don't even run into each other during the day."

The detectives nodded in unison, "Yeah, Sheriff. That's right."

"Coincidence, my ass," said Medrano. "There's ten current cases on the blackboard, and not a damned one has moved an inch forward. Three murders, two missing persons, robbery, assault, you name it. Who's minding the store, people? Maybe we should open another substation next to the donut shop."

Romero stood, eager to change the subject. "The tox screens came in on our murdered mariachi. My guys have started to interview family, friends, and acquaintances. Sanchez was a well-known musician in these parts. Been with Mariachi Sunrise for a couple of years."

Sheriff Medrano glared at him. "What else?"

Romero continued. "Nothing seemed to be missing from his pockets. He had thirty-two bucks and some credit cards in his wallet, and a few dollars' worth of spare change. He was wearing a couple of gold rings and an expensive watch. It's obvious that robbery wasn't the motive, and our perp didn't bother trying to make it appear that it was."

As if he was in a classroom, Chacon raised his hand. "Yeah," he said. "Word on the street is that Sanchez considered himself quite a ladies' man. Had a different woman on his arm every week. Chicks fell all over him. Maybe one of them did him in. What's that they say about a woman scorned?"

"Well, someone out there knows something," said Medrano. "We're speeding down nowhere-road and there's a fork up ahead. Somebody better come up with some info pretty damned quick. Not only on this case, but on the rest of them."

Romero stood again. "According to Ruben Mares, the band's manager, Sanchez was supposed to be on his way to Mexico to pick up a new mariachi outfit. Mares said the guy was a clothes freak and had ordered a new get-up with boots to match. Must have had a sudden change of plans. Apparently he never made it out of the county."

Medrano gave a snort. "Whatever. You people need to get your butts in gear. And stay the hell out of Dunkin' Donuts.

Get your wives or girlfriends to cook you up some oatmeal or something for breakfast. Now get your carcasses out of here. No use everyone hanging around scratching their behinds. Bring me something I can work with. A list of suspects would be good. An arrest warrant would be better." Medrano turned to refill his coffee cup and gestured them off.

Out in the parking lot, Romero leaned against the wall and offered Chacon a cigarette. "Damn, Medrano's in rare form today."

"Yeah, he sure can get his shorts in a twist. He spends more time eating doughnuts than the rest of us," Chacon sneered.

Romero nodded. "Them's the perks of being the boss."

"Probably nothing I'll ever get to experience, at this rate," Chacon said.

Romero fished his cellphone out of his jacket to check his messages and the time. "The medical examiner's office sent a text. Autopsy scheduled for tomorrow. See you there?"

Chacon groaned. "No chance of me calling in sick?"

Romero thumped him on the shoulder. "Gotta go, Artie. Need to catch up on some paperwork. Clarissa's threatening to throttle me if I don't start keeping up with her."

"Just give her a raise and a promotion and throw in an assistant to get all that work caught up," Chacon said.

Romero laughed. "Hey, her head's already big enough. She runs the place as it is."

Chacon jumped in the driver's seat of the cruiser and headed back to Santa Fe. Romero headed south toward his office. Twenty minutes later, as he pulled into the parking lot, he was almost mowed down by a television crew and a reporter blurting out questions about the case.

A few years earlier, local media had still been old school. They just covered the news and lacked the sensationalism created by national television shows like *Geraldo Rivera* and *Forty-Eight Hours*. Not one to be easily distracted, Romero did a double-take when he saw a woman reporter who looked like a fashion model. Immaculately dressed, she had her auburn hair styled in a sexy upward flip. Her voice was as silky as a Victoria's Secret push-up bra.

"Detective Romero, Janey Velasquez here, Channel Seven." She flipped the ID over on her neck to identify herself. "Would you be willing to answer a few questions, please?"

Romero headed toward the entryway. "I'm a little pressed for time, Miss Janey," he said politely.

She pressed the mic toward his face. "Any progress on the mariachi murder?"

Romero reached for the screen and unlocked the door. "Just going through the preliminary motions. As soon as we have something solid, I can assure you'll be hearing from the department."

The reporter batted her luxurious eyelashes and said, "Could it have been a jilted lover or an angry husband?"

He could feel himself getting caught up in her good looks and deliberate ploy to extract information. He cleared his throat. "Nothing in the case to indicate that. Now, if you'll excuse me, I have a meeting to attend."

The reporter's exaggerated pout was hard to resist, but it didn't work on Romero. Long before he'd started dating Jemimah, he was involved with a woman who had the same magnetism as this reporter. Turned out the last thing she was interested in was monogamy. That taught Romero a few hard lessons, one of which was that love and loyalty go hand in hand.

Chapter Ten

———•———

FOLLOWING THE DISCOVERY of the body, crime techs processed the rooms of Sanchez's condo with the proverbial fine-toothed comb. They packed up his computer, iPad, and DVD collection. A microscopic amount of cocaine was found on the glass tabletop, gathering dust, hardly enough for a hit, but worth mentioning in their report. A 9mm Beretta sat next to a full clip in the drawer of the desk in the hall. The tech dusted it for prints. There were none. It appeared the weapon had never been fired. A white manila envelope with over ten thousand dollars in hundred dollar bills was found stuffed behind an armoire in the bedroom. A small keychain with what appeared to be a key to a safe deposit box was also taken into evidence. After the techs tagged the items and wheeled them out, Detectives Chacon and Martinez stayed behind to search for anything that might point to the reason for Sanchez's untimely demise.

Questioning neighbors bore no fruit. Residents of the adjoining dwellings indicated they barely knew the man, and neither was aware he was a popular musician. They were also unaware he had been the victim of a homicide. The condo was located on the upper east side of Santa Fe near Fort Marcy, just off the main road to the ski basin. It was a one-story unit in the compound, with gleaming Saltillo floors and smooth Venetian plastered walls. The hallway was decorated with framed posters from key Santa Fe events for the last ten years: the Santa Fe Opera, Indian Market, and Spanish Market along with a few Georgia O'Keeffe prints thrown in for good measure. There was a forty-eight inch television in one corner and a to-die-for sound system in the other, both top-of-the-line brand names. Everything appeared to be in its place, neat as a pin. Tidiest bachelor pad around.

Detective Chacon browsed through the medicine cabinet in the master bathroom. Several brands of moisturizers, face masks, dermabrasion pads, lip balm, anti-aging cream, sunscreen, a Bactrim prescription for a bladder infection, and various brands of painkillers. "Geez, Floyd," he hollered out to Martinez, "Never seen so many cosmetics in a guy's bathroom."

"Guess he liked to keep his skin soft and supple, Artie," Martinez quipped from the hallway. "My wife said when they were neighbors during high school, Sanchez had really smooth skin for a guy. Never a pimple or a zit."

"That explains it. Not much else here but beauty products and an old prescription for Tylenol with codeine."

Chacon closed the medicine cabinet and headed to the master bedroom. He slid the door of the walk-in closet to the side and found it filled with an array of clothing—mariachi costumes, hats, boots and belts. "Man, Floyd. Take a look at these boots. Tony Lama, Lucchese, Justin. Sterling silver tips on these suckers, every one of them."

"Almost identical to the pair he was wearing when they found his body," said Martinez.

Chacon whistled. "Wonder how much boots like these cost? There's gotta be a dozen pair."

"Custom with a capital C. I'd say our mariachi was a bit of a clothes horse," said Martinez. "Same high quality as his outfits. Guess money wasn't an issue with this guy. I imagine those designer boots can cost a couple of thousand a pair, and that probably doesn't include the tips. All hand-crafted out of silver."

On a corner of the dresser sat two foam mannequin heads, each wearing a hairpiece. One curly, one straight, both dark. Chacon sifted through the contents of the desk. The bottom drawer contained a stack of letters, opened but stored in their original envelopes. He placed them in a plastic evidence sleeve and marked them with the date and time.

"Looks like Sanchez had a pen pal. These are all postmarked *Mexico*," he said.

"You can never tell. Might be something in them. The guy's always had girlfriends coming out his ears," said Martinez. "Never could figure out what they saw in him."

A cursory check of the kitchen and hallway produced nothing out of the ordinary. The cupboards were neatly stacked with boxed and canned goods, beans, brown rice, *sopaipilla* mix for making frybread, and spices. In the refrigerator were aging vegetables, limes and avocados, several containers of yogurt and a long-expired carton of skim milk. The digital clock on the microwave flashed two pair of zeros. A stack of bills sat in a file box on the counter, including a receipt for a custom outfit. Chacon marked those as well. "Maybe his credit card statement will shed a little light on this guy's comings and goings, in addition to what the techs get off the computer."

Detective Chacon placed everything they gathered into a file box. Taking one last look around the room, he said, "Looks like we're done here. Amazing how a person's entire existence can fit into a twenty-four by twenty-four inch cardboard box."

Chapter Eleven

———•———

As PART OF the new judicial complex, the county morgue was housed on a side street in downtown Santa Fe. Romero and Chacon wound their way down the hallway toward the medical examiner's office. At the front desk, the secretary directed them to the basement where the autopsy on Eduardo Sanchez was scheduled for ten o'clock that Thursday morning. With time to spare, the detectives stepped out onto the covered deck, where county employees gathered for their mandatory fifteen-minute breaks.

Romero lit up a smoke and offered one to Chacon.

Chacon leaned against the rail and exhaled. "You know, I'd rather eat dirt than be subjected to an hour with Donlon," he said.

Romero chuckled. "Are you intimating that Harry Donlon, our esteemed chief autopsy technician aka medical examiner, isn't on your list of favorite people?"

"Esteemed in his own mind," Chacon said. "He's not even on my list. Not by a long shot."

"Why, Detective Chacon, do I detect a note of disrespectful sarcasm in your voice?"

Chacon blew a puff of smoke through the side of his mouth. "The guy's an asshole. Should have retired or had his ass fired a long time ago."

"You're not getting an argument from me on that," Romero said. "I've known him for years and his bedside manner has yet to improve. In fact, I'd venture to say it's gotten worse."

"He's a dyed-in-the-wool bigot. The only reason he keeps his job is that his brother is chairman of the county commission," Chacon said.

"Yeah, and it's a total white bread commission. Only thing is he's always been that way and nothing we have to say about it is going to change things."

Romero had pressed Chacon's buttons. "Every sexual harassment case against him has been dismissed," he ranted. "He's violated just about every rule in the book and they still blow smoke up his ass."

Romero couldn't keep from laughing. He raised his eyebrows and slapped his forehead dramatically. "*Aiii, Chihuahua.* You're on a roll there, Artie. Good thing we don't have to be around him for a while. With your current mood, you might be placed on leave for insubordination."

"Yeah. Donlon could care less if anyone likes him or not. I'd like to see him get his comeuppance one of these days." Chacon flipped the ashes from his cigarette.

"*Comeuppance?* I see you're still doing those daily crossword puzzles," Romero chuckled.

Chacon flushed. "Hey, I know a few big words, boss. Just never get a chance to use any of them. Not with these dorks."

They spent the next fifteen minutes chatting about recent changes in county administration. "Too bad none of those changes affect Donlon," Chacon said.

Romero couldn't help but notice Chacon's pained expression and snuffed out his cigarette in the receptacle. "Come on, we might as well get this over with."

The desk clerk handed them some powder blue scrubs,

hairnets, disposable masks, and booties and directed them to the dressing room in the corner. Romero pulled out the Vicks VapoRub from his pocket, dabbed some on his nostrils and offered the container to Chacon.

"I brought some Noxzema. I heard it works better," Chacon said.

"Nothing erases that smell, so whatever you prefer," said Romero.

As they shuffled into the room, Donlon looked up, horn-rimmed eyeglasses resting at the tip of his nose.

"Well, if it isn't the Chicano Hardy Boys," he said, looking over at them through the plastic lenses.

Romero bowed his head. "Delighted to see you again, Donlon. Though I keep thinking you're going to retire to a condo somewhere … not here."

"No, I kind of like the old *barrio* where I live. Bought my house for a song from some *Mehicano* who probably should have held on to it. It's worth a *huevo* right now," he said. "Lucky me."

"With the fat retirement check you'll be getting, I thought you'd rather spend your days squatting on a sandy beach somewhere," Romero said.

"What do I have to look forward to in retirement, anyway? Gout, hemorrhoids, and erectile dysfunction? No thanks. I'm keeping this job until I die," he scoffed.

"There's always Viagra," Chacon quipped.

Donlon huffed and shifted his attention back to the body on the exam table. It was draped in a green sheet, the empty blue body bag folded neatly on the adjoining table. He gave his spiel about the purpose of an autopsy, "I'm stating the obvious here, but in case some of you don't get it, my job is to figure out what caused the death of the victim. This examination follows a series of DNA tests, total body X-rays and a complete external exam." He then rattled off the date, time, and who was in attendance.

Chacon took a deep breath and whispered, "Here it comes; hold on to your hats."

"And by the way, gentlemen, keep your hands to yourselves and your masks attached to your head. Can't have one of you sneezing all over the evidence and cross-contaminating everything." Donlon paused, as if to make sure he had everyone's attention. "Male, aged approximately forty. Six feet tall, black curly hair. The white tag on his toe reads 'Eduardo Sanchez,' date of death, unknown. Liver temp conducted at the site was inconclusive. Imagine warm weather had something to do with that." He paused again. "No further need for this vanity wiglet," he added, as he brusquely popped the toupee off the dead man's head and flipped it into a plastic bin.

His assistant, whom Donlon always referred to as *Hey You*, jotted notes on the clipboard as the ME rattled off his findings. At times *Hey You* wished he had a recorder in his pocket to pick up the vile profanities that Donlon spewed along with them. Once it was on tape, there could be no denial. *That would fix his wagon, bastard that he is,* the man thought.

"You seem a little perplexed, Romero," Donlon said. "This is pretty cut and dried. One of *your* people murdered another one of *your* people. Ethnic cleansing, I believe they call it in uncivilized countries. Not too different than the old west side of Santa Fe, eh?"

Romero clenched his fists. He knew this jerk thrived on pushing everyone's buttons. Today was no exception, but he had to admit, the man was showing his true colors more vividly than usual. It took a good bit of self-control to keep from grabbing him by the collar and throwing him across the room.

"Let's move on, Donlon," he said. "Some of us have jobs to attend to."

"One of those plastic bags over there has a religious medal of some sort that the vic was wearing around his neck. Let's see … the note says, *sterling silver Our Lady of Guadalupe medal on chain*. Didn't look like it helped him much." Donlon rearranged the organs in the victim's stomach cavity. "Well, looky here," he continued. "This guy has so much fat around his heart he more than likely would have kicked the bucket in ten years or so. I imagine he probably ate a lot of them *chicharones* you people like so much."

Donlon reached for the X-ray film and placed it over the light box on the wall. "See this break here at the left wrist? Looks like he might have broken it as he fell or when he was already down. The wallop on the back of the head … more than likely post-mortem. The shot to the head took one-third of his skull and surely would have killed him; the second one to his side, which lodged in the spine, was either a reflex shot or the shooter wanted to make sure he was dead. They followed in quick succession. Both would have been fatal."

"Lot of maybes there, Donlon," Romero said.

The slugs made a loud 'ping' as Donlon dropped them in the metal tray. "Somebody didn't like this guy. Teeth look as though they were knocked out after he was dead, probably by a swift kick to the face. Maybe as an afterthought."

"Ouch," Detective Chacon said under his breath. Even wearing a jacket, he was shivering, thanks to the cold temperature in the lab. Feeling the contents of his stomach making exit overtures, he put his hand over his mouth, trying not to appear obvious.

Donlon glanced up at him. "Getting a little queasy there, Chacon? I haven't even started."

"To a normal person, some of these visuals are pretty gruesome," Chacon said.

"You look like you might have been in a gang at one time or another. Surely you've seen a few brutal ass-kickings," Donlon said, not looking up. "You know, where there's blood all over the sidewalk?"

"Not hardly. I was one of the good boys," Chacon said.

Donlon examined the heart, spinning it around for effect.

"Oh, I forgot. Some of you Mexicans can't stand the sight of blood and guts."

"Not when it's so in your face, we can't," Chacon said.

Romero threw him a look to chill it down a bit.

Donlon enjoyed being goaded, especially by someone he considered beneath him. From experience, Romero knew that once his chain got rattled, he was relentless.

The autopsy continued as Donlon removed a length of the victim's colon and held it up in the air like a trophy. "Didn't you guys know that that *menudo* stuff you eat at those greasy spoons on Cerrillos Road is cow stomach? Pretty much like we have here," he said.

Chacon glared, but said nothing.

"Or is it *La Raza*, whatever you people call yourselves," Donlon plowed on.

Romero gritted his teeth. "Americans, Donlon. *Spanish* Americans."

"Mexican, Spanish, Chicano. *No difference.* They all eat out of the same bowl of *free-ho-les* around here," he chortled.

"Speaking of Chicanos," Romero interjected. "Weren't you married to a *beaner* from Española?"

Donlon's face reddened. "Rosario? Oh, she found herself a Mexican laborer and went to live with him at some trailer park."

"Couldn't take the pressures of your job, I take it," Romero said, "or your stellar disposition."

"No, she couldn't live up to *my* standards, if you must know," Donlon said. He pulled the gloves from his hand, tossed them on the floor and slipped out of his gown. "Okay, we're done here. Wrap it up, kid." Without another word, the medical examiner had left the building.

Romero looked at Chacon. "He can dish it out but can't take it," he said.

"Most assholes can't," said Chacon.

With the autopsy complete, the detectives could set the wheels going full blast on the investigation.

Chapter Twelve

———————•———————

A FEW HOURS after the autopsy, Romero met with Jemimah and his two detectives to plot out the course of action. Around noontime, they were seated in the conference room of the substation in Cerrillos. Clarissa brought in a tray with coffee and an assortment of small frosted cupcakes from Dulce Bakery.

"I thought you guys might like something different than chocolate-covered donuts," she said, as she distributed small plates and napkins. "Cinco de Mayo is coming up, and I thought it would be nice to get an early start."

Chacon winked at her. "Ooooh, fancy. Just like a birthday party. Do we get to blow some candles out?" He reached for a cupcake and raised his pinky finger high before plunking it in his mouth.

Clarissa clucked. "If you'd like, Detective, I can run over to the general store and pick up some Neapolitan ice cream."

Jemimah took a sip of coffee as Romero waited patiently for Clarissa to return to her desk. "We have a lot of work ahead of us," he said. "Someone needs to check the victim's financials to see if there's any money out of synch with what's normal for him. Let's start racking up some evidence here. Somebody killed this guy and there's got to be a damn clue somewhere. No such thing as the perfect murder. Check all his known relationships, old girlfriends, groupies, anything at all that smacks of suspicion." Romero paused. "Man, I just realized how much that sounded like Sheriff Medrano."

Jemimah leaned forward. "I'm convinced that Sanchez's murder wasn't a random event. The culprit doesn't appear to be a predator or serial killer. He met someone at the site for an unknown reason, something happened, and he ended up dead. He was dressed in his mariachi garb, as if he was headed to or from a gig. I'm sure he intended to change into something more comfortable for the long drive to Mexico."

Not to be outdone, Chacon piped up, "So far all I've been able to dig up is that before he was going to take off on his trip, he was scheduled to perform at a Mariachi Mass at the *Santuario* in Chimayo on Saturday. He never made it."

Jemimah looked at her tablet. "The fact that his wallet or jewelry weren't missing rules out robbery. As much as he was blinged out, something would surely be missing."

Romero nodded. "He was out there for another reason and we need to figure out what it is. Whoever did this wasn't too concerned about the body being found. A piss-poor job of digging a hole and barely burying him below the surface. Or maybe they thought the area was too remote and nobody would ever find him."

"Not to worry, boss. We're on it," said Chacon. "Me and Floyd here have been putting in the hours. This is a tough one. Don't seem to have any real evidence to point us in the right direction."

Martinez nodded, finishing off the last sip of coffee.

Romero rubbed his hands together. "Well, keep at it. There has to be something out there." He looked at Jemimah. "Dr. Hodge, I understand there was a stack of letters from someone in Mexico?"

"Yes. I'll take a look and see if there's anything that might help us start to unravel this mystery."

"Has anyone considered that our killer might be a rival musician?" Martinez said. "Someone who has deluded himself into believing he's just as talented as Sanchez and would be the obvious replacement?"

Chacon scribbled a note. "That's a good point, Floyd."

"Might not be too far from the truth, so check it out," Romero said. "We all know that ninety percent of murders are committed by someone known to the victim. So where does that scenario leave us?"

Jemimah said, "We have at least thirty members of different bands who couldn't stand the guy for a number of reasons. But most of them have admitted that Sanchez was the best entertainer they knew, and nobody else could make that trumpet sing like he could."

Romero paced across the room. "Somebody knows the truth about what happened to our victim. Maybe we're not asking the right people. Could be the only one who knows is the killer himself."

Detective Martinez peeled the liner from a cupcake not much bigger than his thumb. "Bunch of people wanted this guy dead. From all reports he was an arrogant asshole. Of all the preliminary interviews we've conducted, very few of them exhibited any remorse after hearing about his death. One of them actually remarked that the SOB finally got what he deserved. Of course that guy has an alibi, as does anyone else who had a snide comment to make."

Ever conscious of how the detectives tended to intimidate her, Romero paused and looked at Jemimah. "It might be a bit early in the game, but how are the interviews stacking up, Dr. Hodge?"

Before she could answer, Chacon tapped his pencil on the desk. "Nothing viable so far. Couple of people didn't bother to return my calls. One guy said it wasn't worth it for him to take time off to talk about someone he didn't like anyway. I'll get in touch with them again. Impress them with the civic duty spiel."

Undaunted, Jemimah stood and walked toward the window. "I think this is our first interview pulling up now," she said. "He looks pretty manly. Maybe you should take this one, Artie." She handed Detective Chacon the file as she turned to Romero and winked.

The group watched through the glass door as a paunchy man dressed in snug Wranglers, pinstriped Western shirt, and snakeskin cowboy boots ambled up the gravel driveway. Chacon guessed he was in his late thirties, although the beer belly made it hard to tell. He pushed against the metal screen door and entered the waiting room.

Chacon stepped into the reception room. "Gilbert Gomez?"

"Yes, I am," the man responded.

Chacon greeted him with a handshake and directed him to an office in the back. The small room was sparsely furnished with a wood table and three folding chairs pushed into a corner. None of the amenities.

"Have a seat, Gilbert. Thank you for agreeing to stop by and give us a statement. I know how hard it is to take off work during the week. Can I get you a cup of coffee?"

The chair scraped noisily against the wood floor. "No thanks. I've had my fill for today," he said.

Chacon refilled his cup, took a seat across from Gomez, and pressed the button on the recording device. "Well, I'll get right to the point, then. As I mentioned over the phone, as part of our ongoing investigation of this case, the sheriff's department is interviewing anyone who might have been involved in any manner with Eduardo Sanchez."

"Yeah, so I heard," Gomez said. "What's that got to do with me?"

Chacon raised his hand. "Let me finish, sir. We're hoping to gather some insight into just what made this guy a target. How would you characterize your relationship with Mr. Sanchez?"

Gomez straightened his back and puffed out his chest. "I wasn't crazy about him, if that's what you're asking. I can't say we had any kind of relationship. I knew him. That's all."

"Would you consider yourself a friend?"

Gomez looked straight at him. "Not really. More like an acquaintance. We didn't hang out together or anything like that."

"So how long have you known him?" Chacon said.

"We attended different high schools. He was a grade ahead of me. I went to Santa Fe High and he went to St. Mike's. I think he lived somewhere off Paseo de Peralta and I live in the Casa Solana area."

"All right, then," Chacon said, scanning down a sheet of paper in the file. He noted that Dr. Hodge had printed out a list of questions for the interview. "I understand from one of the band members you had a disagreement with Mr. Sanchez in the recent past?"

He was silent for a moment. "Yeah, I had a fight with him. So what?"

Chacon noticed the man's hands were clenched into fists. "Was there a particular reason for the altercation?"

"None other than he pissed me off. Said something chicken shit to my date and I popped him one. He deserved everything he got, and as far as I'm concerned, he didn't get enough."

"What exactly did he say that set you off?"

Gomez put his elbows on the table, cupped his chin with his left hand. "I don't remember his exact words. I had a few drinks under my belt—maybe more than a few—but I'm pretty sure it was slimy."

Chacon took a sip of his coffee. "Slimy sexual or just slimy in general?"

Gomez shifted in his seat. "Look. We were sitting in the front row. The sniveling son of a bitch made a remark about my girlfriend's boobs—referred to her as the hot chick with the big knockers wearing a red dress. Said he wouldn't mind having a piece of that."

"So you just hauled off and popped him one?"

"I reached for his boot and pulled him off the stage, and then I punched him." As if to illustrate, he punched his right fist into his left palm.

Chacon tossed the empty Styrofoam cup in the trash. "Sounds like quite a brawl."

"We were the last couple on the dance floor. Had it been earlier in the evening, every guy in the place would have enjoyed getting a piece of him."

"Why is that?"

Gomez paused, looked around the room. "It's never been a secret around Santa Fe that Sanchez thought he was hot shit, and that every woman he met wanted to jump into bed with him. He was that way in high school, strutting around like the cock of the walk. Nothing ever changed," he said. "Other than as a musician, he never worked a day in his life. At least that's what I heard."

"So what happened after the fight started?"

"The bouncers broke it up before I could get too many licks in."

Chacon leaned forward. "I assume you didn't care for the guy," he said.

"Don't know too many people who did," he said.

"So did you have occasion to run into Sanchez after that?"

Gomez leaned back in his chair. "Nope. Decided I'd better cool it. Didn't want an arrest on my personal record. Can't get a job, you know, if there's crap like that in your file. I have a Q-Clearance from Los Alamos, and that would go down the tubes."

Chacon smiled. "You decided that all by yourself?"

"No, my girlfriend decided that for me. She threatened to break up if something like that ever happened again, and she was dead serious."

"Sounds like a smart lady, that one," Chacon said, closing the file folder and setting it aside.

"Yeah, that she is," Gomez said.

Chacon pushed his chair back. He stood and offered his hand. "Well, Mr. Gomez, thank you for coming in. If you remember anything else that you think might be helpful, I'd appreciate you giving me a call."

"Will do."

Chacon directed him through the reception area to the exit. He placed the CD from the interview in a plastic sleeve and slipped it into the case file. It was late afternoon as he tapped on Romero's door jamb. Jemimah and Martinez had left earlier.

Romero looked up. "How'd it go, Artie ... anything worth pursuing?"

Chacon scratched the back of his head. "Nothing that's going to break the case. He's so pussy-whipped he'd be the last guy I'd suspect of murdering anyone."

Chapter Thirteen

———•———

IT HAD BEEN hours since the twilight curtain dropped like liquid velvet over the Ortiz Mountains. The wind zigzagged around the juniper bushes like a whisper, gently pushing up against the wind chimes in the portal. Tim McCabe squinted at the clock on the desk. It was three o'clock Friday morning. The television flashed images of a leggy blonde in an infomercial demonstrating a too-good-to-be-true belly fat eliminator. He flicked off the remote, stood, and stretched.

Peeking into the bedroom, he saw that his wife was fast asleep. They were spending a few days at the ranch, where Laura wanted to add a few touches to the new addition. He was relieved she had no problem falling asleep away from the comfort of their Canyon Road home. Feeling a pang of guilt, McCabe reached for the folder on the desk. Sleep was an elusive commodity for him these days. Nighttime had taken on an unwelcome presence. The comfort of snuggling up to his wife and falling asleep next to her was hampered by the results of a recent ultrasound test. It had shown a mass in one of her breasts that required a biopsy and led to a tension-filled week waiting for the results. The doctor told them they would know where things stood by week's end. McCabe stared at the file for a short time, rearranged the pages, and retreated to the bedroom. *Gotta snap out of this. Laura can read me like a book and she's not going to like what she sees.* Unable to imagine life without her, he spent too much time in worst-case-scenario mode.

Just a few weeks before, he had returned to work after a six-month sabbatical he had taken to put together a treasure hunt with his long time buddy, Foster Burke. Being in the limelight for six months had finally grown tiresome, but he still looked forward to the excitement of some determined person lucking out and finding the hidden treasure, which so far had eluded everyone. His post office box overflowed with letters. Each day the postman deposited numerous requests for additional clues and glowing testimonials of how the treasure hunt had changed peoples' lives. It did his heart good to know that—especially when parents took their kids along for the adventure. The hunt spirited them away from the daily onslaught of information generated by the Internet and the news media.

McCabe appreciated that after the musician's body was discovered, Romero took him off the task of serving papers and asked him to spend some time on a number of the county's cold cases. It took his mind off his wife's medical condition.

In recent months the couple had sold their ethnographic and Indian art gallery and kept their main residence on Canyon Road in Santa Fe. They planned to spend a lot of time at the ranch house near Cerrillos. It was quiet and peaceful, adjoining the Indian ruins, so McCabe didn't have to make as many trips out when he wanted to dig for artifacts.

He quietly crept into the bedroom, slipped under the covers, and fell asleep. He didn't even hear Laura getting ready to drive into town for an early meeting at the museum that morning.

***

THE SUN WAS at full strength when he opened his eyes. He

smelled the coffee and padded into the kitchen, where Laura had left him a note on the counter. She would see him in town later that day. As he poured himself the first cup of coffee of the day, McCabe heard a horn honking like crazy outside and looked out the window to see what the ruckus was about. The dog was in Mach One attack mode, wagging his tail and barking his head off, uncertain if the intruder was friend or foe but giving it his all nonetheless.

Driving over the cattle guard near the ranch house, Detective Romero felt the wheels of his 4WD cruiser vibrate as he rolled to a stop by the retaining wall in front of the greenhouse. This place was very familiar to him. Almost two years before, five gruesome murders had taken place on the Indian ruins adjoining the ranch. It was also where he first met Jemimah Hodge when he responded to her frantic 911 call after she found McCabe shot in the chest. That was an event that would be embedded in his memory for a long time. He was happy for two things, though: he had gotten together with Jemimah, and McCabe had survived.

Seeing McCabe at the kitchen door, Romero waved. "Hey, McCabe, some killer dog you've got there. I was about to hightail it out of here." He laughed. "Come on, boy," he said to the dog. "Looks like you need to find yourself another profession." He tossed a chicken treat at the dog, who immediately snapped it up and scampered away.

McCabe came down the steps. "When we bought this ranch a while back, we inherited that poor guy, and animal lover that Laura is, she fell in love with him. Didn't have the heart to take him to the shelter, so we let him retire out here. Confused old thing was hiding out in the barn when we moved in. Almost skin and bone, that one. Even the old Manx cat and the owl in residence felt sorry for him. Cat used to plop a dead mouse in front of him every so often."

"Is he that same dog the Cooper fellow had when he lived out here?" Romero said. "I thought the county dogcatcher came out and picked him up."

"Hey, I'll bet it was. Probably found his way back. You know how intelligent animals are, especially Border Collies and Australian Shepherds. He's just a little older and a lot friendlier, especially when he gets those expensive treats I know you carry around."

"Have to," Romero said. "It's a dog's world out in this area. Although I'm sure if there's occasion to be out on Kennedy Hill you have to carry more than a treat; otherwise one of those pit bulls will attack first and ask questions later, just like their owners."

McCabe nodded. "So what brings you out this way? You want to come in for a cup of coffee? Just brewed up a fresh pot, and there's some baked goodies Laura brought in from town."

Romero gestured around him. "I was going out to meet Jemimah and thought I'd come by to check out the new wing you added. Didn't have a chance to talk to you first part of the week when that body was found. Hadn't heard too much, other than you were finished with construction and spending a little more time out here. Looks like you guys are pretty well settled in." Romero shuffled his feet. "How's Laura doing, anyway?"

As they stepped into the kitchen, McCabe ran his fingers through his hair. "She had a biopsy a few days ago. We're hoping that the results will be negative and she won't need to have surgery or any other treatment. The doctor said he'd get back to us as soon as he got the results. I've been sitting on the phone like a mother hen."

Romero took a seat at the counter. "I'll keep a candle lit for her."

McCabe filled two cups and set them on the counter, pushing one toward Romero. He stirred cream and sugar into his. "I'm sure that will help. She's got that old *santo* at the house in Santa Fe working overtime. Every time she passes by, she shakes her finger, telling him he'd better come through for her or he's going to end up as kindling for the fireplace."

"Yes, I remember my mother had her own cavalcade of saints she called on every time me and my brother got out of hand," Romero said. "Traditionally, native New Mexicans prayed to their patron saints for favors."

"Laura got into the habit when our elderly cleaning lady would tap the old *santo* on the head, reminding him she was expecting an answer to her prayers," McCabe said. "Seems to have worked."

"I'd been trying to call you. No service out here?" Romero said.

McCabe jiggled the house phone. "Landline's been down on and off this past week. Craziest thing to have to deal with. Luckily I have my cellphone; it works pretty well out here."

"So I noticed. My phone has full bars. That's a good thing, since we don't want any of our deputies getting caught out in these areas without service. County Commission's been talking to some of the pueblo officials to see if there's any chance of putting in a few more towers. Looks like they've had some success."

"Wouldn't be any worse than the billboards they've allowed to pepper the view along I-25 over the years." McCabe slid off the kitchen stool. "Hey, where are my manners? You got time for the grand tour? There's a new sunroom with a hot tub. Hope to invite you and Jemimah over for a barbecue sometime in the future."

Romero rose to his feet. "Maybe another time, Tim. I won't keep you," he said, placing his cup on the counter. "Just wanted to stop by for a few minutes and see how you're doing."

"Well, I'm trying to adjust to a lot of things, Rick. Some of it's not too easy. I'm used to Laura handling all the paperwork. I never had to do much more than sign a check or two. I can't wait for this to be over." McCabe's voice cracked. "That woman's the love of my life. I don't want to think about losing her."

Romero put his arm around McCabe's shoulders and squeezed. "Hey, buddy, I'm here for you. Anytime you want to talk, just find me."

"Thanks, Rick, I appreciate that," McCabe said.

"In case we haven't loaded you down enough with those files you picked up last week, I've got some other stuff I could use your expertise on. Once Laura's situation is all worked out, swing by the substation," Romero said.

"I was planning on doing that this afternoon on my way into town, *compadre*, and thanks," McCabe said. "I appreciate your coming by."

The dog waited in anticipation as Romero walked toward his vehicle. He couldn't resist tossing him another treat.

"If only dogs could talk. He's probably seen more gruesome details than most humans see in a lifetime."

McCabe reached down and ruffled the dog's neck. "That's why he deserves a good home, and we aim to give him that."

Chapter Fourteen

———•———

LATER THAT FRIDAY, McCabe took a drive to the substation in Cerrillos to catch up on his caseload. The heavily graveled driveway crunched under the wheels of the Hummer. It was a welcome sound. A half hour after Detective Romero left, the phone rang.

"Honey?"

"Laura, are you all right?" he said.

"Her voice trembled. "Yes … yes, I am," she said.

"Don't keep me in suspense. I'm a wreck here," he said.

"I stopped by Doctor Chan's office to give them my new insurance card. She came out of her office and said she had some news."

"Good or bad," said McCabe.

"She said the tumor appeared benign and it would only require minor surgery to remove it."

McCabe pulled over to the side of the road and let out a whoop. "Damn, that's the best news I've had all month. I'm coming into town to get you."

Laura laughed. "Tim, there's no need for that."

"Yes there is. I'm not having you drive all the way back here. I'll see you at the house."

"All right, *dear*. You're the boss."

"And you are the love of this boss's life. I'm going to drop some files off and then I'll see you there. We're going out to celebrate."

He drove the rest of the way to the substation with a big smile on his face.

Clarissa greeted him with a fond embrace and a smile. "So how you doing, Tim? Seems like you've been gone a year. I take it you managed to get a little rest?"

"Hardly. Laura's uncle was running a few horses at the track in Ruidoso last weekend and we spent most of our time urging them on. Now we're looking forward to getting Laura up and running."

Clarissa hugged him again. "Oh, that's great to hear. I'm happy for you both."

McCabe's blue eyes clouded over. "Thank you." He cleared his throat. "So, is the boss in? I told him I'd drop by first chance I got."

"Let me buzz him for you. He's back there with Dr. Hodge. They're beginning to focus all their efforts on that body found on the ranch next to yours."

McCabe nodded. "Yeah, I've been eager to get back on it. A lot can happen in a short time. Any action so far?"

"Seems to me he said something about going nowhere fast, so that tells you something." Clarissa reached across her desk and buzzed Romero to let him know McCabe was in. "Go on back, Tim."

Romero met him at the door and motioned him in. "Hey, Tim," he said. "Come in and have a seat." Jemimah hugged him and patted the chair next to her.

"Rick mentioned you were coming by," she said. "I think he was about to deputize me and hand me that pile of unserved subpoenas and eviction notices that have been piling up. I haven't seen you since the day you headed out to Kennedy Hill and ran into the guy who found the body with the boots."

McCabe sat next to her. "Listen, I'm almost ready to get back to work, even if it involves serving papers on all the crazies. After I reviewed the stack of cold cases, I had time on my hands, and you know what they say about idle hands and the devil."

Romero laughed. "Glad to see you again, Tim. Grab a cup of coffee and let's get with it. I'll bring you up to date on what's going on in the county, including our murdered musician." He smiled at Jemimah. "And you can catch Jemimah up on any developments regarding Laura's health."

McCabe set his coffee on the desk. "I've only got about thirty minutes. I'm heading to town to meet Laura, and I have great news for both of you." He related his conversation with his wife and told them how relieved he was. After an awkward silence, he pulled his chair forward. "Enough about that. Let's talk about murder."

"Yeah, but before that how about bringing us up to date on whatever happened to that treasure you and Foster Burke buried. You remember Jemimah and I searched every square mile from Santa Fe all the way to Yellowstone at the end of last summer."

Jemimah squeezed McCabe's sleeve. "And all I got out of it was a nasty case of sunburn and a slew of mosquito bites," she laughed.

A big grin formed on McCabe's face. "The only thing I can say is that you guys were headed in the right direction." He looked at Romero. "But in your case I'm sure spending time with Jemimah was far more fulfilling than digging through the countryside searching for an elusive treasure."

Romero smiled. "Well, we did have a pretty good time, no doubt about that. Treasure or no treasure, it was still an adventure."

"Speaking of murders, back to the guy you unearthed east of

my ranch. Any suspects?" McCabe said.

Romero shook his head. "Unfortunately, no. It appears as though we're going to be conducting another investigation right on the edge of your property, Tim. I thought you sent all the evil spirits running after that batch of corpses was found in the tunnel under the ruins on your property?"

"Well, I sure thought we'd accomplished that with the elaborate cleansing ceremony the tribal elders conducted," McCabe said. "I might just have to gather them up again for a redo. Don't want any more nasty spirits lurking around now that we've settled in part-time at the ranch."

"Amen," Romero said. "And don't you worry about things here at the office. We'll just play that by ear. Once things are level again, give a call. Most important now is getting that sweet lady of yours back to optimum health."

Jemimah gave him a fond embrace. "I second that. Those cold cases can wait a little longer for you to work your magic on them."

McCabe reached for his hat. "Well, you know you can call me anytime," he said.

Romero stood. "Hey, Tim. Do you and Laura want to join us tonight for a Cinco de Mayo celebration? We're thinking of maybe dinner at La Choza. Lot of goings on downtown, too. They're having a chile pepper eating contest and live music."

"I'll have to take a raincheck on dancing in the streets, Rick. We're going to spend a quiet night at the ranch celebrating on our own. Knowing that she's going to be all right will be the best Cinco de Mayo we've ever had."

McCabe waved to Clarissa as he stepped out into the parking area. He unlocked his vehicle and sat in the driver's seat for a few moments, relishing the thought that the weight of the world had been lifted from his shoulders.

Chapter Fifteen

——◆——

O N ANY GIVEN morning before eight o'clock, eighty to
one hundred Native American vendors huddle together
under the shade of the long portal of the historic Palace of the
Governors in downtown Santa Fe to participate in a lottery
to determine who will be fortunate enough to set out their
handcrafted wares. Each individual plunks their hand into a
glass jar containing numbered and blank chips. The prize is
acquisition of a two-by-four-foot space to hawk their goods that
day. On that particular Monday morning, fans and followers of
the deceased mariachi gathered to set up a makeshift shrine
against a wall of the Plaza bandstand across from the historic
building. A Navajo silversmith setting up his jewelry on the
brick floor of the portal looked over at his neighbor and said,
"Who died, Paul McCartney?" He pointed to the commotion
across the street.

In the center of the shrine, someone had placed a life-
sized photograph of Sanchez, dressed in the trademark fitted
black outfit worn by mariachis. The photo was surrounded
by a multitude of vases filled with cut flowers and dozens
of red and white roses. Snapshots, notes and trinkets filled

every remaining space. Interspersed along the edges was an assortment of votive candles that illuminated the usually dark Plaza well into the night. The shrine had grown since the news about the mariachi's death first spread. At nightfall, bereaved fans sat as sentries, holding flickering candles in their laps. It was a somber place to be.

After several days of watching the crowds build, a number of the Native American vendors complained to each other and anyone who would listen that the dead guy was getting more attention than they were as they observed tourists walk around the plaza toward them, pause and then turn to join the crowd. Sad voices blended together as they sang along to Sanchez's music piped through the audio system on the stage.

There was one person in the audience who didn't appear to be in mourning, however. He leaned against a tree taking long drags of his cigarette and watching the trail of smoke evaporate into the air. While waiting for his sister to give him a ride, he'd wandered onto the Plaza for a smoke. Most everyone else in the crowd was moved to tears. He was fascinated by the overly emotional fans. Like the Native Americans, he wondered, *Who the hell was this guy, anyway?*

As daylight dissolved into a jelly bean sunset, the downtown area darkened and the streets surrounding the park emptied. A few skateboarders plowed across the pavement taking advantage of the deserted streets. Only two types of characters populated the Plaza's murky hours after midnight— skateboarders perfecting their moves and a few homeless people waiting to crash for the night on or under the wrought-iron benches along the grassy area of the park. As they drifted off to sleep—some in sleeping bags, others in hand-me-down jackets—it didn't matter one iota to them who had been kidnapped, murdered, or maimed.

Chapter Sixteen

———•———

IT HAD BEEN almost a week since the discovery of the body. The Monday morning air was cool and filled with the pungent fragrance of lilacs sprouting across city neighborhoods. Jemimah planned to attend the slain mariachi's funeral later in the afternoon. One never knew if a potential suspect might show up to see the results of their handiwork, although even so she felt it necessary to pay her respects.

She walked out into the parking lot across from her office and swung her briefcase into the front seat of her 4Runner. Setting the coffee mug in the holder, she cranked the engine. She had two appointments that day. One was to attend the funeral service with Detective Romero; the other was to meet with Sheriff Medrano, who was bound to chew on her about the overall lack of progress in pending cases.

Certain she couldn't face either one on an empty stomach, she stopped by to pick up an apricot scone at the Tea House on Canyon Road and chatted a while with the new owner as she waited for a refill. She glanced at her watch, muttered a few cusswords to herself about being late, and said her goodbyes to the coffee crew. Out in the parking lot, she balanced the

Styrofoam cup and the scone in one hand while she fumbled for her keys with the other. She took a bite out of the scone while she fastened her seatbelt and started up the engine.

Jemimah cut across a few side streets on the east side heading toward the county compound on Highway 14. The Acequia Madre followed her along the side of the road, crystal clear waters meandering down the center, gently splashing against stone sidewalls built hundreds of years before from stone quarried miles away at Galisteo. This revered stream of water had flowed through Santa Fe for more than a century, with residents using the water to irrigate their fields. Now it was a part of the city's charm, especially noteworthy each time the spring runoff began.

Her meeting with Sheriff Medrano lasted for less than an hour—about what she expected, though less painful. After pleasantries were exchanged, it proceeded predictably. They discussed recent cases and then he patted her on the back lightly and told her what a good job she was doing. The guy never changed. By periodically summoning her to his office, he was demonstrating to staff and detectives that she was under as much scrutiny as they were and didn't have a free pass as they suspected. He dismissed her with a wave of his hand, returning his focus to the paperwork covering his desk.

Jemimah said her goodbyes and bounded down the steps, dialed Romero's number and left a message that she was on her way to meet him. Traffic around the Plaza was heavy, and she pulled her car into a space at the La Fonda parking lot across from St. Francis Cathedral. He was waiting for her in a pew at the back of the church.

The historic Catholic Church in downtown Santa Fe was laid out in a cruciform pattern—the shape of a cross. It was a magnificent structure, with stone walls and vaulted ceilings supported by massive marble pillars. The early adobe church had been destroyed during the 1680 Pueblo Revolt, but the present building had been the vision of French Bishop Lamy in 1850. His imported stonemasons built the church with stone quarried from the Village of Galisteo. Light filtered through majestic stained glass windows flanked by painted contemporary Stations of the Cross in polished mahogany frames. An intricate Gothic stencil ran along the walls of the entire church. A large polychromed altar screen with painted and gold-leafed panels of modern saints stood behind the sanctuary.

As they waited for the funeral service to begin, Jemimah's thoughts wandered back to her childhood in Salt Lake City and the occasions when her family attended services in the LDS Church in Temple Square before her father joined a fundamentalist sect. With its gleaming white quartzite façade and multiple spires that soared heavenward, the edifice had been far larger and more splendiferous than this Santa Fe church. LDS rituals were not unlike those practiced by other religions. She assumed their *Heaven* might be similar to the LDS *Celestial Kingdom*, but doubted if Catholic *Hell* was akin to the *Telestial Kingdom* in her religion, which was reserved mainly for those who refused to repent.

Similarities aside, she knew it was a stretch to even compare the two. Yet at that moment she was drawn to the piety of the parishioners and observed with awe as they entered in single file through the bronze doors, walked toward the front of the church, crossed themselves and genuflected at the altar. Watching Monday night football, she had seen players cross themselves when they made a touchdown. Now she was witnessing this ritual in person, in a much more somber setting.

She glanced up at the life-sized plaster statues of saints and wondered what they represented, especially the one pushing a plow flanked by two oxen. Romero explained that was Saint Isadore, the patron saint of farmers. Jemimah nodded. In more ways than she could ponder, there had been no saints in her religion.

Next to her in the pew, Romero was also pondering the subject of religion. He was a cradle Catholic, much like Jemimah was a cradle Mormon. He wondered if their religious differences would affect any serious relationship they might pursue. As far as he could tell, she shied away from the subject of religion altogether. He guessed if she had a need to discuss the matter, she would do so in her own time. This was one of those pointless discussions he engaged in with himself. He was no expert on religious beliefs. The only time he entered a church these days was for funerals, and even then, he had forgotten more than he remembered about prayer and ritual. Oh sure, he still believed in God. He just didn't believe he needed to express his beliefs in a church run by man-made rules. He wondered if he would ever feel at home there again. It wasn't a question of faith … it was a question of forgetting he had been betrayed by a priest he'd arrested for engaging in a forbidden relationship with a minor.

By the time the service began, there was standing room only. Through the magnificent bronze covered doors, the casket was wheeled into the church, flanked by dozens of mariachis decked out in colorful attire and standing guard around their fallen brother. Jemimah imagined that some of them had set aside their personal feelings about the man. After all, he had been the victim of a horrendous crime. It no longer mattered what they'd thought of him while he was alive.

The first three rows were occupied by friends, primarily women. Jemimah wondered how many of them might have been romantically involved with Sanchez. His only sibling sat in the first pew, inconsolable, and wiped tears from her eyes. As the mass progressed, a group of mariachis sang "*Las Mañanitas*," accompanied by guitars and violins.

Jemimah whispered to Romero, "What are they singing about? It sounds both sad and happy."

He cupped his hand over her ear. "It's actually a traditional song generally dedicated to someone's birthday or a saint's day, but around here, it's also performed at funerals, since most everyone has listened to it at one time or another." He translated part of the lyrics:

> *De las estrellas del cielo tengo que bajarte dos, una para saludarte y otra para decirte adios.*

> Of the stars in the heavens I will lower two for you. One with which to greet you and the other to tell you goodbye.

Jemimah felt her heart sink when she heard muffled sobbing coming from the front pews. "It is very sad, indeed," she said.

At the conclusion of the service, several individuals stood at the pulpit and eulogized Sanchez as a talented musician who was popular with fans of all ages. Everyone agreed that his demise came far too early. Then the priest blessed the casket and the congregation again knelt, crossed themselves and turned to leave the church. A long cortege of vehicles gathered behind the hearse, ready to wind its way around the Plaza, its final destination the local Catholic cemetery across from DeVargas Mall.

Romero and Jemimah were the last to leave the church. She took his hand as they walked in silence toward the parking garage. A flock of tourists with cameras hanging from their necks bounded up the steps to the church, unaware of the solemn occasion that had just concluded.

Following the service at the cemetery, the couple stood next to the ancient stone wall that encircled the gravesites. Romero wondered who made the decision to build a shopping mall across from an active cemetery. He found it odd there was no plaque to indicate that in 1680, the area on which they stood had been the site of several major battles during the Pueblo Revolt. He knew that particular subject was still touchy for both Native Americans and Spaniards. Sanchez would rest in peace here, or would he? At this stage in the investigation, no viable suspects had surfaced, and from watching television, everyone knew that if cases weren't solved in forty-eight hours, they would soon go cold.

Jemimah leaned up against him. "This is really sad. From the outpouring of affection this guy received, it's pretty hard to paint an accurate picture of him. It's apparent he was well liked, or there wouldn't have been so many people in attendance."

Romero agreed. "I'm glad that's over. Now we need to put the pedal to the metal and dredge up a few suspects. What's on your schedule for the rest of the day, Jem?"

"I spoke to his sister briefly before the service. She's going to call me to set up an interview. I hate to pressure her so soon after the funeral, but she might have something to add to enlighten us a little. You?"

"It's already after three. I need to clear up a few things at the office, then I'll probably head home. You feel up to dinner and a movie?"

She squeezed his arm. "How about just dinner at my place? I have to drop some papers by my office and then I think I'll take the rest of the day off. I might just clean out the barn or do something constructive until you show up. Maybe work off some of this tension."

"Well, wait until I get there. I've got all kinds of tension-relieving moves," he said, "and they'll work better in the bedroom than the barn."

Chapter Seventeen

———◆———

B Y THE TIME Jemimah reached the turnoff to her ranch, it was four o'clock and her energy had returned. *Must have been all that sadness at the funeral service.* She needed a break to clear her head. She set her briefcase on the counter and went into the bedroom, where she changed out of her work clothes and slipped on a pair of faded jeans, long-sleeved shirt, and cowboy boots. She looked around for Molly and decided she must be out chasing rabbits, one of the dog's favorite pastimes.

She walked over to the barn and saddled up Mandy, her Appaloosa. A good ride usually helped to recharge her. She hoped galloping at a steady pace might give her some insight on the present case. She had plenty of time before Rick would show up.

Within a half hour, she was riding the horse through Waldo Canyon. It was almost five as she guided Mandy through the rocky trail on the outskirts of Cerrillos, her hair flowing in the breeze. Jemimah was in her element and grateful she finally had an opportunity not only to exercise her horse, but also to take some time to enjoy the scenery. Periods of serenity had been sparse lately, and she welcomed the mixed aromas of blooming wildflowers and pine trees. Up ahead on her right was Cerrillos Hills State Park, more than five miles from her ranchette. She leaned down to stroke Mandy's neck and whispered, "Easy girl," as the path took an upward and rocky slope.

It took less than an hour to make the climb to the top of Devil's Throne, a massive rocky outcropping protruding from the south side of an equally large mountain that wasn't as intimidating from the back side. She felt no ominous foreboding as she normally did when she drove along on the gravel road between Interstate 25 and Highway 14. Jemimah pushed aside any thoughts of the unsettling experience she'd had in this same area the previous year when she was accosted by a fugitive suspect hell-bent on fulfilling a contract on her life. This was another day, and she was determined to enjoy it to the fullest.

The view from the top of the mountain took her breath away. She could see the entire expanse of the thousand acre park laid out before her, and the Ortiz Mountain Range and the Sangre de Cristos surrounding Santa Fe. Dismounting the horse, she tied her to a tree and retrieved a bottle of water from the saddlebag. Then she sat down on a grassy patch surrounded by hundreds of small wildflowers in every color of the rainbow. Jemimah breathed in the fresh air, closed her eyes, and leaned against a wide tree trunk. Taking a sip of water, she watched in awe as the peach red sun began to dip toward the horizon ever so slowly. Reddish hues seeped into the surrounding clouds, providing a breathtaking Kodak moment.

Although Jemimah's work as a forensic psychologist could at times be an emotional drain, transitory events such as this one made up for it in spades. She cornered a fleeting thought about her relationship with Detective Romero, where it had been and where it was going, and redirected it to the *don't want to deal with it now* file in her brain. Her surroundings were much too beautiful to be spoiled by random worries.

She replaced the cap on the plastic bottle and stood up to stretch. Leaning down, she picked a purple aster and stuffed it in her pocket. A lone horny toad stood still, stared in her direction, and then darted between two rocks. She looked at her watch and couldn't believe another hour had elapsed. There was still enough light to make it home. She untied Mandy from the tree, put her foot in the stirrup and pulled herself onto the saddle. The horse shook her head, scraped the ground, and gave a friendly neigh. Jemimah smiled. *Just like in the movies.*

On the way down the trail, she took a wrong turn and found herself in an unfamiliar area. She looked up at the sun and determined she was going west instead of east.

"Damn," she muttered, "I guess that wasn't the shortcut I thought it would be." She needed to change direction. About a quarter mile in, the rolling juniper savanna became thicker, with spiky branches on the far too narrow trail scraping against her boots. She was looking for a place to turn around when she heard a loud rustle up ahead. A heavy-set man wearing a red-checkered shirt stepped out of the shadows onto the path in front of her. The sudden movement startled Mandy and she reared back on her hind legs. An experienced rider, Jemimah held onto the reins as she squeezed her knees against the horse to keep from being thrown off.

She bent toward Mandy's head and soothed her mane, finally managing to calm her down enough to turn around in the small clearing, a space barely wide enough to accommodate a horse. The man didn't move a muscle, but continued to stare Jemimah down. He moved his hand inside his shirt. She saw the glint of a gun barrel reflecting off the sun.

"This is private property, lady. You got business out here?" His voice was brusque.

Jemimah stiffened. "No. I got lost coming down the mountain and was looking for a way back."

"Well, this isn't it," he said.

From her vantage point atop the horse, she could see

hundreds of bright green plants growing between the evergreens. She estimated they were at least eight feet tall. She took a deep breath and recognized the overpowering smell that invaded her nostrils. *Marijuana.* She realized she'd better keep any other questions to herself and make her way to safety.

The man motioned with his palm facing her, apparently discouraging her from moving forward. "Just keep to the left."

As if to make sure Jemimah rode away, he stood his ground. For a fraction of a second she thought he moved his hand closer to the gun. She chastised herself for not taking time to slip her pistol into the saddlebags, not that she could have retrieved it at this point. She usually kept a weapon handy on her outings just in case she encountered a rattlesnake or other denizens who occupied the dark areas around rocks and bushes.

A few hundred feet down the trail, she looked back over her shoulder. The man was no longer in sight. It was as though the trail had disappeared, closed in by the heavy overgrowth. Jemimah reached the bottom of the hill and saw the analemmic sundial to her left. She knew Cerrillos wasn't too far beyond the solar calendar and breathed a sigh of relief. She galloped across the highway and cut through Tim McCabe's land to shorten the distance to her ranch. What had started out as an innocent country ride had turned out to be a harrowing experience. She couldn't wait to see her house off in the distance. As she flew into the driveway, she spotted Rick's car. He was sitting on the front porch bench, the cat on his lap and the dog at his feet.

"Hey, Jem. I was worried about you. Everything all right?" he said.

She walked the horse to the water trough and unlatched the saddle. "Give me a minute. Mandy needs some water."

"Here, let me help you," he said, taking the saddle from her arms. "Now tell me what has you so worked up."

She folded the saddle blanket and placed it over the fencing. "After the funeral service, I was pretty stressed out about the case. I needed a change of scenery, so I took my horse out for a ride. I knew it would be a couple of hours before you came by. I left my phone in my purse."

"I figured. I've been trying to call you for over an hour but your cell kept going to message. So tell me what happened."

Jemimah related the details of her misadventures after she became lost on the trail and wandered into an unfamiliar area.

"You're sure those were marijuana plants?"

"I think I've been exposed to enough drug raids that I know what I'm looking at."

"Do you think you can direct one of the guys from DEA to the place where you spotted this fellow?"

She pursed her lips and exhaled. "I'm not sure, maybe. It was about to get dark and both my horse and I were disoriented. I just wanted to make you aware of suspicious doings not too far from town."

Romero went to his car and pulled out a map from the glove box. "See if you can at least pinpoint it, and then I'll contact drug enforcement. They have their ways of zeroing in on these guys. Probably be able to do it from the air."

Jemimah marked a red line in the areas she had been initially. "It was beyond the park. When I started down the trail from the top of the mountain, I must have taken a wrong turn somewhere in this vicinity. From there on, it was all unfamiliar territory. I'm not even sure I could find it again. The guy said it was private property and you know how it goes once sundown sets in. Nothing looks the same."

Romero made a few notes and rolled up the map. "Thanks, sweetie. I'll see what I can do with this. In the meantime, would you please stick to places you're familiar with? I don't want to be worrying about my best girl running into bad guys after dark."

She smiled. "Yes, *sweetie*. Anything you say. I need to clean myself up and then I'll see what I can throw together for dinner."

He slid open the living room door. "You let me worry about

that. I'll run over to the pizza place in Madrid and pick up dinner and a six pack."

"Sounds good to me."

By seven thirty, they were sitting on the couch with their feet propped on the hassock, an empty pizza box on the coffee table next to half-full glasses of beer. Jemimah stretched her arms and yawned. "I think I'm ready for you to show me those moves, Detective."

He laughed and pulled her toward him. "Come on. You know you don't have to ask me twice."

Chapter Eighteen

———•———

Iᴛ ᴡᴀs ғɪʀsᴛ light, Tuesday morning, and off in the distance a rooster crowed. Jemimah opened her eyes and rolled over on her side. Yesterday evening she had arrived home physically and emotionally exhausted. After her sensual night with Rick, she felt rested and invigorated. She knew he was already up from the smell of fresh coffee that permeated the air. She reached for her robe and padded to the kitchen.

He kissed her on the forehead and poured her a cup of coffee. "Glad to see you so chipper this morning," he joked. He knew it took a moment for the caffeine to take effect. "Breakfast?"

She playfully rumpled his hair. "I think I'll just have a quick bagel and then get going. I've got a busy day."

"Me, too. I'll jump in the shower while you're charging your batteries," he said.

She creamed her coffee and returned to the marble island to split a bagel. The toaster popped out her breakfast and she sat on the leather stool reading the newspaper until Rick walked into the kitchen.

"As much as I'd like to hang around and watch you get

dressed, I have an early meeting," he said. "I'll catch up with you later in the day."

She stood and wrapped her arms around him. "Do I need to send you flowers for last night?"

"That was definitely a chocolate moment," he grinned.

Jemimah watched him leave. *God, how I love that man.* And she knew the feeling was mutual, if only the idea of commitment wasn't so terrifying.

After showering, she slipped into her work clothes—dark slacks and jacket, white shirt and comfortable shoes. When she was ready to leave, she gave the dog a quick nuzzle and checked the doors. Finally, grabbing her mug, she got in the 4Runner and drove off. Traffic was light on Highway 14 as she sipped the remainder of her coffee. It was almost eight in the morning, and as she passed the satellite office, she saw Romero's car was already in the parking lot and blew a kiss in that direction. By the time she reached downtown Santa Fe and made her way to her office, it was nine o'clock.

Carol Ortega was sitting in the waiting room. She was a thin woman with an outdated pageboy haircut, devoid of makeup and dressed in a black skirt and a crisp white over blouse. Jemimah introduced herself and directed her to a chair at the table next to her desk. She clicked on the recorder.

"Thank you for coming by, Carol. I know how difficult it must be for you," she said.

"Yes, it is. Such a shock."

"I'll try to make this as painless as possible," Jemimah said, "but I'm sure you know that as part of our investigation, we need to delve into your brother's personal life. It might help to fill in some of the gaps."

"I understand. What is it you need to know?"

"Were you and your brother close?"

"Not really. We didn't communicate much in recent years."

"Why is that, if you don't mind my asking," Jemimah said.

Carol looked down at her hands. "For the most part, he was

very family oriented. But he also had a bit of a mean streak that reared its head periodically."

"Can you expound on that a little? Are you saying he could be sadistic?" Jemimah said.

"Oh, no. I wouldn't go that far. Sarcastic would be a better word. It's part of the reason we drifted apart."

Jemimah waited while the woman seemed to struggle. It appeared she didn't want to put her brother in a bad light, particularly now that he was dead.

"I don't mean to say that he was mean to everyone. Maybe it was just a sibling thing. We always got along until about ten years ago when I decided to get married. I had been a schoolteacher since graduating from college and hadn't met anyone I wanted to spend my life with. I didn't date a lot." She paused to wipe her eyes. "He always joked that I was going to be his spinster sister."

"Can I get you some water?" Jemimah said.

"No, it's all right. It's hard to talk about old struggles. So my fiancé was coming to ask our father for my hand in marriage, you know. It's an old Spanish tradition, and my father was very old fashioned."

Jemimah nodded. "Yes, I'm familiar with that."

"It feels a bit petty for me to say this, but on that occasion, Eddie happened to be visiting my folks in Roswell. They moved back after we graduated from college. He leaned over and told my dad that he might as well give his permission for us to get married, because nobody else would want me, and that I was lucky to have hooked this guy." She put her hands over her eyes and wept softly. "He always thought I was such a wallflower, just because I wasn't out partying all the time like he was."

Jemimah handed Carol a box of tissues while she took a moment to regain her composure. "I've been carrying that around a long time. We never talked about it, so maybe he didn't realize I held that against him." She wiped her eyes. "And then he goes and leaves me his condo and his personal belongings."

Jemimah patted her arm. "Maybe that was his way of saying he was sorry. I'm sure he cared deeply about you. Sometimes men have a hard time expressing their feelings. I'm sorry, but I have to ask. Did he have a life insurance policy?"

"Yes, but I believe the beneficiary was that woman he had met in Mexico. Since we never saw each other, I didn't know much about her."

"Tell me a little about his childhood. How did he become a musician?"

"Eddie was a rambunctious child. He was always watching scary movies and reading about UFOs and alien beings. My mother never said anything to him; in fact, he could sit for hours listening to the old folk tales she would tell about *La Llorona* and other bogey people roaming about the arroyos. In his teens, Eduardo sought out psychics and fortune tellers, believing they could provide him with answers. In an uncanny series of events, every psychic—even those perceived by others to be charlatans—convinced him he was destined to be a musician.

"He bought a used trumpet at a flea market on the outskirts of town. After practicing for two years he was hired to entertain at every wedding, baptism, and *quinceanera* in the county. You know, the coming of age celebration for young girls of fifteen. Each summer he traveled across the state to attend concerts in El Paso, the mecca for mariachi music. When he was fifteen, our family moved to Santa Fe. In his senior year at St. Michael's High School, he found a job as a busboy in a Mexican restaurant which featured mariachi music on weekends. That summer he scored an audition with Mariachi Sunrise after filling in for one of their musicians. The rest is history, such as it is." She dabbed her eyes with the tissue and sniffed loudly.

"Do you know what happened to his belongings?" Jemimah said.

"I donated all his outfits to a group in Mexico. I'm sure an inspiring young musician can use them. The furniture and the rest of his stuff went to one of the homeless shelters. I had no use for any of it."

"Did you find anything unusual, anything the detectives might have missed?" Jemimah said.

"No. He had a lot of clothes and a lot of jewelry, and he kept everything in place, very neat."

"Did you know anyone who would have wanted to harm your brother?"

She shook her head. "Not that I know of. As I said, we weren't in contact that often, and after our parents died, he seemed to focus more on his music career. I would read about him in the newspaper and occasionally go watch him entertain on the Plaza, but that was about it."

Jemimah closed the file in front of her and stood. "Mrs. Ortega, thank you for coming by." She reached out to shake the woman's hand. "I appreciate your giving us a few moments during these difficult times."

"I'm sorry I couldn't be of more help. You must think it's terrible for families not to know what's going on in each other's lives," she said.

Jemimah walked her to the exit. "Not at all. It's human nature. We all express love in different ways."

Chapter Nineteen

———◆———

THE NOON TRAFFIC around the plaza was noisier than usual. The sound drifted up through the single pane windows of Jemimah's office above the Plaza Café. She closed the door to the inner office, tuned the radio to 95.5, her favorite classical station, and returned to her desk. Settled into the chair, she tried to refocus by separating the contents of the Sanchez file and spreading the various elements across the desk. Her interview with the victim's sister had not added anything of substance. She pored over each notation, adding her thoughts on a new pad. *Seems like everything in here leads to a dead end.*

She picked out a familiar business card in a plastic envelope and noted it had been retrieved from the victim's wallet. The card read:

Sister Rita. Psychic Consultations. Clairvoyant.

There were two dates and times on the back. She checked her calendar and found that one date was in mid-March and the other was two weeks before the body was found. She smiled, because she was definitely familiar with Sister Rita.

They'd met the previous year when Jemimah was profiling suspects in the murder of New Mexico's state archaeologist, who coincidentally had also engaged the services of this well-known psychic.

She dialed the number and waited. After the fourth ring it switched to a recording. Jemimah grinned. The message had not changed over the last year. Sister Rita's inviting voice still conjured up promises of good things to come, if one was willing to take the journey. She left a short message requesting a callback. Jemimah revisited her encounter with the psychic, who had an uncanny resemblance to carnival fortune tellers she had seen portrayed on the History Channel. It wasn't easy to forget the petite woman adorned with rows of gemstone necklaces, bangles, cuffs, turquoise bracelets and other jewelry. Dark ringlets peeked out from under the colorful bandana wrapped around her head. Handcuff-sized hoop earrings hung from her earlobes, and multicolor Mardi Gras-like beads encircled her neck. The shelves in her lair were stacked with hundreds of decorative containers filled with potions designed to heal the lovelorn, conjure up new relationships, or be rid of old ones. Jemimah wasn't sure she was prepared to visit the psychic again, since on that first occasion she had been subjected to over an hour of unexpected aura cleansing and chakra realignment. She had to admit, however, that she'd felt tons lighter as she walked out to the parking lot that afternoon.

Sister Rita returned her call at the end of the day. Delighted to hear Jemimah's voice, she inquired whether there were wedding bells in the future, a question Jemimah skillfully sidestepped. They arranged to meet the following day.

***

ON WEDNESDAY JEMIMAH drove down the gravel road alongside the centuries old cemetery—smaller, but not unlike the cemetery where she attended the mariachi's funeral. Shadows danced around her vehicle as gigantic Siberian elms swayed with the wind. The dark granite of freestanding mausoleums appeared even darker from recent sprinklings of dime-sized raindrops. She drove into the parking space in front of the pitched-roofed adobe building, slipped her small backpack into the trunk, and set the alarm on the vehicle. Not much had changed since the last time she was here. The wrought-iron screen door was ajar, waiting for her to enter into the small living room. Inside, the setting and its atmosphere with its hundreds of candles flickering in unison still reminded Jemimah of a classic Vincent Price thriller.

Sister Rita's broomstick skirt swayed in the breeze as she entered, separating the beaded strings hanging from the arched doorway. As Jemimah returned her greeting, the only word that came to her thoughts was *flamboyant*.

"Please remove your shoes, my dear, so we can begin," she said. Jemimah complied and followed the psychic into a small anteroom, its walls saturated with hundreds of hanging silver Milagros. Reflection from a string of colored lights danced across the room, washing a surge of dazzling color over the myriad strings of crystals hanging from the ceiling.

Sister Rita sat in one of the blue-backed chairs and motioned to Jemimah as she patted the seat of the other. She placed a deck of cards on the table.

Jemimah shook her head. "Sister Rita, this is not a social call. I am in the midst of a murder investigation and I need your help."

The psychic shuffled the deck and arranged five cards on the table before her. Jemimah pulled a photo from a manila envelope. "As I recall, you don't read newspapers or listen to news on television, but do you remember meeting with this man sometime during March of this year?" Jemimah asked.

Sister Rita leaned forward and pulled a pair of reading glasses from her cleavage. "Ah, yes. The mariachi. How could I forget *him?* He was very handsome." She looked away from the photo, put her hand on the table, and turned over the first card.

"The gentleman had an ongoing conflict he wanted to resolve."

"Do you remember the exact date he came to see you?" Jemimah said.

Sister Rita flipped through a few pages of her datebook. "I saw him on the fifteenth, the Ides of March. As I recall, he didn't get the connection."

Jemimah raised her eyebrows. "That Julius Caesar was stabbed to death after being warned by a seer to be careful? Not too many people would have gotten that."

"And the next time was about a month later, in April. On what day was he killed?" asked the psychic.

"The body was discovered on May second. I'm not sure I can provide much more information, but I assume he was murdered a day or two before," Jemimah said.

Sister Rita looked up. "I told him there were evil persons lurking in the shadows around him. He needed to be careful where he ventured and wary of whom he trusted." She turned the second card over.

"Did he mention any problems he might be having?" Jemimah said.

Sister Rita tapped on the third card and flipped it over. "It involved money, moving from one place to the other. He had no idea how to stop it. He didn't go into great detail, and I had the impression he was holding back. You know, some people are suspicious of psychics and palm readers. They think we're charlatans, fortune tellers, gypsies. A whole gamut of labels has been tagged on my profession. He was a little antsy that day and at one point mentioned that on second thought he wasn't sure he was even interested in a reading—much like you indicated the last time you were here—but he stayed to the end."

"*Something* brought him to you. Do you know what that was? Was he just curious?" Jemimah said.

The psychic reached across and pondered the remaining cards. Jemimah waited patiently. "On the earlier visit, he seemed content and asked questions about his career. But on the second visit, he indicated he was experiencing some kind of interference from the same woman—someone he thought he cared deeply about." She gazed at the fourth card. "He wanted out. Whatever had occurred between them had served its purpose to make him realize she was not the person for him."

"Did he tell you what happened?"

Sister Rita adjusted her silk scarf and waved her fingers in the air. "He said very little. I relied on the cards to give me answers." She stared at the fifth card. "Whoever was trying to influence him wanted him to stay, to continue with whatever he was doing. He was torn, unable to make a decision that was going to work for him."

Jemimah's expression was blank. Sister Rita touched her hand. "Like your profession, my dear, the tarot is only a form of counsel, not a predictor of the future. Many individuals misinterpret that fact."

"Did he give you any specific idea of what was going on in his life?" Jemimah said.

The psychic shook her head. "He was searching for answers. All I can tell you is that he seemed unnerved. He drove here in a friend's vehicle. I detected an imbalance in his chakras that indicated he was involved in something dark and disturbing and wanted to get out. I cleansed his aura a number of times and it kept relapsing back to a dark haze. That had never happened before."

"Why do you think that was?" Jemimah said.

Sister Rita rearranged her scarf. "When the mind is prevented from cooperating out of fear, it generates an impenetrable shield. I had nothing in my bag of tricks to break through the layers. There wasn't enough time in one visit and he wasn't willing to return for another. I had very little to work with."

Jemimah pushed on. "Was he having problems at home or with his career?"

"I got the impression he wasn't married, but was presently

involved with a woman whose name he didn't mention. I sensed that she was making demands on him and he was uncomfortable and ready to break it off. The relationship had run its course and he knew that."

"Were you able to gather any other impressions?" Jemimah said, intrigued by her own developing fascination with this woman.

Sister Rita waved her hands in the air as if summoning a spirit guide. "I was sure there was another woman. Someone a long distance from here. A lover, perhaps. But he didn't mention her name."

"Is there anything else you can tell me?" Jemimah said.

"Only that there was something he wanted to say but I wasn't the person he needed to say it to," she said.

"What do you mean?" Jemimah said.

"Somewhere along the line he realized he had made a dire mistake, and now he was afraid," she said. "He wanted to get as far away as he could from the situation."

Jemimah leaned forward. "Afraid of what, did he say?"

"My dear, you must understand that these are just impressions. I have nothing scientific to base them on. He was just sitting there with his head in his hands. He wasn't saying anything. His entire aura had taken on a dull haze. When he did look up at me, I could see that he was no longer in the room and it was impossible for me to reach him. I tried to rein him back in, but he stood up to leave."

"Did he say anything more as he left?" Jemimah said.

"He mumbled something about having to man up and take care of business and thanked me for my time. He reached into his pocket, placed a few twenties in my hand, and hurried out into the parking lot. I watched as he peeled out onto Cerrillos Road and drove off into the traffic. To answer your next question, I never saw him again." She paused, thinking, and then her eyes lit up. She stood and walked to a cabinet in the corner. Jemimah waited with curiosity while the petite woman rifled through a drawer. Coming back to the table, she placed a small manila envelope on top.

"What is it?" Jemimah said.

"It's a short recording of one of our early visits. Mr. Sanchez talks about an event which played a big role in his belief system regarding anything supernatural. He left before I could return it to him." She sat down. "I generally provide clients with a recording of their visit in case they want to review what the cards showed. It saves me from later calls asking questions. You know, I rarely recall an entire session, but visits with Mr. Sanchez were very compelling. I don't know if that will help, but it might give you some insight into his character."

Jemimah thanked her and asked if she could pay for time spent.

"No, my dear. You cannot. I am in hopes that whatever information is there may be of some use to you."

"I'm sure it will," Jemimah said.

"And now, my dear," the woman leaned forward, "tell me what has transpired in your life since I last saw you." She lifted Jemimah's left hand. "I would have thought there would be a diamond on this finger by now."

Jemimah chuckled. "That subject hasn't come up recently," she said.

"Yes, I see your work still takes center stage. One final word. Whether you wish to acknowledge it or not, there is serendipity and magic in our surroundings. All you have to do is be quiet and observe. Just listen and the answers will reveal themselves."

Jemimah found herself humming as she unlocked her car. She couldn't put her finger on it but just being in the presence of this petite woman whose adornments weighed more than she did seemed to have a calming effect.

Chapter Twenty

———◆———

As JEMIMAH DROVE out onto Cerrillos Road, her cellphone rang. She pressed the remote control on the dashboard without looking up to see who was calling.

"Hey, sunshine, where you headed?" Detective Romero said.

"Hey yourself, Rick. I just finished an interview with Sister Rita, and was thinking about grabbing a quick lunch before I head back to my office."

"I'm just leaving the substation. If you like, I could meet you somewhere and we could have a bite."

"I'm sorry, Rick. Can I take a rain check on that? There's some stuff I need to do on the Sanchez case, so I might just grab a burger and a shake and head back. Do you mind?"

"I do mind, but I understand. Just wanted to hold your hand for a while and maybe sneak in a few kisses."

She laughed. "Believe me, I could go for an hour of that. I'll send you a text and maybe we can get together later in the day."

"Damn, Jem, it's really hard not to get all romantic every time I see you," he said.

She made a *tsk tsk* sound. "Sorry, Detective. Those are the perils of dating a fellow employee. Maybe I should get a job with Santa Fe PD, you think?"

"We'll just have to keep things hush-hush as long as we can," he said. "Medrano addressed the topic of inter-departmental dating, among other things, at our last meeting. There should be a memo out soon."

"How harsh was it?" she said.

"Typical Medrano. He said he's had to turn a blind eye to us sharing more than criminal cases, and that like it or not, we were going to have to continue living under the microscope."

"I'm sure he'll agree that what employees do in their off-hours is pretty much their business," Jemimah said.

"That he does, but he stressed that he doesn't make the rules. The county commission does. Anyway, sweetie, Tim McCabe's just driving up. I guess I'll invite him to lunch."

"Chin up, dear. I'm sure you two have a lot to catch up on."

"Yeah, but I wasn't in the mood to talk shop, if you know what I mean," he said.

"You'll just have to settle for second best. Gotta go," she said.

***

As SHE DROVE into the city parking lot off San Francisco Street, Jemimah kept thinking about the CD in the manila envelope on the seat. She couldn't wait to listen to it. She tossed her keys to the valet and crossed the street to the two-story adobe building that housed a restaurant, an Indian arts shop, and a few random offices. She trudged up the steps, and as she walked through the door was greeted by her part-time assistant.

Katie Gonzales had worked for Jemimah for over a year. In her thirties, she was petite with a well-rounded figure that included a bosom ample for her size. She attracted men without effort, a fact Jemimah found intriguing. Her straight dark hair was styled in a fashion-forward shoulder length bob, not unlike that of trend-setting sitcom stars.

"What's up, Doc?" she said. Katie rarely addressed her by

name and preferred to allude to the Bugs Bunny and Elmer
Fudd cartoon characters.

"A little of this, a little of that, Katie. You know how this
business is," Jemimah said.

"I'm working on getting these Sanchez files in order. You
have something to add? I understand you interviewed his
sister," Katie said.

"Yes, but I haven't had a chance to compile my notes yet. I do
have something I want to listen to, though. Don't we have a CD
player somewhere around here?"

Katie went to the storage room and returned with a small
radio/CD player, which she plugged into the outlet near
Jemimah's desk. "A little outdated, since everything is now
Bluetooth, but it still works."

"Great. Let's have a listen." She popped the CD into the
player and sat down at her desk.

"I'll take a few notes. But first tell me what this is," Katie said.

"As far as I can tell," Jemimah said, "it's a conversation Sister
Rita the psychic had with the murdered mariachi some time
ago when he first came to see her. It might give us an idea of
what this guy was like."

Jemimah turned the volume up on the CD, which was, to
her surprise, of decent quality. The mariachi's voice sounded
distant, as though he had been transported back to his
childhood. It curled the hair on her arms. The psychic asked
few questions and let him ramble on:

> When I was a child, my mother always told us stories
> full of mystique and superstition. At the end, she would
> warn me to never sell my soul to the devil, because my
> life would be filled with pain and sorrow. I believed
> every word she said. You've heard the stories of alien
> beings landing in Roswell? Well, believe it or not, I had
> my own experience. My Uncle Fred was a police officer
> and he used to let me ride around town in his patrol car.

One time we were out in the hills looking for a stolen vehicle and we wandered through the maze of roads until the sun dipped into the horizon. We had already circled around and turned to go home.

All of a sudden there was a brilliant flash of light, and then the sky went dark. The heat from the blinding light came toward us. My uncle hollered for me to get out of the car. We sprawled on the ground, the cactus spines sticking us all over. And then I couldn't see my uncle. I was afraid if I hollered for him that whoever was responsible for the light would come and get me. I crawled over to a small grove of trees and reached for him. We waited a while and then slithered like snakes across the sand. About fifty feet ahead of us in the clearing, we saw a triangular shaped metallic object propped up on a steel platform. It wasn't a plane or an automobile. Two tall, thin figures milled around near the ladder. And then a blue flame erupted beneath the vehicle and the area glowed brighter than any light we had ever seen. The ground shook and the hair on my arms tingled.

Afraid of an explosion, we ran for cover near the patrol car. We watched as the object lifted up off the ground, hovered for a few minutes, and disappeared into the sky. It left a burn mark the size of a baseball field. We jumped in the car and hightailed it out of there. We never talked about it to anyone, because we knew we would be laughed out of town. That event made a believer out of me. As I grew up, I spent a lot of time reading about UFOs and all things supernatural. That's why I came to see you, Sister Rita, because I believe you can give me insight into things that have happened in my life that have no explanation and continue to haunt me until this day. I seem to be caught in a vortex of bad energy. About the time I think everything is going along all right, things shift and I end up involving myself with individuals of questionable character.

The CD ended with a short discussion about his experiences with various psychics and palm readers and how they had not always led him on the right path. He expressed hope his experience with Sister Rita would be different.

Jemimah scratched her forehead. "I would imagine an experience like seeing a flying saucer would certainly affect how a person thinks. I can see where he would find it difficult to keep a story like that inside, knowing that if he said anything, he would be considered a little nuts."

"Unfortunately there's nothing on that CD that's going to help with this case," Katie said.

"I agree. It would have been more helpful if she had one for each time he came to see her. Apparently she did give a CD to him after each visit, all except this one, but there wasn't any mention of random CDs on the detectives' list."

Chapter Twenty-One

---•---

ON MONDAY, THE noontime warmth radiated through the south side windows of Detective Romero's office in Cerrillos, and cranking up the evaporative cooler didn't help much. He reached into the desk drawer for his cellphone and speed-dialed Jemimah's number. Her phone switched directly to message. He had hoped they could leave work early and take a drive up to the Santa Fe ski basin, where it was always twenty degrees cooler than in the lower elevations. He left a short message indicating he would catch up with her later in the day. It was May 16th, two weeks since the discovery of the mariachi's body, and he knew Jemimah and his detectives were in the process of conducting interviews.

Clarissa's voice popped through the intercom. "Detective Martinez is here to see you, Rick."

He pressed a button on the console. "Send him back, and hold my calls until I tell you."

Within seconds, Detective Martinez tapped on the door jamb. "You got a minute, boss?"

"Yeah, just a couple. I'm up to my ears in daily reports."

Romero motioned him to the chair near his desk. "What's up, Floyd?"

Martinez didn't move and continued to stand in the doorway. "Got some lunch and some bad news here, Rick."

Romero frowned. "*Bad* as in the diner's out of *chicharron* burritos, or *bad* as in I'd better sit down."

Martinez shrugged his shoulders. "Bad as in maybe you'd better sit down." He placed the paper bag on the desk, reached in for a burrito and handed the other to Romero. He pulled back the wrapper to expose the warm tortilla enfolding the juicy interior. They both knew that eaten often enough, the deep fried chunks of pork smothered with refried beans and chile and wrapped in a tortilla could eventually cause a coronary, but at the moment, Martinez didn't care. The first bite was delicious. This was comfort food straight out of the barrio. It was also his way of dealing with job stress. Working under Romero was no easy task. He silently vowed to hit the gym twice this week to make up for it.

Romero thrummed his fingers impatiently on the desk, his food still in the wrapper. "All right, Floyd. Don't keep me in suspense. What's this news you seem to have difficulty spitting out."

The detective ambled over to the kitchen, grabbed a Coke from the fridge and popped the lid as he sat down in the chair next to Romero's desk. He leaned back and took a long swallow. "Ah, that hits the spot. It's pretty damned hot out there. Don't know what's going on with this weather. Way too warm for this time of year." Not quite sure how to approach the subject, he belched noisily and looked around the room, then finished his Coke in three large gulps.

Romero swiveled in his chair. "Dammit, Floyd. I'm getting tired of playing footsie here. Give me the news and let me enjoy my lunch before it gets cold," he said.

Martinez crushed the empty can and hurled it toward the trash bin. "Hokay. Just trying to figure out how to say this.

But here goes. I just spent a couple of hours at the courthouse offering the usual testimony trying to get a few convictions on last year's rash of burglaries in the county."

Romero was impatient. "Yeah, so?"

"Well, you know Officer Tommy Gonzales?"

"Sure I do. We go way back. What about him?"

"We were both testifying in District Court, so when the hearing recessed, we sat outside the building on one of the benches and shot the shit for a while."

"And?"

Martinez fidgeted in his seat. "And it turns out your brother Carlos had a nasty run-in with Sanchez, our homicide victim, about a week before the body was discovered."

Romero waved him off. "That's a crock if I ever heard one. Where'd he hear that BS?"

"Apparently one of the Mariachi Sunrise band members is also acquainted with your brother." He reached over and handed Romero a file. "This was part of the interview the guy gave. Tommy G is going to fax us the rest."

Romero quickly scanned down the pages. "In a nutshell, what's the rest of the story?" he said.

"It appears as though Carlos and his *date* or whatever she was, the woman he was with, were having drinks at the lounge in the La Fonda Hotel. Sanchez was on the stage performing *"La Bamba"* with the band. He kept ogling this woman while she was on the dance floor with Carlos, kind of directing the song at her.

"So during the break, Sanchez walks over to talk to her while Carlos is in the john. When he returned to their table, Sanchez was leaning a little too close to her."

Romero let out an exasperated grunt. "Don't tell me. Carlos lost his temper and busted his chops."

"Almost. According to the witness, Carlos shoved Sanchez against the wall. The guy picked himself up and started toward Carlos."

Romero shook his head in disgust. "Was there an actual fight or just a pissing match?"

"For a minute there, it looked as though all hell was going to break loose, but the guys in the band broke it up and pulled Sanchez back on stage."

"So did my dear brother stick around?"

"No. He wrapped his arm around the woman and they walked out into the parking garage."

"And Sanchez?"

"Can't really say. The band packed up their gear and went their separate ways."

"So how many nights did Sanchez perform after that?"

"Dr. Hodge spoke with some of the band members, and the group performed together at the lounge the following evening. It was a Friday night, but nobody seems to have seen him after that," Martinez said. "He didn't show up for a Mariachi Mass at the Santuario in Chimayo the following morning. Everyone figured he found himself a one-night stand that turned into a weekender, which was par for the course. Everyone knew Sanchez had quite a reputation as a playboy."

Romero stood up and slammed a file drawer shut. "Dammit, I know Carlos has a temper, but he'd never do anything this stupid. His probation for that idiotic stunt he pulled a couple of years ago is almost over. He'd be a fool to get into any kind of public altercation."

Detective Martinez propped his feet up on a chair. "I have no doubt about that, Rick, but according to the witness, Carlos and Sanchez exchanged some pretty harsh words. Everyone figured they were taking it out to the parking lot, but then Carlos and the woman got up and left."

Romero sighed. "Is that it?"

Martinez had a sheepish look on his face. "I wish it was, buddy. I have another shock wave for you."

Romero wiped his brow. "Jesus. How much worse can it get?"

"Sheriff Medrano says you're going to have to butt out of the investigation."

"You're shitting me," Romero said.

"Nope. Too close to home, he says. And from where I stood, he was dead serious. You know that stubborn look he gets on his face. Magnify that by a hundred."

Romero rolled his chair back and stood. "Let me work it out. I'll talk to Carlos and see what his side of the story is and then I'll get back to Medrano. Thanks, Floyd. You ruined my day but I appreciate you coming out here."

Martinez rapped his knuckles twice on the desk. "I'll let you know if anything else comes down the pike."

Romero dialed his brother's cellphone. After a few rings, it clicked over to message. "Carlos," he said. "I need to talk to you, *pronto*. And don't blow me off. It's important." He slammed the phone in the cradle with a loud bang.

By day's end, Romero had everything that had to be done wrapped up. He cleared his desk and tossed the half-eaten burrito in the trash. The phone jangled just as he reached for his briefcase. It was Carlos.

"What's going on, big brother? What's so important you have to leave a command for me to call you?"

"Serious business here, Carlos. I don't want to discuss it over the phone, so get your butt over to my office. I was about to go home, but I'll wait." Romero hung up and tossed his briefcase on the couch. *So much for a quiet drive home.*

His plan had been to spend some time with Jemimah, but this Carlos situation was more pressing. His brother had unknowingly tossed a monkey wrench into his social life, such as it was. Ever since he and Jemimah had returned from their vacation at the end of last summer, he hadn't quite known where they stood. Things were still good between them, but he wondered if his not-so-veiled attempt at a marriage proposal had thrown a curve ball into the playing field. She was still on first, but he felt like he was caught somewhere between bases hoping for a steal.

Although Carlos had finally moved out in recent days, it hadn't come soon enough for Rick. He would have liked to spend more time fixing meals and hanging out with Jemimah at his place, but Carlos was always under foot. If he wasn't out and about, he was on the phone, having long conversations with his latest girlfriend. Carlos seemed to attract women in their twenties who looked great hanging onto his arm, but beyond that had little to offer intellectually.

The brothers' dating style was different. Rick liked intelligent, family-oriented women who had interests other than checking themselves out in a mirror. That's what he liked about Jemimah … she was down to earth and didn't have to put on airs.

Chapter Twenty-Two

———•———

OUT IN THE south parking lot of the Cerrillos substation, Detective Romero leaned against his cruiser and nervously puffed on a cigarette. He was more frustrated than usual as he waited for his brother. He was tired of mollycoddling this thirty-something adult male and wished he would grow up. Looking up, he saw a shiny black Lexus turn into the drive and edge into the handicapped space. His level of irritation escalated as the driver rolled the tinted window down and waved. It was Carlos.

"Hey, Bro. How's it hanging?" Carlos chirped.

"You driving this?" Romero huffed.

Carlos exited the vehicle, twirled around like a matador with a cape. "*Sí, Señor*. Most awesome ride I've ever had. Just opened her up on the highway past Golden. Hugged those curves near Madrid like a jaguar." He reached into the driver's side window and retrieved a leather jacket. "Lucky for you I was just on my way into town when you called."

Romero ducked his head in the driver's side window and took a look at the dashboard with all the bells and whistles only a luxury car would have. "Jeezus, Carlos. Who you trying to impress?"

"Obviously not you, Loo-tenant," he chuckled. "You're not my type."

"Are you nuts? This is way out of your league, like most of the women you date."

Carlos smiled. "Oh, excuse me. The world according to Rick. Don't you know it's all about image? It's either this baby or that Harley over at the shop on Cerrillos Road. Now *that's* a bitchin' machine."

"If you say so." Romero turned and headed toward the entrance of the building. Carlos followed behind, jingling a set of keys and strutting to some inner beat in his head.

"You should try it, Brother. There's nothing like the wind blowing through your body, a sexy chick hanging on for dear life, and a thousand pounds of sheer power between your legs."

Romero spun around to face him. "Yeah, well, I don't want to be the one to scrape your carcass off Highway 14, so make sure you wear a damned helmet on that test drive. Christ, Carlos, I thought the time you spent in prison taught you to dispense with all this foolishness. About time you grew up."

"To you, foolishness; to me, adventure. That's where we differ, Brother dear."

"Believe me, I'd just as soon ride down the rapids naked than take my chance on a motorcycle skidding across an icy highway."

Carlos laughed. "Now that's a compelling visual there, Rick. But that never-try-anything attitude of yours is what separates the men from the boys. Besides, I haven't decided yet if I want a snazzy car or a snazzy bike, and I'm just test driving that ultra-cool Lexus you already convinced yourself I bought. So what's on your mind? Your girlfriend out of town and you want a little company?"

"This isn't a social visit, Carlos. There's some serious stuff that just came up and we need to talk about it." Romero snuffed out his cigarette and stepped through the entrance of the building.

Carlos followed suit and tossed his jacket on the couch in the reception area. Clarissa, who was rearranging files in Romero's office, looked up and did a double take as Carlos came toward her.

"Wow, Carlos, I hardly r-recognized you," she stuttered.

Carlos was dressed in black leather pants, a gray pullover, and motorcycle boots. He flashed a smile at her. "Hey, Clarissa, long time no see."

"I know. You don't get out here much," she said.

"Give us a little privacy, Clarissa," Romero said, "and put your tongue back in your mouth. You can catch up with the filing and my brother later. It's almost five o'clock, so go home early."

Clarissa's face turned beet red and she turned her head to the side. "It's just a bit warm in here. Hot flash or something," she mumbled. She left the room and closed the door behind her.

Romero sat back in his chair.

"Sit down, Carlos. This is going to take a few minutes."

"Can we forgo the drama and get to the point? I've got things to take care of in town before dark, and I need to arrange the furniture in my new digs."

"That can wait. Now listen to me. I just spent a grueling hour with one of my detectives, and he had some interesting news."

Carlos wiggled to get comfortable. "What's that got to do with me? I haven't had a traffic violation or parking ticket for over a year, and you know I'm still on probation and I'm careful about driving and drinking, so no chance of any DUIs."

"I'll give it to you in one sentence, Carlos. It has come to the attention of the investigators on this mariachi murder case that you had an altercation with Eduardo Sanchez at the La Fonda Lounge a few days before his body was discovered."

The smile turned to a frown. "*What*? Yeah, we had words, but that was the extent of it. He was hitting on my date and I didn't like it. So maybe I had a negative reaction. What's the big deal?"

Romero wearily shook his head. Carlos never seemed to take life seriously. "That's the least of your concerns. This little snit of yours managed to propel you right to the top of the suspect list."

Carlos was silent. "You gotta be kidding. That's all they have? *An argument over a woman*? That's a load of crap, and you know it."

"Christ, Carlos. The hotel surveillance tapes show you all over the guy. Of course it doesn't show what happened after that, but law enforcement can always assume you two went out into the back lot of the hotel and had it out or that you followed him into the hills at some later point and did him in. The DA's office doesn't have enough hard evidence to take it to a grand jury, but they're sure as hell going to try. The body was discovered in a semi-remote area right outside of Madrid, and since you're always barhopping in the Cerrillos/Madrid area, bottom line, you're right in the crosshairs."

A worried look traipsed across Carlos's face. "So what happens now, Rick?"

Romero didn't answer for a moment. He was surprised how quickly Carlos's demeanor moved from annoyance to sincerity. "If things follow the normal course, the DA will probably be issuing an arrest warrant soon. It's an election year and he's duty-bound to make a move. *Any move*. What's more newsworthy than the brother of a sheriff's deputy killing someone in the heat of passion, for Christ's sake?"

Carlos slumped in his chair. Beads of sweat appeared at his hairline. "You gotta make this go away, Rick."

"What you need is an iron-clad alibi. Something that you can back up."

"All I can tell you is that I was hanging out with this new chick, Annae. Not the one I was with at the La Fonda that night, but one I met later in Albuquerque. We drove back into town the next day, had lunch and drinks at DeAngelo's, and the next morning we took a drive up to Taos and then meandered

back down the back road. Took us a couple of days to land
back in Santa Fe. We spent some time at the casinos, got to
know each other a little. You know how it is. I'll spare you the
details."

Romero leaned back. "Well, that's a relief. So what's the
problem with her coming forward to give a statement?"

"I will ask, but I know for a fact she doesn't like cops," Carlos
said.

"Are you serious?" Romero said harshly. "She just doesn't
like cops. I think I've heard it all. Christ, they're not going
to *arrest* her, they're just going to *talk* to her. Does she have
something to hide?"

Carlos bristled. "Hell no, Rick. It's not like that. Pull out of
detective mode for a second. She's had some bad experiences
with cops because she's such a good looking woman. You know
the drill. Cop pulls a pretty girl over for going five miles over
the speed limit and then wants to get laid to make the ticket
disappear."

Romero was incensed. "Whatever. That's a lame excuse if I
ever heard one." His lips tightened. "I'm only going to say this
once, Carlos. She can come in, give her statement, and that'll
be the end of it. Otherwise, your butt's going to stay on the
line. This is damned serious, and it's not going away by itself.
Circumstantial evidence has convicted a boat load of innocent
people. The incumbent DA is a cutthroat barracuda, and I
don't doubt for a minute that Medrano's opposition for Sheriff
is going to keep this case dangling in front of the media for as
long as they can."

Carlos pushed his chair back. "I might raise a little hell
every so often, but you of all people know damned well I'm not
capable of hurting anyone, let alone killing someone. Dammit,
Rick, if I learned anything from all the time I spent in prison, it
is that I never want to go there again. You've incarcerated a few
more criminals, and they'd like nothing better than to get even.
I'm not ready to be some psycho's girlfriend. I'd rather eat dirt."

"That's all good and well, Carlos, but these politicians don't give a crack about whether or not you're innocent. They're happy as long as anything sensational involving our department stays on the front page of the morning newspaper and it gets spun every which way. Medrano ends up being the goat for any little thing that goes amiss, and it trickles down to us."

Carlos folded his arms over his chest. "Well, dammit. I'm innocent."

Romero shrugged. "I believe you, but in the big picture, my opinion doesn't count for diddly. My hands are tied on this one. I've already been pulled off the investigation. I'm going to talk to Sheriff Medrano about it in the morning."

Carlos wrung his hands. "So what do I do now?"

"Get that friend of yours to come forward and give a statement, and she sure as hell better be credible," Romero said.

Carlos sunk back into the chair. "So I'm guilty even if I'm not guilty?"

"Something like that. But we both know that this isn't the first time that fiery temper of yours has landed you in hot water."

Carlos popped a wad of gum into his mouth. "I'm sorry. Did I miss something here? I thought it was innocent until proven guilty."

"In an ideal world, maybe. Not in an election year. Now get out of here Carlos. We're done."

As Carlos walked out to the parking lot, he wondered what the real reason was that Annae didn't care for cops, a thought that immediately went south. *Nah, she was too damned beautiful for there to be anything shady about her.* He leaned against the driver's side door and dialed her number.

After Carlos left his office, Rick walked out to the patio and lit up a smoke. *I hope to hell Carlos hasn't gone and gotten himself involved with another ditsy broad.* He knew Carlos had always been a serial dater. For every relationship Rick had, Carlos had ten. He dialed Jemimah's cell.

"You got a minute?" he said.

"Sure, I'm just getting ready to head home. What's up?"

"I thought we might spend the night at my place for once. We can throw something together for dinner and then talk a little bit about this case. I have a few things I need to settle in my mind," he said.

"I would love to, Rick. It's been a while since we've done that."

"Great. Now that Carlos is out on his own, we don't have to be driving all the way out to your place, especially if we take in a movie. Do you want me to pick you up?"

"Let's just meet at your place. Around seven okay? I need to call the neighbor boy and have him run over and make sure the animals are fed."

"See you then, Sunshine," he said.

Chapter Twenty-Three

———•———

Romero's house was on an unpaved side street with large cottonwood trees standing like sentries on each side of the road in the South Capitol area of Santa Fe. The old adobe was built by his grandparents in 1930 and passed on to his parents. After their deaths, it was passed on to him, and Carlos received a vacant lot on the east side of the city. In recent years, he had remodeled the entire house, updating the electrical and plumbing to bring them up to code. The thick walls had been replastered and the wood floors refinished. It was now typical of the much sought-after residences in the area. It was still his childhood home, only better.

By the time Jemimah arrived, he was ready to take the cornbread out of the oven and smother it with pinto beans, onions, cheese, and red chile to make his favorite tamale pie. It was his grandmother's favorite recipe.

After dinner, the couple sat on the living room couch. Jemimah slipped out of her shoes and sat cross-legged on the Navajo rug covering the floor. "I think I need to unbutton my pants," she said. "That was quite a meal."

"You being here made everything more delicious," he said,

as he sat down next to her. He finished off the remainder of his beer.

"Before we get too comfortable, Rick, what was it you wanted to mull over about the case?" she said.

"I brought home copies of the letters Sanchez received from the woman in Mexico. I thought we might take a look at them and see if anything stands out. Something's been gnawing at me. Why would he save them if they weren't important? If he was such a player, why didn't he just toss them?"

"That sounds reasonable. Let's take a look," Jemimah said. He handed her a file folder and she pulled out the first couple of letters. He did the same.

After a short time, Jemimah said, "This woman, Carmen, has a good command of the English language. Her writing is very poetic. The first letter seems kind of stilted, as though she doesn't want to express too much of what she's feeling. She just asks about how things are going for him, his concerts, the weather, etcetera."

Rick pointed to a letter. "The dates seem to be about two weeks apart. We can assume Sanchez responded in between. This one starts out with 'so nice to hear from you again,' and she mentions having gone to a mariachi concert with her sister in Guadalajara. She adds a little bit more small talk and ends with *con cariño*."

"What does that mean, Rick?" she said.

"It can mean 'with love,' or something more than fondness. I guess a guy could interpret it either way, depending on how the romance was progressing. We have to take into consideration that these two were also talking on the phone regularly."

Jemimah rattled another letter. "About the fifth letter, it seems to me as though things are getting a little more personal. She's asking how he's feeling and whether he'd be able to come for a visit soon. Says she is looking forward to seeing him again."

Rick paused, then said, "So you agree that these two might have had more than just a friendship?"

"As something of a romantic myself," she said, "I would interpret her letters as a prelude to a blossoming romance, fueled by regular telephone conversations. From her responses, it's clear he was encouraging some type of a relationship, otherwise she probably wouldn't bother to write so regularly. And I agree with you that most guys wouldn't save letters from a woman unless they meant something. What do you think, Rick?"

"I'm thinking about taking a trip to Mexico to visit with her. There's no doubt in my mind that she might be able to shed some light on this case. She also may not know of Sanchez's demise. I plan on seeing Sheriff Medrano in the morning and see if I can talk him into approving the trip."

He tossed everything back in the file and set it on the table. "So much for that. I appreciate your input, Jem."

She tugged on his arm. "Come on. I'd like to give you some input about the satin sheets on your bed."

He grinned. "Pleasure after business. I'm all yours."

***

ON TUESDAY MORNING, he drove to the county offices to meet with Sheriff Medrano about scheduling a trip to Mexico to determine if he could jar anything loose on the investigation, which was starting to look like a cold case. In law enforcement circles, two weeks was considered too long a time for there to be so little progress on a homicide.

Medrano skimmed through the travel request. "Is this your way of weaseling yourself back into the investigation?" he said.

Romero sat back in the chair. "Well, I haven't received an official notice that I'm off the case. Cleared out all my emails this morning, and there was nothing there to indicate I was being excluded. Besides, we're already so understaffed, I'm sure you wouldn't want me spending my time tied to my desk if I couldn't work the Sanchez Investigation."

Medrano looked down at his empty cup. He walked to the

kitchen, and after pouring himself another, he said to Romero, "Lucky for you that girlfriend of your brother's came in this morning to give a statement. She also produced a credit card receipt for a double-nighter at the Taos Inn. They didn't check out until late in the afternoon, and then on their way down 285, stopped by the Buffalo Thunder Casino at Pojoaque Pueblo and spent a few hours playing blackjack. I'm sure the casino's security cameras will back that up if we need to go there."

Romero grinned. "Good detective work there, Bobby."

"Have you forgotten I was a detective when you were still in diapers? Now get your butt over to accounting with the purchase order for your tickets. And let's not make this a vacation on the playas of Mexico courtesy of the county."

"Now, *Je-fe*'," Romero chided, "you know I would never do anything to draw the attention of all the vultures out there just waiting for you to screw up so they can rake your ass through the coals."

"Yeah, yeah. Get out of here. I'm on a roll pretending to be a detective."

* * *

ROMERO'S PALMS WERE covered with sweat as he alighted from the inter-city shuttle in front of the terminal of Albuquerque International Airport on Wednesday morning. He hadn't ever been crazy about flying and preferred to drive, no matter how far the distance. Traveling by car into the Mexican interior wasn't an option this time, especially for law enforcement who might be confronted by highwaymen on a remote stretch of road. But something about being thirty-thousand feet in the air and not strapped to a parachute unnerved him. He was sure that Jemimah, with her background as a psychologist, would assure him his fear was unwarranted. He knew it went much deeper than that, but he wasn't about to share that information with her. For that reason, he hadn't taken her up on the offer to drive him to the airport and opted for the shuttle instead, citing the early hour of departure. In reality, he didn't want her to see him shaking in his boots.

He was seventeen the first time he had occasion to be in an airplane. When the Santa Fe Airport was built in the mid-seventies, its purpose was primarily to serve small plane traffic. His friend Leroy worked there on weekends and was acquainted with all the pilots who hung around waiting to score a charter flight. Leroy talked Everett Wilson, one of the pilots, into taking him and a few of his buddies up for a quick flight in a vintage plane.

That Sunday morning, Leroy, Rick and another friend crowded into the small single-engine Cessna. Romero felt the joyous exhilaration of being high above the piñon-dotted landscape. Twenty minutes later the plane gently glided to a stop after a short pattern flight near the state penitentiary and around the edges of Santa Fe.

"Hey, you guys," said Everett. "Next weekend I'm taking a sweet little Beechcraft Baron 58 up for a test flight. Any of you want to come along, you're welcome."

The boys looked at one another and nodded in unison. "Sounds like fun. Count us in."

The following Saturday, Leroy and Rick showed up at eight in the morning. Everett was waiting at the terminal. Since his first experience was uneventful, Rick had decided flying was something he could get into. He and Leroy strode eagerly up the steps and into the second row of seats in the double-engine airplane.

Everett jumped up into the pilot seat. "How do you like this, boys? Eight-seater. A little bigger than that itty-bitty plane we were in last week."

"Pretty neat," Romero said.

Everett dusted off the dashboard then meticulously folded up the cloth and returned it to the cubby hole. "Planes like this one were used after the attack on Pearl Harbor. I'm sure you've studied that at school, hey?"

"Sure have," said Leroy. "And working around here, I've learned a lot about airplanes."

Sitting in the glass cockpit, Everett craned his neck to the left and then the right. He scanned the runway and radioed the tower with his flight plan. Turning to look at his passengers, he chuckled at their boyish anticipation. "Well, get them seatbelts fastened, boys. We're about ready to take off." He skillfully maneuvered the plane to complete a ninety degree turn. The tower cleared him and he taxied down the runway.

Five minutes after takeoff, they were coasting north toward the Tesuque hills, the horizon holding steady. The plane had two 300-horsepower engines and could reach a top cruise speed of 230 miles an hour.

"That's the national cemetery down there, boys. Notice how every one of those white headstones sits in perfect rows. Look just like dominoes, don't they?"

The two teens were smiling ear to ear. This was quite an adventure. As they flew, they looked out the windows in awe. "That's pretty cool," Romero said, pointing to a train winding its way through Cumbres Pass. Leroy agreed.

Everett leaned forward and clutched the wheel in an exaggerated gesture. "You've been around the airport a while, Leroy. Did you know a plane like this can climb over two hundred feet a minute?" He pulled on an imaginary gearshift. "*Vroom, vroom.* Let's see what this baby can do."

Before Leroy could comment, the plane was careening through the Rio Grande Gorge northwest of Taos, flying at top speed. The cagey pilot glanced in their direction and doubled over in laughter. "What's the matter, boys? Thought you were ready for some real fly time."

Rick and Leroy were both hunched over on the floor behind the seat, holding on for dear life while the plane flew straight up in the air and then through a series of loops before nose-diving straight toward the ground. The plane was going down, down, down, as though it would crash into the earth below.

Romero wasn't sure if he was screaming or if he had already died.

With a devilish grin on his face, the pilot lifted the nose up at the last minute, leveled out the plane and turned in the direction of Santa Fe. After what seemed an eternity but was less than twenty minutes later, the plane made a smooth landing on the concrete strip. Romero could still hear Everett laughing as they disembarked from the plane, his knees almost too weak to hold him upright.

Everett had a Cheshire cat grin on his face. "Come on, guys, loosen up. Just a little sky cruise. Let's do it again sometime."

"Yeah, sure," the boys responded, both green in the gills as they bounded toward the bathroom.

ROMERO SHOOK HIS head to clear the fog. That childhood incident had been stored in his mind a long time. He followed the passengers out of the shuttle. Even for early morning, the air was hot and smelled of exhaust fumes. He paid the driver and retrieved his luggage.

Chapter Twenty-Four

———•———

AT ALBUQUERQUE INTERNATIONAL Airport, Romero checked his luggage at the Aero México counter. He had arrived just before eight thirty in time to retrieve his boarding pass. He settled in a seat toward the back of the plane and fastened his seatbelt. Taking a deep breath, he tried to relax his neck muscles. He had no choice but to suck it up. It was about a five-hour flight with a short layover in Dallas. He patted his chest pocket to assure himself the prescription bottle of Xanax was still there. He closed his eyes through takeoff, as the noise of the engines rumbled through his head, vibrating through the walls of the plane.

Endless hours later at two in the afternoon, a petite but portly flight attendant in a gunmetal gray uniform announced both in English and Spanish that Aero México Flight 273 would be landing in less than ten minutes. Romero felt himself being sucked into the backrest of his seat as the plane shifted into descent mode. He squeezed his eyes shut for a moment, and when he opened them, watched the terminal buildings zipping past as the plane hovered over the runway. For a long moment he thought it was going to continue its forward motion and crash into the terminal.

As the plane taxied up to the gate of Guadalajara Miguel Hidalgo y Costilla International Airport, Romero's fingers loosened their vice-like grip on the armrest. The airport terminal was a welcome sight. He had never been this far south into Mexico and never by plane; mostly he'd taken occasional trips to Juarez by car to spend a few days in the sun and pick up a few bottles of Kahlua and tequila on the return drive.

Despite the Xanax he'd swallowed before takeoff, the flight to Jalisco aged him by at least ten years. His palms were clammy as he waited for his heartbeat to return to normal. His body felt as though he was still in motion. He couldn't wait to plant his feet on good old Mother Earth. Grabbing his backpack, he alighted from the plane and walked down a wobbly ramp on wheels held by two attendants dressed in mechanic's uniforms. He breathed a sigh of relief as his feet touched ground level and took another deep breath, dismissing the thought of the return flight. *Too early to worry about that.*

He was overwhelmed by the size of the airport. Compared to Albuquerque's, this one had forty-eight gates and served almost two million travelers. Fellow passengers pushed forward to claim their baggage. Airport security appeared more stringent than in the U.S., and Romero noted there were plenty of armed *policias* around securely holding the leashes of drug-sniffing German Shepherds. He headed out of the giant terminal into the bright sunlight and hailed a white roofed lime-green Volkswagen taxi, figuring that even as crazy Mexican cab drivers go, it couldn't be half as bad as flying.

The driver skidded to a stop, exited his vehicle and rushed to Romero's side. He was wearing khaki pants and a white tunic. Bending forward in an exaggerated bow, he said, "Juan Ramirez at your service, *señor.*"

Romero climbed into the back seat and fastened his seatbelt. "*El Guadalajara Hilton, por favor,*" he said.

"*Por su puesto, señor.* For sure. Is not too far from here. Maybe twenty minutes. We should be there in a little *momento*," the driver said in broken English.

Romero smiled as the driver peeled out onto the main drag. Hundreds of pigeons scattered as the taxi wound its way around the Mercado. He looked out the windows. "This is a beautiful city," he said.

"Oh, *sí señor.* I have been here all of my life and I never get tired of driving around every day."

Another block and they were on Avenida de las Rosas in front of the World Trade Center. The Guadalajara Hilton was nestled in the complex. At first glance, Romero was stunned by the size of the hotel. Some county bookkeeper had obviously screwed up and placed him into a situation that definitely wouldn't be workable. He could hear Medrano bitching about it: *You stayed where?* This was a bit much luxury for an information gathering trip. Juan Ramirez reached for the luggage.

"Hey amigo, *un momento.* Can you find me a hotel around here that isn't so big and expensive?"

The driver laughed. "*Por cierto, señor.*"

"I just want something small, where I don't have to go up and down in an elevator."

"I know a good one. El Tapatio Hotel. It's more better. *Vamonos!*" The driver took the ramp at Mexico 23, a few lefts and rights and drove up in front of an impressive colonial-style building at the top of a green hill. The hotel was painted a stark white, with bright blue shutters and wrought-iron balconies. Rows of foot-high dahlias lined the walkway. Colorful feathered macaws perched in cages hanging from the portal ceilings. He left the engine running as he collected Romero's suitcase from the front of the VW.

Romero reached for his luggage. "Wait for me, *hombre.* I just have to check in and then there's another place I need you to take me to."

"*Sí*, that is all right. I'll be here," said Ramirez.

Romero walked into the lobby of the 150-room hotel, which was about the size of the Santa Fe Hilton. He checked in, retrieved the key, and took a moment to call and cancel his reservations at the larger hotel. As he exited the lobby, the driver was waiting as promised, leaning up against the hood of the cab.

"I need to go to 74 La Paz Street. Do you know where that is, Juan?" Romero said.

"It's not too far from the hotel, *señor*, maybe ten, twelve blocks," he said.

The drive was circuitous, the taxi skirting around brightly painted tourist buses and horse drawn carriages. Once off the main drag, Romero wasn't surprised to see the graffiti on the buildings, a stark contrast to the pristine multi-spired cathedrals on the previous blocks. He commented to the driver about the brightly colored bus carrying everything but the kitchen sink on the roof.

"They call that a chicken bus, *señor*."

Romero snapped a photo with his phone. "Strange name for a bus."

The driver laughed a hearty laugh. "It's because not only people ride on it but also cats, dogs, and chickens, too."

Another few blocks and the driver slammed on the brakes in front of a small house dwarfed by two adjacent imposing residences. Romero chuckled, wondering how long it would take to adjust to the precarious driving habits of this country.

"You are here, *señor*," the driver said in fractured English. "Fourteen dollars American."

Romero handed him pesos in the equivalent of twenty dollars. "*Gracias, amigo*. Keep the change, *to'me la feria*," he said in perfect Spanish, a sheepish grin on his face. "I need for you to return here in about an hour, around four thirty."

The driver tittered. "*Aiieee*, I thought you were a *gringo turista*," he said. "I will be happy to return and wait for you. I am at your service."

Romero sensed the driver meant every word. He waved him off and stepped onto the sidewalk.

The house had an ornate iron gate and a terraced courtyard bordered by ceramic pots filled with hibiscus flowers and cactus plants. As he pulled the cord on the outside bell, he could hear roosters crowing and a dog barking incessantly in the neighboring yard. He wasn't sure what connection Carmen de la Torre had to the case he was investigating, but he had come this far and hoped his interview would bear fruit. From the letters the detectives had recovered at Sanchez's home, he was still under the impression that her relationship with Eduardo Sanchez might have been much more than casual.

He was momentarily stunned by the woman who walked toward the gate.

Chapter Twenty-Five

⸻

THAT SAME WEDNESDAY afternoon, Jemimah parked her 4Runner SUV and traversed the ramp leading from the parking lot to the double doors of the county sheriff's compound in Santa Fe. A pair of piñon jays jabbered back and forth in the trees bordering the building. Earlier that morning she had stopped by the substation to say goodbye to Rick before he departed to Mexico. He had graciously refused her offer to drive him to the airport, stating the county had already booked the shuttle service. He promised to call her for a ride home on his return.

At the county compound, she flashed her ID to the security guard, who waved her in. After climbing the steps, she stopped in the hallway to grab a soda. Cellphone to one ear and satchel hanging from her arm, she made her way toward the office she shared with several detectives. As she reached the doorway, she was greeted by an extended wolf whistle coming from the bench outside her office. She looked up to see a man with long braided hair and a beard and moustache. He was wearing tight black jeans and a satiny black shirt embellished with intricately embroidered skulls. Finishing off the outfit was a pair of polished motorcycle boots. The guy was handsome in a *Milagro Beanfield* kind of way, with a confident demeanor and a mouthful of sparkling white teeth. Even from fifteen feet away, she could smell his musky aftershave. Jemimah could only assume he was her four o'clock appointment.

He stood up and whistled again. "*E-ho-lay,* are you the shrink?" he said.

"I am Dr. Hodge, yes," she said.

"If I knew a shrink who looked like you, lady, I'd be on her couch every week," he laughed, a gold incisor gleaming in his mouth.

She forced a smile. "Mr. Barela, I gather?"

He did a mock tap dance. "You gather right, pretty lady."

Jemimah directed him toward the door. "Come in. I'll be just a moment." She placed her purse and briefcase on the desk closest to the entrance. "Thank you for coming to Santa Fe," she said.

"Oh, I come a lot," he smiled. "No problem."

She sidestepped his double entendre. "I'll try not to take too much of your time. I know it's a long drive back to El Rito."

"My pleasure, believe me, lady. You can take all the time you want. I got nowhere to go. Maybe I'll play tourist for the rest of the day. Might find me some chicky baby wandering around the plaza."

Jemimah sat at the desk and motioned for him to take a seat on the couch. She knew sitting anywhere near this character would give him ideas. His forward manner unnerved her, and she took another deep breath. She hoped he would settle down once she started the interview.

She opened a file and placed the recording device between them. "All right, Mr. Barela. As you are aware, the SFCSO is conducting interviews as part of the investigation into the death of Eduardo Sanchez. His body was found about fifteen days ago in a remote area near the Town of Madrid. I understand you were acquainted with him?"

"Yeah, I knew the mariachi dude, if that's who you're talking about. I read in the *Rio Grande Sun* that they found his body somewhere."

"Yes, that would be the person we're discussing here," Jemimah said.

Barela fiddled with his bolo tie, caressing the large hunk of turquoise in the center. "I knew him, but not real personal like. We both play with mariachi bands around town, and for a while we were dating the same broad."

"And who would that be, Mr. Barela?"

"This Annae chick."

"A-N-N-A? Is that how it's spelled?"

"No, she spelled it different. Said it separated her out from the ordinary chicks. A-N-N-A-E, I think it was. Only reason I know that is 'cause I was going to tattoo her name on my butt, but I changed my mind." He laughed out loud at his own joke. "No, seriously, she had one of those silver ID bracelets with her name engraved on it."

Jemimah nodded. "And Mr. Sanchez was also dating her?"

He raised his eyebrows in mock indignation. "Well, not really at the same time, but right after," he said. "Like a few minutes, or an hour, or something like that. You never know with some of these broads."

"Did you date her for an extended period of time?"

"Nah. She was a crazy bitch, man. All she wanted to do was hang on to me everywhere we went. She wouldn't let me finish my gig in peace. A guy expects Spanish chicks to be like that, all possessive; we're used to it. But this was a *gringa* chick, and she wanted to be the center of attention, even during our performance, throwing me kisses and shaking her boobs. We can't have stuff like that going on. We like pretty women in the audience, but we also know most of them are off limits, and just like to flirt around to make their boyfriends jealous." He paused as his mouth formed into a grin. "You could come and watch us play sometime."

Jemimah uncapped a water bottle and offered him one. He waved his hand. "So what happened to her," she said, ignoring his invitation.

"I dumped her ass. Told her I didn't want to be in a relationship with her. She was too, how do you say it, volatile."

"What happened after that?"

He ran his palm over the top of his head. "She got all hysterical and came at me with a beer bottle. She was feisty, that one," he said. "Looked to me like she needed to be the breaker-upper."

"What do you mean by that?"

"When I told her I didn't want to hang out with her anymore, she told me 'You can't do that.' So I said, 'Well, I'm doing it.' "

"Anything happen after that?"

He laughed. "She threw me the finger and told me to go to hell."

"Did you ever see her again after you had your disagreement?" Jemimah said.

"Not for sex, if that's what you mean," he chortled.

Jemimah held her tongue. "I mean socially, Mr. Barela, for whatever reason," she said, emphasizing each word.

He leaned forward and grinned. "Call me Nick. All the chicks do."

"I hardly consider myself a chick."

"Hey, man. You're right up there with all the tens, lady. You got nice chrome. Maybe me and you could catch a beer after this. All this talking is making me thirsty."

Jemimah rolled her eyes. This guy was exactly the macho type she'd never even consider dating. "I don't think so, but thank you," she said. "Have some water."

"You hooked up with some dude, or what?"

She reminded herself to practice tolerance. "Let's continue with our interview, all right? I have just a few more questions."

"Suit yourself, Professor. You don't know what you're missing. You could be running your fingers through my hair. See, touch it, it's soft, *que no?*" He laughed.

Jemimah stifled a smile and a sigh. *This guy's something else.* "So, did you see her again in a social setting?"

"Nah, not really. She hooked up with Eddie Sanchez right away. Before my tears had even dried."

"This was another mariachi?"

"Yeah, you know, the dead guy," he said.

"Oh, yes. Eduardo Sanchez. Tell me again, was he just a casual relationship or a good friend of yours?"

He thought for a moment. "Look, we were buddies for a while, but he was too full of himself. He thought he was hot shit, if you know what I mean."

"No, I don't. Can you elaborate?"

"You know, the ladies would fall all over him every time he was on stage. I guess all those years of playing trumpet made him think he had some magical powers with women, if you get my drift."

Jemimah continued, "So how did they meet ... did you introduce them?"

"At the La Fonda Hotel, in the lounge. Sanchez had a weekly gig there with a group him and a couple of the guys formed. Totally different from the stage performance."

"In what way?"

"You know, closer, more couples dancing belly to belly, that kind of thing. Not the big old band thing like playing in a concert or on the plaza bandstand where everyone dances on the grass or the street."

"More a night-club atmosphere, smaller stage, more intimate, is that what you're describing?" Jemimah said.

"Yeah, 'intimate,' that's the word. He would pick out a hot chick from the audience and sing directly to her, like he was Antonio Banderas or some big celebrity. Didn't matter if there was a guy around. By the end of the song the woman he was singing to would get all hot and bothered and melt right there." He rubbed his hands together.

"So did you and Mr. Sanchez ever perform together?"

"Not if I could help it, but a couple of times my friend Danny Gonzales scored a hot date, and he would ask me to fill in for him at the La Fonda. I couldn't pass up the bucks, so I helped him out anytime he asked."

"And Sanchez met her—this A-N-N-A-E woman—there, during a performance?"

"Yeah, I spotted her when she came through the lobby, so I got all prepared, you know, smoothed my eyebrows and stuff. I thought she was coming over to make up with me after we got back from our break, but she zeroed straight in on Sanchez. She started fawning all over him, like he was so great."

Jemimah looked straight at him. "Mr. Barela, did that make you jealous?"

"Oh, hell no," he said. "I was done with her. Once I give a chick her walking papers, she's gone. I don't invite them back for seconds. That's not my style. You're either in or out, and she was out."

"So did Annae and Mr. Sanchez start seeing each other after that?"

"As far as I know. Any time we had occasion to play dueling trumpets—you know, our guys against his group—she was right there in the audience acting like some teeny bopper watching Elvis."

"Did he ever mention her to you?"

"Like I said, we weren't that good of friends and I'm pretty sure he knew I had slept with her. He never said anything. But every time they were together, she would point her nose up in the air at me and give me the evil eye." He put his finger on the edge of his eye and pulled it to the side to indicate a malevolent expression.

"So how did that make you feel—angry enough to confront him?" Jemimah said.

"It was no skin off my back. I was pretty sure it wasn't going to last. It wouldn't take long for him to discover what a crazy broad she was."

"So did he?"

Barela raised his eyebrow. "Did he what?"

"Find out what a crazy broad she was."

Barela smirked. "Well, he's dead, ain't he, so we'll never know."

Jemimah's cellphone vibrated, and she reached into her jacket pocket to take a quick look at the screen. She pushed her chair back and stood up.

"Excuse me, Mr. Barela. I have to take this call. I'll just be a minute," she said.

He watched as she walked out of the room, whistling under his breath. "*Mama Mia,* what a body on that one. I wouldn't mind strumming her guitar for a while," he said, adjusting the silver clip on his braided hair.

Jemimah stepped out into the hall and answered the phone. She told Katie she was in the middle of an interview and would she let her next appointment know she was running late. She hung up and returned to her desk.

"Mr. Barela, thank you for coming in. I think we've covered all the questions I had."

He reached for his jacket and moved toward her. "I have a question," he said.

"And what is that?" Jemimah said as she gathered her file.

"Do you want to go cruisin' in my lowrider? I'll show you a real good time."

Jemimah closed the desk drawer and grabbed her keys from her jacket. She directed him toward the door. "Again, thank you for your time."

Chapter Twenty-Six

———•———

CARMEN DE LA Torre was hardly the type of woman Detective Romero expected to answer the door. As a seamstress, she would typically be a brown-skinned Mexican woman, somewhat matronly, with dark hair pulled back in a tight bun secured at the nape of her neck. Quite to the contrary, the woman standing before him was of medium height, light-complected and dressed in a bright floral shift that accentuated her supple curves. She had shoulder-length dark hair and hazel eyes that sparkled when she smiled. Romero found himself temporarily tongue-tied.

"Señora de la Torre? *Gracias por tomarse el tiempo para visitar conmigo,*" he said, thanking her for agreeing to see him.

"Detective Romero, Carmen de la Torre. I'm glad to see you made it here safely," she said with a smile. "And I do speak English."

"Uh, y-yes," he stuttered. "I'm sorry, Mrs. de la Torre. I forget that English is a second language for many."

"I am widowed. You may call me Carmen, if you're comfortable doing so."

It took Romero another minute to compose himself.

"Come in," she said.

He followed her across the courtyard to the living room, which was modestly furnished with *equipale* furniture. Large tin mirrors and candle sconces adorned the walls. Colorful ceramic trees of life stood side by side on the fireplace mantle. Romero took a seat on the couch across from her. Through the open window facing the street, the sounds of traffic were almost deafening.

She stood and pointed toward the kitchen. "I was just about to have my afternoon coffee. Would you care to join me?" she said.

"Yes, thank you, I would."

Carmen returned with a tray, poured two cups of coffee from the carafe and placed them on the table along with a plate stacked with sugar cookies. She stirred cream and sugar into her cup and handed it to Romero, who followed suit.

She spoke first. "When you called a few days ago, you said you wanted to discuss a matter regarding one of my clients. Can I ask what this is about?"

Romero set his cup on the table. "As I mentioned, I am a detective with the Santa Fe County Sheriff's Office in New Mexico." He handed her his card. "We're investigating the death of a mariachi who we believe might have been a customer of yours."

She smiled and placed his card on the table. "Detective Romero, over the years I've created a good number of outfits for mariachis in New Mexico and have several regular clients from Santa Fe. Can you tell me a little more about this person? I can pull out my invoice file if that will help."

Romero reached into his briefcase for a folder. "No, that won't be necessary. The man's name is Eduardo Sanchez. This is a recent a photograph of him." He placed the picture in front of her.

She glanced at the photograph, and as if she couldn't believe her eyes, leaned forward and looked closer. "Oh, my God, *Dios mio*," she gasped. Her hands shook as the photograph tumbled to the floor. She turned to Romero in shock.

He watched the color drain from her face. It confirmed his suspicion that they had been more than friends.

He moved closer to her, his hand reaching to keep her from falling over. "Are you all right?"

She attempted to regain her composure by inhaling deeply. "Yes, yes. I'm so sorry. The photograph caught me by surprise."

Romero slipped the file into his briefcase. "I take it you knew him?" he said.

The woman's eyes were downcast. "I met him about two years ago ... excuse me," she stammered.

Romero rose to his feet.

Carmen de la Torre stood and turned toward the hallway. "Just give me a moment, please. Sit," she said. She braced her hand on the wall as she walked toward the back of the house.

Romero waited. He looked at the decorative elements on the walls, then walked to the window. Ten minutes later, she returned to the room and sat next to him. It was obvious she had been crying. Her eyes were red and slightly swollen. "I'm sorry about the news," he said. "Can I call someone for you, perhaps a friend?"

She twisted the lace handkerchief in her hands. "No, no. I'll be all right." She sighed. "How terrible this is. I would have never known. He always called me at least once a week. If you hadn't come ..." her voice cracked.

Romero spoke in a hushed tone. "When was the last time you heard from him?"

"He wrote me in early April that he would be coming for an extended visit and also to place another order for a jacket, but he didn't want to do this by phone because he had some specific ideas in mind. And then he called again about two weeks ago. We were on the phone for a long time. He sounded tired. He said to expect him at the end of the month, but he would call first and let me know exactly when his plane would arrive. I hadn't heard from him since. And now …."

"I'm sorry to have to ask such a personal question, but were you two lovers?" he said.

She dabbed her eyes. "We had become very close in recent months. Yes, I guess you could say that." She burst into tears. "My God, yes. We *were* in love. He said he wanted us to be together for the rest of our lives. We were making plans for the future."

Romero reached across the space and gently placed his hand on her arm. "We found a packet of your letters at his home. That's where we obtained your address."

She blinked and turned to look at him. "Can you tell me what happened? Who would do this to him? He was a good man."

"Right now we're in the middle of the investigation. We have no suspects. I can't go into detail, but it is being treated as a homicide investigation. His body was found in a remote area outside of Santa Fe."

She put her hands on her cheeks. "This is so hard to believe. My whole life has just been turned upside-down. We had made so many plans. And my poor Eduardo—"

"Mrs. de la Torre, Carmen, I'm so sorry I had to be the bearer of this bad news. I can't imagine your pain," he said. "If you prefer, I can come back tomorrow to give you some time to process this."

She shook her head. "I appreciate that, Detective, but I'll be all right. Let's get this over with."

Romero pulled out a tablet and scribbled a few notes. "Can you think of anything that might help us determine what was going on in his life? He didn't appear to have any close friends he could confide in."

"Eduardo told me that after his next concert at the Mariachi convention in Las Vegas, Nevada, he was quitting the music business. He was coming back to Mexico to look at a small ranch in Aguascalientes, where he wanted to retire and raise a few horses."

"Did he ever discuss his finances with you?"

"Not in any detail. He did say that in recent months he had been investing his money and that it was starting to pay off. I had the impression that he was a wealthy man. That's not the right word. He had worked hard and lived comfortably. But the money wouldn't have mattered to me."

"At any time during your conversations did he ever mention what these investments consisted of?"

"No, these were just casual comments he made in passing. He never went into detail," she said. "Just that he was about to finalize a transaction and he would be coming into a substantial amount of money. This would allow him to pursue his dream of retiring to a small ranch, where he could raise quarter horses and race them at the tracks in El Paso and Santa Fe."

Romero wasn't sure how to ask the next question. He was silent for a minute. "I know this might be a little personal, but did he ever speak of any of his past relationships with women?"

"Yes. He was very open about the subject."

"Did he say anything specific?"

She looked down at the palms of her hands. "Nothing other than he had recently broken up with a woman who was very demanding of his time and seemed to be more interested in money and material things than anything else. When he did speak of her that one time, it seemed to anger him."

Romero's eyebrows raised. "In what way?"

"Just that his tone of voice changed. I assumed it had not been a friendly breakup."

"Did he say anything else? Who she was or anything about her?"

"No. He was determined to start a new life here in Mexico and didn't want to dredge up the past. It was what it was."

"Just a few more questions. Did Mr. Sanchez ever give you any indication at all that he might be involved with drugs?"

Her eyes widened. "*Drugs?* Oh, no. I never got that impression. He appeared to live a clean life. In fact, when we went out to dinner, he never drank more than a few sips of wine. He was very devoted to being a musician. He loved the music and I was under the impression he had a large following of fans."

Romero shook his head. "I'm sorry. I apologize. I didn't mean to imply he was taking drugs. But that maybe he was involved somehow in buying and selling them?"

"I couldn't say for sure, but I doubt that very much," she said. "I've seen drug dealers in our country and he acted nothing like them. They are all criminals. No, I'm sure he wasn't involved in anything like that. I consider myself a good judge of character, Detective, and I found him to be a good man."

"Had he spent any other time in Mexico that you were aware of?" Romero said.

She wrung her hands. "You must understand it wasn't until several months ago that we began to develop a relationship. I'd been sewing his outfits for some time before that, and I was also aware that he was involved with a woman there."

"So since that time, had he also traveled to Mexico for other business that you know of?"

"Yes, I believe he had. On a previous trip he met with a man in Aguascalientes. I understood it was to talk about buying property. He was planning to see him again on his next trip."

"You wouldn't happen to know this man's name, would you?" Romero said.

She walked over to the desk in the corner of the room and returned with a small card in her hand. "On his last visit, he left a suit jacket here to have the buttons replaced. The card was in one of the pockets. I saved it to return it to him on his next visit. I guess there's no harm in you having it, considering the circumstances."

Romero placed the card in his folder. He looked across at her and noticed the tired look in her eyes.

"Could you walk me through the process Sanchez followed to obtain his outfits from start to finish? It would help me understand what his visits consisted of."

"Well, he would bring his ideas to me about fabric, color, decoration, size, etcetera. Since I had all his measurements, I would then create the outfit to his specifications. On the next visit he would try on the finished product and either approve it or make suggestions for changes."

"Would he then take the outfit home with him?" Romero said.

She shook her head. "No. When everything was said and done, my final task after I made any alterations would be to take the suit to the local dry cleaner, who would press the outfit and sew on the silver adornments. He would then encase it in plastic sheeting and return it to me for delivery. This is a standard practice, since most seamstresses don't have the large equipment required for professional ironing and pressing."

Romero scribbled a note on his tablet. "So then Sanchez would pick up the order from you, already sealed in plastic. On another topic, did he ever mention having difficulty at the border crossing?"

"Oh, no. The guards at the crossing in Juarez all knew him well. They would just let him through, especially when he gave them autographed photos and CDs of his music."

Romero circled his notation about the border. At that moment he didn't know why it mattered, but something was gnawing at his insides. He wondered about the possibility Sanchez was smuggling drugs in the sealed outfits whether he was aware of it or not. He looked over at Carmen.

"Carmen, I know this has been very difficult for you and I want to thank you again for meeting with me. You have my card, and if you think of anything at all that might be of help, please feel free to get in touch."

She smiled weakly. "Yes, I will do that. I pray you will be successful in bringing justice for this man."

She walked him to the door and thanked him. He couldn't help but notice that the sparkling eyes she had greeted him with when they met over an hour earlier had gone dim. *That sucked.*

Out in the sunlight, the cab driver was parked at the curb. Romero was pensive on the drive back to the hotel. The conversation with Carmen de la Torre had pulled his heartstrings.

The beautiful seamstress had nothing negative to say about Sanchez. But then again, she was in love with him. *Love does funny things to people. What was it they say about rose-colored glasses?*

Chapter Twenty-Seven

———◆———

LEANING BACK IN the seat of the small taxicab, Romero pored over a map of the surrounding area. Aguascalientes appeared to be over a hundred miles from Guadalajara, near Oaxaca. The driver informed him the distance was about 172 kilometers and should take about three hours by car. They would be there around seven thirty.

As the taxi headed out on the highway, Romero mentally rehashed his conversation with Carmen de la Torre. He regretted blindsiding her with the news of her lover's death. No way could he have known. He wondered how she would handle the additional predicament of having no closure, no funeral to attend, never seeing him again. What a terrible thing to happen to such a beautiful woman. He dialed Jemimah's number, wanting to fill her in on his meeting, but his phone dropped the call.

The scenery along the highway blurred into a long green ribbon as he closed his eyes. It was early evening when the driver's voice broke into his thoughts. The sun had not yet begun to set.

"*Señor*, we have reached our destination. This is

Aguascalientes." He pulled over to the side of the road. Traffic was heavy.

Romero rolled the window down and took in a deep breath. The strong odor from the Pemex gasoline refinery that had blasted through the atmosphere earlier in the afternoon had dissipated. The city of Aguascalientes had a population of over a million residents, but if he didn't know better, he'd think he was in the middle of northern New Mexico. This was an area famous for its hot springs, much like *Ojo Caliente*, about fifty miles from Santa Fe, where he and Jemimah had spent occasional afternoons soaking in the mineral-saturated waters. He wished he had time to do that here. He also wished he could hold Jemimah's hand right now. Recalling Carmen de la Torre's sadness weighed down his soul.

"This is beautiful country, is it not, *señor*?" said the driver.

"It sure is. Reminds me of Nuevo Mexico." Romero pointed to the north. "What is that green mountain?"

"That's the Cerro del Muerto. If you look at it from the right direction, it looks like a dead man spread out on the grass."

Romero put his sunglasses on top of his head and squinted. "It sure does." He snapped another photo. "Well at least I got to see one tourist attraction."

Reaching into his shirt pocket, he retrieved the card Carmen de la Torre had given him and leaned forward. Putting his hand on the front seat armrest, he pointed to the address on the card. "Do you know this area?"

"Oh, *sí*. My wife has relatives in Aguascalientes. The place you're looking for is somewhere in the countryside, up there on the hill, where all the *ricos* have their haciendas."

Romero looked at his watch. "Listen, *amigo*. It's been a long day and you've been a great help. Do you mind taking me to a hotel?"

"*Sí, señor*. There is a nice one nearby, and I can stay with my *compadres* for the night."

"Of course. It's too far to return to Guadalajara. I will be happy to reimburse you for your time. So can you pick me up at nine in the morning?"

"*Por su puesto, sí, señor.*"

"Just come to the front desk and have them call me. Now let's find this hotel you mentioned. I'm beat."

The driver popped the car into gear and sped toward the center of town. He dropped Romero off in front of a small hotel with white brick walls and a red-tile roof. The manicured grass was bordered by straight rows of flowering dogwoods, which reached into the arches of the portal. Romero waved the driver off and found his way into the lobby, where a jovial rotund man checked him in and handed him a key.

Settled in a room at the corner of a long porch, he was about to kick off his shoes and relax but decided he needed something to eat. He tossed his luggage and cellphone on the bed and walked down the hallway to the restaurant, where he sat at a small table and scanned the menu. He settled for a quick bowl of *caldito* and a plate of chicken tacos. After he finished the meal, he paid the tab and stuffed the receipt in his back pocket. *So much for fine dining in Mexico.*

The walk back to the room was refreshing. His senses were overwhelmed by the fragrance of an immense white flower hanging over the walls of the fountain. He stood next to a couple admiring the blossoms.

The woman smiled and looked over at him. "That's *La Reina de la Noche*," she said. "The Queen of the night. It only blooms between eight and midnight."

"Glad I caught it," he said. "It's uncanny how similar it is to the Datura flower that blooms in New Mexico. That one also blooms at night, but of course it's also poisonous." He waved as he unlocked the door to his room.

He was about to turn off the lights when he noticed his cellphone blinking and remembered he hadn't checked his messages. There was a text from Jemimah. *Don't be looking at any pretty señoritas. Miss you. J.* Romero chuckled and typed in a quick response, aware she was probably down for the count. *Fat chance. Nobody here as pretty as U.* Since his calls weren't going through, he hoped the text would.

***

EARLIER THAT EVENING, Jemimah sat cross-legged on the sofa, her dog resting its black and white head against her leg. She was dressed in checkered flannel PJs and fleece-lined slippers.

"No use for sexy underwear tonight, Molly. Might as well be comfortable." She laughed as the dog placed her front paws on a slipper, pulled it off Jemimah's foot with her teeth and ran off to the bedroom. Jemimah bolted from the couch and caught the dog just as she was about to begin gnawing on the slipper.

"Hey, bad girl! You already have a box full of your own toys. Go shred one of those." She plunked herself on the couch and tossed the dog a stuffed animal. She had rescued Molly from the Santa Fe Animal Shelter the day after closing on her ranch. One look at those soulful eyes, the white stripe running across her forehead, and the silky black coat, and Jemimah was hooked.

A half-eaten pizza sat in a box on the table. She opened a bottle of Coors Light and made a face as she took a swallow. She didn't enjoy drinking alone, although it wasn't a regular occurrence. Tonight was the two-year anniversary of meeting and then dating Detective Romero, and where was he? Off in Mexico chasing leads on the mariachi case. As much as she would have loved to accompany him, he hadn't asked. Jemimah assumed Sheriff Medrano had made it clear that the county wasn't paying for a romantic interlude for the detective and his girlfriend, even if she was a county employee and a vital part of the criminal investigation. She could almost hear Medrano's voice. *Fly in, do the interview and fly back. And don't you go playing tourist in between.* She chuckled at the thought.

She knew Rick took his job seriously, but hey, it would have been nice to walk along a beach in Mexico. *Just sayin'*. She took another swallow of beer and wondered how he had fared on the flight. Although they had not discussed his fear of flying, she was in the room when Clarissa made mention of it to McCabe. Her watch tolled the hour. It was nine o'clock in Santa Fe and she knew Mexico was an hour later. She reached for her iPad as it chimed in a message. It was from Rick. She smiled and typed out a text message, attaching a photo of herself and her dog. *Two girls missing you. How lucky can you get? XOXO.*

She waited a few minutes, expecting a quick response. When it didn't arrive, a nostalgic smile crossed her face. At some point in their relationship she needed to answer the question he'd posed on the final day of their vacation at the end of last summer. Her sleepy mind flashed back to their stay at the small motel near Yellowstone National Park. As they were packing the SUV, Romero had made a veiled reference to the location being a perfect spot for a honeymoon. She asked if that was a proposal, and he asked if that was a yes. Some six months later, neither of them had revisited that conversation. She wondered if they ever would. *Oh well.* She had a whole slew of reasons why she might say yes, and another batch of reasons why she might not.

She flicked the remote to the PBS station, where Pavarotti was singing his heart out. She thought it was an absolute shame that there were so many reality shows on cable TV lately. Between a chubby seven-year-old redneck beauty queen and her family, some rich and bitchy housewives from New York, Atlanta, and Beverly Hills, and another vacuous woman named Kim something or other who was totally famous for nothing other than participating in a racy sex tape that had gone viral on YouTube, it was a wonder there was anything at all for viewers who just wanted to see what was going on in the world that day or be entertained for half an hour. She wondered how long it took before viewers tired of one drama and moved on to the next peek into some other instant celebrity's life.

Jemimah had to admit, if only to herself, that she was guilty of watching at least one off-beat reality show that had piqued her interest—*Sister Wives*. She'd stumbled on the program one night when basketball season had taken over most channels. After that she caught herself looking forward to watching the weekly episode about four FLDS Mormon women who were married to the same man. As she viewed the first episode, she thought about her birth mother. The program echoed the exact situation she imagined her mother had been caught up in. Talk about déjà vu. She was thunderstruck as she listened to several of the teenaged daughters in the group discuss their feelings about the potential for being in polygamous relationships like their parents were. She almost cheered out loud when one of them confided, *No way. I'm going to marry ONE man, and he's only going to have one wife. Me.*

She gathered up the remaining pizza, wrapped it in foil and put it in the fridge, then turned to Molly and said, "Come on, girl. Time for us to call it a night." The Border Collie leaped off the couch, stretched out a classic downward dog yoga pose, and with her long black tail swaying rhythmically followed Jemimah into the bedroom. Before flicking off the lamp, she dialed Rick's number, hoping to catch him before he went to bed. After three rings, a recording clicked in. There was no service. As she sighed and plugged her phone into the charger, it dawned on her that her phone plan didn't include international service.

Chapter Twenty-Eight

————•————

ON THURSDAY MORNING, the sun was creeping through the windows of the hotel room as Romero stretched, yawned, and looked over at his phone to check the time. He noticed the missed call light flashing, tapped on the icon and retrieved a message from Carmen de la Torre.

"Detective Romero, I remembered something. Please call me when you have a moment," the message said.

He decided it was too early to call, that he would wait until breakfast. He got out of bed, fumbled through his suitcase and pulled out a clean pair of jeans and a long-sleeved shirt that he set on the bed. The shower was long and refreshing, and once dressed, he found his way to the hotel restaurant. The hostess directed him to a table, and as he waited for the waitress, he returned Carmen's call.

"Carmen, Detective Romero. I received your message. How are you doing?" he said. Her voice was small, lacking the confidence he'd noted when they first met.

She exhaled audibly. "I'm all right. Thank you."

"You said you remembered something that might be helpful?"

She told him that in one of their phone conversations about a month before, Sanchez had complained about the lining of one of his jackets having become unraveled. She repeated to Romero that when she was done with the sewing, the outfits went to the tailor, where they were professionally steamed and then returned to her covered in plastic, ready to go.

"I was so embarrassed. I would never let something go if it wasn't perfect," she said. "I called the tailor and he denied knowing anything about it. He claimed the suit was in perfect condition when it left his shop. In fact, he remembered making sure the back seams were always ironed flat on each outfit she delivered to him. I relayed this to Eduardo and he told me not to worry about it. He had an idea of what might have happened, but didn't expound on it."

Romero thanked her for taking the time to contact him. He hung up the phone with an uneasy feeling in his gut. Somewhere in all this confusion was the truth. All he had to do was figure it out. He suspected Sanchez might have been more involved in something shady than he originally thought.

He looked around the restaurant, surprised that it had filled up while he was on the phone. Skimming the menu, he decided on *huevos rancheros* and coffee, and afterwards was satisfied that it was as good as any he'd had back home. He paid the tab and left a tip, then stopped by the front desk of the hotel to check out. As he walked out into the bright sunlight, he fumbled for his sunglasses. The cabbie was waiting at the curb, as promised. Romero greeted him and slipped into the front back.

"*Hola, señor.* How was your evening?" he said, hoisting the suitcase into the trunk.

"I was asleep five minutes after my head hit the pillow. It must be the altitude," Romero said.

"We are at sea level here. What is it in your city?"

"Seven thousand feet in Santa Fe, Nuevo Mexico."

"*Aieee*, that's pretty high," he said. "It would take me a month to get used to that."

Romero nodded. "Yes, sometimes the *turistas* experience symptoms for a few days." He clipped on his seatbelt. "Okay, my friend, before we return to Guadalajara, we have one more stop to make. Remember when we were looking at the hill with all the beautiful houses yesterday? You said you were familiar with the area."

The cab driver removed his hat, placed it on the passenger seat, and turned to face Romero. "*Señor*, last night I mentioned to my brother-in-law who we were going to see and he was a little disturbed," he said.

Romero was puzzled. "For what reason? We're just looking for information."

The cabbie wiped sweat from his forehead with his sleeve. "He said this man was known to be one of the most powerful men in Mexico. His compound is heavily guarded and nobody is allowed to even come close. He said maybe you should inquire of the *policias* instead."

"Well, let's just take a ride up there anyway, since we're in the vicinity," Romero said.

The driver maneuvered the cab into the heavy morning traffic. As they reached the posh neighborhood, he moved up the hill at a pace more cautious than they had traveled the previous day. Ahead of them was a massive wrought-iron gate. Romero motioned for him to approach. Within seconds an armed soldier stepped forward and all but aimed his rifle at the driver's side window.

He spoke in rapid Spanish. "Are you blind, or what, *stupido?* Can't you read the signs? There is no trespassing beyond this point. What are you looking for?"

The driver hunched his shoulders and sank into the seat, breathing heavily.

In exaggerated English, Romero spoke from the back seat. "Sorry, sir. We are just out for a drive and got lost. *Turista* looking at pretty houses."

The soldier glared at him. "Well, turn around and go back

where you came from. No pretty houses here." He pointed to the driver. "*Andale, cabron,* turn around before I lose my patience and hide you where your family will never find you."

The driver did as instructed, beads of sweat dribbling down his forehead. By the time they reached the bottom of the hill, he was visibly shaken.

Romero patted him on the shoulder. "Your brother-in-law was right, my friend. That's no place for us to be snooping around. This falls under the category of none of our business. Let's get back to Guadalajara." When he was back in Santa Fe, he would follow up on whatever connection Sanchez had to this man. Who knows? It could very well have been something as harmless as a real estate transaction. After all, Carmen de la Torre said he was seeing the man about a ranch negotiation. Coincidence? He wondered.

Chapter Twenty-Nine

———◆———

HAVING ACCOMPLISHED WHAT he set out to do in Mexico, Romero prepared for the return flight. Before six o'clock on Friday morning, the driver dropped him off in front of the airport terminal. Romero thanked him for all the help he had been the past few days and palmed a generous tip in his hand. The man blushed and smiled. He opened the trunk and handed off the luggage. "*Adios, amigo.* If you ever return to Guadalajara, look me up."

Romero patted him on the back. "You were invaluable to me, *señor. Mil gracias.*" He checked his boarding pass and strolled through the lobby of the airport. He was to depart from Gate 45, which the giant monitor seemed to indicate was miles away. He looked at his watch and stepped on the escalator. It moved slowly in the direction of the gate but arrived in plenty of time. He took a seat near the boarding area, checking his jacket pocket again to make sure he had his tickets. He tried calling Jemimah, but his phone showed no bars. Instead, he sent her a quick text about his arrival time. He figured if she didn't receive the text in time to pick him up, he would take the shuttle back to Santa Fe.

He slumped back in the chair and closed his eyes. Deep in thought, he jumped as the PA system announced that his flight was boarding twenty minutes later. He reached for his carry-on, took a deep breath, and got in line behind a family of four. He was certain everyone around could hear his heart pound as he boarded the plane for the return flight. Once seated, he calmed down a bit. *Hey, I made it here without falling apart, and I'll make it back just the same.* He closed his eyes, recited a couple of Hail Marys, and dozed off. He awoke as the plane taxied down the runway of the Albuquerque airport. When the plane came to a stop near the end of the runway, Romero reminded himself to swing by St. Francis Cathedral and light a candle to St. Anthony, his mother's favorite saint, for bringing him home safely.

Jemimah was waiting under the canopy of the Southwest Airlines terminal. He hurried toward her, arms outstretched. Taking her in his arms, he held her close.

She laughed and quipped in her best Mae West voice. "Is that a revolver in your pocket or are you just happy to see me, Detective?"

He grinned. "Why, Doctor Hodge. How very cliché of you. I am absolutely happy to see you."

She reached up to his face and lifted his sunglasses. "I don't see any tan lines, so I assume you weren't lying on the beach somewhere without me."

"Didn't dare. I knew Medrano would hang me from the rafters." He rolled out his luggage. "Come on, let's get out of here. I've had enough airports to last me a while."

As Jemimah guided the vehicle through the access ramp onto Interstate 25, Romero settled back into the passenger seat. "I'm dying to know, Rick. How did things go? Were you able to find this woman? What was she like? Did you get any valuable information from her?"

He chuckled. "Hey, one question at a time, sweetie. I haven't had time to assemble my notes, but I did have a meeting with

Carmen de la Torre. Man, I felt awful about dropping the news of Sanchez's death in her lap. I'm no doctor, but I would say she went into shock."

He told her about his trip into the hills and the defective costumes. "I think Sanchez was involved with the Mexican drug cartels somehow," he said, "maybe doing some smuggling in the seams of his jacket. If that's what got him killed, it's a dead end for now. He'd have to have been working with someone here, and who knows when it all started? For now, we should continue to look into his connection to Mexico and also figure out the identity of the woman he was having problems with."

"So you were right in thinking they were more than casual acquaintances?" Jemimah said.

"Definitely. She admitted as much. It really tore me up to see her so broken up." He turned to look out the side window.

Jemimah smiled softly. Rick's compassionate side was one of the reasons she cared so deeply about him. She changed the subject and talked about her recent interviews, particularly the one with the fellow from El Rito who occasionally played guitar with the Sanchez group. She maneuvered through traffic, positioning herself in the right-hand lane to take the Waldo exit. The back road, a shortcut to Cerrillos, was as rutted as usual. They traveled at a much slower pace for the next fifteen miles.

Arriving in Cerrillos, she drove down the main street and came to a stop in front of his office.

"I'll just let you off here, Rick. I have a meeting at one fifteen and just enough time to get there," she said. "Do you want to get together tonight?"

"I could use a home-cooked meal," he said. "I did a lot of eating on the fly. But can we leave it open? I don't know what's waiting for me at my desk. And I'm bone tired." He gave her a quick peck on the cheek, grabbed his things from the backseat and waved her off. "See you later, sweet cheeks."

"Ya betcha! Maybe tonight, maybe tomorrow. We'll talk later." She waved as she drove off.

He dragged himself through the substation door carrying his gear. He unzipped the backpack and pulled out his briefcase as Clarissa emerged from the kitchen, coffee cup in hand.

"You're early, boss. Did your plane land in our driveway?"

"My lead-footed girlfriend picked me up. Coffee smells good. I could sure use a cup." He looked at the stack of files on her desk. "Did you bring over the entire filing system from the main office, or what?" he said.

Clarissa handed him a cup. "Believe it or not, these are all the cold cases Sheriff Medrano wants solved, *now*."

Romero groaned. "Get in touch with McCabe and have him stop by next time he's in the area. He's good at digging through evidence files. At least it will be a start. He can figure out which cases have potential and which are hopeless."

"Roger Dodger, boss." She handed him a stack of phone messages. "This ought to keep you occupied for at least an hour."

As Romero thumbed through the messages, Clarissa returned to her desk, and for the next ten minutes, thoughtfully sipped on the cream-diluted coffee. She was feeling uncertain. *Might as well go in and tell him. He's not going to be thrilled to hear this.* She finished off her coffee and then walked down the hallway and tapped on Romero's door. "You got a minute?"

He looked up. "What is it, Clarissa? I was about to make a few calls. Looks like everybody and their mother called while I was out. Christ, you'd think I was gone for a month."

She hesitated and then placed three additional pink message sheets in front of him. "Two of these were on the machine and the last call came in this morning," she said.

Romero stared blankly at the slips of paper on the desk. The name *Julie* stared back at him. *Three times.* The ex-wife he hadn't heard from for as long as he could remember had all of a sudden popped back into his life. His mind raced back through the years. He'd never thought he would get over her leaving him. Every inch of his heart had been trampled. After that, he assuaged his misery by swimming in a pool of beer and bourbon. He landed in rehab, delivered there by Sheriff Medrano, who unceremoniously informed him: *Don't even think you're getting out of here in ten days. No rehab. No job.*

Clarissa stood near his desk for a moment, started to leave and then turned around. "Look, boss, it's none of my business, but you need to address this now. Otherwise it might all blow up in your face."

Romero scowled. "Hey, Clarissa, give me a minute. You just dropped this in my lap. I'm still jet-lagging and I haven't even finished my first cup of coffee. What did she say?"

"Not much other than she wanted to talk to you and did I know where you could be reached. I didn't give her anything to go on, just that you were out of town."

He shoved the messages into the drawer. "Well, I'm not going to drop everything just to call her."

Clarissa pulled up a chair. "Julie also left a couple of messages with the sheriff's secretary and the receptionist. You need to call her, whether you feel like talking to her or not. Lord knows I'm still not crazy about conversations with my ex-husband after what he did to me. One thing for sure, if you ignore the calls, the next thing you know, Jemimah will hear about it through the *mitote* grapevine and she'll get all upset and you won't be able to explain it away."

"Yes, mother." Romero smiled weakly. "I'll take care of it."

"You make sure you do."

His brow furrowed. "Clarissa, I said I'd talk to her. I didn't ask for Julie to pop back into my life. I can't guess what she wants. I doubt she's looking to hook up again. I've moved on. Now get your butt back to work."

Always needing to have the last word, Clarissa continued, "I'm not going to let you live it down if you lose Dr. Hodge over this. Mark my words, Rick, women can be pretty unpredictable if they don't get what they want, and Julie is no exception."

He smirked. "Do I hear your shrink talking, Clarissa?"

"Hey, deal with it. You're the one who suggested I see one. Gotta learn something from these monthly visits."

Romero stared out the window at a squirrel busy stashing provisions in a cottonwood tree as he unconsciously lit a cigarette in the no-smoking office. His mind drifted as he remembered the day Julie announced at breakfast that she wanted a divorce. He hadn't even finished the first cup of morning brew, which usually served to rev up his system. The last time he saw her was months after their divorce, following his stint at rehab for a long alcoholic binge. She had stopped by to tell him she was moving to California. He shook his head and threw himself into catching up on his work load; he would wait until mid-afternoon to place the call.

Hours later, he looked at the message again. She was staying at her mother's. He dialed the number, almost by memory, pausing between each digit. She answered on the first ring.

"Julie? Rick. I understand you called my office. What do you want?"

"My goodness," she said. "*Hello Julie how are you* would be nice."

"Quite honestly, I don't think I have much to say to you," he countered.

"C'mon, Rick. It's been a long time. Can we at least meet for coffee somewhere?"

He hesitated, crumbling the message slips in his free hand and tossing them in the basket. "Yeah, I guess," he relented. He would much rather have gone home to rest up from the trip.

She laughed. "Don't sound so enthusiastic. How about we meet over at Dulce? If it's too much trouble for you to come into town, I can drive out to where you are. I understand you're heading up the new satellite offices. Surely there's a coffee shop in Cerrillos."

He gathered she had indeed been talking to someone else besides Clarissa. The lilt in her voice reverberated in his ears. He thought he had forgotten how she sounded. He found himself grinning. "Unfortunately Cerrillos is still not a bustling metropolis. That's all right. I have to go into town at some point to drop a file off at the DA's office on my way home. How does four thirty sound?"

"I look forward to it," she cooed.

As he placed the phone in its cradle, he remembered how her voice could melt butter. *I hope I don't live to regret this.*

Clarissa winked at him as he left the office. "Attaboy, Rick. Make sure you kick her to the curb."

Chapter Thirty

———•———

For a Friday, afternoon traffic moved at a steady pace and Romero cut across to Santa Fe in less than twenty minutes. As he drove, he once again found himself feeling anxious, and cranked the volume on the '50s radio station. He wondered what the hell was causing these surges of anxiety. Maybe he was still tired from the whirlwind trip to Mexico. He hadn't even had time to go home, empty his suitcase, and chill for a while. He would still love to go to Jemimah's for dinner. She didn't really expect him, but he didn't want the information from the trip to grow cold before he had a chance to assemble his notes. He parked the cruiser in front of the barber shop at the small strip mall in the South Capitol area of Santa Fe and walked a short distance to Dulce, the latest in a slew of trendy coffee shops. The smell of baked goods permeated the air. The place had been a pet store in its previous life—quite a different smell. He vowed to just have a quick cup of coffee with Julie and then head home.

He pushed against the glass door. A sugar rush flooded his nasal passages as he walked past a counter laden with freshly baked pastries. It was a small establishment but apparently popular, as almost every table was occupied. The walls were decorated with colorful paintings of multi-layered cakes and frosted cupcakes. He couldn't miss Julie. She was waving her arm and then stood as he walked toward her table. She reached out to embrace him. He noticed the recently showered scent he used to love about her. It appeared she hadn't gained an ounce of weight over the years.

"You look great, Rick. We have so much to catch up on," she tittered. "Life must be treating you well."

They walked to the counter, where he ordered black coffee and Julie ordered a large vanilla latte with extra whipped cream. He took a seat across from her at a corner table. They sat in silence as he sugared his coffee and gave it a stir. She was even more beautiful than he remembered. She smiled at him. Her lips were full and moist, her eyes an intense green darker than jade. Her hair was a deep piñon brown, laced with golden highlights. Her skin was smooth and flawless. She looked younger than her age. But why had she returned to Santa Fe? They had lived together the entire five years of their marriage. She hated that he was a cop. Her figure was perfect.

In a whirl, his mind shifted from one thought to another. He recalled he had been drunk most of the time following their breakup and still hadn't forgotten the day she left.

There was a faraway look in her eyes … or was he just imagining things? She was smartly dressed in tailored pants and a loose silk jacket over a contrasting shell. Conservative, yet she managed to pull off a certain effortless sexiness.

She broke the silence. "When I came back to Santa Fe a week ago, I wasn't surprised to hear you were still on the force and that you had moved up the ladder."

He looked up at her. "Probably be a lifer."

"You always did like being a cop."

He methodically stirred his coffee. "And you always hated it."

"Yes, I have to admit I did. I could never see much of a future in it. You were gone most nights." She reached over and put her hand on his. "You're going to stir a hole at the bottom of that cup."

Romero felt his temperature rising. "I guess you wanted to meet to discuss which one of us was to blame for the breakup of our marriage?"

Her lips curled into a crooked smile. "Sorry. Old habits die hard. I guess I'm still pretty good at pushing buttons."

"I'll say," he said dryly. "So why *are* you here, Julie? Granted, I have no say about your being in Santa Fe, but why the urgent need for us to meet?"

She tilted her head and looked straight at him. "I'm going to be honest, Rick. After all these years and a number of relationships that went nowhere, I slowly began to realize in the back of my head that I might have made a mistake in leaving you ... that there might still be hope for us."

He blinked but said nothing. His insides churned. She talked nonstop for the next half hour, giving him a wordy capsule of her life as it existed. His head started to spin. Finally, he raised his hand and motioned for her to stop.

"Come on, Julie, you can't be serious. All of a sudden out of the blue you want to come back into my life and we take up where we left off .... Is that what you're saying?"

"It's not as crazy as it sounds, Rick. Lots of couples get back together after being apart," she said, "and their relationships become stronger than ever."

He frowned. "We aren't *lots* of couples. We're *one* couple who probably should have never been together to begin with."

Her gaze searched his face. "Are you saying you regret ever being married to me?"

He made a gesture of impatience. "No. I'm saying that you left the marriage because it wasn't working for you, and so much time has elapsed that I've moved on. I'm still a cop, and that's not going to change."

"All I ask is for you to think about it, Rick. You don't have to answer right this minute."

The sun blazed through the twelve-foot windows at the front of the shop as it made a slow descent into sunset. He glanced at his watch. He hadn't made definite plans to meet with Jemimah, but he'd said that he would at least check in. He dialed her cell. There was no answer; then the mechanical voice said her message box was full. He'd try again later.

"Can we continue this conversation over dinner, Rick? I'm getting kind of hungry and eating a cupcake just won't do it for me."

"Don't think so. I have other plans."

"From the look on your face when you hung up the phone, it looks as though those plans might have changed."

"Maybe, I'm not sure."

"It's just dinner. Surely it won't upset your personal applecart to have an innocent meal with your ex-wife. Besides, there's something else I want to tell you."

"What?" he said sharply.

Her brow furrowed. "I need time. It's not something I can say in a hurry."

He didn't know what was pulling him in her direction. *Maybe this will close that book once and for all. But then again* …. "All right, Julie," he said. "But no dinner. Just a quick drink, maybe an appetizer. Where do you want to meet?"

"How about that new restaurant on Galisteo Street? I'll call for reservations and meet you there at six thirty."

Romero drove home in silence. How idiotic it must be, he thought, to want to repeat history knowing the result will always be the same. He had heard somewhere that was the definition of insanity. After the divorce, loneliness overwhelmed him and the prospect of getting back together with Julie would have put him over the moon. He would have done whatever it took to get her back in his life. Now he wasn't so sure. He was certain it would be a disaster waiting to happen. He looked down at the speedometer and pulled his foot off the pedal. Why was he in such a hurry? Was he about to jump in head first and get his ass kicked? *Exactly what was it Julie was after?* He turned into his driveway and paused before reaching for the door handle. *Geez, I should have my head examined.*

Jemimah still wasn't answering her phone. He left a quick text message: *Can't come over tonight. See you tomorrow?*

Chapter Thirty-One

———————•———————

IN THE PARKING lot of Restaurant Martín, a trendy establishment a few blocks south of the plaza, Romero clicked the keypad to alarm his vehicle. Julie was waiting in the entryway. She reached for his hand. He hesitated, as if to pull away, and then clasped his hand over hers. A surge of emotion trickled down from his brain. He remembered how much he had loved her, where they met, and their wedding day, when he had reached for her hand in much the same way.

They entered the restaurant in awkward silence. The maître d' bowed as if they were royalty, introduced himself and directed them to an intimate dining cell toward the back. The room had a low ceiling and was dimly lit. Wall niches were decorated with colorful Madonnas carved by a local artist. A large contemporary Native American painting hung above the warm and inviting kiva fireplace.

"This is nice," she said. "I remember this place when we walked to Santa Fe High. It was the Frank Ortiz residence. Wasn't he an ambassador to the UN or something?"

"Something like that. And then about ten years ago it was some kind of hippie hangout. Broken cups and plates attached all over the walls, inside and out. Some folks believed the place was haunted, but Chef Martín has proved them all wrong." Romero fiddled with his napkin and serving utensils.

The waitperson brought them each a glass of wine and took their order—Romero ordered some lamb skewers and Julie a main course. As they waited for the server to bring their food, Romero willed himself to relax. Pangs of remorse pinged off his brain. *What was he doing?* Julie leaned toward him and touched his face. "You seem a little tense, Rick."

"Is it that obvious?" he said.

She slid her hand over his wrist. "Take a chill pill. We're just sharing a little supper, not engaging in a romp in the backseat of your cruiser."

He took a deep breath and sipped his wine. He didn't drink much these days, and certainly wouldn't finish off more than just a glass of wine in her presence. "What did you want to tell me?" he said.

She leaned her head toward his and answered his question with a question. "Can I ask you something?" she said.

"Sure, as long as I have a choice about answering."

"I'm curious why it's so difficult for you to even consider us getting back together."

He took a sip from his glass and paused. "Well, let me ask something. Why me? Why not one of the guys you dated after our divorce? Why not someone in California? Lots of *beaners* there, if that's what you're looking for."

"You were always special to me, Rick. It just took me a while to realize you were one of a kind. I know it's a bit of a stretch …."

He flinched. "Bit of a stretch? It's more than that. More like crazy."

Julie pouted and put on her best *I'm so hurt* face. "Look, Rick. It's not as crazy as I sound. We were young. We were in love. Somehow things got screwed up. But we're both older now and smarter. The same things don't matter."

He looked her straight in the eyes. "The more we talk about

it, the more I realize I shouldn't even be here. We were done then and we're still done. I'm not even sure we could be friends."

She jerked her head. "I can't believe you're saying that. We had some great times together. Your work just got in the way."

"And you were the longsuffering wife who wanted her husband home twenty-four/seven, and when you couldn't have that, you walked away."

"Maybe this will change your mind." She leaned over and kissed him passionately.

He gently pushed her away. "Stop, Julie. This conversation is absurd. You need to get it through that stubborn head of yours. I am not interested in re-establishing a relationship with you. I assumed we were just here to have a quiet dinner and catch up on what's transpired in our respective lives. I don't think I agreed to an interrogation or a seduction. What was it you wanted to tell me, anyway?"

"Nothing," she said, "I just wanted to be with you." She emptied her glass in one swallow. "What I don't understand is why you won't just give us a chance, that's all."

Romero shook his head in disgust. He reached into the bread basket, buttered a chunk of piñon cornbread and took a bite. "Because there is no *us*. I'm not interested in revisiting the past, particularly since it took such a long time to get over you. That's a can of worms best left closed."

She smoothed a lock of hair over her ear. "We had a lot going for us then. I made a big mistake. I've never stopped caring about you and I'm sure you still have feelings for me if you would just give yourself a chance to explore them."

He sighed. "How many ways can I say this, Julie? I'm in love with someone else and I'm not about to give up that relationship just to conduct an experiment with you which is destined to fail from the get-go."

Her voice dipped into a sarcastic tone. "Ah, yes. The *gringa* doctor? I heard she's just stringing you along. How long have you known each other ... a couple of years? From what I've heard, it doesn't look like you're even considering wedding bells in the future."

Romero finished off his glass of wine, glad he couldn't help himself to the bottle. "Leave her out of this, Julie. I don't know or care where you're getting your information, but there's one thing you can take to the bank: I am not interested in taking up where you and I left off. End of story."

She persisted, ignoring his hesitation. "It wouldn't kill you to give it a try. I know there's still something there. I can feel it."

"Maybe for you there is—and if so, I'm sorry—but I'd be a damned fool to give it a trial run just to determine if I still had feelings. So, no, Julie. Now can we talk about something else and enjoy our food?"

The waiter set the plates before them. Romero picked up the fork and skewered a piece of lamb.

Julie smiled, her lips taut. "I get it, Rick. Just like in high school. All the jocks wanted the blond cheerleader, and you're no different. You're not ever going to get this chance again. Mark my words: you'll be sorry. You are going to regret refusing my offer."

He chided softly, "We're not in high school anymore, Julie. Most of us are full-fledged adults. I'm beginning to think you never made it there. Chrissake, you suddenly show up in town, chase me down like a hound, propose that we get back together, and expect us to ride off into the sunset like nothing ever happened? That's not very realistic, you think? Take a step back and look at what you're doing. Whatever I felt for you then no longer exists and you're not going to be able to wish it back."

She yanked the napkin off her lap, stood up, and tossed it on the table. She reached for the water glass and flung it at him, nearly hitting his head. "*You* take a step back and kiss my ass, Rick." Her hair flipped to the left as she turned and walked out of the room.

He looked around as he wiped the water from his face and

the front of his shirt, certain everyone at the adjoining tables had witnessed her meltdown. "Ouch, that was harsh," he said.

He motioned to the waiter for the check. He paid the tab and stepped out into the parking lot. The night was cold and rainy with a biting breeze. He rubbed his hands together and walked to his car, started the engine and clicked on the heater to ward off the chill. For a moment, the thought of Julie stomping off made him chuckle, but then he shivered. *What the hell was that all about?* He remembered his jacket was still draped over the chair in the restaurant. More than ever he realized he should have paid attention to the voice in his head that told him he shouldn't meet up with her. Now he wasn't sure what he was going to tell Jemimah. He debated about driving to her house, knowing it was already past eight. He dialed her number several times in succession. She still wasn't answering. He took a deep breath. They were both off for the weekend. He would drive over to her place early in the morning and face the consequences of his now obvious poor judgment.

Man, whoever said you can't go home again sure as hell knew what they were talking about.

Chapter Thirty-Two

━━━━◆━━━━

EARLY SATURDAY MORNING, Romero awoke to the sound of his doorbell ringing. Sheriff Medrano was at the door.

"Hey, Rick. Get your stuff together. We need to take a trip to Flagstaff to pick up a couple of suspects who are being extradited here to stand trial."

Romero rubbed his eyes. "Aw, shit. It's my weekend off, Bobby. Why can't Martinez or Chacon make the trip?"

"Suck it up, Rick. They're working a case out in Tesuque. You can make up for it next weekend. If we leave now, we can be back by Sunday night."

Romero pushed open the screen door and motioned him in. "Give me a couple of minutes to get dressed," he grumbled.

"Got any coffee?" the sheriff said.

"Should be brewing. Help yourself." He grabbed his clothes from the dresser and went into the bathroom for a quick shower. When he was dressed, he looked at the clock. It was too early to call Jemimah. He texted, *Had to go 2 Flagstaff with Bobby on a case. Hope 2 see U Sunday.*

***

ON MONDAY MORNING shortly before eight, Jemimah drove into the county sheriff compound on Highway 14. She circled around a couple of times before finding a parking space. Her intent was to drop off a file with Sheriff Medrano's secretary and then meander downstairs for a quick cup of coffee. She chastised herself for being happy Sheriff Medrano wasn't in his office. She was already in a foul mood and didn't want to listen to any of his rants at this moment. For whatever reason, Rick hadn't bothered to check in Friday night, even though he'd texted that he would. She reasoned that maybe he had been too tired from the Mexico trip and decided to call it an early night. And then that morning he'd texted that he had to go to Flagstaff, and Clarissa had explained that he had gone to Arizona with the sheriff on Saturday and had gotten in pretty late. A late-night movie starring Brad Pitt had grabbed her attention the previous night and it was long after midnight by the time she packed it in.

A good jolt of caffeine would rev her engine up. For more than a year, her office had been located upstairs in the compound, but even though the county provided that office space, Jemimah found that the downtown location was far more suited to her needs. She didn't have to deal with the constant comings and goings of the sheriff's office, which included not only the detectives, but booking and lockup as well.

She scribbled a note for the secretary, attached it to the file and laid it on her desk. She was thinking about working at home the rest of the day to catch up on processing recent interviews.

Downstairs, she took her place in line at the cafeteria, poured a large cup of coffee into a Styrofoam cup, and browsed the baked goods while she waited to pay the cashier. Two women standing ahead of her were deeply engaged in conversation. It was impossible not to hear their exchange, as they carried on as though they were the only ones in the room. At first she couldn't believe what she heard.

"I hear Detective Romero is back with his ex-wife."

"You're kidding me."

"No, seriously. Someone saw them having drinks and holding hands at that fancy restaurant on Galisteo Street, and earlier they were seen cozying up at the coffee house on Cordova Road."

"*Ah-lah.* Doesn't he have a girlfriend?"

"I heard he was dating some Blondie. I highly doubt if she knows. Women are so tunnel-visioned when it comes to love."

"Yeah. Poor thing. Men are scum."

They continued to chat as the line crawled forward. Jemimah lowered her head, paid for her coffee and rushed out of the building to the parking lot. She dialed Katie's number.

"I'm not coming in today, Katie. Reschedule any appointments I might have this afternoon," she said.

"Are you feeling okay, Doc? You sound congested," Katie said.

"It's nothing, Katie. I just heard something that upset me," Jemimah said.

Katie frowned. She knew it had to do with Rick and his ex-wife. Clarissa had told her she was in town and suspected she was going to cause trouble. "Can I help?" she said.

"No, I'll be fine. I had planned on spending the morning catching up on my work load, so I need to get on it." She hung up before Katie could say another word.

Seated in her car, she felt tears sting her eyes as she started up the engine. She could barely contain herself as she drove through morning traffic on Highway 14. As she passed the substation, she noticed Rick's vehicle parked in the driveway. She was too upset to stop and ask him about the gossip she had heard. She continued on to her ranch house, not slowing down until she reached the driveway. Once in the house, she sat on the couch and stared out the living room window, oblivious to any activity in her yard. At that moment she wouldn't have noticed a stray grizzly bear.

***

DETECTIVE ROMERO SAT in a corner of the substation office, his chair facing the mountains. A red-haired woodpecker tapped diligently on the windowsill. He dialed Jemimah's office, surprised that her assistant picked up.

"May I help you?" Katie said.

"Hello, Katie. Rick Romero here. Is Dr. Hodge in her office?" he said. "Her cellphone's been going straight to message."

"I'm sorry, Detective. She isn't. I don't believe she's coming in today," she said.

He detected an iciness in her voice. "Is everything all right, Katie? She's not sick or anything, is she?"

Katie hesitated and her voice softened. "Well, it's not my place to tell you, but if you must know. I understand she heard a rumor that you were out partying with your ex-wife," she said. "I'm not here to judge, but if it's true, I imagine you're in a crapload of trouble. I haven't heard anything other than she wasn't coming in today."

He exhaled a long breath. "Oh, Christ. Thanks Katie."

He stared out to the long expanse of craggy hills. He was worried and his mind told him he had good reason to be. If it wasn't for back-to-back meetings, he'd leave the office right then and park himself on her doorstep.

He heard tapping at the door to his office. He didn't budge.

"Knock, knock. Anybody home?" McCabe said.

Romero slowly spun the chair around. "Hey, Tim. Come on in. Have a seat."

McCabe rolled a chair forward and sat down. "You were looking a bit preoccupied there, Rick. Hated to interrupt you. Everything okay?"

He turned to look away. "Don't I wish. Truth is, I might have just screwed things up royally."

Tim clucked. "This have something to do with Jemimah?"

Romero laid his hands on the desk, palms up. "What else do I tend to screw up on every so often?"

McCabe pulled his chair closer. "I've got time if you feel like unloading. I might not have a lot of suggestions, but I can sure listen."

Romero told him the whole story about spending time with Julie, being dragged off to Arizona with the sheriff, and then talking to Jemimah's assistant that morning only to discover she'd drawn all the wrong conclusions. "We were doing pretty well, and then I had to go see Julie. I should have just said no, but something inside me wanted to hear what she had to say. Time got the better of me and when we were done, it was too late to undo anything."

McCabe whistled. "I guess you really put your foot into it this time."

Romero nodded. "You could say that. I'm just not sure how to get my foot out without breaking it."

"Have you two talked yet?"

"She won't answer my calls."

"Damn, Rick. I can't say I blame her. That's quite a load you dumped on her. You must have really pissed her off this time."

Romero leaned back in his chair. "That's about the size of it. Before I had a chance to explain, she had already heard an exaggerated version from the grapevine. She's got a seminar tomorrow in Albuquerque, so I've been trying to reach her before she leaves. To top it off, I'm booked solid with meetings all day and there's no way I can get out of them. Medrano would have my ass."

McCabe stood and faced him. "I'm sure you know this, *amigo*, but you need to get over there and fix this. I've told you before: Jemimah is a keeper. My wife and I love her like a daughter and there danged well better be some wedding bells somewhere in your future. Laura's not going to have it any other way. It wouldn't surprise me if she's already booked the church."

Romero's shoulders heaved. "You're right, Tim. I just have to figure out how to go about it. Probably have to wait until she's back from her seminar. That will give me another day to figure out my approach, although the tension might just kill me in the meantime."

McCabe patted him on the shoulder. "You made a mistake, Rick. We all do that at some point in our lives."

"I don't think Jemimah is going to forgive me, Tim. No amount of damage control is going to fix this."

McCabe jangled his car keys. "You won't know until you face it head on. I'd suggest you do it sooner rather than later. You give that filly too much time to think, and she's likely to get a burr in her tail and ride off."

Clarissa popped her head in the door. "Sorry to interrupt, boss, but if you don't leave soon, you're going to be late for the county commission meeting."

He walked out into the parking lot with McCabe. "Damn, knowing how long these meetings usually run, I'll be lucky to be out of there by midnight."

***

BETWEEN SESSIONS WITH the county commission, Romero tried without success to reach Jemimah. Each time, his calls went unanswered. He also touched base with Detectives Chacon and Martinez to see if anything had transpired on the Sanchez case. As he hung up, Sheriff Medrano came out into the hallway and pulled him back into the meeting room. Romero nodded and stuffed his silent phone in his pocket.

He headed home at nine thirty that night, physically and emotionally exhausted. All he wanted to do was flop down on his bed and pass out. Like it or not, everything would still be waiting for him in the morning.

Chapter Thirty-Three

———•———

EARLY WEDNESDAY MORNING, Romero waited impatiently for the coffee maker to pop its ready light. He needed a good dose of caffeine to jar his senses enough so he could face the day. He hadn't slept a wink, anticipating Jemimah's perceived reaction to his explanation and apology, which he intended to make the first chance he got. He was terrified that his stupidity might be impossible to make up for.

Finally it was ready. He poured himself a cup, sat at the table in his roomy kitchen, and tried not to think. As the sanitation trucks out on the street clanged and banged their way through the neighborhood, he decided it was time to get moving. The steaming hot water in the shower served to soothe his nerves. He was scheduled to testify in court later that morning, and he pulled a dark suit, white shirt, and tie from his closet. The district courthouse was just ten minutes away from his house, so he returned to the kitchen and tidied up before he left.

***

JEMIMAH ZIPPED INTO her space at the municipal parking garage a block from her office, climbed the steps, and tore down the hall, almost colliding with the janitor mopping the floors. As she stormed through the door, her assistant Katie looked up.

"Geez, Doc. You look awful. I'm guessing nothing has changed since Monday?"

"No, Katie. It hasn't. I've been an absolute wreck. I can barely focus."

Katie looked surprised. "Anything interesting happen at the state police seminar yesterday?"

"Don't change the subject, Katie. Did you not hear what I said? Why do I get the feeling you know something about this? You avoided me last Friday afternoon, and now I think I know why."

Standing at the counter, Katie poured herself another cup of coffee and eased herself into the chair next to Jemimah's desk. "What brought all this up? I thought you guys were doing fine," she said.

"I'm not really in a conversational mood, Katie. Can we save it for another time?" She reached for a stack of files to put in her briefcase. "Truth be known, I'm a little bugged at you right now."

"Hey, wait a minute. We need to clear this up," Katie said. "Sounds like things have gotten out of hand."

Jemimah pursed her lips and sighed. She pulled the desk drawer open and pretended to rearrange the contents. "All I need to know is why you kept this from me. I would have expected more from you."

Katie's brow furrowed. "I didn't keep it from you. I just didn't tell you. I didn't see where it would do any good."

"Same difference."

"Look, Doc. I feel pretty awful about this. I didn't want to hurt your feelings. I knew you and Detective Romero were still seeing each other," she said. "I hadn't heard that you were having problems."

"That's what's so annoying. We aren't having any problems."

Jemimah paused. "At least we weren't. It's not as though we're engaged or anything. We're not dating other people. Damn, this is so junior high. I've been a complete wreck not knowing where our relationship stands. I really care for the guy."

Katie interrupted her. "So let me finish. On Friday afternoon when I took a break, I saw Rick sitting across from his ex-wife at the coffee shop. I couldn't wait to tell you. But then I remembered this look you get on your face any time you mention his name, and I realized you two were deeply involved, whether you admit it or not. I didn't want to burst that bubble. So when I came back to work, I kept it to myself. I didn't want to make it something bigger than it was."

Jemimah tossed her head. "Well you *didn't* tell me. I'm sure even Clarissa knew about it, but I had to hear it from the gossip mill, and it hurt me to find out you already knew. This goes beyond employer/employee relationships. I thought we were closer than that."

Katie lowered her voice. "We are. It was stupid of me to think you wouldn't hear it from someone else."

"I did, and that's what hurt. It sideswiped me and threw me off balance. I didn't know what to believe. Coffee was one thing and dinner on top of that, according to the gossip mill, was a bit much."

"Doc, I am so, so sorry. It was very inconsiderate of me. What else can I say? Have you asked Detective Romero for his side of the story?"

"No. I just haven't been answering his calls."

Katie pushed her chair forward. "I wish I could shake some sense into you, boss. Just because he shared a meal with his ex-wife doesn't mean he's still carrying a torch for her. I know I was going to make a big deal about it, but that was before I knew how you felt about him. And honestly, I would have told you that all I saw them doing was talking. It wasn't as though they were holding hands or anything."

Jemimah clapped her hands to her cheeks. "I feel like a jealous schoolgirl."

"There's something about being in love and insecure that makes most women react that way. I'm sure if that happened to me, I would have pulled out a sledgehammer and gone out looking for a car to put a few dents in."

Jemimah forced a smile. "And I'd be putting up bail to get you out of jail. Nothing too discreet about that."

She knew Katie was more than an assistant and was grateful their misunderstanding had been ironed out. No use blaming her for Rick's inability to face the music. She had a few bones to pick with him, too, and the sooner she picked that carcass clean, the better.

***

IT WAS LATE afternoon and most of the offices in the complex were empty. Jemimah glowered at her ringing cellphone. Checking the caller ID, she saw it was Rick calling her again. Ordinarily it warmed her heart to hear his voice. She would jump at the chance to spend a few minutes on the phone with him. Not this time. She was still angry about everything that happened the past few days. The events had waylaid her focus on pressing cases. She knew it was unprofessional to put her romantic life before her job; never before had she allowed herself to be that vulnerable. It took all she had to get her work done.

The phone went silent. She stepped out of her office and walked down the hall to the soft drink dispenser, put in a few quarters and slid out a can of soda. She was surprised to see Romero coming toward her.

"Jemimah," he said. "I just called your cell."

"Did you?" she said. "I must not have heard it. What can I do for you, Rick?"

He felt an icy chill. "Can we talk?"

She popped the top on the can and said nothing. She well

knew if she gave her emotions full rein, she would probably walk away, leaving him standing there. But at the very least, she owed him the opportunity to explain himself. She swiveled about, intent on returning to her office. He tugged lightly at her sleeve and forced a laugh.

"Hey, what's the hurry? You mad at me for something?"

She pulled away and closed the door behind them. "That's an understatement if I ever heard one."

Romero loosened his tie. "Hey, I've called you a dozen times since Friday and I texted you the whole time I was in Arizona with Sheriff Medrano. We haven't spoken since I returned from Mexico ... not because I haven't called, but because you haven't bothered to answer any of my calls."

She clenched her fists. "I was hurt, Rick. Can you understand that? I was too angry and confused to talk to you. I didn't know if you were calling just to tell me you blew me off to hook up with your ex-wife, or what."

The color drained from his face. "I intended to tell you, but by the time I did, you weren't picking up on your calls. It's no excuse, but I was exhausted from that trip and hadn't had a thing to eat, so we ended up going to dinner. I just had a glass of wine and an appetizer. You and I hadn't made definite plans. I figured I would eat something light and then head over to your place. Nothing happened."

Jemimah set the soda can on her desk and walked to the window. "This is not the time, Rick. My workload is pretty backed up. I don't want to talk about it."

He stood next to her. "Well, I do. We need to talk this out before things get any crazier. Come on, sit." He led her to the couch and sat next to her. He reached out and took her hand. "Jem, I don't know what you're thinking, but I won't blame you if you want to call it quits."

They shared an awkward silence. "I'm not sure I understand it myself, Rick," she said. "We went from dinner at my house two weeks ago to no contact at all. Then I get blindsided by gossip at the main office. I'm sure by the time I heard it that wasn't the first time it had been around the pike."

He looked into her eyes. "Look, Jem, I don't know who started all the gossip, but there was nothing to it. My ex-wife returned to Santa Fe with some absurd idea that we could just take up where we left off after our divorce became final years ago."

Jemimah returned his glance. "I have to ask, Rick. Did you consider it?"

He looked away for an instant and took a long breath. "Ten years ago, I would have given my right arm to reconcile. I was devastated when she left."

"And now?"

He squeezed her hand. "And now, since meeting you, my life has changed. I love you, Jemimah. I would never deliberately hurt you. Yes, I met her for coffee, thinking I owed her that much. It started to get late and I let her talk me into having dinner—I just wanted to get everything straight in my mind—but after she told me what she was thinking, everything went south. I realized how determined she was to make it happen."

She relaxed her shoulders. "I'm sorry I reacted so strongly, Rick, but I wasn't sure what was going on. I hate to admit I felt threatened. I knew nothing about this woman other than she was obviously your first love."

"That's my fault. By the time I looked at my watch, I realized you were already off work and probably headed home. I had no idea she was bound and determined to get back together. Years ago, you could have knocked me over with a feather when she said she wanted a divorce. I never knew what hit me. She gathered all her things and moved out and I went into a tailspin. I tried everything I could to patch things up, but it was no use. She would only reconcile if I quit my job. Guess she wanted me to work at a nine-to-five job with some state agency, whether it suited me or not. After the divorce I spent the next three months drinking myself into a stupor. If it wasn't for Sheriff Medrano and Detective Chacon pulling an intervention, I probably would have imploded. That's what got me into believing in psychologists. I've managed to see one periodically since then."

A smile crossed Jemimah's lips. "Everyone has a few skeletons kicking around in their closets, Rick. None of us is perfect."

"I don't think I've heard rumors about you gallivanting around with any ex-husbands lately."

"You're right on that count. But not to sound trite, it appears as though your ex-wife has a few problems," she said.

"I just want you to know how sorry I am for putting you through this. It won't ever happen again."

Her forehead touched his. "Apology accepted. I'm sorry I gave you such a hard time." She put her hand on the side of his face, pulled him close, and kissed him passionately.

"Oh, my God. How I've missed you," he said. After a long embrace, he reached for her hand and pulled her off the couch. "Come on. Let's get out into the sunshine. Maybe take a ride up to the ski basin?"

"Sounds like what the doctor ordered. Maybe we can throw something together for dinner at my place after."

***

THE BRISK AFTERNOON air at the ski basin worked its magic. Romero followed Jemimah home and parked his cruiser next to hers in the driveway. After washing up, he walked into the kitchen and saw that she was pulling stuff out of the refrigerator.

"Whatcha doin'? Need some help?"

She shook her head and chuckled. "I just realized the package I thawed is pork and not chicken."

"You open the wine and get the peppers and onions sliced. I can make pork fajitas as well."

He reached around her for the knife and began slicing the meat into thin strips. He seasoned it well and tossed it into the pan with the onions and peppers. Jemimah poured two glasses of wine and slid one in front of him.

"This should be ready in about ten minutes," he said, giving the mixture a good stir. He wrapped some tortillas in foil and put them in the warm oven.

"I had forgotten you were such a whiz in the kitchen, Detective. I'm a lucky girl," she said.

He leaned over and kissed her. "If I wasn't so hungry, I'd try to spirit you into the bedroom."

She nuzzled his earlobe. "Plenty of time for that."

He threw back his head and laughed. "Yes, you do serve up the best dessert."

After dinner they sat on the wooden banco on the back porch and watched the crimson sky envelop the last remnants of the sunset. She leaned back and snuggled against him as he put his arm around her.

"I was hoping we could catch up on the status of the investigation," she said, twirling the chest hair peeking through his V-neck t-shirt.

" 'Fraid not," he said, reaching for her hand. "At this hour, I believe dessert trumps work." She held onto him as they wound their way to the bedroom.

Later that evening, with Jemimah cuddled in his arms, Romero found it easy to fall asleep. Out in the country there was a peaceful silence, free of noisy traffic and honking horns. He slept solidly from the time his head hit the pillow. When he awoke, her side of the bed was empty, but he could smell the coffee. He went into the bathroom to shave and shower. Then, dressed in the previous day's clothes, he walked into the kitchen.

"Good morning, sunshine. I hope I wasn't making too much racket," she said, leaning over to kiss him. "I noticed you were still sawing logs when I got up. I figured you could use another thirty minutes."

"Very thoughtful of you," he said. "You could have pounded

on a drum next to my ear and I wouldn't have heard it."

She handed him a mug of coffee and motioned him toward the island. "Breakfast?"

He brushed his lips against hers. "Just coffee, thanks. I need to get going. McCabe's coming by the station at eight thirty."

Chapter Thirty-Four

———•———

IT WAS THURSDAY the first of June, twenty-seven days into
the investigation, and Jemimah's desk overflowed with
paperwork. It had already been a long week. She yawned and
stretched, still feeling the mellow glow of her night with Rick.
So far her day had been filled with endless phone calls and
boring meetings. She walked to the window and watched as
droves of tourists milled around the plaza, some standing in
line to order food from Roque's Carnita Cart. The lip-smacking
meat and chile mixture wrapped in a hot tortilla was worth
the wait. Jemimah's mouth watered as she debated whether to
run downstairs and join the line or wait and have lunch with
Detective Romero. She decided to wait and returned to her
desk.

She was deep in thought when she heard a knock on the
door jamb. She looked up from her desk to see a tall, wiry man
with a prominent nose, dark pomaded hair and shifty eyes. He
was impeccably dressed in a casual suit and wearing Armani
glasses with tortoise shell frames.

"May I help you?" she said.

"Mind if I sit down? Long walk from the parking lot. Wasn't

sure where your office was," he said.

Jemimah removed the reading glasses from her face. "Excuse me? Exactly who were you looking for?"

The man entered the room and plopped himself down in the leather chair. Pulling a wad of gum out of his mouth, he placed it in the wrapper and hurled it toward the trash can. Then he took another stick of gum from his pocket, rolled it into a neat pinwheel and popped it into his mouth. He smiled at her across the room.

"So, Jemimah, long time no see," he drawled.

It took her a moment to recognize Byron Mills, someone she hadn't seen since the Buckaroo Ball a couple of years ago, shortly before Tim McCabe was shot at the Indian ruins. She pushed her chair back as she stood. "What do you want, Byron? I have no wish to take a journey down memory lane with you."

Byron wagged a long finger at her. "Now hold on a minute there, missy. You don't even know why I'm here. Don't go dismissing me like one of your demented clients."

"No, I don't know why you're here, but I'm just fine with that. Please leave, or I'll call Security and have them escort you out. You are in a private office complex, you know." There was no love lost between her and Byron Mills. He had been one of her father's closest friends and a staunch supporter of the FLDS polygamist lifestyle. She imagined that by now he had his own covey of young sister wives.

Mills moved from the space on the couch and sat in the chair next to her desk. "How about we start over," he said. "I apologize for barging in on you without calling for an appointment. I know you're a very busy person, what with all you seem to have accomplished since you left Utah. I half expected to find you waiting tables in some hole in the wall, but I must say I'm impressed. PhD, hmmm."

Jemimah sat in silence. It took everything she had not to run to the bathroom and vomit. "Apology aside, you can barge right out the way you came in," she said.

"There's no need to be so hostile, Jemimah. I don't deserve to be disrespected. I came here to possibly mend some fences. Being as we live in the same community now, and all."

She stared at him, and her revulsion toward this man magnified. "I like the fences just the way they are, thank you. I see no need to be reminded that someone like you lives anywhere near me."

He ignored her comment. "Look, Jemimah. Your parents are getting up there in age. They've always been concerned about you. It's taken me a long time to find you, and that happened only because I ran into you at that fundraiser a while back. Imagine my shock at seeing you."

"Believe me, the shock was mutual. So you're expecting me to thank you? And by the way, Byron, just how many *parents* are you talking about here? As I recall, my father's newest wife before I left was just about my age, and I never did get to know her. I'm sure he's added a few more young things by now." She shuffled the papers on her desk, and hoped he wouldn't notice her hands shaking.

"You sound a bit resentful, Jemimah," he sneered.

She glared at him. "You are fully aware that at one time my father was a devout Mormon who found his way into a Fundamentalist lifestyle, which included polygamy. He destroyed our family. But of course, you followed that same path, and I'm sure without conscience or consideration of how your original wife felt."

Mills fiddled with his cufflinks, pulling his sleeves down to expose the gold squares. "Can I assume that you're not interested in having them contact you?"

"Your assumption is correct. How perceptive of you. That's all behind me, and quite frankly I don't want any of it dredged up. I'd prefer that the past stay buried with all the rest of the skeletons."

Mills cleared his throat and stood up abruptly, almost knocking the chair over. "Well, I can see you haven't changed much. Nobody would have wanted you for a wife. They would have had to beat you regularly to make you conform," he snarled.

Jemimah had a determined look on her face. "Well, guess what, Byron? No amount of beating would have made me conform. That's why I left and I've never looked back. Now why don't you just return to your own harem, which I assume by now is fairly sizeable, and leave me the hell alone?"

Mills turned on his heel and stomped out of her office. She pretended not to notice. Once he was out of sight, she burst into tears. The confrontation made the thoughts whirl around in her mind. In the past, she had moments where she dwelled on her childhood, recalling their happy family life before her father began entertaining a polygamist lifestyle for their future.

She never knew what the family's reaction had been to her leaving, but assumed she had been immediately ostracized. Didn't matter. She never planned on going back anyway. She knew then that if she ever returned to Utah, she would be shunned. No telling how things had changed there. It was likely all her combined siblings had children and grandchildren of their own by now.

At an early age, she decided the lifestyle her parents embraced would never work for her. Confused and disgusted, she didn't believe in that mode of living, no matter how her father spun it. She wanted a life and identity of her own, not to be dependent on a man chosen for her by individuals who knew little about her, other than that according to their standards she had reached a marriageable age. Her father insisted it would be a *spiritual experience*, once she rid herself of the notion of *independence*. The last discussion she'd had with him almost escalated to a screaming match, but Jemimah knew better. She would be punished severely, then closely watched to make sure she complied with his requests.

How surreal to suddenly hear about the father she once loved and cherished wanting to make contact with her after all these years.

She shuddered in disgust. He had to have an ulterior motive. With several FLDS scandals still in the news after all these months, many polygamist fundamentalist cults were being exposed and ostracized both by the government and the media. It wouldn't be long before some of them would creep into remote areas of New Mexico and set up camp. She wondered if that was the reason Mills was in Santa Fe.

His untimely visit shook Jemimah to her core. She had just denied him the opportunity to ply her with information on the family of her past. *Fat chance that he would respect her wishes about not informing them of her whereabouts.* She would deal with that situation if it ever came up.

On the drive to meet Rick for lunch, she wondered if the planets were out of alignment. First Rick's ex-wife had dropped into his life and then she'd experienced her own blast from the past. She smiled as she thought about the detective. *Now I understand how he must have felt having someone walk back into his life after so many years.* In her case, it was a shock, to say the least. Still in a daze, she parked her car and alarmed it. As she rounded the corner, he was waiting at the door.

The couple had a quick lunch at Sweetwater Harvest, a new restaurant on Pacheco Street whose focus was on healthy, farm-grown menu items. She opted for the tri-color quinoa cakes and he ordered the Santa Fe wrap smothered in green chile. After the meal, while they sipped on hibiscus tea, Jemimah was silent.

"You're not your usual chatty self, Jem," he said.

"Sorry. I had a visitor earlier today and it threw me for a loop. Byron Mills dropped by my office to see me."

"Isn't he the guy who approached you at the charity event a couple of years ago?"

She took a sip of her tea. "Good memory. That would be him. I was shocked to see him and wasn't interested at all in making chitchat. He's a very obnoxious person."

"What did he want?" Romero said.

"Wanted to tell me all about my father and his family and how they were hoping to make contact with me. So he could tell them how I was doing."

"Strange that after all these years they would want to see you, considering the circumstances, don't you think?"

Jemimah shuddered at the memory. "It was all I could do to keep from shaking. It really freaked me out. I listened as best I could and told him I had no interest and to get out of my office. He wasn't too happy that I wasn't willing to let bygones be bygones and start communicating with these people. Does that make me an awful person, Rick?"

He reached over and touched her hand. "Not just no, but hell no."

Chapter Thirty-Five

———•———

BEFORE SUNSET, JEMIMAH spent an hour staring out the living room window of her ranch house. Any other time, she would have enjoyed the view while watching hummingbirds flit around the feeder, stopping for nano-seconds to taste home-brewed sweet nectar. She stared beyond them, out into the vast desert landscape abutting her property. A moment before, the sun had been shining, but as happened often in the area, clouds had moved in to darken the sky. Her mood dampened as she thought of her encounter with Byron Mills. Added to that, she was at odds with herself over the lack of progress in the Sanchez case. Detectives Chacon and Martinez seemed to be focusing their efforts on other pressing cases. Who could blame them? This one had more dead ends than a trout had gills.

She thought about the letters found in Sanchez's apartment and how devastated she would be in Carmen de la Torre's *shoes*. She concluded that Carmen knew nothing more about Sanchez than what she related to Romero. What a painful blow it must have been to have her world shattered by the news of her lover's death. Jemimah had also reevaluated her own thoughts about Sanchez. Who's to say he hadn't been serious about this woman? Her training had taught her when guys like Sanchez wait until their forties to settle down, it is a big deal. Maybe he was tired of short-term relationships, and the Mexican seamstress captured his heart. She kept shifting all the available pieces of the puzzle, but couldn't get them to fall into place. *What was missing here? Motive?*

She shook her head to clear it. She forced herself to refocus on the files laid out neatly on the coffee table. No need to chastise herself. She sensed this case had rattled her emotional state more than any other. *Was it because she disliked Sanchez from the moment they were introduced?* Professionally, she knew better than to let her personal feelings or first impressions enter into a case, but hers had been a human reaction.

Her cellphone rang, pulling her out of a momentary slip into the past. She glanced at the ID and punched the talk button. It was Katie, letting her know she had finished transferring recent interviews into PDF files and had emailed her a copy. They chatted for a few minutes and then hung up. Jemimah returned to the task at hand, twirling her pen thoughtfully as she reviewed page after page of handwritten notes.

From an earlier telephone conversation with the manager of the La Fonda Hotel, she discovered that they had a state-of-the-art security system in place. All points of ingress and egress in the five-story building were monitored, including all hallways and elevators. Security cameras were out by the pool as well as the parking garage. It was possible to keep track of every guest as they checked in and out. In addition, a computer logged each time the door to a room was locked or unlocked. Beyond that, it appeared to Jemimah that the system was cutting edge and just might provide the information she needed to get the investigation rolling forward. Even if that was the case, she wasn't sure exactly what she hoped to find.

ON HER WAY to work on Friday morning, Jemimah stopped

by the hotel to meet with the security manager and inquire just how long surveillance tapes were kept. On her last major case involving the murder of a prominent state official, she discovered that the Indian casinos in the northern part of the state regularly erased security tapes. She crossed her fingers that it wasn't the case here. She was informed that the hotel stored their videotapes for an entire year since they had been targeted in the past for serving additional alcoholic drinks to already inebriated patrons.

She was delighted to hear the lounge had security cameras that not only kept track of bartenders, but also of belligerent patrons and other potential scenarios that might arise anytime alcohol was served. Apparently the owners believed more was better, and in this case, Jemimah agreed. The hotel provided DVDs for a ninety day stretch leading up to the last time Sanchez appeared in the lounge. After consulting with the manager and providing her credentials, she was given copies of video footage for the time period she requested. She picked up her car from the valet and drove to the sheriff's office, where an evidence tech logged the DVDs in and pressed copies for her.

She returned to her office above the Plaza Restaurant in the downtown square. Katie was already clocked in. Together, they began the tedious process of reviewing the DVDs. On the third one—dated in February, three months before the body was discovered—Katie pointed to a woman who entered the hotel through the front lobby.

"The image is a little fuzzy, but does this look like the same woman who showed up in previous videos?" she asked.

"Sure does," said Jemimah.

"Look here. She's talking to some guy in the lobby, and then walks through the hallway and into the lounge, where she sits at a corner table."

"The bartender seems to know her, as does the waitress, unless they're just overly friendly," Jemimah said.

They watched as the woman got up to dance a couple of times, but always returned to sit alone at her table. Twenty minutes later, she left the table and walked down the long hallway to the bathroom in the corner. Jemimah checked the clock on the video. It was almost ten thirty. Minutes later, the camera again picked up the woman as she returned to her table. As the evening wore on, she accepted a number of invitations to dance.

As they continued to review the video, frame by frame, Katie again pointed to the screen. "See there? The bartender motions for a last call. The crowd's starting to break up and it appears as though the band members are gathering their equipment. It's about one thirty. Now she stands as if she's about to leave."

"And there comes one of the mariachis," Jemimah said. "Aha! It's Sanchez. Looks like he's flirting a little."

They continued to review the video as Sanchez sat down and chatted up the woman. Then she appeared to write her phone number on a napkin. She left the premises through the front lobby. Sanchez and a couple of musicians rolled their equipment out into the first floor of the parking garage.

Katie scribbled notes on a tablet, returned the video to its sleeve, and slipped the next DVD into the port on her laptop. "So much for that night. Seems pretty tame. A few fluttering eyelashes, seductive winks, and each one left alone. Story of my life," she quipped.

Jemimah walked into the kitchen. She pressed the switch on the Keurig, which poured out a cup of steaming hot chocolate.

"Handy gadget you got here, Katie. You want anything?"

Katie shook her head; her focus was on the next video. "According to the time stamp, February fourteenth, this looks like the following Thursday, Valentine's Day. See here, Doc, our subject is sitting at a table right next to the stage, no longer hanging out at the back of the room. Sanchez seems to have changed his usual position. Instead of standing toward the right corner, he's in the center. Looks like he's singing directly at her."

Jemimah pulled her chair in. "How romantic of him."

"Ooh," said Katie. "See? He tossed her a rose; she throws him a kiss."

Jemimah looked at her watch. "Darn. Just when this is getting interesting. I have a dental appointment, Katie, so I need to leave. Keep checking the videos and let me know if you see anything substantive, other than obvious flirtations between the two. I'll see you on Monday."

"Will do, Doc," Katie said as she waved her off, her eyes never leaving the screen. She spent the remainder of the afternoon closely scrutinizing the videos. It was considerably easier now that she knew what she was looking for. She noted dates and times where the subject appeared with or without Sanchez and the corresponding number on the video.

"Hmmm," she said aloud. "These two seem to be moving pretty fast. Wish we had videos of what went on after they left the lounge." She looked up at the clock on the wall. It was after five as she gathered up her belongings and bopped down the steps.

***

AFTER HER APPOINTMENT, Jemimah swung by her house to pick up some clothes for the weekend. She and Rick had planned to drive to Ojo Caliente for a soak in the mineral waters and a two-night stay at the bed and breakfast. They promised each other it would be a no shop-talk weekend. They were determined to rekindle all the romantic feelings they had for each other. Difficult as it would be, she left everything related to work, including her phone, on the kitchen island and grabbed her overnight bag as she heard the knock on her door. Molly barked her *I know who that is* greeting and as Rick entered, waited for him to toss her a treat.

Chapter Thirty-Six

———◆———

A T NINE O'CLOCK Monday morning, Katie bounded into Jemimah's office, dropped her backpack on the floor and flopped into the easy chair next to Jemimah's desk.

Jemimah glanced up from her laptop. "You look exhausted, Katie. Hot date over the weekend?"

"Don't I wish. I took the DVDS home with me and watched them until my eyes glazed over." She lugged her backpack off the floor and emptied its contents onto the desk. "I'm sure yours was much more exciting than mine."

Jemimah pretended to swoon, placing the palms of her hands over her heart. "It was fabulous, dah-ling. Need I say more?"

Katie laughed. "No details, please. I'm already envious."

Jemimah pulled her chair closer. "What's new with the romance captured on video?"

Katie scrolled down her iPad. "Here's what I found, Doc. According to the time stamps, the couple started dating shortly after the first video where she wanders into the lounge. That puts it about early February. After that, Sanchez makes it a practice of sitting at her table during the break, holding her hands and fawning over her in general. When the bar closes, they leave together, walking out into the parking lot behind the hotel."

"Sounds like a budding romance caught on tape," Jemimah said.

"For the next couple of months, this woman shows up every time Sanchez is performing, usually on weekends, and they act like a couple. She enters the lounge about an hour before closing time, has a few drinks. He directs a few songs at her, performance ends, they leave together. Videos generally show them leaving the lounge, walking through the parking garage into the back lot and getting into his car."

Jemimah scooted her chair back. "Good work, there, Katie. You should be a private eye."

Katie raised her hand. "I'm not done yet, boss."

Jemimah leaned forward. "There's more?"

"Yeah. Here's the kicker. At the end of April, about three nights before Sanchez goes missing, or at least doesn't show up for a performance, things don't appear to be so friendly anymore. On several of the close shots, she appears to be glaring at him across the room. It looks as though he's singing to someone else, and he doesn't come to her table."

"So all was not well in paradise, I gather."

"Seems that way," Katie said, "and then there's an altercation. There's not too many people on the dance floor, so you can clearly see a guy pull Sanchez off the stage."

"I remember reading about that in one of Detective Chacon's interviews," Jemimah said. "It involved Sanchez serenading the guy's girlfriend."

"Yes, that would be a Mr. Gomez. I printed out a copy of the interview and slipped it into the file."

"The video confirms pretty much everything he said," Jemimah noted.

Katie tapped a fingernail on the desk. "Well, it looks as though they broke up about a week before his body was found, but she continued to frequent the lounge a few more times. I wonder why?"

Jemimah shrugged. "I would suppose she didn't feel it necessary to stop going to places she enjoyed just because of the breakup, or maybe she wanted to make up and renew their relationship. Does anyone know her name?"

"Funny you should ask. On Friday, after you left, Detective Chacon stopped by to drop off something for the file. He sat around for a while as the videos ran on my laptop, and get this …. He recognized her as the woman Carlos introduced as his girlfriend when they ran into each other having coffee at Downtown Subscription."

"Did he remember her name?"

"Yep. Annae Rivers," Katie said.

Jemimah made a face. "Why does that name sound so familiar?"

"You know how trendy it is to change the spelling of a name, just to be different. So do we know when she hooked up with Carlos?"

"That's our next million-dollar question. I'm thinking maybe I should just ask. After all, it is part of an investigation. Carlos shouldn't be intimidated by his brother asking a personal question." She reached into her purse for her cellphone.

"Hi, sweetie," he said. "I'm on my way out the door. What's up?"

"Just a quick question, Rick. It has come to our attention that your brother has been dating a woman who might be the same woman involved with Eduardo Sanchez before he was murdered."

"You're kidding. The only person I know he's been dating recently is the one who alibi'd him out when the DA got wind of his altercation with Sanchez."

"Do you know anything about her? Her name, maybe?"

"Can't say that I do. We've never been formally introduced. He's kind of kept her in the shadows, or at least we haven't had occasion to run into each other of late. Why do you ask?"

"It seems that Detective Chacon ran into Carlos and his date a while back and he recognized her as the woman on the videos from the lounge at LaFonda, who at the time was making goo-goo eyes at our victim."

"I'll give Carlos a call and get back to you on that. Anything else?"

"That'll do it," she said. " 'Bye, Rick." Jemimah ended the call and turned to Katie. "He'll get back to me soon as he finds out."

"Ooh la la," Katie chuckled. "I was waiting for you to blow him some kisses. I gather the fire was rekindled over the weekend? Way to go there, Doc."

Jemimah rolled her eyes upward. "I guess you could say that, Katie."

Katie jiggled her eyebrows. "Hey … everyone knows you two are a hot item."

Jemimah shrugged. "Maybe so, but protocol dictates no hanky-panky between county employees."

Katie snorted. "Yeah, as if anyone adheres to that rule. You two are just one of many trying to keep a secret, believe me, and some of them are not as subtle."

She closed the file in front of her. "Again, Katie, excellent work as usual. Looks like we might start making some headway on this case."

Katie gathered her iPad and slipped it into its case. She was all aflutter from Jemimah's compliment about her work, which she knew was genuine. "I'll get this all typed up and put a copy in the file before I leave this afternoon," she said.

Chapter Thirty-Seven

———•———

MIDWEEK, JEMIMAH WORKED at home, due to some unexpected repairs on her office building. Although she didn't consider herself a nine-to-fiver, it wasn't unusual for her to spend evenings tapping away on her laptop to bring her files up to date. This was something an assistant couldn't do. It was too personal. The case file on the mariachi's murder was spread out on the kitchen island, next to a big bowl of salsa, blue corn tortilla chips, and a tangerine margarita in a Mason jar. Her dog sprawled on the floor next to her feet, paws twitching, far away in dreamland on some fantastic canine adventure.

Katie's review of the hotel surveillance videos and their combined input had provided an interesting twist to the case. Jemimah finally had something to dissect in hopes of pinning down a viable suspect. To date there was nobody at the top of the list, but she hoped to pull one out of the sky. Fortunately, Detective Chacon recognized the woman in the video as the same person Carlos introduced him to a few weeks before as someone he'd been dating for a little over a month. Carlos's girlfriend, Annae Rivers, had apparently also dated Eduardo Sanchez, confirmed by the interview with Mr. Barela. Sanchez was dead. It probably hadn't entered Carlos's mind, but he might find himself in a shitload of trouble if he continued to date this woman—although just having dated the victim did not of itself make Annae a suspect.

Jemimah dialed Detective Romero's office. No answer. She tried his cell. He answered on the first ring. "You must be psychic, sweet thing. I just drove in from Farmington and was thinking about you. What's up?" he said.

She smiled and smoothed a few loose strands of hair over her ear, as if he could see the mess she thought her hair was in. "In your absence, I've been rehashing this Sanchez case, Rick. Did you have a chance to ask Carlos about his girlfriend?"

"I did and he indicated he didn't pry into his girlfriends' pasts … who they dated and why they broke up. He said if she had dated Sanchez, that was nobody's business but her own. He did mention that her name was Annae, though."

Jemimah filled him in about the security tapes and how coincidental it was that Annae had dated both men and Barela before that. More evident was the fact that she started dating Carlos within a week, or even the same week, of the discovery of Sanchez's body.

"No wonder she was hesitant to provide an alibi for Carlos when he was first considered a suspect," Romero said. "His excuse was that she didn't like cops, although Sheriff Medrano said she ultimately came in and provided credit card receipts for their hotel stay."

Jemimah agreed. "She was probably concerned law enforcement might have made a connection between her and Sanchez. That would have resulted in her being a suspect early on or at least being subjected to questioning. Fortunately for her, nobody linked anything together at the time. Another thing … I don't believe she was ever questioned for being one of his previous girlfriends."

"Someone must have slipped up there," Romero said, "although I'm sure it's because he kept his relationships private.

His fellow band members knew he was dating, but they didn't know anything about her, including her name. It was well-known that he moved in and out of relationships with ease." He cleared his throat. "On another subject, Sanchez had a lot of cash in his apartment and more in a safe deposit box at the bank. Sure as hell didn't earn it on his weekly gig with Mariachi Sunrise. It had to come from somewhere."

"Maybe he won it at one of the casinos," Jemimah said. "I understand he liked to play the tables."

Romero paused before answering. "That kind of money … maybe in Vegas, but hardly possible around here. Besides, the IRS would have a record of any casino winnings since they're pretty swift about collecting their pound of flesh right off the top. Any time a player wins more than a thousand dollars, the casino has them fill out a W-9 tax form, which goes straight to IRS. I don't recall anything like that in the papers collected from his apartment."

She slid off the stool next to the kitchen island and paced the floor as they spoke. "Maybe, but we may never know. Sanchez seems to have been under the radar with everything, including his personal relationships. Nobody knows much about him. In a way it's intriguing to explore his private life. There's a lot of information hiding in the rafters waiting for us to link it up."

Romero listened with admiration at how at ease Jemimah sounded when discussing a case. His mind wandered as she talked on about Sanchez. What he loved most about her was her hands. Her fingers were long and soft and she wasn't afraid to get them dirty on her small ranchette. She shoveled manure in the horse corrals on a regular basis, but she still smelled sweet as honey every time they were together. He pulled himself back into the present.

"I'm sorry, Jemimah. What was that last thing you said?"

"I'm beginning to think there's hardly enough here to formulate a profile," she said. "I'd like to narrow down the suspects, but that's impossible, since we don't really have any yet. Any one of a dozen people could have snuffed out this guy's candle, but there's no solid evidence to connect any of them. Just because he was disliked by a lot of guys who knew him doesn't give them motives for murder."

"Well, keep at it. I'm sure you'll come up with something." Romero's beeper buzzed. "Hey, Jem. I gotta go. I'll catch up with you later."

Jemimah laid her phone on the counter and returned to her paper trail, spread out in sequence across the island. She found that if she talked her way through a puzzle, a light bulb would usually go off in her head. She felt a sense of urgency as she was going to be gone for a few days to attend another seminar.

She thrummed her fingers on the hard surface and said aloud, "Hmmm. This is a complex case. On the one hand we have our victim, shot through the head and buried in a shallow grave in the remote desert. A week or two and the coyotes would have dug him up and scattered the bones from hell to breakfast, which would have made our job even more difficult. Thank goodness for the ranch hand wandering down the pike looking for a broken fence.

"Then we have a number of individuals who hated the victim's guts, and didn't care whether he was alive or not, although much of it was probably envy.

"Then comes the Mexican connection. Pretty lady in Guadalajara with hopes of making her relationship with the victim permanent, but fate intervened. Maybe he's smuggling stuff in his jackets, maybe not. Maybe he has a connection to a drug cartel. Or the connection really is about real estate.

"Added to that is the victim's ex-girlfriend who seems to make it a practice of dating men who are tall, dark and handsome. No record to speak of, just a beautiful woman apparently out looking for love on the yellow brick road."

Jemimah filled a tablet with additional notes. She was determined to make some sense of the case by rereading all the reports in the file. Nothing glared out at her. She pulled a pizza box out of the freezer, unwrapped it and stuck it in the oven, and returned to her files. She poured herself another margarita from the pitcher and headed to the couch, where she was joined by her dog.

A rainy deluge dropped the late afternoon temperatures into the sixties. The cooler pre-summer weather reminded Jemimah of the fall, the season she disliked most. It involved winterizing her place, a task she preferred to delay as long as possible. When she first moved to New Mexico from Dallas, she was surprised to learn that winters in the Northern New Mexican *desert* sometimes meant a foot or more of snow.

The oven timer jingled. She put the files in her briefcase and retrieved her dinner, peeling off a few pepperoni slices and slipping them into Molly's bowl. The rest of the evening consisted of watching *Hangar 45* on the History Channel and learning how the government had misled the public about the UFO sightings in New Mexico for the past fifty years.

During a commercial break, she thought about the Mexico connection. If Sanchez had been smuggling something, who was his connection here? The money in his account had to come from somewhere, and there was no paper trail.

Chapter Thirty-Eight

———•———

THAT WEDNESDAY AFTERNOON, Carlos Romero glanced at his watch as he waited in the parking lot of the Madrid tavern for his girlfriend to arrive. He checked the rearview mirror and ran a comb through his hair, then scrolled his phone for messages. He saw a white BMW Z3 drive into the lot. Carlos liked nice cars and he checked it out from bumper to bumper. The car idled as the driver pushed open his door and then walked to the passenger side to let the woman out. Carlos did a double take. The woman was his girlfriend Annae.

She was wearing a clingy turquoise shift and heels. She wrapped her arms around the driver's neck and kissed him, then turned and waved goodbye and walked toward the entrance of the tavern. Carlos exited his car and caught up with her.

She turned her head as she saw him approach. "Carlos, you startled me!" she said.

"I waited so you wouldn't have to walk in by yourself, but I see you managed all right," he said.

"A friend dropped me off. I didn't want to leave my car here in case you had plans for dinner," she said.

Carlos sneered. "A little out of the way for a friend to drive, don't you think?"

He guided her inside and waited for his eyes to adjust to the darkness. The barmaid motioned them to a table and took their order. After she left, he turned to Annae. He was visibly irritated.

"You know, I've been getting really bad vibes from you lately," he said.

For a moment, her green eyes darkened. "What does that mean? I thought we were getting along just fine."

"It means that you've been acting kind of distant for the past couple of weeks."

"Like what? I haven't treated you any differently. We're still enjoying each other's company, aren't we?"

"I don't know. Sneaking around. Hanging up on calls when I come in the room ... that kind of shit. I'm beginning to think you lead a double life. For instance, who was that guy you drove up with?"

The barmaid set their drinks in front of them. Carlos handed her a twenty and told her to keep the change. Annae took a long sip of her drink. "Look, Carlos, he's just a friend," she said.

"From where, Hollywood? The way the guy was dressed makes me wonder what you're involved in."

"What do you mean, 'involved in.' "

"He smelled of money ... and lots of it. Maybe drug money."

She tossed her head back and laughed. "Come on, Carlos. Just because someone has good taste in clothes and cars doesn't mean they're dealing drugs. You've been hanging around your brother for too long. Let's talk about something else."

Carlos tipped back in his chair. He wasn't about to let it go. "So how do you know this guy? Well enough to kiss him on the mouth, I gather."

Annae was exasperated. "What's with the third degree? I don't question you every time some chick falls all over you."

"I guess I'm feeling like I'm being played. Like I've been

thrust into this role of second fiddle, and I don't like it. Lately you spend more time with your friends than you do with me, and even when we are together, you don't quit texting long enough to carry on a conversation."

She leaned toward him and put her head on his shoulder. "That's crazy. I'm not seeing anyone else but you. I don't know where you could have gotten that idea."

He scraped his chair back, causing her to move her head. "For starters, the late night phone calls, your sneaking off when you think I'm asleep ... stuff like that."

"We're not living together. I shouldn't have to explain every little move I make. We might be dating, but that doesn't mean I don't have a life," she retorted. "And sometimes I like to wake up in my own bed."

"For the past couple of weeks you've been acting like I'm no longer a part of that life," he said.

She put her arm through his, and again he pulled away. "Hey, that's a little harsh," she said. "What the hell's going on with you? I can't believe you're jealous of a friend giving me a ride."

"You know, to be honest, I've been thinking it's not going to work out with us. We've drifted apart and our relationship has become unpredictable. I'm the one making all the calls, all the plans, and half the time I can't get in touch with you."

Her eyes widened. "You're kidding me. So what is this, an overture toward a breakup?"

"I can't stay in a relationship that's so damned one-sided. I guess the attention I shower on you isn't enough. You seem to be looking for it somewhere else."

Annae's featured tightened and her cheeks grew pink beneath her makeup. "Seriously, Carlos. Let's talk this out. I enjoy hanging out with you. We always have a great time. Maybe I have been a little distracted. I'll try to be more conscious of your needs."

He motioned the barmaid for another drink. "I don't think so. I'm at the point where I've come to realize it's time to move on. No point in investing any more energy." He took a big gulp of his drink and abruptly stood up to leave.

She looked at him, fire in her eyes. "Blow it out your ass, Carlos. I don't deserve this treatment. You think you're Mr. Perfect, but I'm sure there's no point in enlightening you about that either."

"Obviously." He turned and walked toward the entrance.

***

FOR THE NEXT ten minutes, Annae just sat there, dumbfounded by the turn of events. She reached down and grabbed her purse, then ran to the ladies room. A well-dressed attractive woman with blond-streaked brown hair who looked to be in her late thirties was at the sink. She dried her hands and turned to Annae.

"What's the matter, honey? Looks like you're having a little man trouble," she said.

Annae splashed cold water on her cheeks. "Something like that. The jerk caught me off guard, accusing me of indifference. Then he said it was over and stomped out."

The woman handed her a wad of paper towels. "Come on. Let me buy you a drink and you can tell me all about it," she said.

Annae nodded. "I could use a shoulder to lean on." She checked her reflection in the mirror, touched up her lipstick and smoothed her eyebrows.

She took Annae by the arm and led her back to a side table at the bar. "Come on. We can both cry in our beer. I'm a firm believer that misery does love company."

Chapter Thirty-Nine

————◆————

O N FRIDAY, THE weather looked promising for the
weekend. It was general knowledge that around Santa Fe
the sun could shine all week, but by Saturday, the rain gods
would gather up a group of clouds and rain on the parades of
all the public employees.

Detective Romero sipped on a container of iced coffee as
he leaned back on the leather recliner in his office and stared
out the window. It felt good to relax for a few minutes. He
was looking forward to his first weekend off in months—the
one Sheriff Medrano promised for his trip to Arizona—and
debated whether he should spend the time around his house.
He could maybe clean the yard or hike up one of the trails near
the ski basin. Of course he would have to wait for Jemimah,
since she was in Albuquerque attending the tail end of a two-
day confab on personality disorders and human relations. Not
a great subject to discuss over coffee.

Better yet, maybe he would drive up to Pecos, about thirty
miles northeast of Santa Fe, and do a little fishing along Cow
Creek. Romero loved that place. It was completely isolated
from the hustle and bustle of cop work. When Rick was a

teenager, his father took him to meet Greer Garson, the Hollywood actress who owned a huge spread of land in that area. He had been hired to remodel Miss Garson's kitchen, and she graciously invited them to fish the river anytime they wanted. There were some fine fishing holes along the banks adjacent to the ranch, where they'd usually caught their limit in less than twenty minutes.

The property had changed hands in recent years, when Val Kilmer, another well-known movie star, purchased the place. Romero wasn't sure Kilmer would be open to allowing strangers to fish on his property, but what the heck, there were other places a few miles north of the ranch where a couple of prize-winning trout could be pulled out of the water just as easily using either bait or fly.

Clarissa's voice blared through the intercom, interrupting his daydream. "Boss, Billy Pacheco is on the line. He's looking for Carlos," she said.

Romero raised his head and stretched. "I'm getting ready to head out, Clarissa. Did you give him my brother's cell number?"

"Yeah. He says there's no answer. He still wants to talk to you. He's holding on line one."

Romero spun his chair around and reached for the landline on his desk. "Hey, Billy, what's up? I've only got a couple of minutes. I'm about to take off for the afternoon." Pacheco had been Carlos's probation officer since his release from the detention center almost a year before.

"I know you're not your brother's keeper, Rick, but Carlos didn't show up for our scheduled meeting. He misses this one and I'll have to report him. He knows better. He's only got ninety days left of his probation—three more meetings. I'd hate to see him screw it up now."

Romero paced the floor as he talked. "Let me see if I can track him down, Billy. It's not like him. Can you just reschedule this one time?"

Pacheco thought about it. "Yeah, no problem. I just don't want it to get out of hand. You know I have to file reports on all these guys, and sometimes keeping track of them can be a full-time job."

Romero thanked him. "I understand completely, and I want you to know how much I appreciate it, Billy. You're a good friend."

"You owe me one, Romero."

He breathed a sigh of relief. "Thanks. It won't happen again. I'll try to look sideways the next time I spot you speeding down the highway. I promise."

Clarissa stood next to his desk as he placed the receiver in its cradle. "Maybe he's just out somewhere on an extended date," she said. "You know how involved he can get when a pretty woman's around."

Romero wasn't so sure. He had never known Carlos to blow off something as important as meeting with his probation officer. He dialed Carlos's cell three or four times in succession. Every one of the calls went directly to message. He scrapped the idea of heading to the mountains. He had to be back in time for dinner with Jemimah; then they could decide what to do for the weekend. In the meantime, he took a drive to clear his mind and see if maybe Carlos was at home. He wasn't. He returned to his office to make a few calls.

Chapter Forty

———•———

ROMERO STEPPED OUT into the open air through the French doors in the back office and dialed Tim McCabe's cell. He answered on the third ring.

"Tim, Rick Romero here. How's it going?"

McCabe yawned audibly. "I didn't sleep worth a crap last night," he said, his fingers trembling as he lit a cigarette, a vice he was fully aware his wife disapproved of. "That'll teach me to brew that extra pot of coffee in the evening. I'm thinking of going back home and catching a few Zs."

"You'll have to scrap that thought for a while, Tim," Romero said. "What's your twenty right now?"

McCabe pulled his Hummer to the side of the road. "I'm up at Kennedy Hill, still trying to serve a couple of warrants. These guys have a way of disappearing into thin air whenever a cop car comes within five miles. Haven't served a damned one yet."

Romero paced a circle on the overgrown grass outside next to the porch. "Just drop those for now. I'll have one of the rookies take care of it. It will be a good exercise in perseverance for them. Can you meet me back here at the office? I need your advice on something."

"Sure. It'll take me about twenty minutes, but I'm on my way." He snapped his phone shut and slipped it into his shirt pocket.

Romero sat on the stone bench and gazed out at the Ortiz Mountains. A flock of blackbirds flew toward the horizon, cawing their way across the hazy afternoon sky.

McCabe stopped at the Shell station to fill up on gas and poured himself a cup of stale coffee, justifying it by telling himself it might help shake the lethargy he was experiencing.

"Damn. This cup of java better work," he muttered as he turned the key in the ignition and maneuvered onto Highway 14, balancing the paper cup with one hand.

Arriving at the satellite office, he parked and hurried up the steps. Romero was waiting for him.

He poked his head in the door of the office. "What's so urgent I had to drop what I was doing, Rick?"

Romero motioned for him to sit. His brow was furrowed. "I don't know if I'm acting like an overanxious mother hen or if something's really wrong, Tim. I've just got this damned feeling in my gut and I can't seem to shake it."

McCabe sat across from him. "This must be about Carlos," he said. "He's the only person I know who can get you into mother mode. What's going on?"

Romero walked to the kitchen, poured his drink into the sink and reached for a Coke from the fridge. "I'm not sure whether it's just a bizarre coincidence or if there's something suspicious going on with Carlos. He missed an appointment with his parole officer this afternoon. He's never done that before, and besides that, if his iPhone doesn't remind him, his computer does. No way could he have forgotten."

McCabe stroked his chin. "Maybe something came up, Rick. You know how Carlos is, especially if there's a pretty young woman involved."

"Clarissa mentioned that, too. I know he usually has his head up his ass when it comes to women. He's always been attracted to the bad apple in the bunch. Something about the danger. For a second, I thought that might be it, but Carlos and I have discussed the subject enough times, and he knows what the consequences will be if his PO reports him to the court. It can land his butt back in the clink. I'm pretty damned sure he'd avoid that at all costs."

McCabe shrugged his shoulders. "So what are you thinking?"

Romero turned his glance to the window and then at McCabe. "Before I called you, I went over to his place. His car was sitting in the parking lot, windows open, just like he was getting ready to head out somewhere. I checked around and there was no sign of him."

"I know I'm stating the obvious, but maybe someone picked him up," McCabe offered.

"Doesn't matter. He knows what will happen if he misses this appointment. He'd better have one hell of an explanation. It's going to take more than *I'm sorry* to wipe this one off his slate." He checked his phone for messages, in case he had missed a call.

McCabe moved his chair closer. "Let's try to get this into some kind of perspective, Rick. How long ago since you tried calling him? Maybe he's already back home."

Romero ran his fingers through his hair. "I tried calling him a dozen times. There's still no answer, and there's no messages on my phone. I don't like this one bit, Tim. I know Carlos can be stubborn and bullheaded, but he's not stupid. Not by a long shot."

The two friends sat in silence for a short while, neither having the words to express their frustration.

McCabe finally spoke. "How about this, Rick. I'll head out toward Madrid and check out the bar. I've heard him mention he hangs out there on occasion just to get away from the Santa Fe crowd. In the meanwhile, maybe you can check out his apartment and see if anything has changed."

Romero stood up and reached for his jacket. "All right, Tim. Doesn't seem like there's much else we can do. Can't file a missing person report on him since we don't even know if he's missing."

On his way to the parking lot, he dialed Jemimah, knowing he could count on her to put everything into perspective. There was no answer. He realized she was probably in the middle of a lecture. Besides, she would be home in a couple of hours.

As he unlocked his vehicle, a coyote howled in the distance. The sound made his skin crawl.

Chapter Forty-One

———◆———

A T MID-AFTERNOON THAT Friday, Romero maneuvered at
a snail's pace through the east side Santa Fe neighborhood
where his brother had recently moved. From his vehicle, he
conducted a quick survey of the premises. None of the tenants
seemed to be around. He surmised they were mostly working
class like Carlos, although his brother hadn't worked a regular
job for some time. After he moved from Romero's house into
the condo, his needs were met by the proceeds from the sale of
land he inherited from their parents. Romero didn't know how
much he had remaining and didn't ask.

His heart dropped when he saw that Carlos's vehicle was
still parked in the same place adjacent to the condo. He guided
the cruiser in next to it and walked toward the vehicle. He
observed that the driver's side window was still open; Carlos's
sunglasses were propped on the dashboard, his wallet in the
glove box. The laptop was on the floor in plain sight. To top it
off, the keys were in the ignition. No sign of his cell phone. *At
least that was one good thing.*

Romero gathered the belongings and placed them in the

trunk. He peered into the backseat for any sign of foul play. Finding none, he rolled up the windows, locked and alarmed the car and headed up the walkway to the entrance of the condo, keys in hand. Just as he entered, the alarm began to beep, slowly at first and then picking up speed. He hurried to the keypad in the entry hall and poked in Carlos's birth date. The alarm continued to pierce his eardrums for at least thirty seconds more. He remembered that Carlos sometimes used 7734 as his password, since when viewed upside down it spelled *hell*. He keyed the numbers in as fast as his fingers could move, as he knew it wouldn't be long before the security center notified the police. He didn't have time for that. He held his breath and pressed *enter*. Five seconds later the alarm stopped beeping. *Jeezus.* He sat down at the kitchen table to catch his breath.

He walked down the hallway to the bedroom and bathroom, and then back toward the kitchen. No sign of his brother's cellphone. He was surprised at how neat the place was, as opposed to his housekeeping habits while he'd inhabited a room in Romero's house over the past year. He'd spent most of his time calling Carlos out for his messiness. Walking through each room, he noticed that much of the furnishings were new. The bedroom set and living room furniture looked expensive. Two fifty-inch television sets occupied entire walls in both rooms. Satisfied that everything was normal, Romero dialed McCabe's cell.

"Tim, I'm out here at Carlos's place. There's no sign of him. Looks as though he was getting ready to drive off. Have you heard anything out there?"

"Not anything of substance. After I left the substation, I stopped in at Mary's Bar in Cerrillos. Heard some scuttlebutt there that Carlos preferred to hang out at the lounge in Madrid, but I wasn't sure it was your brother they were referring to. Took a while. I had to down two Ginger Ales and buy a few drinks to get just one tidbit of information. I'm about to head out to Madrid now. Why don't you meet me out there? Maybe we can stir something up."

"All right. I'll be there as soon as I can," Romero said. He re-alarmed the condo, locked the front door and walked down the path to his cruiser. Entering the vehicle, he rested his head on the steering wheel and closed his eyes.

Carlos. Where the hell are you?

ROMERO HEADED UP St. Francis Drive, turning onto the Highway 14 exit. Zipping past the Town of Cerrillos, he drove straight to the bar in Madrid. It took him about half an hour, even with lights flashing on his cruiser. It was three thirty. He rolled into the parking lot of the bar and parked facing the door. As he waited for McCabe, he observed two men emerge from the back of the building. Romero could spot a drug deal from a mile away. He could hear their conversation through the passenger side window.

"That was some heavy stuff, dude. How much?"

Before he could answer, the younger of the two looked up and saw Romero staring at them.

"Oh, shit," he yelled. "Cops!"

The two took off running in opposite directions.

Romero decided to let it pass. Right now his focus had to be on locating someone who had information about his brother's whereabouts. Somebody had to know something; he could count on it. *But who*? He looked around the lot as he waited for McCabe. He remembered his previous visits there. The building was the size of a small church. From the number of cars in the parking lot, one would think services were being held. Square tables on each side represented the pews. At the back was the altar, the long bar with twelve stools representing the Apostles. The small unisex bathroom on the left side was about the size of a confessional. A lot of praying went on in that bar, especially during sports night. Maybe ten or eleven parishioners hung around at different hours of the afternoon, drinking beer, not wine.

Chapter Forty-Two

———◆———

SITTING IN HIS cruiser in the middle of the parking lot, Romero was deep in thought as McCabe tapped on the windshield.

"That's pretty ballsy to come out here in the cruiser, Rick. Nobody's going to come forward when they spot you."

He switched off the ignition. "Yeah, pretty lame. I realize now I'm like a neon light sitting out here. I was too preoccupied in getting here to pick up my car at the office. Go on ahead and see what you can fish out of there, Tim. I'll head back to the station." He looked at the time. "I need to call Jemimah to let her know what's going on. She should be back in town by now."

"I'll give you a buzz if I have any luck," McCabe said. He patted Romero on the shoulder. "Things will work themselves out, Rick."

"I sure as hell hope so." He started up the engine and headed toward the exit.

McCabe strolled toward the dimly lit bar. It was broad daylight outside. Wearing a Western shirt and cowboy boots, he fit right in. As he entered the lounge, it took a few minutes for his eyes to adjust. He picked out a small table in the corner where he could sit and observe without being too conspicuous. A woman with bright red hair dressed in a pink tank top, frayed denim shorts, and high-heeled boots smiled and winked. As he watched her saunter toward the bar, McCabe figured she was somewhere in her fifties and at some time in her life had probably been quite a looker.

It went against his grain to take advantage of the woman's interest, his being a happily married man and all, but he thought a conversation with her might bear fruit. He asked the waitress to take her a drink. Smiling broadly, she jiggled over to his table and eased herself into the seat next to him, drink in hand.

"Well, hello handsome. Haven't seen you in here before," she cooed. "You new in town?"

"First time in these parts," McCabe lied.

"I'm Penny." She smiled and offered him her hand.

Shaking it, he said, "Tim."

She fluttered her mascara-laden eyelashes. "Does Tim have a ball and chain?" she said.

McCabe winced. "Are you a cop, asking so many questions?"

"Who, me?" She laughed. "Not by any stretch of the imagination." Her attention was quickly diverted by the sight of a tall cowboy striding through the doorway. Before McCabe could ask another question, she stood up and turned to him. "Excuse me, honey. Nice talking to you. Thanks for the drink. Maybe another time."

McCabe took a sip of his soda. He looked around the bar and recognized the lanky fellow who stumbled over the threshold and then stopped to get his bearings.

A few years before, Bart Wolfe had been a thorn in law enforcement's side during the investigation of the San Lazaro Pueblo murders. His girlfriend had been one of the five victims discovered in the tunnel below the Indian ruins. More recently, he was involved with the state official who had been murdered while searching for McCabe's treasure. Wolfe's life was a series of misguided events that seemed to propel him toward the wrong place at the wrong time. It took months before he was exonerated as a suspect in both cases. McCabe wondered if this was another situation where Wolfe might be implicated. He hoped not. Extracting information from him was worse than picking cactus needles out of your behind.

McCabe scooped up his drink and ambled toward the bar. Pulling out a stool, he sat next to Bart, who glanced at him out of the corner of his eye.

"Buy you a drink, Bart?" McCabe said.

Bart slowly rotated the barstool and faced McCabe. "Who's asking? Do I know you?"

McCabe reached out to shake Bart's hand. "Name's Tim McCabe. I own the San Lazaro Indian ruins outside of Cerrillos. You and I have had a few run-ins in the past."

A glazed look crossed Bart's face. "Oh, yeah, I know who you are," he said. "You work for the sheriff's department. What do you want with me? I ain't done nothin'. Clean as a whistle."

McCabe maneuvered the barstool closer to Bart. "What you drinkin'?" he said.

Bart straightened his back and puffed out his chest. "Well, I never pass up a *Cuba Libre*," he said, with a heavy drawl.

McCabe motioned to the bartender for a rum and Coke. The ghosts of Monday night football floated across the TV monitor above the bar.

Bart pointed at the screen. "Damned Cowboys. They ain't never going to make it to the finals at this rate." McCabe knew the game was a rerun from last season but didn't mention it to Bart. It would be months before the start of football season, but that didn't matter to these mostly inebriated hard-core fans.

He reached into his pocket and pulled out a recent photo of Carlos. "Hey, Bart, I'd like to ask a favor."

"Sure, as long as it doesn't involve anything illegal," he slurred.

McCabe slid the photo next to Bart's drink. "Nothing like

that. Just need you to take a look at this picture and tell me if you've seen this guy around here recently. I imagine an observant fellow like you knows all the regulars."

Bart craned his neck toward the light over the bar. "He looks like somebody I've seen somewhere. Don't he drive some kind of fancy car? Kind of tall fellow, maybe not that tall, nice dresser."

"I believe he was driving a black Lexus with a dealer sticker on the back window. Think it was a four-door. You know them shiny cars they sell out at the dealership way down Cerrillos Road," McCabe said.

"Yeah, that's it. You don't see too many fancy cars around this place. Too hoity-toity to hang out with us lowlifes."

McCabe leaned in. "So you've seen him recently?"

"Damned right. His girlfriend almost ran me over in the parking lot, but they were in a different car that time."

McCabe cupped both hands around his glass. "When was this, Bart?"

Bart cradled his chin in his hand. "I think it was maybe yesterday around noon. I had seen him standing next to that fancy black car the day before, like he was waiting for somebody to show up. Asshole raised hell with me for parking my truck too close to his precious car. Looked at me like I was the scum of the earth."

"Was he alone then?" McCabe asked.

"Well, yeah, until that lady zipped into the parking lot and parked next to him." Bart said.

He was becoming a bit bleary-eyed, having siphoned everything McCabe put in front of him. He took another sip from his almost empty glass and rattled the ice cubes as though expecting the amber liquid to magically reappear. McCabe could see that Bart was more willing to talk if the drinks kept coming, so he motioned the bartender for a refill.

"You remember what this lady looked like?"

"Oh, same woman as always. They've been out here a couple

of times. You'd think she was a little too classy-looking for this joint, if you know what I mean, but she's the kind you don't forget."

McCabe took a swallow from his glass. He knew from past experience Bart wasn't used to a lot of conversation. Seemed he liked to enjoy his drink without too many interruptions. McCabe kept the drinks lined up in front of Bart, and once he was good and buzzed, his tongue loosened up.

"Tell me more about this woman, Bart. You know, the one this guy was waiting for in the parking lot," said McCabe.

"Shit, man, this one was a real looker. Prettiest little filly I'd seen in a long while. They'd sit in the corner and carry on like teenagers," Bart said. " 'Course she kept checking out the guys at the bar every time she had a chance. Didn't look like no one-man woman, if you get my drift. Caught her looking at me a couple of times."

"What did she look like, Bart, aside from being pretty?"

"Like some centerfold chick. You know the kind. Every hair in place, ruby lips, long legs, nice knockers."

McCabe reined in his frustration. "Can you be a little more specific here?"

Bart peered at him with one eye closed, the other glazed over. "She in some kind of trouble?"

McCabe waved one hand. "No, no. I'm just trying to get in touch with her. Got some business to attend to."

"She's nice-sized, not too tall, not too short. Not as tall as the guy was. Maybe five-seven or so. She had long, honey-brown hair, more blond than brown, and green eyes the color of that malachite on this ring here. Did I say that she was nicely stacked? She didn't look like she was too old. Maybe late twenties. Can't tell too much anymore. All the young ones look old and the old ones look young."

"And her vehicle. Do you remember what kind of car she was driving?" McCabe said.

"It was one of those sporty cars. Red. Mazda something or

other. Looked pretty new to me. And shiny. Not a speck of dust on it. Fit her to a T, like it was made just for her." Bart turned his attention to the roar coming from the end of the bar. "Damned Cowboys. Another friggin' fumble. Shit."

Bart didn't hear McCabe thank him. He was staring at the woman sitting on the barstool to his right. McCabe knew this conversation had come to an end. He made his way toward the exit. Out in the bright sunlight, on his way to the Hummer, he patted his chest looking for his sunglasses. He hoped Detective Romero had fared better than he had. All he had managed to glean from Bart was that Carlos and his girlfriend had been in the area the previous day. But with Bart, one never knew if yesterday meant a week or a month ago.

Chapter Forty-Three

———•———

THE RED MAZDA MX-5 Roadster sped south on the Turquoise Trail in the direction of the town of Cerrillos. The attractive brunette with the blond highlights sat in the passenger seat, refreshing her lipstick and checking her hair in the visor mirror. Carlos glanced at her.

"Are we there yet?" he chuckled. "Where is this mystery place you're taking me to?"

She reached over and touched his hand. "Keep driving, sweetie. I'll tell you where to turn off."

"All right. I'm driving, but you're the boss," he said. They drove past Cerrillos. To his right Carlos could see the spire of the historic Catholic church and the equally old adobe residences surrounding it. They continued south on the road that would eventually curve toward Madrid and lead to I-40 on the outskirts of Albuquerque.

His cellphone jangled and he reached for it out of habit, but she smiled and swept it away from him.

"Hey, handsome, just ignore that. We're supposed to be spending some quality time here. No interruptions, remember?"

"It's my brother—might be important," Carlos said.

Her forehead wrinkled. "Since when is anything he has to say important?" She reached across the seat and gently placed her hand on his upper thigh. Carlos almost swerved off the road.

"Okay, okay. I get it."

She muted the ringer on the phone and tossed it into the back seat.

"There, now we can have some peace and quiet." She turned to gaze out the window. "Isn't it beautiful out here? I just love spending time so close to the mountains." She pointed up ahead. "Slow down. There's a road coming up to the left here."

Carlos braked and slowed for the turn. "I didn't even know this road existed. Are we headed to the boonies?" he joked.

"I heard about this place from some guy at the bar in Madrid. It's on the corner of land some old lady named Crawford used to own. She got her kicks taking potshots at trespassers before calling the cops."

"Sounds like a real sweetheart. She still around?" Carlos said.

"Not that I know of. She'd probably be a hundred years old if she was. This is just an old back road around the property. If you follow it long enough, it will get you to Galisteo, across private land, of course. It's been a while since I've been out here. I pulled off the road one time and found an arrowhead. So exciting."

"Somehow I can't picture you scouring through the dirt looking for bright and shiny things," Carlos said. "Hey, on second thought, maybe we shouldn't be trespassing around here either if it's private property."

"Oh, not to worry. Your reputation is safe. That was a while back and I hear the property has been on the market for some time. There's never anyone around. The land goes on forever. I believe the main ranch house is a ways from here, but there's nothing but some dilapidated ruins on this side."

Carlos drove into the desert for another five minutes. The

road had all but disappeared. In the distance he could see remnants of an old building fallen into crumbling ruins. It appeared to be a church, and it had an old metal cross balanced against a decaying post. During the 1680 Pueblo Revolt, marauding Indians destroyed most of the churches in their wake, including the church and convent at San Lazaro Pueblo. Carlos had never been in this area, but remembered newspaper articles about Tim McCabe, his brother's partner, having purchased an Indian ruin somewhere around the Cerrillos area. He wondered if this was it.

She squeezed his arm. "Let's park here, Carlos. This looks like a good spot."

Carlos left the engine idling. "I don't have that much time, so why don't we just talk on the way back?" he said.

She turned to face him and grinned, ignoring his question. "I'd like to apologize, Carlos. The other night when I ran into you I realized I was still deeply attracted to you."

He reached across the seat and put his hand over hers. "That's very sweet. I'm flattered. But I still want to know why we had to drive all the way out here just for a chat?"

She squeezed his hand. "I just wanted to catch up with you. It's been a while since we bared our souls. What better place than this enchanting spot to chill out?"

He raised the visor and looked around the expanse before them. "Enchanting is sure the right description. It's very peaceful out here. No noise other than the chirping of a few piñon jays."

She leaned against him and nuzzled his ear. "There's obviously a great deal of chemistry between us. I can still feel it. What do you say?" she said.

Uncomfortable, he fiddled with his collar. "As inviting as that sounds, I can foresee it would create problems. I'd prefer that we be friends. You understand, don't you?"

She stretched her legs, sure that Carlos noticed her shapely thighs. She slid over and opened the car door. Carlos did the same. "It's awfully warm in the car," she said. "Turn the engine off."

As they stood next to the car, she reached for his hand, pulling him next to her. "Come on, let's walk a little ways up here and get out of the sun."

Carlos glanced at his watch. "What do you have in mind? I've got some stuff I need to do back in town, and it's getting late. We took off before I had a chance to lock my car."

"It won't be long. Just a short ways up. There's a shady spot around the curve. Not too far. I thought we could spend a little time enjoying the scenery before we head out again."

He relented. "All right, but I need to get back to town fairly soon."

"You got a hot date or something?" she said.

"Well, I can't say if it's hot, but yes, I do have a date, of sorts." He didn't mention it was with his parole officer.

She crossed her arms over her chest in mock indignation. "You always were a player. I knew you had quite a reputation with the ladies."

Carlos laughed. "All fiction. I'm pretty laid back when it comes to relationships."

She touched his arm. "I thought we might make a good match. Hanging out with you the other night was pretty special. I'd like to explore the possibilities."

His eyes widened. "Hey, this is kind of sudden. I thought we covered that topic. Things just wouldn't work out between us. I thought you were okay with that. Friends?"

She turned her head so he couldn't see her expression. *Sure, Carlos. BFFF, best fucking friends forever.* "Well, at least we can enjoy a drink and make a toast to whatever each of us goes on to do. I brought some wine coolers," she said, in a sugar-coated voice.

"Sounds good to me," Carlos said, breathing a sigh of relief. He wasn't too enthused about pissing off yet another woman. Of late, his track record was suffering. He also wasn't very happy about showing up to his appointment with alcohol on his breath, although a wine cooler probably didn't pack much of a punch.

They walked another hundred yards to a grassy knoll next to the remnants of the old convent building Carlos had read about. The field was a purple carpet of wildflowers, bordered with bright yellow daisies.

"Wow, this place *is* awesome," he said.

She reached into the knapsack for two ice-cold bottles, uncapped them and handed him one. They sat together on the wild grass. Carlos took a big swallow and leaned back against the rock wall. He saw how attractive she was and found himself momentarily caught up in her web. His watch pinged the hour.

"Hey, listen. I really do need to get back to town. Maybe you could just drop me off at the sheriff's substation in Cerrillos and I can hook a ride into town with my brother."

"Sure, we can do that," she said. "Let me stuff these things back in the bag. Don't want to litter the landscape."

Carlos stood, brushed off his pants, took a few steps forward and lost his balance, falling to the ground. The last thing he remembered was the feeling of being dragged over the rocky terrain.

Chapter Forty-Four

———•———

O N Friday at around four o'clock, Jemimah was relaxing before getting ready to meet Detective Romero for their dinner date. She had spent the previous night at the Albuquerque Hotel and was glad to be home after a full day of listening to psychiatrists and psychologists present papers on personality disorders. She was convinced most criminals would fit the criteria discussed and planned on doing more research on the subject.

Later that evening, rather than review her notes, she had grabbed a sandwich and taken it to her room, where she would have preferred to curl up on the bed and finish reading Michael McGarrity's latest mystery. The main character reminded her of the kind of man she'd like to have in her life. Luckily he was pretty close to Rick. Instead she had pulled the Sanchez case file out of her briefcase and gone over its contents again. Since the day's meeting broke up early, she was determined to spend more time with the file before getting ready for her date.

She stretched out, yawned, and shuffled into the bathroom, then brushed her teeth and jumped in the shower. The warm water was soothing, and she lingered an extra five minutes, luxuriating in the soapy warmth. As she toweled off, the phone rang. It was quarter to five. She took a quick look at the caller ID. It was Rick.

"Hey there," she said. "I was just about to throw on my clothes and head out to meet you. Am I late?" There was a lilt in her voice.

He hesitated for a moment. "We'll have to postpone dinner, Jemimah. Something's wrong. Carlos is missing."

She put a hand to her mouth. "Oh, my God, Rick. Are you sure? What's going on? Where are you?"

"I can't talk now, Jem. I'm trying to put the pieces together. I'll explain later. I'm waiting for Detective Chacon to get here."

She held the phone between her neck and her ear as she slipped into her jeans. "Wait for me, Rick. I can be there in fifteen minutes," she said.

"No, no. That's all right. I'd prefer you go over to his condo, just in case I'm mistaken about this." He gave her the address. "Look, I gotta go. Artie just pulled up."

"Rick, wait—"

"I don't have time to explain, Jem. Just do as I ask. I'll check back with you first chance I get."

Jemimah stared at her cellphone before she tossed it on the bed. She assumed Romero had a good reason for not wanting her to come around.

***

ARTIE CHACON, HEAD of the Criminal Task Force, bounded up the steps to the substation. Romero met him at the door. "Glad you could make it, Artie," he said.

"Got here as fast as I could. Picked up a hint of concern in your voice, boss," he said.

Romero set a folding chair next to the long table. Chacon took a seat next to him and opened his laptop. Romero explained what he thought might be going on with Carlos. He tapped into his contact list and pulled up his brother's cellphone number, wrote it down and handed it to Chacon, who keyed it into his laptop.

"Let's hope the phone is on, Rick. Otherwise our efforts will be for *nada*, zilch."

"I get it, Artie. So how exactly does this triangulation work? I've read about it but have never put it to use."

Chacon unfolded a map of the surrounding area. "There's a couple of cellphone towers between Santa Fe and the village of Golden, a little over ten miles past Madrid. Every cellphone emits a signal, which is picked up by the different towers. In other words, when your cellphone is on, whether you're talking or not, it is in continual relay with surrounding towers. Kind of like the GPS on your vehicle. When your phone drops a call or it sounds like you're in a tunnel, that's because you're not near enough to a tower to get a strong signal. Sometimes it beeps first and then drops the call."

Romero nodded. "So how are we going to determine Carlos's whereabouts, assuming his phone is on?"

Chacon adjusted the screen on his laptop, typed in a few lines and numbers and turned it toward Romero. "Easy. This is a program used by law enforcement and 911 courtesy of the service providers." He pointed to the screen. "See, there are three towers receiving signals from his phone right now. All we have to do is intersect the signals from the towers and it will tell us exactly where the phone is located. When a new digital signal is pinged, it determines latitude and longitude via GPS and sends these coordinates back via the SMS system."

"Which is?"

"Simply stated, similar to the system that transmits text messages," said Chacon.

Romero leaned over to look at the map. "Anything?"

Chacon looked at the screen, placed a ruler on the map, ran a few pencil lines and drew a circle where they intersected. "Bingo. Now all we need to compute is the location on the map and see how far it is from here."

Romero tapped his fingers on the table. "Come on, Artie. Time's wasting."

Chacon whistled. "You're not going to believe this. The phone is pinging about two miles south of San Lazaro Pueblo. Isn't that near McCabe's property?"

"McCabe *owns* San Lazaro," Romero said. "It's the only privately owned Indian ruin in this part of the country. There's more than a thousand acres surrounding the ruins."

"Well, according to the information we plotted out, the location of the phone is about eight miles west of County Road 55A, which puts it smack dab on the fringes of McCabe's property."

Romero took out his phone and dialed McCabe's number. McCabe answered and Romero started to explain the situation.

"Hold on a second, Rick. I'm driving." He pulled over to the side of the road and parked next to the fence. "After you called me an hour ago, I stopped at the ranch to pick up my gear, so I'm not too far from there."

"The ping from Carlos's cellphone puts him somewhere on the outskirts of your property," Romero said. "Three cell towers have picked up the signal, and Artie triangulated it to within a few feet of where the phone should be."

"Wait a sec, Rick. Got a map here in the glove box." McCabe retrieved a map of the ranch. "Even as long as I've had the ruins, I'm always amazed when something new is out there I don't know about—especially now that I've bought the remaining acreage."

Romero stood up to slip into his windbreaker. He reached for his keys and motioned to Chacon. "Take your time, Tim. We need accuracy on this." He put his hand over the receiver and turned to Chacon. "I'm going to head out there, Artie. Get over to the main office and arrange for a SWAT team to be on call."

McCabe came back on the line. "There's an old dirt road that comes into the back of the ruins and leads to the Galisteo side.

The first mile or so is accessible by passenger car, but once you get to a certain point it becomes pretty rough. It depends on how far in he is." He paused. "Maybe Carlos was looking for a place with a little privacy? People use the boondocks around here all the time to get in a little necking," he said.

Romero walked toward his vehicle, pressing the phone to his ear as he fumbled with the keys. "Hard to say, but I would have thought Carlos had outgrown that. What else is out there, Tim? Any buildings to speak of?"

"There's a couple of old church buildings, mostly in ruins, abandoned about a hundred fifty years ago."

Romero reached through the driver side window for the notepad on the visor and set it on the hood. "How do we get there from the substation?"

"You have to find the back road to my property, so drive about five miles past the Cerrillos turnoff. After you pass Jemimah's place on the left, look for a sign close to the ground that says SR 55C. It will also say 'dead end.' It isn't. That's just to discourage cruisers. Follow the road until it ends. There should be a break in the fence where the gate has fallen in. I'll be waiting there for you. I won't go any farther until we hook up, just in case something shady is going on and there's more than one vehicle out there."

Romero climbed into his cruiser. He tossed the tablet onto the dashboard. "I'm heading out now, Tim. Be there as fast as I can. Keep your fingers crossed."

"Shoot, Rick, if I had a candle out here, I'd light that too."

***

AN HOUR LATER Jemimah was parked in the lot of the east side condo, next to Carlos's car. She switched off the ignition and looked around the complex. Leaning back on the headrest, she closed her eyes. A clap of thunder rolled across the sky. She felt a brisk wind blow through the open passenger-side window. She reached into the backseat for her hoodie and draped it over her shoulders, rolled up the windows and sighed. There was nothing she could do but wait. She mulled over a slew of unanswered questions as the rain began to pelt the windshield. *I sure hope Carlos is all right.* She knew it would destroy Rick if anything happened to his brother. She looked across at the condo and watched the rainwater gush from the roof and form waterfalls through the metal *canales* on the side of the building.

She jumped as thunder and lightning clapped in tandem. With the loud racket, she barely heard her phone and reached for it with both hands. "Rick, what's going on?"

"I don't know anything yet, Jem. We've tracked his phone to the outskirts of McCabe's property in Cerrillos. I'm headed there to meet him."

"Nothing going on here, Rick, other than I'm sitting in the middle of a downpour. Carlos's car is still parked and there's no movement at his condo. I'm taking off right now and will meet you."

"Jemimah. Do me a favor and stay there a while longer. Then go straight home. I'll call you when I know anything."

"All right, but promise me you'll keep in touch, Rick. And be careful."

"I will. I promise."

Chapter Forty-Five

———•———

OUT IN THE open, it was still light, several hours before a slow dissolve into darkness would begin. Carlos's shirt was drenched in sweat. He felt a wave of nausea accompanied by the feeling that the sky was spinning. He had been unconscious in a delirious sleep punctuated by short bursts of lucidity where he realized his dire circumstances. But there was nothing he could do. He was helpless. He had no choice but to remain still, listening for something, anything that would give him a clue as to where he was. A shiver ran through his body.

Dammit, what the hell is going on here?

His ears strained to hear a sound, any sound. There was no traffic noise, nothing to penetrate the quiet. The only sound he could hear was his thoughts clanging up against the inside of his head. Everything around him reeked of old garbage. He wondered if he was still in the same place. He didn't remember being moved, but heck, he didn't remember much of anything.

Carlos felt a sharp pain in his head when he tried to peel open his eyes. He was blindfolded and his hands and feet were bound. It was eerily quiet. Through the edge of the blindfold he saw that it was still daylight. His body ached. He was so disoriented, angry, and frustrated that he couldn't move. *Where the hell am I? Sonofabitch! She must have put something in my drink.* Before he could muster up another thought, his eyes closed and he passed out again.

He awoke with a start and tried to force himself upright, but he sank back to the floor. For a moment he thought he had been dreaming. His mind was fuzzy. The moist ground beneath his face smelled musty. Carlos wasn't sure what to think. *Was this some kind of a joke?* The last thing he remembered was sitting on the grass. They'd been bantering about the possibility of hooking up, and when Carlos realized she was coming on to him, he didn't want to go there. She had smiled sweetly as she handed him the wine. After that everything was blank.

He was suddenly aware that he wasn't alone. "Hey," he hollered. "Who's there? What the hell is going on?"

Silence.

He inhaled deeply and struggled to get free. He felt a cold piece of metal press against his forehead.

"Don't," she said.

"Hey … what the …" he began.

"Shut up, Carlos."

He tried to move. His heart was pounding. He started to protest, but before he could blurt out anything, she'd plastered a piece of tape over his mouth.

"Godammit, Carlos. Shut up already," she said.

He couldn't believe someone her size could have taken him down, let alone dragged him. Maybe he hadn't passed out right away. He wondered if she had just helped him over to this space. He searched his mind for the sequence of events. Things were still hazy. They'd been sitting on the grass near a rocky ledge. She handed him a wine cooler. In the middle of a sentence he stood up to leave, when he felt dizzy.

"Oops. This is making me a little woozy," he had said.

She held on to his arm. "Probably too much sun." She had

smiled as he felt the sensation of falling. "Here, let's walk over here to that shady spot."

And now Carlos's wrists were securely tied behind his back. He struggled to sit up but she pushed him down. He fell over like he was made of cotton. He fumbled with the tape. Maybe he could loosen it. He felt disoriented and his head hurt. Now he knew for sure she must have drugged him. His eyes closed again. When he awoke he listened for a few minutes. Quiet. He rolled over and felt the cold, hard wall against his side. He thought he heard someone talking, arguing. He strained his ears. He could only make out part of the conversation and then he was out again.

She was on the phone. "I'll explain later. You need to come and help me. Your sister gave me your number." She paused. "It's not that difficult to get here." She gave him directions. "Yes, just come in on the Indian ruins side and walk about half a mile. You'll see the car there."

Carlos woke up again, this time in a fearful mood. He couldn't tell if it was dark or light. He concluded it must be dark inside where he was—not even a firefly to light up the place. He could feel the ties eating into his wrists. He tried without success to wiggle them loose. The mostly dirt floor reeked of old urine and manure. No, more like something decomposing. He could sense someone nearby. *A different smell. Musty. Masculine?* His mind went blank as he saw a momentary flash of light and experienced intense pain in his head.

Chapter Forty-Six

———◆———

ROMERO TURNED OFF Highway 14 onto the dirt road, barely slowing down from forty miles an hour. His cruiser fishtailed. Up ahead he saw a van straddling the middle of the road and coming straight at him. *Sonofabitch.*

He laid on the horn and hollered out the window. "*Cabron pendejo!*" You stupid ass.

The driver of the van pulled his arm away from the girl squeezed up against him and swerved back into his own lane. Romero blazed the siren and continued on. The driver slowed the van to a crawl and then tore ass when he reached the highway—probably surprised to be spared this time.

McCabe was waiting up ahead in a small clearing. He flashed his lights and motioned Romero forward.

Romero parked and exited his vehicle. He ran his hand across the side of his head and readjusted the collar of his jacket.

McCabe walked over and patted him on the shoulder. "Don't worry, son. We'll work this all out. If Carlos is around here somewhere, we'll find him."

Romero reached for his pack of cigarettes, offered one to McCabe. They lit up on the same match. "I can't wrap my brain around whatever's going on here. This is too doggone bizarre," he said.

"Aside from a little stubborn streak, Carlos always seemed pretty level-headed to me," said McCabe.

"Can't disagree with you there. So let's get on it. Did you observe any unusual activity on your way here? Parked cars, anything?"

"Didn't see a thing. Hardly any traffic coming or going."

"So, that place where Detective Chacon triangulated the phone to, where is it?" said Romero.

"That area is a ways up here. We'll have to walk, just in case someone's hanging around. Watch your step."

They walked about fifty yards when a flash of lightning lit up the sky. The clouds swelled into dark gray pillows. The intensity of the rain increased as they inched forward. There had been no forecast for rain, but that wasn't unusual. Desert storms burst forth without a moment's notice, turning into raging gully washers. This was just the beginning.

McCabe raised his voice to be heard over the din. "There's some water rushing toward us, Rick. Get over on the side there."

The rain continued to pelt the area, filling the arroyo and creating a flash flood that came barreling down the wash toward them. Romero watched as the muddy water rushed in their direction, carrying bushes and branches in its wake. He dragged himself up the side of the hill with McCabe close behind.

"Over there, head toward that cave," hollered McCabe. The overhang was just wide enough to keep them from being pounded by the dime-sized hailstones that had erupted from the sky moments before.

"Damn, where the hell did all that come from? Good thing there was still enough light to see what we were in for," Romero said.

McCabe wiped the top of his head with a handkerchief.

"That type of sudden downpour can cause a torrent that will carry a grown man for miles without effort. They don't call them flash floods for nothing."

As quickly as it began, the deluge slowed to a drizzle. Romero glanced around, checking to see if there was any movement. His radio crackled. It was Detective Martinez.

"Romero here. Go ahead."

"Chacon called us in. We just pulled onto the dirt road. Had to wait the storm out. Where are you guys? I can see your vehicles up ahead."

"About a hundred yards north of McCabe's Hummer," Romero said. "We're standing under an overhang, out of the rain. I imagine the road's kind of slick by now, so take it easy."

Martinez spotted his comrades and motioned for his sidekick to move forward. The four gathered in a small clearing surrounded by juniper bushes. Romero gave them an update on the situation.

"Detective Chacon is headed this way with the SWAT team. I'll give them directions. They'll have no trouble finding us," said Martinez.

It was almost sunset as Romero gathered his men around him and filled them in. He checked his phone for the time. Six thirty p.m. Although the overcast skies made it appear later, it would be a while before it was pitch-black outside.

He spread out a map on one of the vehicles, pointed at an area and circled it with his finger. "McCabe here says we're headed over some rough terrain. Even though it's flat in most places, there are arroyos and ledges that make it a difficult hike, especially once it gets dark. The place we're thinking Carlos is being held is an old church building abandoned over a century ago, so we're not sure what to expect. Beyond that, we don't know anything."

The gravelly ground crunched under their feet. Romero motioned for them to spread out. McCabe stayed next to him.

The group slowly arrived at the area where McCabe indicated

there would be an ancient convent building. About a quarter mile away they spotted a red Mazda parked out in the open. Martinez ran it through DMV and reported it was registered to Annae Rivers.

"That's my brother's girlfriend, or at least she was up to a week ago. I hadn't talked to him since," Romero said.

"That's the type of vehicle Bart Wolfe said Carlos was standing next to while he was talking to a woman," said McCabe.

Lying low, McCabe and Martinez moved slowly toward the car. The windows were open and the doors were unlocked. The interior was drenched from the rain. A cellphone lay in the middle of the backseat, along with an empty Coke can and a pack of cigarettes that he knew to be Carlos's brand.

McCabe picked up the phone, looked at the screen, and waved at Romero. "That's gotta be Carlos's cellphone," he said. "Bunch of missed calls from your number and looks like the battery's almost dead."

Romero slipped the phone into his pocket. "With any kind of luck, it will turn out that Carlos had been on a bender and is all right." He knew better. Carlos never did anything half-assed. Added to that, he assumed Carlos rarely drank alcohol because of the terms of his probation agreement. But then again, most people couldn't party without alcohol. He began to wonder if he really knew his brother.

The ground became slippery as the caliche surface turned into red clay. It made for difficult walking.

"Man, what is this stuff? It's like walking through a mud bog," Martinez said.

McCabe flicked a bug from his arm. "It is red clay. The whole area's covered with it. The Indians used to gather it to make pottery. Probably still do."

Romero turned to see Detective Chacon and his crew closing in on them. He waited for them to catch up, and as the group gathered, McCabe discussed the plan. Each passing moment weighed heavily on Romero's shoulders.

"We don't know what we're up against. So let's split up in two groups. That way we can approach the area from each side. We have to assume that whoever is with him is probably armed. It's impossible to predict what's going to happen."

He turned to Chacon. "No shots fired unless absolutely necessary. Like I said, this could be something completely innocent and we don't want anyone getting hurt."

"Got it, boss," he said. "Martinez, you take the team and go in that direction. I'll stick with McCabe and Romero and go in the other."

McCabe looked at Romero. "If Carlos is where I think he is, there's only one way in. We're going to need the element of surprise on our side."

"You figure we can sneak up from both sides?" Romero said.

"The way I see it, yes." McCabe sketched a diagram on a sandy patch of ground. "Here's the building, or what's left of it. Even though it's fallen apart over the last century, the walls that are left are fairly tall. There are no windows, just a couple of clerestory openings toward the top. Most of the roof is gone. This was a convent, not a church, so there are a couple of small cubbyholes still intact, the largest toward the front."

Chacon knelt at the edge of the drawing. "Is there something that functions as a door?" he said.

McCabe shifted. "No," he said. "Back in the '80s the doors and ceiling beams were salvaged and used to build one of those pricey Santa Fe homes on the east side. There's just a wide opening with most of the room exposed. Looks pretty much like a big cave, as I recall."

"So the front is the only way in," Chacon said.

McCabe drew more lines in the sand and then stood up and pointed to a peak about a quarter mile away. "See that hill? The convent was built up against it, so the lower part of the building is on a different level. Someone could probably stand there and look into the room below. That might be one side we can approach it from. If he's not on that side, then the only way in is through the front."

Romero stood up and dusted his pant legs. "Let's get going here. Take it slow and easy, guys."

As they walked, a thin trail became visible. McCabe pointed up ahead. "There's only one place this leads to. A couple of hundred years ago there was an old church on the corner of the property. It was first destroyed during the pueblo revolt in 1680, but then rebuilt as a convent in the 1800s when raiding Indians were less of a problem. It was abandoned at the turn of the century. Most of the stone has been hauled off over the years for those houses I mentioned in Santa Fe. There's an old stone quarry about ten miles east of here where the rock probably originated."

Artie Chacon stared at McCabe. "*Eholay*, Tim. Do we really need a history lesson right now? Who gives a crack about rocks, anyway?"

"Sorry. Talking takes my mind off wondering what the hell's up with Carlos. We need to get off this main trail. We're sitting targets if anyone is up ahead watching us," McCabe said.

The convent had been built as an outbuilding of the church over 150 years before. The hope had been that the nuns could reach the outlying pueblos and teach catechism to young natives. Now a weathered building overgrown with weeds and high grasses, it had long been abandoned, and appeared dry and barren. Much like the mood of the detectives present.

Since they avoided the dirt road, their only path became a grueling hike over rocky terrain, now slick from the rain. Massive natural rock formations lined the area, some almost impassable. The two groups split up and circled around the perimeter, managing to cover only a few yards at a time.

McCabe stopped and motioned to Romero. "There it is up ahead." A high-walled dilapidated stone building loomed in the distance.

Since they were in an area of mountainous desert, there were no wooded areas to serve as cover. Romero was glad Jemimah wasn't along for the search. He would have overridden that request. He signaled for the group to surround the area.

"Tim, where would the entrance be?" he said.

McCabe drew a sketch in the muddy ground while the clouds overhead dissipated and the sun began to slide behind the Ortiz Mountains. It wasn't long before cooler temperatures crept in to herald the sunset.

They approached the abandoned building from the rear, weapons drawn. The SWAT team and Detective Martinez waved from up ahead. Romero could feel his heart crank up. Random thoughts of Carlos's potential condition blazed through his mind. Each step forward was slow, calculated. *Hold on, Carlos.*

"With all the racket that storm generated, maybe we can catch them off guard," McCabe whispered.

Romero nodded. "We can only hope." He remembered the time Carlos decided to walk home from school by himself. There was a bully who hung around by the bridge across Alameda Street, in the direct path of the way home. Carlos saw him, and in order to avoid a confrontation, snuck under the bridge. When he failed to show up by dinnertime, Romero went out looking. He found him tied up underneath the bridge, a bandana secured over his mouth, his eyes tinged with fear.

Romero was worried. He wanted to believe his brother was all right, but how many times could they tempt the Fates? Carlos had straddled on the edges of disaster since childhood. As the group crept forward, the only sound he could hear was the whisper of the wind gently threading through the low slung junipers. It was getting darker as they inched forward, weapons in hand. Up ahead he could make out a set of tire tracks.

Romero turned to McCabe, about to say something. Just then the unmistakable sound of a gunshot thundered through the air.

Chapter Forty-Seven

———◆———

W ITH DARKNESS HAVING set in, Jemimah started up the engine and headed home. She continued to check her phone as she drove along the highway. There were no texts or messages. She knew there was cellphone service in the vicinity where Romero was initially, but not so sure about the remote area he described. She had ridden her horse through there a number of times. He had promised to call her, and she'd just have to trust him to do that. She just hoped nothing had gone wrong.

She parked her Toyota in the driveway and walked toward her front door. In her haste to drive to Carlos's place, she had forgotten to set the alarm or the timer on the lights. She fumbled with her keys. It was barely seven, but the cloud cover darkened the sky, providing little light for her to make it to the front door. She could hear Molly barking inside, waiting to rush out into the bushes and do her business after two long hours inside the house.

There was nothing on the news channel about anything going on in the immediate area, so Jemimah knew whatever Romero had encountered was not newsworthy or had not become general knowledge. She wasn't sure what to do with herself. She wasn't really hungry and didn't want to start preparing a meal she'd have to abandon if he called. She scoured the refrigerator, pulled out a half-eaten pizza, and stuck it in the microwave. It appeared as though it was going to be a long night.

***

IT WAS EERILY dark in the room with only a flickering candle on top of a beer can as illumination. Only moments before, Detective Martinez and two members of the SWAT team had stormed the building. The woman screamed and fired the pistol, hitting Carlos. Martinez and his men cautiously moved toward her. She pointed the gun directly at them.

"Get out of here," she screamed.

"Ma'am, drop the gun. Everything's all right here," said Detective Martinez.

She continued to point the weapon toward them. "No, no. You don't understand. This man hurt me. He tried to kill me."

Carlos lay in a heap, his hands tied behind his back. Martinez doubted he had been any threat to her. However, he knew the best way to disarm her would be to let her think he agreed with her.

"We're here now, ma'am. Let us take care of it. We'll get this jerk arrested and off to jail. Now please, drop your weapon. I'm going to move toward you and you can hand it to me."

She stopped and looked at him. Her nostrils flared. "Go away!" she screamed.

Martinez took two cautious steps. He thought he recognized that voice. *Who was she*? She pointed the gun toward him. The officer behind him readied his weapon. Martinez leaped forward to tackle her. The officer fired. She screamed again and fell to the ground.

Romero, Chacon, and McCabe reached the entrance as the second rounds of shots were fired. McCabe reached Carlos first and Romero rushed to assist the woman lying in a heap next to him. He knelt down and touched her blood-soaked hair.

His jaw dropped as he gently turned her head in his direction. "Oh, Jeezus ... this can't be."

It was his ex-wife, Julie.

Chapter Forty-Eight

———•———

REELING FROM THE momentary shock of the events unfolding before him, Romero rushed to his brother. Carlos was on the ground, bleeding from a chest wound, as McCabe wrestled with the ties that bound him. Romero panicked as he saw his brother lying still. He knelt next to him, pulled out his pocket knife and helped McCabe cut the cords around his hands and feet. He tossed his keys in Chacon's direction.

"Artie, get my cruiser over here, *pronto!*"

Artie complied and took off running toward the area where the vehicles were parked. It was getting dark as he tore over the landscape. In the moonlight, he could see the outline of the cruiser up ahead. He jumped in, started it up, and maneuvered it toward the site. Martinez directed him as he backed it up as close as he could to the entrance.

Romero turned to McCabe. "Tim, help me get Carlos into the open. We need to get him out of here."

McCabe hesitated. "Christ almighty, Rick. Do you think we should move him? It might be too dangerous. We don't know what his injuries are."

Romero pulled himself up and looked at McCabe. "Got no other choice, Tim. He might bleed to death by the time the EMTs get here."

As a makeshift gurney, Romero arranged a blanket under Carlos. Together they lifted him off the ground. He groaned and dropped his head to the side.

"Easy, Carlos, we're going to get you to the hospital," Romero soothed. He wasn't sure if his brother could hear him.

They carried Carlos to the waiting vehicle and gently lifted him onto the backseat. McCabe climbed in and sat next to him. Romero grabbed another blanket from the back and handed it to McCabe, who wrapped it around Carlos. Romero pulled himself up into the driver seat. As he cranked up the engine, he rolled down the passenger window and motioned to Detective Martinez.

"Floyd, radio in and tell dispatch I'll be headed down Highway 14 with one of the shooting victims. Tell them I'll hook up with one of the ambulances somewhere near the San Marcos Café. I'll have all the lights going. Shouldn't be too hard to spot. They can pick the woman up. I can't take responsibility for moving her, but I can for my brother."

As he eased the police cruiser forward, Romero drove carefully over the uneven terrain of the rutted road. Every jar and jolt of the vehicle caused Carlos to emit a groan. Romero glanced up at the rearview mirror. McCabe was stretched across the backseat with Carlos cradled in his arms. He reached over and snapped open the First Aid kit strapped under the glove box, grabbed a handful of gauze squares and handed them to McCabe.

McCabe pressed the pads into Carlos's chest. He looked at Romero. "I'm getting worried here, Rick. His breathing's pretty shallow and he's lost a lot of blood." He placed his fingers on Carlos's neck. "Pulse is very weak."

Romero kept his eyes glued to the road as he pulled onto the highway. He gunned the engine, his hands clammy as he death-gripped the steering wheel.

"Keep putting pressure on the wound, Tim. The ambulance can't be that far out. We'll drive all the way to the hospital if we have to. We made the right decision to get moving."

McCabe stroked Carlos's forehead. "Hang on, son. You're going to be all right," he said, tightening his hold as the vehicle swerved to miss the carcass of an animal in the road.

Romero pushed the cruiser to the limit. The whine of the siren filled the early evening hour. He drove at ninety miles an hour for the next ten minutes past the Garden of the Gods. Up ahead he spotted the lights of two emergency vehicles coming straight at him. He flashed his headlights and pulled over to the side of the road. One ambulance slowed down enough to make a U-turn and pulled in next to Romero as the other continued on.

Two EMTs alighted their vehicle and opened the rear door. Grabbing a gurney, they headed toward the cruiser. Working at lightning speed, they transferred Carlos to the gurney, took his vitals, and hooked him up to an IV. Romero and McCabe hovered nearby, exchanging anguished looks. Once Carlos was secure in the ambulance, Romero handed his keys to McCabe.

"Meet us at the hospital, Tim. I'm going to ride in the ambulance with Carlos."

The trip to St. Vincent's Hospital took the ambulance a long twenty-five minutes cruising at top speed. Upon arrival, the tech drove up the back ramp to the ER entrance, where they were met by two RNs and an orderly. Romero felt a panic surge through his body as he stepped out of the ambulance. He held Carlos's hand and ran alongside the gurney as the orderly pushed it through the ER doors. Carlos barely moved. His skin had a gray pallor and his eye sockets were sunken. He looked more dead than alive.

Every available seat in the emergency room wait area was occupied. An ongoing flu epidemic had incapacitated a section of the population of Santa Fe. This H1N1 flu wasn't particular who it dragged down. Patients coughed and hacked noisily and waited to be examined, looking up in hopeful anticipation each time a nurse or orderly came into the waiting room to summon the next one to be seen. The police entourage accompanying Carlos and the next ambulance would seriously slow down the line.

The attending physician was well known in police circles. He had patched up more cuts, scrapes, and bullet holes suffered by officers in the line of duty than any other doctor—and that included the injuries of Romero and McCabe. Dr. Amos Hillyer was in his mid-sixties, tall and distinguished. He shook Romero's hand.

"What brings you here, Detective ... working a case?" he said.

Romero shook his head and related details of the shooting.

The ER staff transferred Carlos from the gurney to a bed. They hooked him up to a series of machines, all intended to monitor his vitals. The bed was wheeled down a long hallway into the trauma section of the ER, an eight-by-ten room equipped with multiple life-saving devices. The staff hovered around the nurses' station waiting to take action.

Carlos lay on the bed, unresponsive. He heard a voice somewhere off in the distance. He felt as though he was floating on a cloud.

"Mr. Romero, Carlos, can you hear me?" the voice said.

Carlos tried to nod but his head felt weighted down. He couldn't tell if his eyes were open. It was dark. *Where was he*? He felt his heart rev up and then everything went black.

"Mr. Romero," the voice said once again. "Squeeze my hand if you can hear me". There was no response. The ER physician examined him and glanced up at the nurse.

"His respiratory functions have dropped. Get the surgeon on call in here, stat. There seems to be an obstruction in his trachea. We need to do an endotracheal intubation."

The surgical nurse stepped forward. "Do we have a next of kin in here?"

Detective Romero stepped forward. "I'm his brother," he said.

"We're going to need you to sign authorization papers, Mr. Romero," she said. "He needs immediate surgery to get that bullet out. He's having additional problems caused by the bleeding, and on top of everything else, his breathing is labored."

Romero leaned forward and grabbed his brother's hand. "Hang in there, Carlos. You're going to be all right." He moved aside while the medical techs prepared to transport him to the surgical ward.

Romero met with the surgeon. "What's going on, Doctor? Is my brother going to be all right?"

"We'll do our best. From what I can see the bullet is loosely lodged near the collarbone. This is not the main concern. A chest X-ray shows that as it became dislodged, it caused his lungs to collapse and the trachea to shift within the chest."

Romero wiped his forehead. "How serious is this?" he said.

The surgeon put his hand on Romero's arm. "To be honest, this could be a life and death situation, but we've caught it in time. We'll get in there and see what's going on. I'll find you when everything's done."

FIFTEEN MINUTES LATER Carlos saw the bright ceiling lights spinning past him at breakneck speed. As the lights went out he felt himself drifting away then propelled through the air, coming to rest against a block wall.

The nurse directed Romero to the ICU waiting room. He sat down in the recliner and leaned his head back. He was exhausted. He closed his eyes. The events of the day zipped through his mind, and he realized he hadn't given a moment's thought to Julie. *What the hell had happened there?* He dialed Jemimah's number. He'd never needed her as much as he did at this moment.

Chapter Forty-Nine

———◆———

JEMIMAH PACED THE floor most of the night waiting for Rick to call. She drank an entire pot of coffee trying to stay awake, imagining all sorts of scenarios relating to Carlos. Long after midnight she dozed off, a fitful few hours' sleep filled with nightmares.

It was very early Saturday morning when the phone rang with an update. Exhausted, she splashed some cold water on her face, smoothed back her hair, grabbed her keys from the hook near the door, and dashed out to St. Vincent's Hospital, where Romero's brother was recovering from surgery. Aside from that, Romero had told her nothing else.

While he waited for Jemimah to arrive and for any word from the doctors, Romero sat in the waiting room, browsing through the messages on his iPhone. He sent a quick message to Tim McCabe to fill him in. He Googled the daily newspaper site. The early morning headlines read "Police officer's ex-wife involved in attempted murder." He skimmed down the article, filled with sensational language to make the story more than it was. Quite honestly, even he wasn't sure what had happened.

Nevertheless, this would be the version consumed come morning by the community at large.

He looked up to see Jemimah hurrying toward him. Before he could speak, she leaned over and hugged him, then thumped down in the chair next to him, still holding his hand.

"Oh my God, Rick. What happened? Is Carlos all right?" she said. "I was a complete wreck."

He shrugged. "Not at this moment, but hopefully he will be. He hasn't regained consciousness long enough for me to talk to him."

"This is all so surreal," she said. "Do you have any idea what started it? Where was he?"

Jemimah covered her mouth as Romero filled in the details from the last time he had spoken to her up until they'd found Carlos. "By the time we stormed the place, Julie had already fired a shot at Carlos and another one at Detective Martinez," he said.

"*Julie*? You mean *ex-wife* Julie? I don't understand," she said.

"You and me both. I had been wondering what the hell she was up to, and now we know. We're going to have to do a lot of digging to get the full story here." Romero paused. "All we have right now are bits and pieces here and there. In a few days, Carlos should be well enough to fill in the blanks. At least I hope he will."

"I've been sitting on my thumbs since you called to tell me he was missing," she said. "I sat at his place, even after the rainstorm subsided, praying that by some miracle he would show up. Every car that drove into the lot got me shaking."

He squeezed her hand. "All hell broke loose after that and I couldn't take time to get back to you," he said. "Things started moving too fast."

"What about the girlfriend, Annae? I've been looking at her as a possible suspect in the mariachi homicide."

Romero met her gaze. "Carlos's girlfriend? Seriously?"

"Well, this isn't the place to review the case, but I imagine that initially you suspected she had something to do with Carlos going missing."

He wearily brushed his hair back from his face. "In a way I did, but seeing it was her red Mazda that was at the scene when we got there confirmed that she might be involved. I was hoping this woman wouldn't be crazy enough to let things get out of control."

"So Carlos's girlfriend wasn't anywhere around there?" she said.

"All I saw was a woman crumpled up on the floor who had been shot a few moments before after she fired at Detective Martinez. Let me tell you … when I saw it was Julie lying there, I didn't know what the hell to think. "

"I'm thinking we need to call Annae in for an interview," Jemimah said.

Romero leaned forward to touch her face. "Sweet cheeks, we're going to have to sort that out along with everything else. There's some connection, but my mind's in such a fog right now I can't put anything into perspective."

She squeezed his hand. "When things settle down, I'll go back and review the files. There's little question in my mind that she's involved somehow in the Sanchez homicide."

He nodded. "I thought for sure she was responsible for Carlos going missing. Have to rethink that one too."

"I know," she said, "there's a lot more than meets the eye here. Just a jumble of circumstances and coincidences. I need a little time to sift through the maze and see what comes out at the end."

IT WAS MID-AFTERNOON, and they were deep in conversation when Dr. Hillyer motioned from the hallway. Romero noted the worried look on his face. The doctor walked over to them, and Romero stood as he approached and introduced Jemimah.

"Your brother is coming out of the anesthesia. Might be a good idea for you to be there when he does. His body's had quite a shock," the doctor said, as the couple followed him to the ICU check-in and waited.

Meanwhile, through a door not far beyond them, the nurse checked Carlos's vitals.

He awoke with a start. His vision was cloudy and pain tore through his body as fear gripped him once again.

"Carlos, can you hear me?"

He slowly opened his eyes. "Whoa, someone please stop the room from spinning," he mumbled.

"Carlos," the voice repeated. He groaned in pain as he attempted to roll onto his side. He tossed the blanket aside.

"How are you feeling, Carlos?"

"Like a friggin' freight train just ran over me. Where am I? Where's my clothes?"

Dr. Hillyer turned to the nurse. "Administer 3cc of Demerol. That should help with the pain."

The doctor leaned over and looked Carlos squarely in the eye. "Relax, take it easy. You're in the hospital. We had to perform a couple of surgical procedures on you, but you're coming along nicely," he said.

Carlos tried to sit up. "What happened to me?" he said.

"You were brought in about twenty hours ago. We had to remove a bullet from your chest. You're a lucky man, Carlos. Another inch or two and you would have been a goner. Your brother is here and as soon as I'm finished bringing him up to speed, he'll be back here to see you."

Carlos leaned back against the pillows, relaxing as the medicine took effect.

Romero waited in anticipation as the doctor came toward them. "How's he doing, Doc?"

"He's coming along. As you know, we were able to remove the bullet, but if you had waited ten more minutes to get him here, we might not have been so lucky. His lungs collapsed right before surgery, and that could have been disastrous."

Romero smoothed the top of his head. "Thank God. I was

worried we were doing more harm than good by transporting him by car. I knew it was going to take the ambulance a while to get there. We were pretty far out in the boonies."

"That might be what saved his life," said Dr. Hillyer.

Jemimah hung on to Romero's arm. "So is he going to be all right?"

"He's not out of the woods yet," the doctor said. "He's having some localized pain and discomfort, which is normal in cases like this, but the wound should heal nicely in a couple of weeks. Bullet wounds can be pretty dirty. We had to give him a tetanus shot. The dressing should stay on for another day and then we'll let it heal from the inside out. I'll have my nurse call you for a follow-up. In the meantime, he's going to be our guest for a few days, maybe even a week. You probably should see him now. Don't want him to worry any more than necessary."

Romero paused. "One more question, Doc. The woman who was brought in the second ambulance, can you tell me how she's doing?"

Dr. Hillyer checked his notes. "As far as I can tell, she had just a surface wound to the forehead where the bullet zinged her."

He looked at Jemimah and breathed a sigh of relief. "I thought she was dead. So much blood."

"The bullet hit a small artery. Caused her to bleed more than usual. We cleaned the wound up, gave her a transfusion and sewed her up," he said.

"So she's going to recover?"

"In essence, yes, but I understand she's under house arrest. Since you're a police officer, I'm sure you can go in and talk to her."

Romero waved his hand. "No thanks, Doc. I'm sure there's going to be ample time for that."

"I'll be checking on your brother before my shift is up. I'll let you know if there's any change then," said Dr. Hillyer, shaking both their hands.

At the desk, the nurse in charge indicated that because of his condition, Carlos could only have one visitor at a time.

"Let me just wait for you, Rick," Jemimah said. "I'm sure it's not going to be easy on either of you. You can come back to the waiting room and get me when you're ready."

He kissed her on the cheek.

The nurse escorted him to a corner section where he craned his neck to peer around the curtain. Carlos was connected to a bevy of machines, all whirring and beeping to their own rhythm.

"Hey, Brother. How's it going?" he said.

Carlos shifted in the bed. His eyes were wide. Still woozy from the anesthesia, he blinked, trying to focus. "Rick, what the hell happened? My chest feels like I got hit by a torpedo."

Romero squeezed his shoulder. "*Shhh.* Try not to talk, Carlos. They've got you sedated. You should be cozying off to sleep, getting started on healing up so you can go home."

Carlos reached out and grabbed his arm. "Rick, I don't remember what happened. How did I get here?"

"Ambulance brought you. You were way out on the south end of McCabe's property in Cerrillos. You hooked up with the wrong crowd, so we had to call out the militia to get you out safely."

He forced a weak smile. "Seriously, Rick. Am I going to be all right?

Romero saw tears welling up in his brother's eyes. He heard his own voice crack.

"Hey, relax, little brother. The Doc said you're going to recover from this just fine, and before you know it you'll be good as new."

"All I can remember is sitting on the grass talking to Julie," he said.

"How'd you manage to hook up with that loony?" Romero joked. "She's only been back in Santa Fe for a month and has already caused enough trouble to last a year."

"Ran into her a couple of nights ago at the Mine Shaft Tavern in Madrid. Apparently you really pissed her off. What was that about?"

"Not today, Carlos. There's plenty of time to talk about that. Right now you need to heal up, and when you get out of here, you're coming home with me. I'll tell you all about it then. Jemimah's waiting to see you. All right if I bring her in?"

Carlos's face brightened. "Maybe we can get that pretty girlfriend of yours to be Nurse Betty," he said. "I'm sure she'll be great company."

Romero could tell his brother was already on the mend.

LATER IN THE day, Dr. Hillyer stopped by to talk to Romero.

"Is everything all right?" he said.

"I'm concerned about your brother's ability to understand the seriousness of his injuries," Dr. Hillyer replied. "Will there be someone at home to keep him down so he won't try to move around? He's ready to gather up his belongings and go home. We're not ready to let that happen just yet."

Romero smiled. "It's a Romero thing, Doctor. Hard to keep this family down."

"How so?"

"I'll give you a quick example," Romero said. "In the mid-1950s, my great uncle Tio Genaro suffered frostbite on his feet after he walked from Los Alamos to Santa Fe during a snowstorm in the middle of the night. He arrived home half frozen and doctors had to amputate about half his toes. My grandmother said the next weekend he was out dancing at the local dance hall."

Dr. Hillyer grinned. "I see. Sounds like a tough bunch of menfolk. In any event, I'll leave it up to you to keep him corralled until we release him for light movement. That should take about ten days."

"We'll do our best," Romero said. For the rest of the day and Sunday, he and Jemimah took turns alternating visits to Carlos's room.

Chapter Fifty

———•———

BY NOON ON Monday, Jemimah was at her desk, deep in thought. The events of the previous days had her rattled, but she needed to get back to work. The case file in front of her had become a blur. She looked up as Katie stepped into her office.

"There's someone to see you, Dr. Hodge," she said.

Jemimah glanced in her direction, momentarily unfocused. "Who is it, Katie? I'm in the middle of something. Do they have an appointment?" She tapped the screen of her phone. "I don't see anything on my calendar."

"His name is Karl Rivers. He says he's related to Annae Rivers, Carlos's girlfriend," Katie said.

"Really? That's a surprise. Send him in."

The man who followed Katie in was wearing plaid Bermuda shorts and a Disneyland t-shirt. His oversized canvas hat made him appear to be on a safari in the middle of a jungle, far away from the deserts of New Mexico.

She introduced herself. "Have a seat, Mr. Rivers. Tell me how I can help you," she said.

He slipped off his hat and held it between his knees. "I'm

here about my niece, Annae Rivers. I was concerned she might be in some kind of trouble," he said.

Jemimah looked across at him. "May I ask where you heard that?"

"Well, my wife and I have been visiting friends in Albuquerque. Yesterday we hopped on the Roadrunner train into Santa Fe to do some sightseeing. Sure is pretty around here. Real different than Denver."

She leaned forward attentively. "Yes, it is a pleasant ride, isn't it?"

"Yes, ma'am. We checked into the Hilton Hotel and after dinner I was browsing through a newspaper that must have been in the desk drawer for a while. I bumped into an article on the front page and almost fell out of bed."

Confused, she asked, "And what article was that, Mr. Rivers."

"It was about this musician who was found dead. Toward the end, the reporter included quotes from friends as they came out of the funeral home. Along with several other women, Annae was quoted as saying she had dated him. They didn't give a last name, but I doubt there's another person by that name. I read somewhere that the main suspects in a murder are usually the wife or the girlfriend."

Jemimah smiled. "That's not always the case, but go on."

"Well, there was a computer in the room, so I logged on to the county sheriff's website and looked for more information. Didn't find anything, so I thought I'd come to see if I could discover something for myself."

"You're sure that's who this person is," she said.

"Yes. That definitely has to be my late brother's stepdaughter— my niece."

She offered him coffee. He waved his hand. She got up and poured a cup for herself, remaining quiet as she stirred in the cream. "What can you tell me about her?" she said, setting the cup down on the desk.

"Not a heck of a lot. I haven't seen her for a long, long time.

Didn't know she was in this area. But those two, they acted like they were raised by wolves."

She tilted her head. "*Those* two?"

"Yes, she has a stepbrother."

She scribbled in her tablet. "Can you give me his name?"

"Samuel, but I think he preferred to be called Sammy," he said.

"Do you know where he lives?"

"As I mentioned, we haven't seen hide nor hair of them for a long time, but knowing how close they were, I figured maybe they'd be together."

"You said they acted like they were raised by wolves. What did you mean by that?"

"That's about the best description I can come up with. No manners. Independent. Did whatever the hell they wanted to once they became teenagers."

"Where were their parents?" she said.

"These two kids came from completely opposite backgrounds."

Jemimah took a sip of her coffee. "How so?"

"From the time she came into my brother's life, she seemed to look at everything through the proverbial rose-colored glasses. Peace, love, and harmony. Far as I knew, she grew up in some free-love situation where everyone walked around barefoot and naked, sharing food and everything else."

"What did they do after that?"

"Her mother and some doper boyfriend decided to head to South America to score drugs to resell in the States, so she dragged the kid along. After a few months, she grew tired of having the girl around and sent her to the grandmother in New Orleans. These folks were throwbacks to the seventies. A lot of sex, drugs, and rock 'n' roll all rolled up in flower power. My brother told me that family was beyond dysfunctional. Consequently, that young lady didn't have much of a grasp on reality. She's a poor judge of character, gravitating toward people beyond her means, and dealing poorly with any kind of rejection. She had virtually no friends, other than Sammy."

Jemimah nodded. "So when did Annae's mother hook up with your brother?"

"After six months in Columbia, the boyfriend dumped her. She picked up the kid and headed toward the Southwest. My brother had been a hard-working man all his life. He had a bit of money saved and bought a couple of acres in Colorado. She showed up on his doorstep one day with the kid in tow. Car had broken down about a mile up the road. Truth was, they were broke, hungry, and needed gas," he said.

"Did your brother help her?"

The man clasped his hands. "At first I guess he felt sorry for her. Fixed them up at one of the local churches where they help the homeless. Before we knew it, they were doing church work together, you know, participating in the fundraising, teaching Bible school and all that stuff."

Jemimah took her time asking questions, but she wondered what useful information this man could provide. "How about his son?"

Rivers fiddled with the brim of his hat. "Sammy wasn't really my brother's biological son. Belonged to an ex-girlfriend who abandoned the kid, so he took him in and raised him as his own. He didn't have the heart to give him up."

She had filled a page with notes and flipped her tablet to the next page. "How did this new group get along—two adults and two teens?

He hesitated for a moment. "I guess you'll find all this out eventually. The boy had been in trouble since my brother took him in. Always pilfering or staying out late, drinking and such. But being a good Christian man, my brother continued to work with him. The kid was a real disciplinary problem. I'm not saying my brother was perfect, especially after he took to drinking, but he did his best. I could see he was fighting a losing battle with the boy."

"How did he get along with the daughter?" Jemimah said.

"Oh, it seems that early on he took a real fancy to her. He tried to be a father figure in her life. She was quiet as a church mouse. Did everything that lazy woman should have been doing. Kept the house clean, laundry folded, helped with the meals. She kept to herself, but I could see she was like an explosion waiting to happen. Then, once those kids put their heads together, for whatever reason they began to dislike him, no matter how hard he tried. I guess he turned to drinking to deal with it. He had never been more than a social drinker, but this new lady was a well-seasoned party girl, lots of booze and pot. Never a dull moment."

Jemimah paused. "What happened to the church part?"

He shifted in his chair. "I think maybe she used that to get her claws in him. They still kept that up, but they also spent a lot of time at the local bar most nights, knocking back a few."

She ran a pencil down her notes. "You mentioned they were both deceased. What's the story there?"

His voice cracked a little. "My brother and his wife were killed, but no one's sure precisely when. Him in a hunting accident and her in an apparent home invasion. A passing hunter found his body in a small clearing surrounded by deep brush and tall pines." He turned his head and wiped a tear from his eye. "He was wearing a dark brown camo jacket and someone had mistaken him for a deer, or maybe a ricochet bullet got him."

"And the wife?" Jemimah said gently.

"The state troopers came to notify the family, pounded on the door for a while and got no answer. One of the neighbors said he hadn't seen her for a few days and thought she was out of town, but her car was parked in the garage. They pushed in the back door and found her body in the living room. She had been dead for about a week, far as they could tell. Oddest thing you ever saw, them both being killed around the same time. Crime was never solved. We buried them and just picked up and went about our business."

"Do you happen to remember what kind of weapon he was shot with?" she said.

"Coroner ruled it a hunting accident, so the police records might indicate that. Some kind of rifle. As I recall, she was shot with a revolver. The bizarre thing about it is that she was found with her hand gripping a vodka bottle, as if she was pouring a drink."

Jemimah made a note to check what type of weapon the coroner determined was used to kill Sanchez. "Is there anything else you can add to that, Mr. Rivers?"

He took a deep breath and blew it out. "None other than I know in my heart that little son of a bitch killed my brother. I can't prove it, but I know he did. It was just a matter of time before something like this happened. I'm guessin' that kid did her in too. He never liked being around that woman when she was drunk." Jemimah noticed his hands clutching the arms of the chair.

"And the girl?" she said.

"She was away at college, we thought. But neither of them showed up at the services. Don't know if they even knew. I was left to clean up the mess. My wife and I gave them a decent burial. Good thing my brother hadn't transferred title to the house." He leaned his head back. "Now let me ask you a question, if I may. Can you tell me if this girl has gotten herself into any trouble?"

Jemimah stood. "There's not a lot I can tell you, other than what you read in the newspaper. We're in the middle of a homicide investigation, involving a man whose body was found out in the desert. She had dated him sometime in the past."

"Do you think she had anything to do with it?" he said, his eyes wide.

"At the moment we haven't formed any conclusions," Jemimah said, "but we'd like an opportunity to question her. She's been avoiding police so far."

Rivers had a strained look on his face. "She doesn't know we're in town. Maybe if you have an address for her I can leave a note at her place."

Jemimah hesitated. "I guess there's no harm in that. I believe there's an address for her somewhere in the file." She reached for the phone and buzzed Katie, who returned after a few minutes with a slip of paper.

"If she does contact you, I'd appreciate your getting in touch with me," Jemimah said. "Thank you for taking the time to come in. You've been a great help in filling in some of the blanks." She reached out to shake his hand. "My assistant will see you out."

She returned to her desk and scribbled a series of notes on the yellow pad. *Motivated by money; insatiable need for attention; bipolar, schizo, what? Suffering from delusions? Trivializes trauma; personality disorder? Brother easy to manipulate.* The profile on Annae Rivers was starting to fall into place. Jemimah thought about the stepbrother and imagined that he was vulnerable to Annae in more ways than one could guess. It seemed that in a way she had stolen his life. As a stepsister, she was not off limits; there were no rules about his falling in love with her. Considering that she was enamored with Eduardo Sanchez and then Carlos, and became furious if they rejected or even crossed her, she was apparently the one who needed to be in control in all of her relationships—the one instigating the breakup. But Jemimah knew that didn't prove she was capable of murder.

Chapter Fifty-One

———◆———

ONCE THE DUST settled around his brother's shooting, Detective Romero was back at work catching up. After meeting with his detectives about the backlog of cases, he drove into town to catch a quick lunch with Jemimah. They talked about the case while they waited for the meal to be served.

"What did Detective Martinez have to say", she said.

Romero took a sip of water. "Not much, other than he's been looking into the financial records of our victim," he said.

"Anything interesting pop out at him?"

"It appears that Sanchez was making periodic deposits of about ten grand each in a checking account at Wells Fargo."

"Hmmm. Did they happen to pop into his account after a visit to Mexico?" Jemimah said.

"Hadn't thought about that. What are you mulling around in that pretty head of yours?"

"This might be pushing the edges a little, but I'm thinking maybe Sanchez was getting some kind of kickback," she said.

Romero's eyes widened. "For what?"

"Either smuggling drugs or laundering money," she said.

He paused. "You know, in reviewing my notes, Carmen de la Torre mentioned he returned one of the jackets because the lining had come apart."

"Now see, that makes sense," Jemimah said. "Maybe Sanchez had refused to smuggle the money in for them anymore. After he told Annae, she decided to continue sending it through in his outfits without him knowing."

Romero tapped his fingers on the table. "Hmmm. Martinez said the deposits started sometime in mid-March. Your review of the videos indicated they started dating sometime before Valentine's Day."

"And when did the deposits stop?" she said.

"The last one was about a week or so before the video shows that they'd broken up."

She tapped a few notes into her phone. "She had to be involved. It's too coincidental. She was going to Mexico. He was going to Mexico. There's no indication they ever went together."

"So maybe the lining in the jacket hadn't come apart by itself. Carmen said it couldn't have," he said.

She took a moment then said, "It could have been cut by someone looking for something specific …."

They looked at each other in surprise and both said the same thing. "The girlfriend, maybe?"

They were deep in conversation when the food came. Neither of them looked up.

Jemimah reached into the basket for a frybread and drizzled it with honey. "That's a possibility. But then, you know it's well documented that a person can't make much money running drugs unless he's in the upper echelon."

Romero looked at her. "So what are you thinking?"

"Let's say he's smuggling money. For one hundred grand, ten grand would be a reasonable percentage, don't you think?"

"Wow, I would say so," Romero said. "So if Sanchez made five deposits in the months leading up to his death, that would account for the size of his bankroll. Carmen said he made regular trips to Mexico to order his outfits. Maybe he also made trips she didn't know about."

"Yes, and that's what she probably meant by his 'coming into money,' she said. "He was probably planning to close out his account and move to Mexico. Fifty grand would last a long time in that country, even if he bought a ranch. Last time I heard, you could pick up a thousand-acre spread in Hermosillo for around twenty grand. Not to mention his personal property. If he sold that pricey condo he was living in and all the personal possessions he couldn't take with him, that would add another nice chunk of cash for them to live on."

Romero unfolded the napkin. "For argument's sake, let's say you're right. As I recall, when Carlos was first dating Annae, he mentioned she was in Mexico for about a week. That's when he was walking around with a puppy dog face. So we can assume she was already a player when she introduced Sanchez to her contacts. An attractive woman like her would have little trouble getting past the border guards."

She nodded. "And someone as charming and popular as Sanchez would easily be admitted, especially once they knew he was a well-known musician. You know how Mexicans love their mariachis. He was probably a hero to them, and he might have found a way to cross the border whenever the same guard was on duty."

"Not only that, but Carmen mentioned that he carried photographs and CDS to give out to the guards when he crossed from Juarez to El Paso. We need to explore this link. Since Annae isn't an official suspect, I have to figure out a way to get a warrant to look into her financials. I'll stop by the DA's office before I go back."

Jemimah jotted down a few notes. "Yes, until we have some info on her personal finances and spending habits at the time of the murder, we can't assume anything. I checked with impound and she hasn't bothered to pick her vehicle up after

Julie took off with it. I wonder what's up with that."

Romero lifted an index finger in the air. "*And* we know there was a firearm in her glove box. That certainly shows potential for something suspicious." He looked down at his plate and reached for his fork. "No more shop talk. Let's dig in before lunch break is up."

Jemimah smiled. "Yeah. Kind of hard to eat something this delicious and talk about murder." She smothered a blue corn taco with sour cream and salsa and took a bite.

For the remainder of the meal they talked about Mexican food. "I have to admit I didn't eat anything hot or spicy until I moved to Santa Fe," she said.

"Surely they have Mexican restaurants in Dallas," he said between bites.

"Yes, but after having my first meal here, I would refer to that as *faux food*. San Antonio would be the place to go, but that was a long way from Dallas."

Romero put his hand over hers. "I'm happy to inform you you're not going to run out of options in Santa Fe. I'm sure you've noticed there's a Mexican restaurant every ten blocks."

She laughed. "I, for one, am deliriously happy to hear that."

Chapter Fifty-Two

CONVINCED JEMIMAH HAD made an accurate connection between the slain mariachi, Annae Rivers, and Carlos, he discussed the efficacy of checking into her past with the district attorney and obtained a warrant to examine her records and search her apartment. He met with Detective Chacon to map out a plan and serve the warrant on Rivers. Ten minutes after they drove out of the satellite office, Chacon asked Romero to pull over onto the shoulder.

"There's a cell tower over there that will make it easier to get a connection on my iPad," he said.

Romero pulled out of traffic and pushed the gearshift into park. "You and your gadgets," he said. "What are you after?"

"I'm running Annae Rivers' driver's license through MVD. Need to make sure we're going to the right address. People change residences all the time and don't notify MVD. It's a big pain in the ass to show up to serve a warrant on the wrong person." He tapped a few numbers on the small keyboard. "Got it," he said.

Romero pulled the cruiser back onto the road and headed in a westerly direction. They drove past a row of strip mall businesses that included an AutoZone, an Indian restaurant, and an herb store. Her apartment was on West Agua Fria Street, which translated to "cold water." Romero assumed that at one time in history the Santa Fe River had irrigated farms along the road.

Half an hour later, he pulled into the driveway of an apartment on the corner of a four-plex. Much of the housing on the street was Section Eight—subsidized by the city. The porch light was on and the screen door hung from one hinge. Leaves and debris gathered in the corner. He checked his weapon and walked across the yard with Chacon. They stepped onto the porch and stood outside the apartment door.

Chacon rang the doorbell and waited. No answer. He rapped his knuckles on the door and peered through a side window. It appeared nobody was at home. He checked the copper mailbox next to the door.

"Nothing but a fairly recent gas bill, so it's obvious she's getting her mail here."

Romero knocked harder and the door flung open. Chacon looked surprised, and then followed him in.

"I'll deal with any consequences later, but right now we're justified, since we don't know if she's met with some kind of foul play," Romero said. As if determined to follow protocol, he called out Annae's name several times. "Miss Rivers, hello! Sheriff's department here. Anybody home?"

The apartment was small, messy, and cluttered. The two small bedrooms down the hallway were dark. Chacon moved ahead, checking behind the door and in the closet. "Nothing here," he called out.

The television set in the kitchen was on the QVC Channel, with some model hawking face cream guaranteed to make women look and feel ten years younger, just like her. Chinese food takeout sat on the counter, half eaten.

Romero looked in the sink. "Chinese food for one, looks like," he said. "No indication here that she's moved out. Aside from the lack of housekeeping, the closets are full, toiletries still in the bathroom."

Chacon looked in the spare bedroom. "No computer in sight. Maybe she has a laptop."

"Too bad, it might have helped us pin her down." Romero turned 360 degrees. "Hey, Artie, you have one of those fancy phones. Check and see if she has a Facebook page."

Chacon tapped the buttons on his phone for a few seconds and logged on to Facebook. After a few minutes, he pushed his phone across the counter to Romero. "Take a look at this, Rick."

On the screen was a post uploaded earlier that day. The photo of Carlos was defaced with a thick red line. Annae's status was listed as single. Previous posts indicated she had met the man of her dreams and was falling in love.

"This is an adult?" Romero said. "Sure sounds like something a teenager would write."

Chacon raised his eyebrows. "You'd be surprised how many people use these sites as a sounding board for all their rants and personal observations. Don't seem to care whether the whole world reads them. Pretty narcissistic, if you ask me. Ever since someone coined the term *selfie*, lots of these posts consist of sexy photos taken with a cellphone."

Romero handed him the phone. "Let me run this through Jemimah. She's been working up a profile on the woman."

They exited the apartment, closed the door securely, and walked out into the sunlight. Romero handed Chacon the keys.

"Drop me off at Dr. Hodge's office. I'll catch a ride with her," Romero said. "You can pick your car up at the station and leave my cruiser there."

Chacon grinned. "Are you sure? You might have a tough time getting home."

Romero tapped his forehead. "That's what I'm hoping."

Chacon backed the vehicle out of the driveway and headed

toward the downtown area, where he dropped Romero off at the stop sign in front of the Häagen-Dazs ice cream parlor.

***

ROMERO LOPED UP the wooden steps and through the hallway. The smell of grilled corn and chicken fajitas wafted through the windows of Jemimah's office from the restaurant below.

She was glad to see him again, as evidenced by the embrace they shared. They were both relieved the disagreements of previous weeks had been resolved. It was good to be near each other, even in a professional situation.

"Wow. Two visits on the same day. To what do I owe this special treat, Rick? Criminal activity, or you just wanted to see me again?"

He leaned forward and kissed her on the cheek. "A little of both, and you have the choice of either giving me a ride home or taking me home with you."

She tapped her cheek with her finger. "Hmm. I'll have to think about that. So what's up?"

He pulled up a chair and sat next to her. "Artie and I were checking out Annae Rivers' apartment."

"Find anything?" she said.

"Not really. We still need to officially serve her with a copy of the warrant, but Artie did show me something interesting. Can you log on to Facebook and pull up her page?"

Jemimah did as requested. She clicked on to the profile page and positioned the laptop on the desk between them.

"According to this, Annae's recently single." Scrolling down, she pointed to the screen. "She seems to have dated mostly musicians. In a town this size, most of them probably know each other. Looks like she flitted like a butterfly from one to the other, sampling their nectar." Jemimah pulled up the photo of Carlos with a red line across it. "Wow, he must have really pissed her off. This wasn't here when Katie was browsing her posts last week."

He studied Annae's profile photos and scratched his head. "That is so weird. I can't believe the resemblance between her and Julie. They could pass for sisters."

Jemimah gave him a mischievous smile. "I'm sure that's why Carlos thought it was Annae who had driven into the parking lot and parked behind him. Interesting that both you and Carlos would be attracted to women with similar traits. Then when he realized it was Julie, he would never have suspected she was dangerous."

He poked her gently on the shoulder. "No psychoanalysis, *Doctor* Hodge. What else have you worked up? You mentioned you thought you were getting close to formulating a profile."

"I'm not quite finished yet. Yesterday I had an interview with Annae's uncle, who just happened to be in Santa Fe. I'm checking out a few things he said, just to get the story straight. I should have something in from Colorado State Police soon." Jemimah closed the file. "That's all I've got. Tune in tomorrow."

It was after five. Romero pulled her gently out of her chair and held her by both hands. "Now, are you giving me a ride, or just taking me home? We could go to my house, now that Carlos has his own place."

"I'll flip you for it," she joked. "Seriously, I would love to, Rick, but it's already too late to arrange for the horse sitter. Can't let Mandy go without her feed. The dog and cat fend for themselves, but she's got her own little schedule."

He picked up her briefcase as she flicked off the lights. "Your place it is."

Chapter Fifty-Three

———•———

THE RAYS OF the morning sun filtered through the skylight in Jemimah's bedroom. Satiated but exhausted, she had slept a solid eight hours. She yawned and stretched, expecting to reach out and touch Rick. Instead she felt a sheet of paper crackle on the blanket. She rubbed her eyes and read the note:

> You looked so peaceful, I hated to wake you. Catch up with you later. XOXO *Rick.* P.S. Fed the dog.

A leisurely hour later, she walked down the hallway toward her office.

Katie was on the phone when Jemimah strolled through the door. She grinned a knowing smile and winked at Jemimah, made a few notations on a notepad and replaced the phone in the cradle.

Jemimah unbuttoned her jacket and plopped her backpack on the chair next to the desk. She slipped out of her black loafers, stretched out her legs, and crunched her toes. "Be nice if they'd let us wear sandals around here," she complained. "Did you run into anything that piqued your interest, Katie?"

"Well, I'm sure not as interesting as I'm sure your Monday evening was," she said. "Great way to start a week."

Jemimah blushed. "No comment. I mean about the case."

Katie swung her chair around to face her. "I don't know why you guys don't just move in together. It must be exhausting driving back and forth," she said.

"It's more complicated than that, Katie," she said.

"I know. The county frowns on interoffice relationships."

"Yes, and moving in together would wave a big red flag that someone's bound to notice. You know how the gossip mill operates around here," Jemimah said.

Katie crossed her arms. "I'd be willing to take the chance, just to be together with the man of my dreams."

"Well, that's very admirable, but I don't want it on my résumé that I was laid off for sleeping with my superior," she said, shaking her finger at Katie. "I'd have a lot of *'splaining* to do."

"Okay, okay. Let's get to work. I just spoke to the archives clerk at Colorado State Police. It appears that Annae Rivers and her stepbrother, Sammy, virtually disappeared from the state a number of years ago. Their parents were killed in separate incidents, as we know from your meeting with their uncle Karl."

"I assume you asked for a copy of the files on the case?"

"Sure did. They're going to fax them to us."

For the next several hours they worked side by side in reviewing each section of the homicide file. Between them they finished off a pot of coffee. Katie started to brew another.

"None for me, Katie. I'll be so wired I won't be able to focus," she said.

Jemimah pulled a compact out of her purse and refreshed her lipstick. "I'm meeting with Detective Romero in about half an hour, so I'd best be going. Let me know when you hear from Colorado."

Katie made a clucking sound. "Are you sure I won't be interrupting anything?"

Jemimah slipped into her shoes and dusted off her slacks. "Doubt it. We're still on the clock."

WAVING TO THE parking attendant, she strolled to the corner of the parking garage, unlocked the car, and tossed her briefcase in the back seat. Traffic was light on Water Street as she edged out onto Guadalupe Street and wound her way to the interstate where she would catch Highway 14. It was the kind of sunny day that made it clear why tourists flocked to Santa Fe. Just a handful of popcorn clouds dotted the blueberry sky. Definitely an Ansel Adams moment. Jemimah wished she and Rick could have taken the day off. *Fat chance.* Sheriff Medrano was pressuring his deputies to get some of the pending cases solved. Guess he still believed in magic. Easter Bunny too.

She arrived at the substation, pulled her 4Runner into a spot near the wall, and parked. Clarissa waved at her from the entrance.

Jemimah returned the wave. "Leaving for the day?" she said, pushing the driver's side door open. "I hope your boss is still here."

Clarissa giggled. "I would venture a guess he's waiting with open arms."

She walked down the hallway toward Romero's office, where she heard him banging around in the kitchen. He peeked his head out the door. "Hey, you made it. Thought you might be too busy to drive all the way out here for a meeting. Kind of expected an email instead."

"Busy, yes, but I never pass up a chance to be within touching distance," she said, playfully nudging her elbow against his. "And besides, it's part of my job description."

"I take it you got my note?"

"Sure did, although I would have preferred to say good morning in person."

"You were sleeping like a baby. I hated to cut your dream time short, but I did kiss you before I left," he said, "and you did swoon a little. I sure wanted to stay a little longer."

She put her finger to her lips and smiled. "Enough love talk. Time to hit the bricks."

Romero opened the fridge, peering in as though expecting the contents to have changed since the last time he looked. "Let me get us something cold to drink. Coke?"

She nodded. She spread her file out on his desk. He stepped out of the kitchen and joined her.

"From the determined look on your face, can I assume you've made a little progress?"

"One can hope," she said. "This has been a difficult case from the very beginning."

"So what you got so far, pretty lady?"

Jemimah tapped a sheaf of papers together and paperclipped them. "This is what I've been able to piece together. I reviewed Detective Chacon's interview with your ex-wife. I thought it was more appropriate for him to interview her. It turns out that Julie was in the bar when Carlos and Annae had a falling out. Annae wanted to make up and recharge the relationship. Carlos wasn't open to that. After a few angry words, he stomped out and left her standing there. Julie saw a way to take advantage of the situation and took Annae under her wing. They had a few more drinks and Annae told her all about regretting her breakup with Carlos. She expected Carlos to come back for her. He didn't. She was incensed that he would just drive off and leave her standing there.

"Julie sat around with her for a while listening to her tale of woe. She volunteered to drive her home, and then slipped something into her drink. She helped her out to the car, took her home, and tucked her in. She returned to the bar and picked up Annae's car and parked hers next door at a gallery closed for the season."

Romero swiveled the chair as he listened. Jemimah didn't skip a beat. "Somewhere along the line, Julie decided a good way to get even with you was through Carlos, and I won't bother to mention the expletives she used. The next day she drove to his condo where, according to Carlos, he was getting ready to leave for a meeting with his probation officer. He saw the car drive up, thought it was Annae and figured he might as well talk to her and avoid another scene. Julie spammed up a story about having dropped Annae off at her place and wanted Carlos to return to the bar with her to retrieve her own car; he could drive Annae's car back to Santa Fe. Julie had run into him the previous night and wanted to finish their conversation. Thinking it would only take about an hour, Carlos got in the car. She drove him out into the boonies and you know the rest."

His eyes widened. "Wow. Do you think she intended to kill him? Why would she? Carlos has never done anything to her."

"Obviously that Smith and Wesson pistol she shot him with was serious metal. If her story hadn't been so convincing, Carlos would have never believed her. Both women share that one trait: manipulation."

"You figure she would have shot him if we hadn't shown up?" he said.

"I'm pretty sure she would have. A few minutes before your guys stormed in, Carlos made a strong effort to get loose, kicking and rolling around. The drug had worn off completely by then and he had regained complete consciousness. That threw Julie off guard, and then she panicked when the detectives blasted through the entrance. Initially, she might have just intended to threaten him with the pistol to keep him quiet, but she shot him instead."

Romero took a sip from the soda can. "She pointed the gun at Detective Martinez, and the SWAT team had no choice but to shoot. Fortunately he didn't aim to kill, just to disarm her. By that time, Carlos was already on the ground bleeding and unconscious."

She nodded. "Dr. Hillyer said that a couple more inches to the right and he would have been facing his maker."

Pushing himself out of the chair, he stepped into the kitchen and popped the top on another soda. "Right now we have more questions than answers. And it all started with Julie showing up on my doorstep. I wonder if this would have happened if I hadn't agreed to meet her. I should have listened to my intuition. I had a nagging feeling she might be up to something, but I let my ego override my common sense."

Jemimah held up her hand to stop him. "Don't go blaming yourself, Rick. There's a lot about crazy we don't understand. I'm just grateful things didn't get any worse than they did. After all these years, in a fantasy-filled sort of way, your ex still believed you would drop everything in your life and take her back. When you didn't, it triggered memories of every failed relationship she'd ever had. She turned that anger on the closest target, Carlos. She figured you would go ballistic if you found out she'd slept with him."

He heaved a sigh. "I'm pretty sure he would have never done that. My brother might be a little relationship challenged and girl-crazy, but he does have morals."

"I hate to ask, but as part of the investigation, I feel I need to. What did Julie tell you?"

"Nothing that would lead me to believe she was this angry," Romero said.

"But you obviously spurned her advances at dinner," Jemimah said.

Romero propped his elbows on the table. "Of course, but I figured all that would happen was she would be pissed off for a while, dismiss me from her mind, and resume her life. She stormed out of the restaurant in a huff and I didn't see her again until that night with Carlos."

"I don't know, Rick. You might have added the final straw to her cumulative disappointments," Jemimah said.

"Maybe we'll never know," he said.

"I understand you had a conversation with her mother?"

"Yes, something I wasn't looking forward to. I felt like I owed it to them. I was concerned they weren't going to understand what happened."

"Weren't you a bit worried her family was going to throw the blame on you?"

"Maybe, deep down."

She put her hand over his. "One thing I've learned in my practice and studying the culture around here is that Hispanic families are much more clannish than the Anglos."

"That we are. But she understood. Apparently she had spent a lot more time than she was willing to admit worrying about her daughter. Julie was having serious emotional problems that probably dated from the time she left Santa Fe. Her mother knew she needed treatment, but she couldn't force the issue."

Jemimah slipped the file back in her briefcase. "I'm pretty sure there won't be a repeat of these events anytime soon."

He agreed. "I figure Julie's looking at about ten years, with part of that spent in a psychiatric ward. She'll be fifty by the time she's out."

Jemimah nodded. "At least she was cooperative about being questioned. The legal aid attorney thought we might recommend leniency, based on extenuating circumstances."

"Not up to us," Romero said. "I'll listen to whatever he has to say, though." He stood and stretched. "The day's not over yet. Chacon is interrogating Sammy Rivers."

"I wasn't aware he was in custody," she said.

"Oh yeah. Right before the SWAT team stormed into the building where Carlos was being held, Sammy took off running in the dark. One of the guys tackled him and shackled him to a tree. In all the commotion with Carlos, I forgot about it for the moment. I'd like to listen in on part of that. You got time? We can take my vehicle, if you'd like."

"Sure. He might be able to enlighten us about his sister's comings and goings," Jemimah said.

Chapter Fifty-Four

———•———

AT THE COUNTY sheriff's compound, the couple walked down the steps to the lower level and stopped in front of the two-way mirror in the hallway. At first glance, it appeared Sammy was no longer silent. Chacon asked him about his involvement in the murder of the mariachi.

Rivers's eyes shot up in surprise. "Where did you hear that?"

"Your sweet little stepsister's been telling us a lot of stories," Chacon lied. "Guess she's looking to make a deal with the DA if she gives you up. She says you planned everything."

The room went quiet. Rivers gripped the Coke can and crushed it. Then he let out a loud wail. "It was all her fault!" He wiped his eyes between wrenching sobs. "She got him involved with a cartel out of Mexico, and when he wanted out, she tried talking him out of it. They were still smuggling money in his outfits and she was taking it out of the lining without him knowing. And then he caught her in his closet one night."

"Tell us how it happened. Who shot him?" Chacon said.

"Look, she called me and told me to follow a ways behind her because she had gotten this guy pretty angry and was going to try to smooth things out. They drove out into the hills somewhere out past Cerrillos, like they were going on a picnic or something. She dialed my number, we both left our phones on and I put mine on speaker so I could hear the conversation."

"And what was the gist of that conversation?" Chacon said.

"Far as I could tell, he was pissed off because one of the linings in a jacket was torn out. He said she was the last one in his room when she unpacked his suitcase and hung them up. He asked her what she was looking for. She denied everything. Then she told him that she was under a lot of pressure from the contacts across the border because Sanchez was no longer willing to keep smuggling in the packages. He said he had never intended to let it go that far, just a couple of times for the thrill of it and to keep her happy."

"And then what happened?" Chacon said.

"I had stopped to pick up some smokes at the general store in Cerrillos, and when I got back to my truck, I heard a commotion on the phone, like they were having a screaming match. He was really angry. I know my sister and she could usually handle just about anything, but this time I think she overestimated her abilities. I drove in and parked behind her car, looked around and spotted them about a hundred yards down the way next to a barbed wire fence. I'm sure he didn't hear me, since he had his back to me and they were talking so loud."

"What did you see, Sammy?"

"He was standing up and he had a gun pointed at her. He was laughing and telling her she needed to back off—that she better understand that she was going to be in a shitload of trouble if she didn't get these people off his back. I had my pistol in my hand and I took aim and fired." Sammy's eyes were wide as he recalled the events. "She started screaming at me and called me a fucking idiot. I asked her what was I supposed to do, let him shoot her? I didn't sign up for any of this. I always took care of her, but this time she had gone too far." Sammy wrung his hands. Chacon offered him a cigarette. He lit up and then continued.

"She told me to get a shovel and bury him. It was ninety friggin' degrees out there and she wanted me to start digging a hole. I knew it was pointless to argue with her. She laughed and stuck her tongue out at me. I started digging the best I could."

"What happened to his weapon?" Chacon said.

"She picked his pistol up and wrapped it in her scarf. She said she would wait until dark and then drop it off at his apartment and stash it back in the drawer where he usually kept it. I took my gun and put it back in the glove box of her car, intending to clean it off."

"What did you do after that?"

"We went over to the lounge in Madrid and had a drink. I was pretty shook up." Sammy put his head down on the table, sobbing quietly.

When Sammy regained his composure, Chacon went over the information they had received from Colorado State Police, implicating him in the murders of his parents. For a while Sammy was speechless, then admitted to having committed the murders. He didn't implicate his stepsister, said she knew nothing about them and acted like she didn't care when she found out they were dead.

Chacon told the suspect to take a break. He came out into the hallway, popped a few quarters into the Coke machine and retrieved a bottle of water. Romero and Jemimah waited as he took a couple of long sips.

"Tough to see such a brute of a man reduced to tears. He gave us everything we need to implicate his stepsister for the homicide of Eduardo Sanchez," he said.

Romero ran his hand across his forehead. "Jeez. There but for an instant of sheer luck goes Carlos. If Julie hadn't had a meltdown and kidnapped him, I'd venture a guess that the Rivers siblings would have done him in too. Did he say what he was doing out there on McCabe's property that night? He took off right after the first gunshot was fired. Lucky for us he was spotted and someone took him down."

Chacon leaned back on the ledge. "He said he was having a beer at the tavern in Madrid when he gets a phone call from Julie telling him she was a friend of his sister's and that Annae was in some kind of trouble. She told him how to get there. He came in from the opposite direction, parked at the Indian ruins, and made his way into the building. It was dark, but he could make out Annae wearing her favorite baseball cap. It wasn't until Julie fired a shot at Carlos that Sammy realized it wasn't his sister, so he took off running trying to get to his vehicle before all hell broke loose."

"He knew nothing about it beforehand?" Romero said.

Chacon shook his head. "He admitted to being there, but claims he had nothing to do with shooting Carlos. Julie got spooked when Carlos tried to get up and she shot him."

"Fascinating," Jemimah said. "So if none of this had happened, the Sanchez case might have gone unsolved for a long time. Under a different set of circumstances, Sammy might not have admitted to it."

Chacon nodded. "Try 'forever.' Sammy said he pulled the trigger and helped bury Sanchez while his stepsister looked on. She must be one hell of a manipulator."

Jemimah piped in. "I came to the conclusion that she controlled him soon after their parents tied the knot. Sammy objectified her from the moment he met her and developed a protective personality because of it. Annae was being mistreated by her mother and Sammy was bound and determined to shield her. She was essentially the love of his life; he would do anything for her, and he did. He was just a face in the crowd, but she was a knockout. Even without makeup, she caught everyone's attention. It never bothered him how guys looked at her, until later when she started dating so many different men. He had been the one prominent person in her life and she in his. That was changing too fast for him.

"As far as Sanchez is concerned, I think she was always the brains behind the murder. In her warped mind, she was probably justified in getting rid of him. She'd have tried to kill Carlos off too if Julie hadn't beat her to the punch. I'm sure it didn't fare well with Sammy when Annae dated both Sanchez and then Carlos in quick succession. He's made no pretense of the fact that he's a Class A bigot, particularly toward Hispanics."

"I imagine he's got a whole load of crap between his ears," Romero said.

"You're probably right about that," Jemimah said.

Chacon stared at Rivers through the glass. He was bent over in his chair with his head in his hands. "So how did this Colorado connection come about? It really freaked him out when I pulled out your case file and started asking him questions. He melted like a block of ice. He knew there was no way he was going to get around it. He probably suspected we had enough evidence to hang him, so he might as well 'fess up."

"I had Katie contact Colorado State Police about unsolved murders after I interviewed their uncle," said Jemimah. "According to him, his brother was killed during a hunting trip, and his sister-in-law was killed during a home invasion. At first the father's death was considered a hunting accident, but they changed their minds when they found the mother's body in the family home. Turns out her killer left DNA all over the house, and because the cops didn't know Sammy wasn't this man's biological son, nobody put two and two together. He was never a suspect and the case went unsolved for a long time. We took a sample of his DNA, and with this new rapid DNA technology, had a result in less than ninety minutes. So we ran it through the Federal DNA Database and it matched the Colorado sample. They also sent us photos of a broken fingernail found at the scene; its striations tentatively matched up to his index finger."

Romero whistled. "These two crazies have been roaming around for years and they've managed to stay under the radar.

Wouldn't surprise me if we unearth a few more bodies left in their wake."

She nodded in agreement. "Nothing would surprise me about those two."

Romero jangled his keys. "Well, I'll leave it up to you to make the final connections. You're good at dealing with psychos." He reached up and touched Jemimah's cheek.

Chacon took a last sip of his water. "Hate to break this little mutual admiration society confab up, but I need to finish up here. I'll read him his Miranda rights and take him up to booking. You guys can deal with the other half of the psycho siblings."

Chapter Fifty-Five

———◦———

ON WEDNESDAY, JUNE 7, Jemimah headed to an appointment with her psychologist, Dr. Jerry Cade. She was exhausted from the chain of events over the previous five weeks since the mariarchi's body had been discovered. She had been seeing Dr. Cade since shortly after she arrived in Santa Fe. He was a tall, lean cowboy with silver threads woven through his sandy brown hair. An outdoor lifestyle and Native American heritage gave him a year-round tan. He had just celebrated his sixty-second birthday but had the look and presence of a much younger man. From the first she had been drawn to his laid-back style.

Their sessions had been mostly about exploring her feelings about her childhood and now dealing with her relationship issues and the fallout from her cases. Thumbing through a *New Mexico Magazine* as she waited, she read an article on cemeteries. Before the mariachi's service, she couldn't remember the first funeral she ever attended. *Oh yeah, she could, but didn't care to.* There had been far too many victims of homicide in the past couple of years.

As a psychologist, she was aware that her views on death

should be more progressive, but they weren't. She hated everything about the topic. Dr. Cade would certainly say she had issues and needed to address them, but it was frightening to think about the subject, let alone talk about it. She looked up at the clock. Since she'd arrived early, she would have to wait another fifteen minutes to address anything, death included.

She leaned back and closed her eyes as her mind wandered back to her childhood in Utah. She was five years old. She could hear herself screaming, her eyes pinched shut, but no sound came from her mouth. She imagined the wet grass beneath her feet. Her mind filled with the agony of having lost her younger brother. She looked at the small child in the casket. He appeared so fragile, much younger than three— almost infant-like. Her chest heaved. She hadn't been able to push the memory far enough into the brackets of her mind. That had been over thirty years ago. She surmised that event had affected her present views on death and everything surrounding the subject.

She was deep in thought when Dr. Cade tapped her on the shoulder.

"Earth to Dr. Hodge," he said.

She jumped and turned to face him. "Dr. Cade, oh, I was a million miles away."

She stood up, brushed the front of her skirt, and mumbled something incoherent. Once inside his office, she took a seat on the leather recliner a few feet from the desk. Dr. Cade sat across from her in a newly upholstered wingback chair.

At the beginning of their conversation, he mentioned he was considering retirement. She was silent.

"Say something, Jemimah," he said.

"I'm in shock, Jerry … Dr. Cade. I never expected you'd be giving up your practice. When I think of someone old enough to retire, I think of white hair, stooped shoulders and a hearing aid. You're definitely not in that category."

"Well, thanks for that," he said. "This has nothing to do with age. I'm ready to spend some quality time riding my horse and doing a little fishing and prospecting. Maybe I'll get a wild hair and go off hunting for that treasure your friend McCabe buried somewhere in the mountains." He chuckled. "There's no better time than the present. I've had a lucrative practice, both financially and personally. I've been lucky in the folks I've had the pleasure of giving my honest opinions to."

She felt like a school girl who just learned her favorite teacher was getting married and moving away. "What's going to happen to your patients? What's going to happen to me?"

He smiled. "I was thinking you could also retire from therapy. I can't think of a patient who's come as full circle as you have. We've covered everything from soup to nuts in our sessions over the past two years."

She looked down at her fingernails. "I think we've still got a long way to go," she said.

Dr. Cade leaned toward her. "I'm going to disagree with you on that, Jemimah. I'm sure you're aware that ninety percent of the work in therapy is accomplished by the patient, part of a lifetime process. You've managed to stay ahead of the game, and your training as a psychologist has certainly helped. I'm not retiring for another six months, and if at the end of that time you still feel the need to talk, we can arrange that. I can also refer you to another therapist I feel will be a good fit."

She relented. "All right, but you know it's never been easy for me to rehash my personal life, and starting over seems so overwhelming. I'm not sure I can comfortably revisit the past with someone new."

He met her gaze. "There wouldn't be a need for rehashing. Haven't we been trying to work on the present and put the past in perspective?"

She shifted in her chair. "Yes, I guess we have," she said softly.

Dr. Cade sensed his announcement had triggered a few feelings of insecurity in Jemimah. He reached for his eyeglasses and scribbled a few notes in the file. "So let's get to it before our time is up. What's been going on with you since I saw you last?"

She forced a smile. "Same old, same old. I seem to be stuck in a Karmic whirlpool, reliving the same experience."

"Which experience is that?"

"The one where I seem to prefer to profile the case rather than the suspect," she said.

"And by that you mean …." Dr. Cade smiled inwardly. It had always been a pleasurable task to peel information out of Jemimah. An artichoke came to mind.

She put her hands together, tapping her fingers thoughtfully. "I've been working on a case which necessitated reframing the suspect's profile more than once. About the time I'm satisfied I'm headed in the right direction, things start to go awry. As time passes, I seem to be unsure of my findings, as though I'm not on the right track."

"Are you still playing detective? I thought your focus was on profiling suspects in a case, not trying to solve it."

She shrugged. "It is, but you know I always seem to get in deeper than I'm supposed to. I just can't help it."

"Take a moment and venture back in time. At what point did you start thinking like a detective?" he said.

"Not too long after I was instrumental in discovering a group of corpses on McCabe's Indian ruins, and then helping to solve the case."

"And what set of circumstances did that bring into play?"

She strummed her fingers on the edge of the chair. Dr. Cade's barrage of questions was unsettling. "My curiosity got the better of me and I just had to know what had transpired. What were these women doing when they were murdered and what would cause them to become victims of such a horrific crime? I felt a desperate need for answers."

Dr. Cade paused to take a sip of water. "We've gone over this before. As I understand it, Jemimah, your job is to conduct a preliminary assessment of potential suspects before formulating a profile, is it not?"

"Yes."

"And yet you do much more than that?"

She hesitated. "I have to admit that I do."

He studied her face. "You work with a group of qualified detectives, do you not?"

"Yes, two who are assigned to the Cerrillos substation, and I'm assigned to the sheriff's office. Because of our caseload, I no longer assist the state police in profiling unless Sheriff Medrano requests my help."

"And isn't it the job of these two detectives to solve a case?"

She lowered her eyes. "Of course, but I can't seem to keep from looking further into the matter. Something compels me to dig on my own, to search for answers. The deeper I get into a case, the more of a rush it creates."

"And where does it go from there?"

"It's like a puzzle. You take fragments of information and put them together to try to form a picture. Until I find all the pieces, I can't stop."

Dr. Cade looked at her intently. "And why do you think that is?"

Jemimah massaged her neck. "Because I feel I offer a different perspective than they do. I'm not saying I'm better qualified. I just have this knack for seeing beyond the horizon, if you will. Like reading between the lines. These detectives tend to see everything as black and white, with no gray areas. They're so used to seeing dead bodies, nothing bothers them."

"I would venture a guess that such a perspective would be a plus, don't you think?"

"Not always. The detectives can be a bit territorial. They have their own reputations to protect along with seniority. Sometimes when I ask a question, it's taken as a challenge to their abilities, and since Detective Romero is their boss, I don't need to go crying to him for every little comment they make."

"How does that make you feel?"

She gazed at him for a moment before answering. He could see the wheels turning in her head. "Hmmm. Threatened, uncertain, frustrated, angry. Choose one. And maybe add embarrassed to that list. It certainly has never been my intention to show any of them up. I've learned a lot from them about how cases are investigated and how to interrogate witnesses, but I'm certainly no master at it ..." After a few seconds she added "yet."

"So, let me ask you this. Has anyone expressed any dissatisfaction with your tendency to go beyond your job description?"

Jemimah squirmed in her chair. It was the principal's office in junior high all over again. "Not that I'm aware of. I don't feel as though anyone is sitting there watching every move I make. For the most part, I've received high points on my performance reviews. I *have* heard rumors, though, that some of the men in the department refer to me as the boss's girlfriend or the blond detective."

"Sounds like a bit of reverse penis envy, you think?"

She laughed. "Now that's an interesting theory. Freud would have had a heyday with that."

Dr. Cade emphasized each word with his palms together. "Here's what I'm getting at, Jemimah. At some point in your career, you are going to have to decide exactly what you need from this job. Do you want to be a forensic psychologist, or do you want to be a detective?"

She smiled. "Maybe I could become a forensic detective."

He chuckled. "Now that's a possibility you might want to explore," he said. "We'll take it up on our next visit."

As Dr. Cade saw Jemimah to the exit, he thought that of all his patients, she was the one he was going to miss the most. She was a remarkable woman and he knew she was going to continue to test the waters in every direction.

Out in the parking lot, Jemimah realized what she had said. *Forensic detective ... hmmm. That has an interesting ring to it.*

Chapter Fifty-Six

———◆———

THAT FRIDAY AFTERNOON, Annae Rivers was standing in line at Trader Joe's on Cordova Road when she saw Detective Romero enter the store. At the checkout counter, she turned her head to the side and edged her basket forward, moving next to the dark chocolate display. The detective was the last person she wanted to interact with. As Carlos's brother, he'd surely be curious about their breakup and his kidnapping, such as it was. She smiled at the thought of his ex-wife taking Carlos down. She would have done it herself, but Julie beat her to the punch. The only difference is that *she* would have killed him and left him out in the desert for the vultures and coyotes to snack on. *The nerve of him. Breaking off their relationship.*

As she hurried the cart out on the sidewalk, she pressed the key tab to unlock the door of the car she had borrowed from her brother. Out of the corner of her eye, she spotted Romero coming out of the store. She tossed the groceries onto the passenger seat as she jumped into the car and started up the engine. Fortunately the space in front of her was vacant, and she gunned it out of the parking lot, pretending not to see him. She headed down St. Francis Drive, scooting past the red light.

On the way to her apartment, she felt a pang of anxiety jitter her insides. It was a delayed reaction, but something told her she was now between the crosshairs, particularly since a few days before she had found a card from the sheriff's office in her mailbox. She assumed it had to do with her Mazda, which had been impounded. She hadn't yet figured out how to go about retrieving it without drawing attention to herself. She turned into her driveway and bolted for the door. The key stuck in the lock and she almost sprained her wrist jiggling it until it finally turned. She dropped the bag of groceries on the counter and reached for the bottle of vodka in the cupboard. Sitting on the couch with her feet propped up on the hassock, she took a long swallow and a deep breath. There was a message from Sammy on her house phone that he had been arrested and wanted her to come down and post bail.

There is no way they can connect me to anything. Goddamned Sammy can talk his head off, but he can't prove anything. That little sonofabitch is going to try to save his ass by making me the goat.

She peeked through the curtain in the living room. No sign of the detective. Maybe she was imagining things. He might have just been shopping and wasn't even looking for her. Obviously if he had seen her, he would have made some kind of contact.

She put the groceries away and kicked off her shoes on the way into the bathroom. She looked in the mirror hanging over the vanity. She was going nightclubbing. It was Friday night, and she was ready to latch on to somebody handsome and exciting, maybe a sugar daddy. For all her flirtations and pretensions, she had never been able to stay in a relationship for very long. She frowned as she recalled her stepfather's constant admonitions about her selection of boy toys when she was a teenager. *What the hell did he know?* After all, she was gorgeous and someone tall, dark, and handsome was waiting to shower her with all the good things in life she deserved. No way did she want to be like her mother, who latched onto men who treated her like dirt. She wasn't going to settle again. No more musicians and no more unemployed pretty boys.

She smoothed her eyebrows and brushed her eyelashes with a heavy coat of mascara. A juicy coat of lip gloss rolled over her lips and she stepped back to admire the reflection of the fashion-forward and sexy woman looking back at her. She padded into the bedroom and sat on the corner of the bed while she slipped into the ice blue Jimmy Choo strappy pumps. The doorbell rang as she twirled in front of the closet mirror. Probably the newspaper boy, bugging her again for payment. She reached for her purse and her keys. Might as well just pay the little bastard and be on her way. She pulled the living room door open.

"Annae Rivers?"

Her face flushed. "Yes, who are you?"

The detectives flashed their badges. "Detectives Chacon and Garcia. Santa Fe Sheriff's Department. We'd like you to come down to our office. We have a few questions to ask."

She blinked a few times. "Sure. I'll make it a point to come by sometime tomorrow. How about ten o'clock?"

"I'm sorry, ma'am. You misunderstand. We've been instructed to take you in for questioning on a case we're investigating," Detective Chacon said.

"Oh, I guess this is about Carlos Romero. All right. Let me just grab my wrap. It looks a bit chilly out here."

"Yes, ma'am," Chacon said. "You won't be driving. We'll be accompanying you there."

"It's not as though I'm going to get lost," she said as she entered the back seat.

Chacon secured her door and then hopped in the driver seat. The detectives arrived at the Adult Detention Center and escorted her downstairs to the interrogation room where Detective Romero was waiting. She was surprised to see him.

"Have a seat, Miss Rivers," he said. "Can I get you something to drink? Water, maybe?"

"No thank you. I have plans for the evening, so let's get on with this. First of all, I had nothing to do with your brother getting shot. I wasn't anywhere near him. We broke up a week before that. That's pretty much all I have to say." She stood and reached for her purse.

"That's not why you're here, Miss Rivers. Please sit down," Romero said, thinking that the newly platinum blonde looked very appealing in her going clubbing clothes.

She hesitated, and then sat back down. The interview room had a subtle stink of sweat embedded in the dull gray walls. Annae perched on the edge of the metal folding chair like a bird preparing for flight. Her legs were crossed as she leaned down to adjust the strap of her shoe. She had a cigarette in one hand and fiddled with the ashtray in front of her, spinning it around after she flicked ashes into it. She stared at the detective as she snuffed out the cigarette. Her icy-green eyes darted around the room, taking in every corner. There were no windows and she seemed to sense that the mirrored frames were two-way. She appeared to be closer to fourteen than twenty-four. Her hair was pulled back and clipped with a silver feather barrette around a perky ponytail. She fiddled with the diamond stud earrings and matching necklace she was wearing.

Straightening her back and jutting her chin forward, Annae fielded questions from Detective Romero for more than thirty minutes. He asked about her background, her schooling, employment, and a myriad of other subjects. She answered without hesitation and then became frustrated.

"Is there anything else you need to know? My dress size is six and my shoe size is eight," she said.

Romero reached into a file, leaned forward and shoved a photo of Eduardo Sanchez in front of Annae's face. "Tell us what you know about the murder of Eduardo Sanchez," he said.

She crossed her arms across her chest and turned to face him. "Why are you asking me? I don't know anything about that."

"This is our victim. You dated him, broke up with him, and then killed him in a fit of jealous rage."

She glared at him. "You don't know what you're talking about. I barely knew the man. We only had a few dates. I read about him in the newspapers. Sad. Very sad."

He paused. "You look a little unnerved, Miss Rivers. Would you like a glass of water, or maybe a soda?"

She looked down at her ruby red fingernails. "I'm fine," she said. "Let's get this over with."

"So, are you saying you had nothing to do with the death of Eduardo Sanchez?" Romero said.

Her demeanor calm, she looked at him with raised eyebrows. "That's exactly what I'm saying."

Romero sat down across from her. He knew she was lying. "Would it surprise you that we have proof that you were at the murder site when Sanchez was killed?"

Annae was silent. She stared straight at him. "There's no way you can connect me to anything."

Annae took a deep breath and hoped her escalating nervousness wasn't obvious to the detective. It had been her intent that the body wouldn't be found until years later, vultures and coyotes having picked the carcass to bits, bones scattered for miles. But that didn't happen. She should have hunted down the idiot who accidentally discovered the body and used him as target practice.

He pushed a paper toward her. "Do you know what that is?"

She leaned forward and studied the paper. "No, I don't."

"That is a DNA report on two hairs that were found on Sanchez's shirt sleeve."

"What does that have to do with me? You don't have my DNA and I'm not giving you a sample."

"No matter. We can obtain a court order to get it, whether

you comply or not. I'm pretty sure if we compared these strands to your hair, it would be a match."

She flipped her head to the left. "Good luck on that. I'm sure you're going to find my hair all over his place. We spent a lot of time together, in case you didn't know that."

"A while ago you said that you barely knew him. Are you changing your mind about that now?" he said.

She was having a difficult time projecting the image of a sweet and beautiful, yet innocent, woman. She clasped her hands. "All right, dammit. We dated for a while. Hit the bars, had dinner, you know the drill. He was a boring, narcissistic slob. All he talked about was himself and music. A girl needs a little more intellectual stimulation than football and Mexican music. Things didn't work out so we broke up."

Romero paced around the room. "So you got all pissed off about the breakup and decided to get even?"

"You're grasping at straws, Detective. I told you I had nothing to do with it. I don't care what your DNA report might show. I'm sure you'd find his hair all over my clothing, too."

He sat down again and scooted the metal chair closer to her. "We don't have to wait for the results, Annae. Sammy gave you up. Said you talked him into it."

She sat still. Her eyes widened and seemed to darken in color. Then she erupted into a rage. "That mangy sonofabitch. He's lying. I had nothing to do with that. He's the one. He followed us and then shot him. He's always been jealous."

"We checked your bank accounts, Miss Rivers. You were making regular deposits which seem to coincide with deposits Sanchez made to his account. Only yours were between thirty and forty grand," Romero said.

She looked surprised. "I'm a hard worker," she said.

He stared her down. "I think you were both involved in laundering drug money from across the border."

She stared back. "Again, prove it."

"We don't have to," he said. "We'll leave that up to IRS or the guys at DFA. They'll track it without a problem."

Another round of questioning proved unproductive. She denied everything he asked.

"Is Mr. Sanchez the only person you were involved with at that time?" he said.

She squared her shoulders. "I'm sorry, that's a NO zone. I don't have to answer that."

He flipped through his notes. "All right, we'll come back to that. Are there any other 'no zones' I should be aware of?"

"I'll be sure to let you know," she said. And then she was silent again.

Jemimah watched the interview from an adjoining room. Romero had decided to take a break, maybe give Annae some time to rethink her answers. He joined Jemimah in the video room.

"Did you hear all that, Jem?"

She set her notes aside. "I heard most of it. It's my impression that she probably intended to kill Carlos, but a wild set of circumstances kept her from accomplishing that goal. The DA doesn't have a strong enough case to even implicate her. Your ex is going to take the brunt of that charge."

Romero nodded. "Unfortunately I have to agree with you. I'm more interested in hanging her on the Sanchez case."

"It appears to me her involvement is primarily circumstantial, even though she's probably responsible for the murder. Her stepbrother gave her up, but she insists he's lying. Her word against his. And since we have no official time of death for Sanchez, she conceivably had Carlos as an alibi for her whereabouts."

Romero inhaled deeply. "Maybe we can talk Sammy into telling us what happened to the weapon. He's in so deep, any kind of deal might be welcome."

They observed through the glass as Annae reached into her purse and retrieved a makeup bag. She searched in a leisurely fashion through the contents and pulled out a wand of mascara.

She leaned into a small compact mirror as she swooped the dark liquid across her lashes. She followed with a fresh coat of glossy pink lipstick and shook her head as if to loosen the curls. Satisfied, she zipped her handbag and set it on the floor.

Detective Chacon walked around the corner into the hallway. "Hey, boss, been looking for you. Got some interesting news."

Romero motioned him over. "Right about now any news would be more interesting than trying to squeeze this woman for information. Man, she's a tough one."

Chacon handed him a sheet of paper. "This might help. I just picked up a report from the crime lab. Ballistics confirmed that the gun used to shoot Carlos was the same gun used to kill Sanchez."

Romero gaped at him. "Are you serious, Artie? Julie said she found the gun in the glove box of Annae's vehicle."

"Damn right. And because your ex was the one wielding the gun, we also ran her through records. Turns out your ex-wife did a couple of stints in a psych ward back in California. I put in a call to the psychiatrist in charge, but she has yet to get back to me."

"How long ago was that?" Jemimah said.

"About six months before returning to Santa Fe. She had only been back here for a couple of weeks. Word was that she quit her job in LA and was planning on moving in with some relatives until she found another job," Chacon said.

Romero whistled. "Man, I would never have suspected Julie was capable of anything this bizarre. Her mother couldn't have known, or she'd have mentioned it. I still can't wrap my brain around it. Don't get me wrong. We had our problems, but they never involved more than butting heads or the occasional shouting match."

Jemimah shook her head. "Who knows what Julie's life has been like since she left Santa Fe? She snapped somewhere along the way. Since she's not a suspect but rather a perpetrator, I can't psychoanalyze her that deeply."

Romero turned to Detective Chacon. "Take little Miss Murder upstairs and book her on an open charge of accessory to homicide and anything else you can pull out of the hat."

"Will do, boss," said Chacon.

The couple slipped into one of the vacant cubbyholes. He opened the file to the interview page. What else did you pick up from her answers?"

Jemimah slipped her reading glasses on. "Her behavior during the whole interrogation rings false. I can't tell if she made up her answers on the fly. One of her talents is building an entire story from one thought, embellishing it to the point where the truth blurs and the lie moves to the forefront. She appears to live in a dual reality. Lying is a defense mechanism she uses to keep centered. In order to survive, she has to create a different reality whenever convenient. This woman is a severely egotistical sociopath. No telling what else she's capable of. You saw that sudden change from sweetness to anger. I suspect she also suffers from an intermittent explosive disorder. Takes a lot for her to keep it in, but when she reaches a boiling point, run for cover. Someone needs to keep a hawk-eye on her while she's in custody. Unlike her stepbrother, she's exhibited no remorse at all. Very cold and calculated. I'm sure she believes everything is going to turn out all right."

Romero agreed. "As far as Sammy is concerned, it looks like Colorado will probably attempt to extradite him on the murders of the parents. She didn't have anything to do with that, at least according to Sammy. But we can damn sure charge her as an accessory to murder for her influence on him in the Sanchez case. We're going to get her one way or the other. It may take a while, but it will happen."

It was past seven when they finished discussing the case. On the way home, the couple stopped at the San Marcos Café on Highway 14, the only restaurant open after hours in the Cerrillos area. There were still a couple of stragglers sitting at the wood tables. Romero ordered a beef burrito smothered in green chile, and when the waitress delivered it to the table, Jemimah wished she had ordered the same, rather than the sad-looking BLT resting on her plate.

"We've finally started to connect the dots here, Jem," he said as he forked up another bite.

"Unfortunately it's going to be difficult to figure out what part of Annae's harangue is truth and what is fiction. We may never know what events or circumstances transformed this beautiful young woman into a psychopath unable to take rejection in any form. Or maybe she was just born that way."

"I'm sure you're well-versed on all the studies and articles on this subject," he said.

She sighed. "I doubt they even scratch the surface. Abuse takes many forms, but so many individuals are able to rise above it and become normal functioning adults. With others, like Annae, something snaps in their brain that causes them to become monsters. Over the years they develop skills to keep the Dr. Jekyll side of their personality from surfacing until the circumstances become so convoluted they can't help it."

They shared a moment of silence before the waitress brought the check to their table.

Romero stretched his arms and yawned. "Maybe a good night's sleep will help put it all in perspective. Ready?"

"Sprinkle in a bit of snuggling and I'm in," she said.

Chapter Fifty-Seven

———•———

THE FOLLOWING MONDAY, Jemimah reviewed her final notes with Katie. Detective Romero dropped by to take her to lunch and discuss the remaining elements of the case.

"Didn't you initially have your doubts about Annae being a suspect?" he said. "I did. I figured such a pretty woman could hardly be capable of killing someone."

"Isn't that a bit sexist? Prisons are full of pretty women who have a mean streak a mile long," she said. "I considered that a hired killer might be a more reasonable scenario, but then I figured with a stepbrother like Sammy to do her bidding, that wasn't necessary."

"How reliable did you find his story? He might be trying to protect her."

"I don't think so," Jemimah said. "I believe somewhere along the line he had an epiphany. She was never going to love him the way he adored her. He was just a plaything to her, someone to take care of unpleasant things. Shortly after she came into his life he began to protect her, worry about her and idolize her."

"What do you think changed?" he said.

"She had too many boyfriends in succession. He must have realized he could never match up to any of them." Sammy had a big chest and thick arms. Jemimah imagined he could be an intimidating presence, the kind of guy you wouldn't want to meet in a dark alley. "He didn't seem to have much in the way of friends. Pretty much a loner."

The hostess directed them to a table as they continued the discussion. "Annae never confessed to anything. She still insists she's innocent," he said.

"Those two evil siblings make a good pair. Unfortunately they'll probably get unequal sentences. Not a lot of justice in that," she said. "At least they'll both be off the streets."

After the waiter took their orders, Romero said, "One more question, Jem. What's your opinion of why Sammy Rivers would do something so horrible as killing his parents?"

"My opinion on that would be after the fact and totally worthless."

"It's worth something to me. You've got great insight."

"That's very nice of you to say, but you might be a bit prejudiced. There was no sibling rivalry between these two. Unusual for two young people thrown together under those circumstances. Maybe he figured he had to get rid of the parents in order to keep her, or else she might have gotten fed up on her own and taken off without him. The mariachi's murder was precipitated by Sammy believing the woman he secretly loved was about to be harmed."

"Do you think maybe he overdid it? He could have just tackled the guy, taken away his weapon, beat the hell out of him. I don't think Sanchez had it in him to shoot her—maybe just scare her."

"I don't think Sammy's mind worked that way. He probably figured if he didn't kill the guy, there would still be someone else standing between him and his soul mate."

Romero took a sip of water. "I guess we can speculate all we want, but when it comes down to it, we're just going to have to be satisfied with a conviction for these two. Whatever comes up in the future regarding anything else they might have been involved in will have to be handled then. A jury will have to decide."

The waiter set their entrees in front of them.

Jemimah put her fingers to his lips. "Case closed, my handsome detective." She raised her glass. "A toast. May all our cases be solved and all the bad guys expeditiously put behind bars."

"And may you always be open to my loving you as much as I do at this moment," he said.

They both grinned as their glasses clinked.

***

THE COUPLE'S RELATIONSHIP had grown steadily over the preceding months. Bystanders could easily see they were in love, but they each shared the same trait: caution. Although they spent as much time together as their frenetic jobs allowed, rather than move in together—which might be too much of a commitment for either of them—they alternated weekends at their respective homes. Jemimah hadn't claimed any of Romero's space for her things, and he hadn't claimed any of her space for his. She brought her night clothes and toothbrush in her backpack, and he did the same. Although Romero preferred to sleep in the raw, he purchased a pair of pajamas from the Kohl's store out on the highway, just in case he was staying the night at her house.

They had just finished a romantic dinner at their favorite restaurant, La Choza, a cozy little Mexican restaurant at the south edge of the Railyard in Santa Fe. It was the place they had their first official date a year after driving each other crazy with indecision, hers about romantic involvement with anyone, and his about commitment. When the planets finally aligned, they found themselves wildly attracted to each other. Something in the air made them both realize things needed to change.

Romero questioned if it was time to break out a ring and take it to the next level. He wondered what her reaction would be. *Better think about it some more.* He had given her a diamond heart before they took off on vacation last summer, and it seemed to please her. In fact, he believed she hadn't taken it off since then. Or was that just his ego talking?

After dinner they took a drive up to Cañoncito, a small community a few miles north of Santa Fe. They parked facing west at the top of the hill, climbed on the hood of her car and stretched out, their backs leaning on the windshield. From this vantage point they could watch the brilliant sun about to drop below the horizon, coloring the sky in amber and magenta hues. It was as though a heavenly architect had arranged the voluminous clouds into a cotton crown over the mountaintops, more than fifty miles away. Soon the night sky would be peppered with stars and the full moon would loom above them.

Romero reached over and pulled Jemimah closer. He kissed her gently on the lips. She looked at him and smiled.

He rearranged a wisp of hair near her face. "Jem, I've wanted to ask you this for a while. Have you given any thought to getting married?"

She put her hand up to shield the sun from her eyes and looked toward the Sangre de Cristo Mountains. "There's a cold front moving in. Look how dark the clouds are."

He was momentarily dazed. He turned to face her. "And what, may I ask, does that have to do with anything?"

Jemimah broke into laughter. "It means yes, I will marry you, and it's going to be really nice to have someone to cuddle up with this winter. That's all."

He drew her close and kissed her passionately.

She hugged his arm. "You know, of course, this means that one of us is going to have to quit our jobs. I'm not sure I'm ready to do that, are you?"

"Whatever it takes, sweet cheeks. We'll jump across that creek when we get to it."

He reached into his jacket pocket for a black velvet box. "Very romantic," he said, "proposing on the hood of an SUV."

"There's a first for everything," she said.

He took her left hand in his and slipped an almond-sized diamond ring on her finger.

MARIE ROMERO CASH was born in Santa Fe, New Mexico, to a family that would eventually number seven children, and has lived there most of her life. After graduating from Santa Fe High School, she took a job as a legal secretary, a field that would provide a lifetime of employment. But then, in her mid-thirties, she discovered the traditional arts of Northern New Mexico. After twenty years of creating award-winning art, she began to write about it, but decided she needed a higher education to do so. At fifty she enrolled in college, and five years later, graduated with a degree in Southwest Studies. In 1998, she received the prestigious Javits Fellowship to pursue her education. Since then Marie has written several books about the art and culture of the southwest, including a memoir about growing up in Santa Fe.

The Mariachi Murder is the fourth book in the Jemimah Hodge Mystery Series, which began with *Shadows among the Ruins*.

You can find Marie on the Web at marieromerocash.camelpress.com.

You've read the 4th Jemimah Hodge Mystery.
Now catch up on the series.

Forensic Psychologist Jemimah Hodge has just moved to the foothills of the Ortiz Mountains south of Santa Fe and taken a job with the local sheriff's department. There she expects to assess a few petty criminals a week. Instead, along with two handsome detectives, Jemimah finds herself knee deep in the investigation of a series of gruesome murders that took place in an ancient Indian pueblo.

Forensic psychologist Jemimah Hodge is handling a cold case that concerns the death of a police officer's wife. After she and her would-be beau, Detective Rick Romero, survive separate shooting incidents that seem related to the case, they must put aside their differences and distractions and work together to solve it. Will they be able to identify the culprit in time to save themselves?

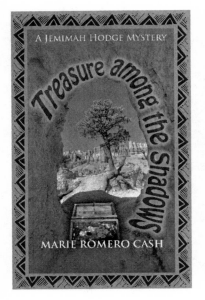

A JEMIMAH HODGE MYSTERY

Treasure among the Shadows

MARIE ROMERO CASH

When prickly Gilda Humphreys is murdered near Santa Fe, there is no shortage of suspects. All Forensic Psychologist Jemimah Hodge and her new boyfriend Sheriff Rick Romero have to go on is a similarity to another cold case, the woman's obsession with a local treasure hunt, and her midlife sexual escapades. In fact, the killer is close by. Too close.

CPSIA information can be obtained
at www.ICGtesting.com
Printed in the USA
FFOW04n2305300516
24584FF